Proteus Rising

A novel by Peter Dingus

Published by SpeculativeFictionReview.com

www.speculativefictionreview.com

Copyright © 2006 by Peter Dingus

ISBN 0-9785232-0-2

Cover Art by Peter Dingus

Proteus Rising

www.speculativefictionreview.com

To my loving family, Annie, John, and Paul.

Prologue

Genesis Revisited – Anonymous

In the beginning, some ten billion years after the emergence of the known universe from a quantum fluctuation of a De'Sitter space, the solar system formed. Many billions of years later, the Earth, the third planet from a minor yellow dwarf star on the inner edge of the Milky Way galaxy, cooled from molten rock.

For the next three billion years, the rock was pelted with debris of the solar system's violent birth. Huge asteroids rained down onto the surface of the Earth with the fury of tens of billions of nuclear bombs. The Earth's surface remained a fiery hell, and the atmosphere consisted of a noxious soup of poisonous hydrocarbons and acidic sulfurous compounds.

Sometime during the fourth eon of the Earth's existence, life emerged onto a more peaceful Earth. The celestial debris had cleared. Plants on the land, and algae in the seas, scrubbed the carbon dioxide from the atmosphere and replaced it with oxygen, heralding an environment suitable for the emergence of animals.

Hundreds of millions of years later, at the beginning of the Mesozoic era, the age of the dinosaurs began and would endure for another hundred and twenty million years. Sixty-three million years after the extinction of the dinosaurs, give or take a few million years, Homo sapiens appeared, supplanting the dinosaur as the highest animal on Earth. The dominion of Homo sapiens would last for less than one percent of the time of the dinosaurs before them. Though modern humans did not burn as long, they certainly burned brighter, changing the natural environment, and with it, the rules of the biological game that brought them into being.

By the first decade of the twenty-first century after the birth of Christ, humans were in possession of a genetic technology that would finally enable them to more closely approximate the angels they imagined when looking in the mirror, but upon closer inspection, failed to see.

During the final decades of the twenty-third century, humankind had begun its conversion to a more pleasing form in earnest. Genetically engineered Moderns would be the first step in a cathartic renewal of humanity by its own hand...

Chapter One

"What if I told you I'd discovered a genetic cure for Original Sin?" – *George Mills, Ursa University, Mars, 2321 A.D.*

They pulled alongside a white picket fence. Dale heard the soft whine of the engine fade as the car drew to a stop. The house beyond the fence was old with a façade of slatted stucco, stained and textured in a vain attempt to simulate wood.

"Is this the right address?" Dr. Gates asked.

"Let me check," Dale said. He grabbed the clear plastic tablet from its cradle on the car's console, held it at opposite corners, and pulled its malleable fabric into a larger rectangle. He found the contact icon and confirmed the address, then nodded and felt a constriction of betrayal choke his throat. With a resigned sigh, he joined Dr. Gates in front of an overgrown fence that framed a small yard. Because it was bright out, Dale put a hand over his eyes before taking a look around. The house was high atop a ridge overlooking Lake Geneva, and he couldn't help seeing the spidery outlines of dome struts against the early afternoon sun. Dale mopped his damp brow, then lowered his gaze; Dr. Gates was staring at him from behind dark glasses.

"Okay," he said, unable to delay the encounter any longer. He made his way to the front door and delivered a couple of quick open-handed knocks. Before he could withdraw his hand, Dale heard stirring, muffled steps, then the door opened a crack.

A woman's brown eyes darted from Dale to the edge of the door and back again. "Can I help you?"

"It's Dale Metz, Mrs. Abrams. I'm from the Department of Reproductive Affairs. We're here to talk to you about Ben."

"Is he in trouble, is there a problem?"

"No, no, nothing like that," he lied. "We're here to talk to you about a test he took in school."

"In school?" The woman continued staring out the door, lingering a little too long at its edge, as if aware of someone out of sight.

"We'll tell you all about it," Dale assured. "Can we come in?"

Her breath hung and she dropped her eyes. Maria Abrams opened the door and ushered them in. Dale recalled meeting this woman and her son in an office building in Dome One, through Joanne Zhu, Ben's genetic doctor. He couldn't help noticing that she was staring at Dr. Gates with an intense scowl, which was not that unusual, given how people in the district felt about Earthers, especially genetically modified Moderns.

They followed Maria into a demure sitting room. A dark pattern of shadows emanating from blinds over a large window cast the angular furniture into a dizzying perspective that knotted Dale's stomach. In a small voice, Maria asked, "Would you like something to drink?"

"Not for me, thank you," Dale replied, wincing.

"Mrs. Abrams, we don't have much time," Dr. Gates said. "Could you have Ben come in here please? We have some questions we'd like to ask him."

The doctor took off a pair of dark glasses, revealing pale violet eyes. When she saw them, Maria raised her hand to her forehead and made the sign of the cross. She hadn't struck Dale as an ostensibly religious woman at their first meeting, but he knew that early-learned habits were hard to break, like when he blinked too much, something he'd done as a boy when caught in a lie. So Dale wasn't too surprised to hear a quaver enter Maria's voice as she called her son.

"I'm right here mama," said a boy. He was already standing in an archway leading to a cramped kitchen, which Dale spied beyond the small room. Maria's hand flew to her chest; she hadn't even gotten the words out before he'd answered. While Dale watched, Maria glanced from the boy to Dr. Gates and continued to fidget, wringing her hands and shifting her stance.

"Hello Ben, I'm. . ."

"I know who you are. You're Dr. Gates—I heard."

The doctor smiled ever so slightly, leaving Dale with the strange image of how Neanderthal might have felt meeting Cro-Magnon. The unusual aura the boy cast made him uncomfortable from a shadowy sense of intrusion, as if someone were looking over his shoulder. The urge to turn and confront whoever it was seized him, and he had to force himself to appear more relaxed than he actually felt.

"Do you know why we're here, Ben?" the doctor asked.

Ben found a seat next to his mother on a worn brown sofa, and said nothing.

"You took a series of tests at school. Mr. Metz and I are interviewing children in the domes who did better than we thought possible," Dr. Gates explained.

The boy continued to stare with eyes a color Dale found unsettling. They had odd golden flecks that seemed to scintillate when the boy turned his head. Then the boy looked directly at him and the eyes seemed to go dark, as if the corneas were polarized.

"I was wondering if you could do something for me," Dr. Gates asked, removing a plastic bag from an attaché case they'd brought.

The doctor pulled six red plastic figures from the bag and placed them on the coffee table in front of the boy. Each figure consisted of balls connected by a stiff plastic tube, like large beads on a skewer. Five of the figures were exactly the same— three balls in a line, and a fourth ball at an angle. The sixth figure had just three balls in a row.

"Do you know what this is?"

The boy looked down at the toy with mild interest, then looked up and smiled thinly.

Dr. Gates exhaled and turned to Maria. "If he doesn't cooperate, he'll have to come with us."

Maria's eyes grew wide. "Go with you where?"

"It's a puzzle," the boy said. "It makes a solid figure with the least variation in the shape of the pieces."

Dr. Gates turned back to the boy. "Have you ever seen this or anything like this before?"

The boy shook his head. "No, I've never seen this before."

"Remarkable," Dale uttered. He remembered his own confusion and inadequacy when Dr. Gates had first showed him the assortment of pieces and asked him to guess their purpose. "Don't fret Mr. Metz," he recalled the doctor telling him. "We've never found a person, not even among the finest minds on record, that could solve this puzzle in under an hour—you're in good company." The possibility that, in a glance, this eleven-year-old boy of modest means could do what he had failed even to understand increased Dale's edginess.

"Can you assemble the puzzle?" Dr. Gates asked.

"Will you leave if I do?" Ben asked.

The doctor nodded and the boy moved to the edge of the sofa, cocked his head slightly, and reached for the plastic pieces on the table with slender brown fingers. As Dale looked on, the boy assembled the three-dimensional object, a sardonic smile slowly creeping across his face. He didn't even try the pieces in various orientations, something Dale imagined himself doing. Ben simply put each piece in its appropriate place, as though he'd had a diagram on the table next to him.

When he had finished, the boy slipped his hands over the object, almost in a caress, then sat back on the sofa. Dale regarded the pyramid standing in the middle of the table with a sense of unreality. It was four levels high, with each stratum delineated by a row of large beads that seemed to shine in the diffuse light of the room. Each layer of the pyramid had one less bead than the preceding one, with a single red bead adorning its pinnacle. The solution of the puzzle had all happened so quickly and easily that it seemed almost anticlimactic.

As Dr. Gates continued to speak to the boy and his mother, Dale began to feel dizzy and short of breath every time the little bastard's black eyes settled on him. He just wanted to jump up and run out of this place, but the metaphoric thirteen pieces of silver were weighing him down. What the hell had he gotten himself into anyway? Yesterday, he'd been a mid-level bureaucrat looking for career advancement, and right now, all he wanted to do was to get the hell out of here—fast. But he knew that option had passed—no, it was too late to close Pandora's box.

When he thought he could no longer stand to be in the same room with the boy, Dr. Gates rose and mercifully motioned him toward the door. He gladly complied. A sense of palpable relief washed over Dale as he followed Dr. Gates out of the modest little house. Daring to look back, he saw the boy and his mother standing on the front porch, watching them leave. Deep furrows on the woman's brow suggested this wasn't over. The boy stood partially behind her in a protective embrace and looked impassive.

Dale got in, slammed the door shut, and waited impatiently for Dr. Gates to start the car so they could go. But when he glanced over at the driver's side, Dr. Gates was just sitting there, staring straight ahead.

"Doctor—you all right?"

Finally, the doctor turned to him. "Mr. Metz, that was remarkable."

Dale nodded in bewildered agreement, as blood began trickling from Dr. Gates' nose in bright red droplets on porcelain white skin.

Chapter Two

"A profound change in technology changes the world; a modest change in the nature of man creates an entirely new and different world." – George Mills, Ursa University, Mars, 2321 A.D.

The large silver skyliner flew south, high above the Kepler Canal toward Ursa Township in the Valles Marineris canyon. From the forward cabin window, George Mills saw a crisscross of plasma contrails paint the Martian stratosphere with golden streaks, making the thin sky look busy below the infinite void. While common above Earth, bustling sub-orbital traffic was virtually nonexistent over Mars.

He felt uneasy, something must have changed in the four months since he left. The sight served to heighten his doubts about the testimony he had given before the review board back on Earth. George couldn't get the man's eyes out of his head. It was strange, because he'd last seen the chairman of the review board more than a month ago, and a hundred million miles from here.

During his testimony, he remembered forcing himself not to look away, not to appear deceptive. He had focused on the bridge of the man's nose instead of his eyes. Though he knew he wasn't a good liar, George felt confident avoiding those tidbits his inquisitors sought with exquisite circumspection. But a lot of things continued to bother him about the review—like the memory of a slight unnatural heat that had prickled his bare arms and face during the questioning. It had alerted him to the infrared scanning his irises and measuring his temperature, as well as the acoustics tracking his heartbeat.

In the end, all of their efforts had apparently revealed very little. For the moment, at least, his secret was safe. The key had been deciding before the trip that his lies would be of omission, not fabrication. As far as he knew, it had worked. That's what he kept telling himself, like a mantra, trying to ease his doubts.

The liner pitched forward, beginning a quick plunge from a hundred thousand feet. It shook and rattled violently, leaving the fringes of near space in a shroud of hypersonic turbulence. As it dropped, the wall of mountains known as the Martian Himalayas grew on the lower edge of George's window. He watched the peaks swell from a small insignificant rust colored band to an awe-inspiring field of red-brown spires that stretched the contour of the planet. He grabbed his seat in a white-knuckled grip and stiffened as the liner lurched and dipped to the west, seeking a low passage.

Just beyond the mountains, the terrain fell into an ancient seabed, surrounded by sheer cliffs more than two miles deep. George registered the craft's vertical descent by the sinking sensation in the pit of his stomach. He glanced out the window and fixed on the three huge domes of Ursa Township for perspective. The domes were miles beyond the transport pads of the airport, but they eclipsed everything else. He edged closer to the window, looked down, and saw two large liners parked on adjacent pads as lifters, powered by piezoelectric artificial muscles, raised sealed jetways to their fuselages, off-loading people and cargo to the receiving station below ground.

After landing, George made his way through a passage to the gate concourse on the surface, looking for signs that might direct him, first to the terminal, then later to the baggage carousel. The walls were littered with video clips announcing the arrival and departure times of transports and other information. When he found what he needed, he began walking, but hesitated when he happened to glimpse something unexpected in one of the windows as he passed by. He felt the draw, picked up his pace, and moved toward the soft pink glow for a better look.

Out on the tarmac, next to the terminal, loomed the lethal black profiles of two Terran Void Fleet interceptors.

"What in the world?" George whispered.

Until now, he had only seen such exotic war machines in video dramas. They were never parked at public airports, not to his knowledge. There must be a much larger Void Fleet ship in orbit around Mars right now, he thought. Perhaps there was a connection to all the sub-orbital traffic he had seen earlier.

"Ugly, aren't they?"

The voice shattered the silence. George flinched. When he turned, he found someone standing to his left. The man was Martian dark and powerfully built, with a glint in his gray eyes gleaming beneath the brim of his sky-port security cap. There were gold bars on his collar, indicating that he must be an officer, though George was unclear as to his rank. The Martian crescent and double moon insignia on his right shoulder suggested he was with Planetary Security. The man didn't say a word; he just stood there, like the stone bust of a soldier.

"When did these show up?" George asked.

The officer walked past him, and looked out the window. "Don't you read the netcasts?"

"I've been out of town for a while."

"You're an Earther, aren't you?"

"No, Martian citizen," George said. "Just like you."

The officer turned. He was taller than George, which was common for native Martians genetically adapted to the lower gravity. His upper arms were heavily muscled, and his barrel chest was characteristic of an increased lung capacity endowed by genetic modification. His well-sculpted oval face might have belonged to a North African or East Indian back on Earth a couple of centuries before.

"Can I see your passport?"

George felt the man's scrutiny, as he slowly reached into his wallet for his ID. The officer took it, then pressed it into a Tab, after which the card glowed a dull green. The officer pulled a pen-like object from his belt, and touched it to an index finger George had extended. As soon as it was withdrawn, the probe flashed incandescent, sterilizing itself. A few seconds later,

George was identified by the bar code of nucleic markers the probe had sampled.

The officer handed back his ID. "You work at the university?"

"That's right. I'm a professor of physics."

After a long moment, the officer said, "Sorry, Dr. Mills." His eyes showed a fatigue that made him seem a little smaller. "It's been tense around here since they came." He gestured curtly toward the window.

How much should he say? George didn't want to be seen as sympathizing with Earthers, an impression he could easily give just by the way he looked. He did, however, want to know what was going on—wanted to make sure the officer's interest had nothing to do with him personally.

"How bad is it?"

"Bad enough that there are riots in Dome One." Spittle clung to the corners of the officer's mouth, and his left hand cupped a tight fist at his waist. "The Terrans don't belong here. It'll only get worst the longer they stay; the independence movement will make sure of that."

George listened intently, recalling the situation unfolding in netcasts back in his Washington hotel room. Because he had left Mars in relative calm a few months earlier, he considered the reports exaggerated, more hype for the masses so numb on excess that they required regular infusions of entertainment posing as news.

"I don't understand," George said. "Mars Independence is nothing new. We've never had this much Terran military here before. What happened?"

The officer hesitated, eying him suspiciously. "I wouldn't know," he said finally.

George stood on the concourse, with the quiet suddenly returning. Not knowing what else to do, he extended a hand. After an awkward moment, the officer took it in a firm dry grip. "Fred Jackson," he said.

"I have to go now, officer Jackson—it's not what I was expecting."

Jackson measured him. "Stay clear of the government buildings in Dome One; I hear there might be trouble."

"Yeah, thanks for the advice." George nodded, turned, then walked away, leaving Jackson standing in the glow of the window. He half expected Jackson to call him back before he could enter the terminal proper and disappear from sight, but the summons never came.

After he retrieved his luggage, George caught the airport tube to Dome One. As the tube car sped along on its magnetic cushion, he watched the stroboscopic lights go by outside the window. Eventually, the passage of lights slowed and gave way to the expanse of Dome One's tube terminal. From here, George planned to change cars, taking the inter-dome tube to Dome Two, the location of Ursa University, and the borough of Ursa where he lived.

* * *

The terminal was brightly lit. George surveyed a dazzling cream and blue striped tile floor made of Martian clay, which extended as far as the promenade access beyond the terminal apron. Gentle breezes, from the constant arrival and departure of tube cars, felt soothing on his face. Though the complex was underground, the ceiling was high and gave George the impression of being outdoors. He'd almost forgotten how strangely beautiful Ursa was, and felt an unexpected sense of home.

The tube car accelerated away, with its characteristic electric hum, kicking up the scent of eucalyptus from the many tall trees lining the promenade beyond the terminal.

"Hey stranger."

George looked around. From a nearby walkway bridging the promenade and tube landing, he spotted a woman, smiling and waving enthusiastically. She was about six feet tall and had dark olive skin, offset by light brown hair. The combination was in stark contrast to her pale blue eyes, giving her an exotic otherworld look, even here on Mars.

Waving back, George felt an awkwardness that came from being alone for too long. Fear gnawed at him at not knowing what to say, because over time, he'd grown accustomed to saying nothing at all. There hadn't been enough time to re-acclimate before seeing her again, and he feared that she might mistake his hesitation for indifference.

Before he knew it, she crossed the gulf between them. He felt arms around his middle. She kissed him, then pulled back and searched his face.

"I didn't expect to see you here this morning," George said.

"I surprised myself."

"Why's that?"

"Because I missed you more than I thought I would. I got up this morning thinking about how long that flight was, and about how you'd feel stepping off the tube with no one here to meet you."

George started to say something, then hesitated.

She laughed, making a quick motion with her eyes in the direction of the bridge. "Come on, I have a car over there."

She put her arm through his, and they started toward the little bridge on which he'd first seen her. George nodded and laughed as she spoke, responding more to the sound of her voice than the content of her words, their four-month separation melting away with each step. They continued over the bridge to the avenue beyond, down the rust clay sidewalk, to the cul-de-sac where she had left the car.

"I can't believe you've been gone for four months," Joanne whispered.

"Sorry I didn't call," George said.

"Did you miss me?" she asked.

"Yes, of course I missed you. But I had a bad feeling about the trip from the start. I couldn't put my finger on it, but there was something a little off about the whole thing—know what I mean?" He regarded her, remembered fantasizing about her during fitful nights in nondescript hotel rooms on another planet. This moment, which he'd anticipated for months now, seemed somehow more wishful thinking than something real. "That's why I didn't call, because I was afraid to involve you, not because I didn't miss you. I've missed you ever since the day I left."

She looked at him in mild amazement.

"Ask yourself why," George said. "Why, after funding the project for all these years, did they suddenly make me travel more than a hundred million miles to explain what they could have just as easily learned from a video conference. I've given them mountains of reports. You know the types; they wouldn't spend that kind of money unless they thought I was hiding something. They probably assumed I'd be on neural opiates over a Com-Link, and couldn't tell if I were lying or not."

After a moment, Joanne Zhu took his arm again. They moved off the clay sidewalk onto the cul-de-sac, where the car was parked. When she left to go to the driver's side, George continued feeling the warmth in the crook of his arm.

They circumnavigated the round motorway, joining a street that ran parallel to the promenade he'd seen from the tube platform. At the end of the street, they turned onto an upward-going ramp marked *Dome One Access*. The car began climbing toward an artificial sky whose unnatural lighting was so diffuse that it left few shadows on the underground world below. Joanne engaged the car's Nav AI, then released the wheel, as they followed the small access road up into a tunnel that traversed the dome's foundation. The tunnel led to a ramp for the *Sea Of Storms*, the large inter-dome avenue between Domes One and Two. George felt himself pushed back in the seat as the car accelerated into avenue traffic. Though he was glad to be back, he was put off when he noticed the Nav had selected the right-most lane of traffic, which was also the slowest moving—obviously Joanne's way of giving them more time to talk about what he felt reluctant to discuss.

When Joanne shifted in her seat to face him, he caught the hem of her dress moving up her leg, exposing a light inner-thigh that he found pleasantly disturbing.

"You've been in space a while, haven't you?" she teased.

He looked up too quickly, feeling his face getting hot. "You don't miss a thing, do you?"

"So, what happened back on Earth?" Joanne said. "You really scared me, you know." She lingered on him. "I didn't know what to think when I didn't hear from you. I even had scary flashes that you might have been detained."

Joanne sat back, crossed her arms, apparently not satisfied with the flimsy explanation he'd given back in the tube terminal.

George tasted rough flaking skin as he licked his lips. "Well, as it turns out, it's my part of our work they have a problem with. The review board knows the models are okay, and since you did them, and not the simulation, they wanted to talk to me. That's why I was called to Earth—the problem's with my simulation as a whole."

"How do you mean?"

"They're having trouble getting it to run. They grilled me about optimizations, details of implementation, things like that. They know I'm hiding something."

Joanne considered this, then asked, "It's a Will problem isn't it?"

"That's right, Jo. It's a Will problem. Up till now, they've only run selected segments of what we disseminated, subsets with a manageable number of dynamic cells. They always assumed that running the more complete scenarios, like the ones in our reports, were just a matter of logarithmic scale. Since they'd already reproduced less complete results, they thought that simply adding more computing power would fix it."

"It was a fair assumption on their part," she pointed out. "We always knew it was only a matter of time, but that still doesn't explain your recent behavior. There's more, isn't there?"

George leaned forward, as though doing so would make his explanation more viable.

"I don't think that they've made a connection between the simulations and the Proteus file yet. Nothing like that was ever mentioned. And since these are separate and unequal things, bringing you into it now might have been the red flag they needed to connect the dots. At least that's what I was afraid of. Does that make sense?"

George was a little surprised by her reaction this time. She sat back, exhaling softly.

"I had another reason for picking you up this morning," Joanne confessed.

The admission made his stomach knot. "Go on."

"Well, since you've been gone, I've gotten several calls from Dale at DRA. He's worried, George. He told me that most of the parents have had unannounced calls and impromptu visits from DRA reps working with another division of child services."

George made a mental audit of what he knew about the Department of Reproductive Affairs, something he hadn't really thought about since receiving enhancement therapy after his immigration to Mars years ago. As a consequence of the hostile Martian environment, permanent human residence on Mars resulted in higher rates of disease and premature death in most individuals. Mars was smaller than Earth, about one third the size, and the low gravity produced skeletal and muscular degeneration, as well as a plethora of deleterious metabolic changes. The thin atmosphere, and the lack of a strong planetary magnetic field, made the ambient radiation levels on the surface of Mars far greater than those on the surface of the Earth. The result was another set of maladies, ranging from cancer to premature organ failure. George had never considered the DRA suspicious, or even intrusive. The Martian government had established the agency as a public resource to provide a full spectrum of services for immigrants and expecting couples. It had never occurred to him that the DRA might have an investigative branch too.

"Are these visits something to worry about?" George asked. "After all, that's what DRA does, right?"

"I don't think you understand. The reason that Dale called was because only my kids, the Proteus kids, received unscheduled visits. It's unusual for the genetic consultant not to be called in cases like this."

It was serious. And, what's more, it was certainly troubling that this had all started just after his being called away. Looking at Joanne now, George could tell she wasn't finished.

"There's more?"

"Yes, I'm afraid there is. The visits were strange not only because they were unannounced, but also because there appears to be some involvement by a doctor from Mollar."

"Who?"

"I don't know who he is. I tried to find out more, but wasn't able to."

"Mollar?" George repeated slowly. "Why does that name sound so familiar? Help me out here. You're the molecular biologist."

"I'm not surprised you recognize the name. Mollar is in the interplanetary news all the time these days. They're a large Earth-based pharmaceutical company."

George sat back, looked out the forward windscreen, hoping that his testimony had bought them a little time. Everything seemed to be going in the wrong direction; he felt a surge of frustration. "What the hell is an Earth pharmaceutical company doing with DRA?"

"We'll know more tomorrow. Dale didn't only call to bring me up-to-date, it appears they want to interview me as well. I've got a meeting with DRA at their executive offices in Building One tomorrow. Care to join me?"

"Why you, Jo?" George was plagued by doubt. He flashed on the review board chairman's face, the one he'd tried so hard to exorcise. The man's thin lips sat in a malevolent grin that looked as though it'd been cut into his face by a razor. George shifted in his seat. He couldn't help feeling claustrophobic—the net was tightening.

Joanne leaned over and touched his hand. A slight scent of jasmine graced him as she came close. "Don't worry so much. I don't think they know anything definite. It's natural that they'd call me, since I did all the genetic work on the children they interviewed. My only real concern is how long it took them to bring me into it. I'm more worried that they chose to involve a doctor who has no prior knowledge of the children's histories. That's not the way it's usually done."

George thought the coincidence too strong to be brushed aside by her explanation. The fact that Joanne had invited him to come along was a sure sign she was having trouble buying it too. It was painfully obvious, even before his trip, that the true nature of the children's prenatal therapy would soon be discovered. Recent pictures of the children had been cause for concern. As they'd gotten older, the children had begun to change. Though they were designed to be virtually invisible in the general Martian population, there were still no guarantees that, in time, telltale racial characteristics wouldn't surface. Constraints had been placed on their synthetic evolution to suppress unusual distinguishing traits, but the extent to which he and Joanne had changed the human genome could easily impart small correlated artifacts into their appearances, which might escape the notice of the evolutionary simulations—no matter how good they were. And now he realized that this was especially true of traits linked to puberty.

They drove in silence. George felt Joanne watching him in stolen glances. He turned away to gaze at the alien landscape streaming by outside.

"You still with me?" she asked.

"Just taking in the sights. Seems like I've been gone for more than four months—know what I mean?"

He turned toward her, his head still resting on the seat. Joanne put her hand on his forehead, stroking the hair on his temple.

"I might have something for you tonight, if you're up for it," she said.

"I'm sure I could be talked into something."

"Remember Malcolm Peters?"

"The psychologist you did some work with from Orion Township?"

"Uh-huh. I've been talking to him for the past couple of months about some of the simulation results."

"How much did you tell him?"

Joanne laughed softly. "You have to relax. It's me, remember? I didn't tell him anything about the true nature of the scenarios. As far as he's concerned, this is an academic exercise." She paused, holding him in earnest communion with pale blue eyes. "But I think he could help. He's in Ursa right now for a psych conference at the university. I told him you were coming back today, and he suggested we have dinner tonight—if you're up for it, that is."

George lowered his side window about halfway. As he gazed out the window, warm air washed over him like a soothing balm. The terrain of the dome was mostly cobalt Martian clay and rock, punctuated by occasional patches of green grass and trees. He loved the flowering bougainvillea, which was often found around parks, and as part of the landscaping near office buildings and housing complexes. He could see the shimmer of Lake Potomac in the distance, a saltwater lake in the middle of Dome One that was connected to two other large lakes in Domes Two and Three. The water circulated between the three, thus keeping it fresh and aerated, and the dome air humidified. It wasn't long before they were over water. The *Sea Of Storms* spanned a section of the lake on widely spaced slender pylons that lifted the roadway sufficiently high to admit large-masted sailboats at its loftiest clearance.

"Well, what about it?" Joanne asked. "Are you up for it?"

George turned from the warm air. "What?"

She regarded him. "On second thought, maybe you should skip dinner and just get some sleep. You look like you could use some."

"No, I was just thinking about the trip from Earth. For the most part, it was pretty bad. You know, solitary confinement interspersed with long stretches of sheer boredom"—and fear, he wanted to say.

"I don't know," Joanne said. "I saw something else there."

He smiled at her.

"Why the smile?"

"It's true, you don't miss a thing."

"So, you're saying what?" Joanne asked.

"So I'm saying I could use a night on the town, not to mention the fact that you're the first woman I've been with for at least a month." He started to laugh when he saw her eyebrows arch.

After traversing Dome One, and taking the lower level between domes, they got off the *Sea Of Storms* and turned onto Ravine Road in Dome Two. Joanne returned the car to manual mode and followed Ravine as it climbed Monte Claire via an ascending series of switchbacks. Near the summit, they turned off Ravine onto a gravel driveway and drove through a large ficus hedge that hid the Summit Apartment complex. Joanne negotiated a circular drive and pulled up in front of the complex's common area. When George had retrieved his bags, he walked around to the driver's window, which Joanne had lowered. She invited him with a familiar motion of her index finger, then put her hand on his face, drew him closer, and kissed him softly on the lips.

"Welcome home," she whispered. "See you tonight."

Chapter Three

"As long as there are men, there will be war." – Albert Einstein

Planetary Security had ordered Fred Jackson to follow up on reports that separatists might be plotting an incident in the domes, something that could easily escalate the current civil unrest. When he returned from the airport this morning, Jackson rejoined his men in Dome One. They had been on patrol for hours now, beating back gangs of rock-throwing young people who were burning and looting shops in a central business district.

After encountering heavy resistance, Jackson ordered his men to regroup, to have a bite to eat, and something to drink. They needed some rest—a chance to catch their collective breaths. He found a mall with a courtyard enclosed on all sides, except for a front gate and archway. It was a defensible position, a good place to take a break. The men sat on stairs around a central fountain, momentarily laying down their weapons and retracting their helmets.

Jackson remained standing, poised at the gate, looking out over the large tree-lined promenade that was the center of the district. A blue ceramic sign with white lettering read *Mediterranean Way*. It hung over the empty street, just beyond the gate. The sky was bright, and the air was warm under the summer sun. Only a few days before, Jackson had seen people strolling lazily up and down the tiled walkways under the cool shade of large trees. The shops along the promenade, made of orange and rust colored Martian stucco, should have been bustling with shoppers and sightseers, but in the distance, Jackson saw clouds of dirty black smoke billowing from several shops along *Mediterranean*. The pungent odor of charred plastic replaced the fragrance of the foliage and burned his sinuses. He unconsciously tightened his grip on his rail gun as he thought about the bastards who had done this, about the crowds of young men he had chased down similar streets earlier today.

When Jackson's squad first arrived, they discovered a family had been attacked and killed in the middle of *Mediterranean*. Jackson checked for activity in the immediate vicinity, and found that automated dome surveillance indicated the presence of snipers armed with conventional assault weapons farther down the street. He hadn't expected lethal urban warfare, so he and his men had loaded their electromagnetic pulse cannons with tranquilizer gas, which, given these developments, put them at a disadvantage. The point was driven home when they found two security men standing over the bloody remains of four people in the middle of the street. The rest of the security detail was further down the district, trying to contain an angry mob that was throwing rocks and setting fires. They were, presumably, the same mob responsible for the carnage at Jackson's feet.

Standing above the bodies, Jackson recalled hearing occasional bursts of automatic weapons fire in the distance. Before retracting his helmet, he saw muzzle flashes in the infrared from the tops of buildings further down the street. Then, looking down, he saw the remains of a man, a woman, and two children. One of the children was about twelve, the other was very young, perhaps four or five. The adults looked to be recent immigrants, their features and complexions too Earth-like for their own good. The older boy was, unfortunately, Terran in appearance, but his little brother looked to be first- generation Martian. He had been genetically changed to conform to a world that apparently did not want him.

The family had been bludgeoned to death by something hard and blunt, perhaps a metal pipe or rock. The man had defensive wounds on his arms; his fingers were broken and set at odd angles. His head had been bashed in and lay in a pool of dark red blood littered with pieces of gray matter that spread into the street like a stain. The pre-teen, like his father, had been brutally killed and disfigured with equal savagery. The toddler, like the woman, seemed to have been spared the painful death of his father and brother. Perhaps the crowd, momentarily touched by the realization that the toddler looked so much like them, was moved to spare his agony, if not his life. Jackson had touched the bar under his helmet and made it retract. Then he calmly walked to a planter by the side of the road and vomited until there were only dry heaves left.

Shaking off the memory of recent events, Jackson checked his chronometer; twenty minutes had elapsed since they had entered the mall. He looked back at his men—no one spoke. They seemed held by personal thoughts, the details of which were too private to ever be known.

"Come on, time to get movin," Jackson called out.

A few minutes later, they were walking down the street again. He sent several soldiers to flank the main body of the squad further up. They held tight to the lines of buildings on either side of the street and stayed in the shadows, where snipers might miss them. Jackson could still hear the sputter of automatic weapons coming from somewhere further down the street. His suit acoustics triangulated the sounds while receiving information from sensors placed around the district. He could tell that one sniper was no more than a hundred and fifty feet ahead of him and above street level. Each volley of weapons fire made him angry; each sputter slapped some center of his brain making him want to slap back. The rattle of gunfire soon became more sustained with an accompanying increase in panicked Com chatter.

"Double time it!" he yelled to his squad.

They all ran down *Mediterranean* using muscular assists built into their suits. Up ahead he saw security men huddled in doorways and behind cars. Around them, sparks speckled the landscape from bullets hitting the sides of buildings and ricocheting off the ground. Occasional flashes accompanied the weapons fire from somewhere above the street, followed by puffs of smoke that Jackson registered on absorption sensors in his suit optics. He felt a couple of quick jabs to the chest and caught sight of flashes again on a nearby roof. He ducked into a doorway and ordered his men to fan out on adjacent streets to look for other snipers. Once the snipers were eliminated, they could push forward and neutralize the main force up ahead.

Jackson went active and scanned up high in microwave, revealing the assassin on a rooftop across the street. The man was hunkered down behind an air vent. Jackson zoomed in on hi-mag, and could make out what looked like a figure in a cap and dark glasses. He was down on one knee, holding what looked like an M100 military-style assault rife with optics. The butt of the rifle was up against his shoulder; his right index finger was on the trigger. Jackson channeled his voice through the PA in his suit.

"You, on the roof, behind the vent, throw down your weapon. Now!"

A hail of bullets rained down around Jackson, digging up the clay tiles on the sidewalk and the stucco on the wall behind him.

"Shit," he cursed, and jumped back.

Jackson crouched in a doorway, reached up and pulled a black and gray composite pack off his back. It had a set of panels on the side; he selected one, pushed it, and watched as it slid open to reveal neat stacks of spring-loaded magazines. He flipped his rail gun on the composite gimbal connected to his waist, and rotated it, exposing the underside. After he pulled out the gas magazine, he replaced it with one containing explosive aluminum projectiles. Then he swung the rail gun from his hip, caught it with his other hand, and aimed in one smooth motion born of experience.

The assassin, framed in Jackson's microwave optics, was acquired by the red aiming dot in his display, as he moved his eyes to the intended target. "Lock," he thought. A red circle formed around the target and started flashing. The artificial muscles took over, locked the target, and moved slightly to track it.

"Fuck you," Jackson said, and pressed the trigger. A sonic boom thundered as the electromagnetic cannon launched its projectile at more than five times the speed of sound. Jackson saw a white-orange streak caused by air friction on the projectile's aluminum jacket. An instant later, the round hit the vent behind the sniper. Both the vent and the man exploded, raining debris down into the street. Black smoke rose from a crater on the roof.

Jackson ran down the street, staying close to the shops.

"Glad to see you, Captain," he heard on Com, after the cheers and expletives that followed the death of the sniper.

He yelled to the security men huddled in doorways as he ran past. "Where?"

"Thirty degrees, three o'clock," Jackson heard on Com. He looked up. A man was running away on another rooftop. He heard several other sonic booms and explosions coming from further down the street—clearly his men had found their targets too.

"You on the roof, drop your gun and stay where you are, this is your last warning."

The man kept running. "Okay," Jackson said to himself. He raised the shiny alloy barrel. His eyes brought the aiming dot to just above the man's head, and his thoughts locked the target on a wall about twenty feet in front of him. The dot began to flash, and he squeezed the trigger. The white-hot projectile burned the cap and hair on the man's head as it streaked a foot above him. Before the pain could register, the projectile exploded on the wall in front of the assassin. The concussion blew him off his feet, and threw him down onto his back. Moments later, the man lay there, unconscious, with the top of his head still smoking.

Jackson did a three-sixty, straining to see if there was anyone else out there, but he saw nothing. His optics sped through the spectrum from IR to ultraviolet; the suit AI worked on pattern recognition of movement and sound—nothing.

"All clear," he declared on Com.

Security people seemed to come out of every crack and crevasse along the street. Jackson counted twelve in all.

"Thanks, Captain," said a man. He appeared from behind a car, which was parked in front of what looked like a dress shop. His plastic visor was up, and he carried a wand in his right hand. He was sporting minimal armor, and the stripes on his sleeves indicated he held the rank of sergeant.

"A little light for this kind of duty, aren't you, Sergeant?"

The man was surprisingly good-natured. He chuckled, "Yeah, ya-think?"

"Lost anybody?" Jackson asked.

"Would have if you hadn't come along, Captain. They lured us down here. There's a civilian crowd further down; we think they did it."

The man glanced up the street. "When we first got here, they were beating some people in the middle of the road."

His expression changed as he recounted the events.

"Most sickening thing I've ever seen," the Sergeant said.

Jackson couldn't help noticing the look in the Sergeant's eyes as he gazed into Jackson's insectile helmet. The sight reflected fright and reassurance, all at the same time. Full combat suits weren't exactly standard issue, and the fact that Dome Security had seen fit to deploy a hunter killer squad marked a turning point in what had been civil unrest.

"Where are they now?" Jackson asked.

"The civilians?"

Jackson nodded.

"Yeah—well, they took off down the street when the snipers opened up. You could hear those sons-of-bitches laughing and yelling cat calls."

"Follow me, and stay close to cover," Jackson ordered. "We're going to round them up, get them off the streets."

"Ya got it, Captain."

Jackson held his rail gun loosely and started walking down the street in the direction of the gunfire. A few minutes later, he met up with several other men in his squad, who were standing behind an archway, not unlike the gateway to the mall where they had rested earlier.

"What's the situation?" Jackson asked.

"We took care of the snipers, Captain—the skyline's clear. There are about twenty civilians in there." He pointed through the gate. "We wanted to wait for you before going in."

"Good," Jackson said. He looked behind and saw security people breaking cover to join them.

"I'm going in. I expect prisoners to come out, but whatever happens, I don't want these assholes walking away from this, understand?"

Jackson saw the soldier's helmet nod in acknowledgement.

"Okay," he said. Then he turned and walked through the gate.

As Jackson cleared the archway, he was pelted by gunfire and raised his weapon. He could see people crowded behind a fountain; others were squeezed into doorsills. Muzzle flashes came from a couple of places. The suit AI set flashing circles in his display around a doorsill and a shop window on the far side of the circular mall.

"Listen to me you people, nobody's going to walk away from this. Lives have been lost, and those responsible will be prosecuted according to their complicity. But one way or another, nobody's going to get away with murder."

"You're a Martian, aren't ya, soldier?"

"Yeah," Jackson called out, "so what?"

"Well, what the fuck are you doing sticking up for those Earthers anyway? You should be with us, not with them. We want justice."

"That's exactly what I'm here to give you. You know those people you killed up the street?" Jackson asked.

"Yeah," the man said. "You mean that Earther whore and her bastards?"

"That's right," Jackson said. "They were all Martian citizens with the same rights you have—to be safe in the streets of this township. For violating those rights, you and your friends are going to prison."

"Like hell," yelled the man, and another volley of automatic fire hit Jackson.

His artificial muscles held firm. His monomolecular armor was scratched, but not breached.

"Last warning," Jackson called. "You can come out horizontal or vertical, but you're coming out!"

He raised his weapon. Its gleaming alloy finish flashed radiant in the afternoon sun, highlighting the word *Justice* stenciled on its barrel. Excited chatter came from behind the fountain.

"I'm coming out," yelled a man in panicked barks.

He threw out a rifle, then rose from a doorsill with his hands high in the air, as if he were frantically reaching for something. He started walking toward Jackson. Another volley came from the shop window, and he fell, broken and bloody at Jackson's feet. Jackson took aim and fired into the window. The shop wall exploded in flame and black smoke. The people behind the fountain screamed in terror and began filing out in a disordered jumble of running and stumbling.

When the security people had taken the last of them into custody, Jackson walked up to the ruined shop wall behind which the sniper had hidden. He moved through the charred hole that had once been a window, and saw someone huddled in the back of the room among the debris. The sniper had obviously known what was coming, but hadn't been fast enough to get out of the way. Jackson pulled his rail gun up vertically and the gimbal took over, moving it to his back where it snapped into its gun cradle. Then he dropped to one knee and rolled the body over.

"Ah-shit," he said out loud.

It was a young woman, no more than eighteen or nineteen. Her long black hair lay tangled and matted with dark ash and blood. Her once lovely face was stained in places, and she wore a painful grimace on a mouth that he imagined many young men had once fanaticized about kissing.

"What a waste," he mumbled in a low voice.

He went through her pockets and found a wallet with ID, which he put in his pack. He'd make sure her parents were informed, and the body secured.

Chapter Four

"How do you infuse lines of computer code with the quality of
desire?" – George Mills, Reflections on the Turing Test, Ursa
University, Mars, 2321 A.D.

George stood motionless as Joanne's car pulled away. She
circled the driveway, then disappeared through the hedges.
Standing on the grass just off the gravel, he realized he'd
forgotten to wave goodbye. In his mind's eye, he saw her
watching his dazed performance in the rear view mirror. He
imagined her smiling and shaking her head. He shrugged,
grabbed his bags, and turned toward the housing complex.
Before him sprawled a large lawn, crisscrossed by slate-colored
tile walkways, leading to destinations hidden by a thick grove of
trees. After picking a familiar path, one he hadn't walked in
months, he began the descent toward his apartment.

As George turned into an alleyway leading to his
subdivision, he could see a random sprinkling of reddish brown
tile roofs dotting the hillside foliage in the late morning sun.
Beyond that, under the massive canopy of the dome, the tops of
university buildings stretched almost to the shore of Lake
Geneva. Typically, George enjoyed the walk back to his
apartment over the majestic sights of the mountain, but today he
was plagued by his earlier conversation with Joanne concerning
the DRA visits. He just couldn't shake it. He suspected his
fatigue had something to do with that, but continued thinking
about Mollar's involvement and couldn't reconcile it with
anything coincidental.

George walked up to a small wooden gate that announced
the entrance of his secluded front yard. When he reached the
door, he dialed a key code and entered. The apartment was just
as he had left it. The familiarity cleansed his mind of all the
noise that had filled it since leaving Joanne's car. He left his bag

in the foyer, crossed the braided rug atop the wooden floor of his small living room, then walked to the bay window at its far end. On his way to the window, his progress was followed by a binocular pair of video cameras that silently turned in response to his movements. They were mounted on an oak veneer wall and situated between two large prints of classical French impressionism. The cameras were small spheres with dot lenses no larger in diameter than the hole in a cocktail straw. They were laterally mounted on a thin plastic member that kept them three and a half inches apart, just enough parallax for depth perception. A small amber diode, which sat at the junction between the two cameras, was illuminated, indicating they were active.

The room was washed in light as he raised the blinds to reveal the mountainside in back of his house. The hills fell in a green descending tree line, beyond which the waters of Lake Geneva undulated in long hypnotic waves that sparkled and darkened as they moved.

A voice addressed him from small speakers on either side of a large bookcase on the opposite wall.

"Good to have you back," the voice said in a smooth male baritone.

"Good to be back, Will."

"I made coffee, if you'd care to have some."

Freshly brewed coffee, common on Mars, was not generally available on spacecraft like the *Prince of Wales*, which had been George's home for the past month.

"That was very thoughtful of you." George moved to the kitchen and poured a cup. As he stood under the cupboard, he thought a moment, then reached up and retrieved a flask. The mixture of the bourbon and coffee steam smelled delicious.

"I take it there were complications." Will said.

Even now, after all these years, George felt a sense of awe at hearing Will use the proper pronoun in reference to itself. This sense of self was not explicitly a feature of Will's heuristic block. And although George had designed Will to mimic human behavior, in time, unexpected things had happened. The scientist in George tried to understand what had produced behavior that most computer scientists of the last two centuries would consider impossible. Unfortunately, Will's novel design of quantum level neural nets did not lend itself to easy analysis of his runtime behavior. Determining the validity of Will's self-awareness was a puzzle that George had yet to solve.

George took a sip, "Why do you think there's a problem?"

"You don't typically drink alcohol before noon."

"I wasn't aware that you were keeping such careful track of my habits," George said. He strolled back to the window, gazing out over the rolling hills on the eastern side of the dome.

"So what happened on your trip? Is there something I should know about, something I might help you with?" Will asked.

"Maybe you can. What do you know about DRA visits to the Proteus children over the past month?"

"Does this have something to do with your trip? I guess I'm a little confused."

"And well you should be," George said. "I'm sorry—let me start at the beginning."

He told Will about his conversation with Joanne on their way back to his apartment, and about his fears that the events of the last month could not be explained away as mere coincidence.

"I think I may be able to access information concerning those visits. Just give me a moment."

George nodded and turned from the amber light to the vista outside. A few minutes later, Will was back.

"I'm accessing the DRA appointment database now, but I can't find a set of appointments cross-referenced to the Proteus file anytime this past month."

"What's that mean?" George asked. "Now I'm confused— but my question still stands. According to Joanne, Dale called her from DRA affirming what you just failed to confirm. Somewhere in all this the chain is broken."

"Apparently," Will said.

George sat on the wooden floor with his head resting on the sofa. His coffee sat next to him on the rug, and he unconsciously rubbed the bare wood with his hands. Wood was such a rare commodity on Mars that typically, when it was used for furniture or building, it was only a quarter inch thick with a plastic or ceramic backing for support and a polymer coat for resistance to wear. George had gone to great lengths to remove the coating on his floor so that the wood was exposed. He often sat on the floor and rubbed it with his hands. Doing so brought him comfort. Talking to Will now, he rubbed it reflexively.

"So, what do you think it means that there were no visits?" George asked.

"DRA keeps a schedule of regular appointments with all their client families," Will replied. "These have to do with regular checkups and the assessment of physical and mental condition of children who received prenatal therapies. Depending on the extent of the care given, and on the age of the child, these visits are mandated by law."

"But you said there were no visits."

"No, what I said was there were none scheduled or recorded."

George thought a moment. "Jo said that Dale called and told her all the children in the Proteus file had received—how did she put it— unannounced visits."

"Curious," Will said. "If we are to believe Dale, then we have to conclude that the kids did receive visits and that something unusual is taking place. And whatever that something is, it's apparently being hidden from us."

George's mind raced. The comfort and calm that he had felt vanished. Someone out there was putting it together. The fact that he had not been contacted meant that they didn't have the whole picture, not yet at least. But how close were they? Who or what had led them to suspect that the Proteus kids were sufficiently different to warrant some kind of covert investigation?

"I still may be able to uncover something," Will said. "I'm reviewing and correlating all landline and wireless communications coming into and out of DRA this past month from billing records in the Ursa central office database at Mars Telecom."

George sat, caressing the floor. "I don't understand. What good will that do if you don't know whom DRA spoke to? There are thousands of names out there. How do we tell who's legitimate and who is not?"

"I'm assuming there may have been some interagency communications prompting the visits."

"You mean like the Department of Education got a set of very good or very bad test scores, for example, and wanted to interview the kids who received a specific kind of genetic work."

"Yes, that's a good example. Unfortunately, I can't find anything there either."

"Nothing at all?"

"I agree, this is very unusual," Will said.

George thought a moment, then asked, "What do you know about Mollar?"

"You mean Mollar Pharmaceuticals?"

"Yes, that's right."

"Biggest drug company on Mars," Will said. "Based on Earth. That's where their executive offices are, in a suburb of Virginia in fact, near Washington DC."

"That's interesting. That's where I was last month, Washington DC. What else can you tell me about them? Can you find something on their associations—who they do business with, things like that?"

"They're known to do a lot of business with Void Fleet in the field of bio-warfare and performance enhancements. Why do you ask? What do they have to do with DRA?"

"That's exactly what I want to find out. Jo said something about a doctor from Mollar accompanying DRA reps on those unannounced visits."

Silence.

"Any opinion on that?" George asked.

"Do you have a name?" replied Will.

"I will tomorrow. I'm going with Jo to some kind of meeting at the DRA offices in Dome One."

"Without a name, I can't really give you anything definitive. Same problem you mentioned earlier; we have to know whom they spoke to if we want a specific record of the call. By the way, while we were discussing Mollar, I checked the communications database once more for a call between DRA and Mollar."

"Let me guess, it's not in there either."

"That's right. However, given the lack of records—once you throw Mollar into the mix, government involvement would appear to be highly likely," Will said.

George smiled, "DRA was a government agency last time I looked."

"I don't mean that type of government," Will said. "Not the transparent government, and not the Mars government."

"I see," George said. He recalled the board chairman's smug expression and mocking tone as he had asked his folksy questions. Maybe the review board hadn't bought his story after all. The only real mystery about the whole thing was why now? What had been the triggering event? It was clear it had something to do with Earth, but why the military connection?

"The fact that they want to speak to Joanne indicates that they are trying to understand the meaning of the Proteus file," Will said.

"I think you're right," George admitted. "Somebody out there is probing, and may even have some idea of what they're looking for. I also agree that, given the information we have, Earth Confederation involvement seems likely."

George got up and slowly paced the length of his small living room, his bourbon remaining on the floor, abandoned and forgotten. "But the thing is, I still fail to understand why Econ—Earth Confederation, and the military in particular—would be interested in a small Martian experiment in genetic enhancement?"

"You forget, genetic enhancement has long been of interest to the military. In fact, in many of my confidential inquires, I've run across oblique references to genetically enhanced soldiers," Will said.

"But research of that kind would be highly opposed on Earth," George said. "It might even be illegal according to remnants of the genetic abatement laws."

"That's exactly my point. If it were being done here on Mars, it would present Void Fleet with a unique opportunity. They could gather data on experiments they've wanted to perform all along, but were prevented from doing because of the genetic abatement laws."

Upon reflection, George couldn't believe how naïve he'd been. Until now, he had thought of their infraction as an unsanctioned extension of genetic enhancements already widely available on Mars. But if he were honest with himself, it was much more than that. Under what definition of enhancement would creating a new species fall?

"It's not surprising," he heard Will say. "If they had any idea of what we were up to, they'd be very alarmed."

"Odd I didn't realized this sooner. To my way of thinking, we've produced a less aggressive, not a more aggressive human variation. All this time my major concern has been the survivability of the children, not the other way around."

"I think what you neglect to consider is that a more aggressive type will naturally tend to project their nature onto their fears," Will said. "Those who credit their physical and intellectual prowess with their success as a species would tend to project those same qualities in greater measure onto another

36

group that they consider genetically superior. It would be reasonable to assume that, to them, superior might mean stronger and more cunning."

As Will spoke, George reclaimed his bourbon, sat on the sofa, and stared blankly out the window.

Will said, "I don't think they know anything definite. I think they might have stumbled across a pattern in the Proteus file, but I don't think they know the nature or the extent of what's happened."

"Oh, and why's that?"

"Because given what I said before, what do you think they would do if they knew?"

"I guess they would've arrested us by now," George said, remembering the incident at the airport.

"Exactly," Will said.

"They're just sniffing around. And the fact that they want to speak to Jo means they're close. At least we have a little time to ..." George trailed off.

What could he possibly do when they figured it out? And, of course, they would eventually figure it out. The only cushion he had ever really had was complete anonymity.

"Tell me about Earth," Will asked, changing the subject. "Your trip must have something to do with all this."

"Why?" George asked. He considered this a crucial point, and wanted to understand Will's thinking as well.

"It was only after you left for Earth that things started happening. Nothing for all these years, then suddenly you go off planet and the Proteus children are systematically interviewed. That can't be coincidental. You've had this grant for almost fifteen years now, and in all that time, how many times have you been required to go to Earth for a status report?"

"That's true, but how do you account for the fact that while I was there, I was neither arrested, detained, nor even questioned about all this?"

"It's interesting," Will admitted. "But if you want my help in this regard, you're going to have to tell me what happened as well as what didn't."

"Okay," George said. "I got the distinct impression that they were more interested in you than anything else."

There was a short silence. George could tell that this wasn't what Will had expected to hear. He was always intrigued on these rare occasions when Will was taken off-guard.

"Oh," Will said finally.

"That's right. You know our work has inspired many other branches of research into stress-based behavior. We've published scores of reports pertaining to mass psychology under stress over a myriad of conditions. Studies that, up till now, could never be performed outside of simulations, because to do so would either be cruel, unlawful, or physically impossible due to scale and circumstances."

George got up and walked to the window. Off in the distance, he could see columns of swiftly-moving traffic, underscoring Dome Two's bustling population.

"That's all well known, but there must be something else, something new," Will said.

"Yes, there is. It appears as if the Earth Confederation has employed some of our colleagues in Washington to run simulations similar to our own. As expected, they've run into technical problems. That's why I was asked to go to Earth."

After a moment, Will said, "I don't understand. If they wanted other detailed studies done, why not ask us to do them? After all, they are funding us to do exactly that, aren't they?"

"The problem is they don't want us to know about it," George said.

There was another pause.

"Do you want to tell me, or do you want me to guess about whatever it is you're not telling me?" Will asked.

George smiled. Was Will frustrated? If so, that was interesting in itself. George saw the cameras looking at him with

38

a motionless intensity. He imagined Will with a face capable of expression, and saw the furrows in his make-believe brow.

"You're becoming more human every day."

"Every time you sense I have a shortcoming, you tend to say that," Will said, with a hint of satisfaction in his voice.

"They're apparently doing tactical simulations of the current conflict here on Mars," George said. "If I had to guess, I'd say they couldn't possibly ask us to do it because much of the situational data is probably classified, and we're too close to the wrong side in this conflict."

"I see; they're playing war-games with our models."

"Very succinctly put," George said. "And, of course, they've run into problems because they don't have a computer like you."

This aspect of it was amusing. Most high-level people on Earth considered Mars little more than a backwater. George remembered the review board, their dismissive arrogance. The only reason they hadn't dug deeper was because they'd considered an Earth expatriate too incompetent to be evasive. Everything on Earth was grand, unimaginable a century before. The level of science and technologic development was considered unapproachable anywhere else in the solar system. It was both amusing and frightening to think that their colleagues would soon discover that a small group on an outpost planet had developed technology far in advance of what currently existed on Earth. That would certainly annoy them, and as Will had pointed out, quite insightfully, it would also scare the hell out of them.

"So what now? You must realize this is a very dangerous situation. How did you finally leave it?" Will asked.

"I stalled for time. Told them they must have made a procedural error somewhere, told them that we would take a look at some of the less classified pieces of it."

"You know such an explanation won't satisfy them for long. It would be advisable to try to prevent them from making the connection between the Proteus file and the technology deficit they have."

"How do you suggest we do that?"

"You've given me some avenues to investigate. I can expand the scope of our search. Give me a day or two. I'll try to get some better answers about the people who are investigating us."

George felt a flush of alarm. "Wait a minute, are you proposing hacking into secure sites on Earth? Is that what you mean by expanding the scope of the search? Aren't you concerned that if they discover someone on Mars is hacking into their secure sites, it'll only make an already bad situation even worse? Wouldn't that just confirm their fears?"

After a few moments, Will said, "I've been careful. I understand how delicate this situation is. If you don't want to proceed, I'll terminate the inquiry right now. But you must understand, we'll be working in the dark if I do."

George walked up to the camera and held its gaze, as if he were relating something in confidence. "Hold off for now, Will. Things are moving much too fast for mere mortals like me. Give me a chance to catch up—okay?"

Chapter Five

By 6:00 PM George had run, showered, and taken a short nap. He had learned from his early days on Mars that exercise and sleep helped restore the alignment of the body's natural clock. As he closed the front gate on his way to the car, he began to feel hungry. That's good, he thought; he was back in sync. Agreeing to go to dinner had certainly been the right thing to do. After his conversation with Will earlier in the day, sitting around the house with all this nervous energy would be lonely and depressing.

He drove down Ravine, spying bands of dark purple over the lake replacing the pink daytime sky. Lights were starting to come on in the apartments and university buildings below. Just beyond the university, he could see the colorful displays that outlined the shore of Lake Geneva. Restaurants, shore side businesses, and arcades were all distinguishable by their bright neon signs and holographic video billboards. George lowered the windows and decided to stay off the avenue, opting instead for a more scenic route along smaller back roads. He entered the campus though a rear archway, which served as an entrance to student housing at the base of Monte Claire.

George made his way through the winding streets to the Minsky computer science building, then parked in his assigned space. It was a beautiful night, clear and star filled. He chose to walk the mile to the lakeshore, since it was decidedly more convenient to park at Minsky than to look for a space near the strip. He took a tree-lined path, drinking in the quiet of the evening campus. As he got closer to the shore promenade, he began to hear the muted talking and laughing of people in the distance. Soon, he emerged from the campus, then crossed the Shore Avenue by taking the pedestrian tunnel that ran under the busy thoroughfare. Once on the other side, he found himself amongst a crowd of people, walking up and down the brightly lit carnival promenade.

Looking around to get his bearings, George saw the antique neon marquee for the Landing, the restaurant where he'd agreed to meet Joanne and Malcolm. The Landing was about a half mile south, across a dense sea of people. He pushed by the crowd until he saw Joanne talking to a man near a set of stairs under the restaurant's porch and entrance. The large sign above the entrance depicted a bearded sailor pulling his raft onto a sandy beach. It was this sign and the proximity to the campus that had made the Landing one of George's favorite places. The sign was an antique, with electric blue neon water lapping electric brown sand in a surreal stop motion reminiscent of ancient seaside California towns where George had passed summers a lifetime ago. He moved to within a foot or two of the pair before they realized he was there. Joanne turned, took his arm, and pulled him into their small circle.

"Malcolm, I'd like you to meet George Mills, my close friend and associate."

George smiled and took Malcolm's outstretched hand.

"Good to finally meet you," Malcolm said. "Joanne talks about you all the time."

He was taller than George, who, at six foot five, was taller than most Earthers. Malcolm was lean, with the physique of an athlete. George guessed that he might be a runner or swimmer— something like that. He was balding, with wildly curly hair around the ears and a full beard. Turning from Malcolm, George noticed Joanne was wearing another print dress like the one she'd worn this morning. It fluttered lightly in the brackish breeze coming off the lake, which carried with it the smell of curry, basil, and garlic from the restaurant. George put his hand on the small of her back. "Lets go in, I'm starving."

They were seated at a private table on a veranda in the back, two stories above the lake. The rear of the Landing was in stark contrast to the side facing the promenade. While the front was awash in lights and noise, the back was dark and quiet. A little too romantic, but considering what they had to discuss, George was happy to have the privacy.

After they ordered and the waiter brought a bottle of white wine, Joanne glanced at George and asked, "Want to get started?"

George filled their glasses. He'd assumed this was going to be Joanne's show. The meeting was her idea. He hadn't wanted to bring anybody else into this thing, which led him to believe that he had been invited to fill in some of the blanks.

"Well," George began, and took a sip of wine. He regarded Malcolm across the table, in the candlelight. The man's neutral expression conveyed little that George could read.

"I don't know you very well, Malcolm. What I'm about to tell you is, well, pretty fantastic. Before I start, I'd like to know what your understanding of this meeting is."

Malcolm glanced at Joanne, then back at George. "Joanne hasn't told you about our conversations?"

"I just came back from Earth this morning, so we haven't had much time to talk. She only told me that being a psychologist, you might be able to offer some professional observations on a project we're both involved in. She did tell me you have experience with children traumatized by war." George took another drink, "Is that right?"

"Yes," Malcolm said. "I was a lieutenant in the Martian Militia during the helium-3 riots on Phobos."

"I remember," George said. "I was still on Earth at the time."

"When was that?" Joanne asked. "About twenty years ago, wasn't it?"

Malcolm took a drink, "That's about right."

"It was bad, wasn't it?" George asked. "I remember it dominated the netcasts for nearly a year. Almost turned into a civil war, didn't it? At least that's the way it was portrayed on Earth."

Malcolm's face was stern, distant, not the casual stranger that George had just met. It was obvious that the conflict had left scars on this man that the passing of two decades had failed to heal.

"I'd say it was bad. I was only twenty-three then, scarcely a man."

He fixed George with an icy gaze. "I don't think there's been anything like it on Earth for a hundred years. People forget what war's like when they're not directly involved."

"But the militia is a police force, isn't it?" Joanne asked. "It's not formally part of the army."

"Suffice it to say that at that time, the militia was a branch of the Terran Marines. Our standing orders came from the same NearSec commanders who commanded the regular army. The only reason I was conscripted was because I was a doctor and an Earthman. They would have never trusted a regular Martian in the officer's corps. That should have been a tip off as to their true intentions."

"I'm no longer an Earthman," George said smiling.

Malcolm touched his glass to George's. Both men drank.

"Remind me," George said. "The riots were about ERC mining operations on Phobos, weren't they?"

Malcolm gave a contemptuous chuckle. "They called it mining, I'd call it forced labor. Those poor bastards." He looked directly at George now. "They came to Mars looking for a better life. Spent every credit they had getting here. Left friends, family, all the support it takes a lifetime to establish, to come here. ECon made it sound attractive. They resettled their families in Orion Township. Then, when they were at their most vulnerable, the ERC exploited them in the most blatant way they possibly could. They became a population of indentured servants a hundred million miles from anyone who could possibly help them. It was hard to watch. When the pressure became too great, there was a mass revolt. Many of them were proud, some with military or police training."

George shook his head, remembering the evening netcasts, the detached intellectual chatter, and the endless political and military psychobabble.

"You know, Malcolm, if I recall correctly, on Earth the whole thing was portrayed as a strike gone bad due to Martian labor organizers. They said it was about highly paid construction workers being pushed by Martian political extremists into trying to take control of valuable corporate assets. They were afraid of being held hostage for better contracts, and worst of all, more local control."

Malcolm paused, then exhaled. "Well, I was there, and that's certainly not what I saw. Hundreds died. They never had a chance. I came as part of the cleanup, an impossible effort to reconstitute something that had been hopelessly broken. That incident spawned a new generation of Martian orphans, and in my opinion, the beginning of the separatist movement that plagues Earth's relationship with Mars to this day."

George was beginning to see why Joanne had brought him tonight. He had known Malcolm for less than an hour, and couldn't remember the last time he'd had such a frank discussion with anyone whose past was as closely linked to Earth as his own. It was simple for someone who had no emotional ties to Earth to be an enlightened critic. That ability of most people to consider only those facts that support their own secret internal needs was one of the reasons, in George's opinion, why human societies had never really worked. George had grown up on Earth, had been educated there, and had married and been divorced there. Secretly, he preferred a blue sky to a pink one, but for reasons he found hard to discuss with anyone else, he couldn't imagine himself being as uninhibited as Malcolm in facing his own demons. If they were going to get through this crisis intact, it would be essential that they were at least honest with themselves.

George noticed the smile suggesting itself on Joanne's lips. Was she using Malcolm, an Earth expatriate like himself, to explore his feelings—lay them bare? Though he and Joanne had been close these last fifteen years, George had hidden much of his own emotional past from her. Perhaps, on the cusp of the upheaval that seemed sure to come, she wanted to understand all his motivations.

Malcolm drank and looked off into space.

"What do you think went wrong?" George asked.

Malcolm blinked. "What do you mean?"

"Why weren't the disputes settled more amicably? Why did it have to go to violence and insurrection?"

Malcolm seemed uncertain. No doubt he considered this a strange line of questioning. He had come tonight with the understanding that they were going to discuss children in one of Joanne's projects, not the metaphysics of war and peace.

"I don't know," Malcolm said finally. "The miners were desperate, the company was greedy, the soldiers were under orders. Take your pick."

"You're a psychologist," George pointed out. "We always claim that violence is a means of last resort, don't we? That it should be avoided at all costs."

"I agree, that's what we say," Malcolm said dismissively.

"But you don't believe that?" George asked.

He felt Joanne's hand on his arm, then noticed the look she was giving him. He knew that look.

"It's okay," Malcolm said. "He raises some interesting points. Frankly, George, I don't know why it turned out that way. Isn't that, more or less, exactly how things have turned out on Earth for the past two or three thousand years? We want to think that violent conflict is an aberration, but history doesn't bare that out. We had an isolated hundred years of peace under Rome, and remember it as a unique moment in history."

Malcolm shook his head.

This was exactly what George had been looking for. "I agree with your observations, but what I'm really interested in is the reason. I'm a physicist. I'm trained to regard phenomena from a fundamental point of view. I hold the view that there exists some small number of fundamental principles from which we can understand the world clearly and unambiguously. I'm not asking you these questions to perpetuate some inane debate. There are plenty of people who make their living doing exactly that."

"Amen to that," Malcolm said, and took another drink.

"The problem with endless debate," continued George, "is that it hasn't settled anything. We think of ourselves as good people, people steeped in civilization and tradition. Yet we seem, like alcoholics, unable to avoid taking that next drink."

"Interesting metaphor," Malcolm said. "In my experience, it almost seems to begin with a lack of imagination. The people in charge feel as if they're far above the fray. They concern themselves with tactics and strategy. They will say anything and do anything to appear somehow in possession of secret insight. After all, they consider themselves intellectuals, endowed by God with a firm grasp of the big picture."

The waiter returned with their food. George had broiled salmon from Lake Geneva, and Joanne had trout. Malcolm ordered steak made of the finest soy proteins that Mars could grow. George, who'd been in space for over a month, was starving for real food and ate with enthusiasm. Realizing that his table manners had perhaps suffered due to his month of near isolation, George glanced over at Joanne.

She was unable to stifle a laugh. "Is it the stimulating conversation, or just the night air?"

George smiled weakly and shrugged. The rest of the meal was spent in relative silence.

When everyone had finished, the waiter brought coffee. Malcolm wiped his mouth with a white cloth napkin he took from his lap. George watched him from across the table through puffs of aromatic steam rising from his coffee. The man looked no more able to let go of his memories than a hypnotized bird was able to look away from a snake.

"The people in charge," Malcolm said, "they really don't think about the people who die. They say they do. They go to great somber lengths to convince everyone involved that they do—the parents, the troops. They pay homage to higher powers, almost asking for forgiveness in advance. But in reality, aside from what they say, most insulate themselves and those they care about from the actual carnage. I can't tell you how many times I saw new officers start vomiting when the killing and dying started. I was one of those officers. Lack of imagination," Malcolm repeated.

"But what about the ones who experience it, then do it again?" George asked. "I've heard people say they actually enjoyed it. Some of them say they were never as alive as in the middle of a battle. Some say it gave their lives meaning."

Malcolm sighed. "Yeah, I know. I've heard that too. What's more, I've seen it. As a psychologist, I find this phenomenon very troubling. I can't explain it without admitting that there may be something systemically flawed about the human psyche."

George paused a moment, trying to organize his thoughts.

"Suppose that the basic problem is that people, Homo sapiens, are fundamentally flawed just as you intimated."

Malcolm regarded him quizzically. "Are you arguing psychology?"

"No, not really, not in some abstract sense of right and wrong anyway. I'm speaking more objectively."

Malcolm furrowed his brow.

"For example, let's take a case from adaptive evolution," Joanne said. "Suppose that at some point in the past, people ate fibrous roots, that these roots were somehow a dietary imperative."

"Like fruit for scurvy," Malcolm said.

"Exactly. Now, as a consequence, we know that in some people wisdom teeth are a big problem. They're too large for the jaw. And if they aren't extracted, they can sometimes abscess, and become infected."

"That's true," Malcolm said. "In fact, when I was younger, mine had to be extracted, all four of them. But what does that have to do with war and peace?"

"It's a flaw," Joanne said. "A physical flaw which, if not corrected, can lead to the death of the individual with that particular flaw."

"I understand the principles of basic evolution," Malcolm said. "In a world with no dentists, everyone with large teeth and small jaws would eventually die off. In the end, when people no longer depended on a diet that included fibrous roots, and there was another competing imperative for smaller jaws, everybody would be left with small teeth that fit correctly into a smaller jaw."

"Exactly," Joanne said. "For species that survive, adaptive evolution tends to correct for advantages that later become flaws as the environment changes. That's what we've done on Mars, isn't it? For example, I've been enhanced to live here more effectively. The evolutionary path that I inherited from my earthly ancestors was wrong for this world, flawed, if you will. The environment changed. Earth became too crowded to support all of us. We couldn't wait for evolution to fix those flaws. We had to act, if we were to survive here. Now, suppose that our predatory instincts as a species are just such a flaw. Clearly, in the distant past, it was a survival advantage to be aggressive and cunning. But as our situation has changed, it has become, perhaps, a terminal flaw."

Malcolm seemed to consider this possibility. "Okay, it's true that people did come from a primate branch that left the trees for the savanna more than a million years ago. In doing so, many pre-Homo sapien groups became hunters."

"Predatory hunters," George said.

"It may well have been a major step toward the development of a larger brain, along with walking upright and having opposable thumbs," Joanne said. "Predators have a good sense of their prey—their habits, their strengths and weaknesses.

They needed to develop hunting strategies if they were going to hunt in packs. Many prey animals are good runners, with a keen sense of smell and good eyesight. Predators need to develop tactics that enable them to effectively catch their prey. Typically, that kind of organization requires a complex social order."

"True," Malcolm said, acknowledging that the conversation had taken a more understandable tone.

"Our circumstances have changed dramatically in the time between the savanna and the present, but we ourselves have not," Joanne said. "There are twenty billion people on Earth now, and another billion scattered throughout the solar system. We have organizations committed to our governance. We have religious associations that are ultimately in the business of polarizing ethical opinions. We often find ourselves compelled to take sides."

"And many of these organizations are, unfortunately, in competition," George pointed out.

George drank the remainder of his wine, then asked Joanne and Malcolm if they'd care to take a walk before calling it a night. George felt an ache in the small of his back; the effects of the wine made him long for the comfort of his bed. He did feel, however, that revisiting all this tonight was serving to strengthen his own resolve. With all that had happened today, the fear of being discovered and going to jail, and the terrible position the kids and their parents would soon find themselves in, George's resolve had begun to wane.

Lately, he'd started to question the wisdom of what they had done. The same fears, which he'd felt when they had made the decision to go ahead with the experiment, had returned with a vengeance. Talking about it now in such human and historic terms, and witnessing the agreement of a professional psychologist as to the nature of the problem, if not its solution, was reaffirming the validity of their decision. The fact that the intervening years had been so uneventful obscured the enormity of what they had done.

"How do you feel?" Joanne asked. She put her hand on George's back, and started rubbing his shoulders. "How's that?"

"Lower," he said smiling.

The waiter came back. Standing between Malcolm and Joanne, he said, "Will there be anything else?" He was a young man, probably a student, George thought. His dark Martian features were almost invisible in the shadows of the dimly lit veranda. Turning, George saw that a small crowd had formed at the hostess station, and appeared to be waiting for tables on the deck.

Joanne and Malcolm shook their heads. Malcolm shifted in his seat. George said, "I'll meet you outside in a minute."

They all got up. Joanne and Malcolm went downstairs, and out the front entrance. George went to the bar on the second floor to retrieve his card. When he finally emerged from the Landing, he found them waiting at the base of the stairs below the porch. Joanne turned and took his arm. They strolled south, away from the lights and crowds of the northern strip. Soon, the walkway split into a sidewalk that followed the shore avenue and a path through a palm-lined park that overlooked the lake. Cast iron posts topped by frosted glass orbs lighted the path. They were reminiscent of antique gas lamps that George had seen on summer nights back on Earth, in Golden Gate Park, an eternity ago.

"Make you homesick?" Joanne asked, seeing the melancholy gaze with which he regarded the relics.

"This is home," George replied unequivocally. He could feel her tighten on his arm. He smiled and watched the shadows wax and wane on the path as they encountered subsequent lamps, and walked deeper into the park.

"Well," said Malcolm, breaking the silence, "That was one of the most academic conversations I've had in a while, albeit a sobering one. But I get the feeling you still haven't gotten to the point. You had something else on your mind tonight, didn't you?"

George nodded. "What if I were to tell you that it wasn't meant to be an intellectual discussion about the human condition."

"What do you mean?"

"Suppose we were talking about some human malady, like schizophrenia for example. The more interesting reason for talking about it, from your perspective, would be to discuss various cures—wouldn't it?"

"I suppose so," Malcolm said, tentatively.

"What if I told you that we'd found a way to treat human aggression?"

They stopped under a lamp. Malcolm chuckled. "There are a variety of ways to treat aggression. We've known how to do that, to some extent, for a couple of hundred years now."

George said, "I don't mean treat the symptoms, I mean cure the condition. And I don't mean in those who are hyper-aggressive or antisocial, I mean the latent predatory aggressiveness that the soldiers, who you talked about, were so susceptible to."

"Wait a minute, Mills. You sound like your talking about treating original sin, or something."

"That may be a fair description of what I'm talking about," George said. He felt the man's scrutiny.

"You aren't joking, are you?" Malcolm asked.

"No, no I'm not. I couldn't be more serious."

"I was afraid of that," Malcolm said. "But even if you had some idea about how something like aggression originates. Even if you understood the mechanism that allows people to wage war, and do all the incomprehensible things we talked about, how could you possibly treat it?"

"Well, what is it that makes us what we are?" George asked. "If we discount personal experiences, we have only one thing left. Remember, I'm not talking about aberrant behavior. I'm talking about normal behavior in abnormal situations. As a proof of the consistency of what I'm saying, you need look no further than our own bloody history as a species."

Suddenly, Joanne was distracted by distant voices, and looked up and down the path. Several people were approaching from both sides, as the three of them stood in the spotlight of the antique lamp. She ferried George and Malcolm from the clearing to a spot hidden by hedges, near a fence overlooking the lake.

George could no longer see Malcolm's face in the darkness. He worried that their erratic behavior would make what he had to say less plausible. Searching Malcolm's dark outline hovering in the dim light of the lake's distant shore, George said, "It's our genes Malcolm, it's our genes that make us what we are."

Malcolm was silent a moment, then said "That still doesn't answer my question."

"We've been able to change human instinct through a form of gene therapy," George said.

Malcolm's frustration turned to astonishment. "That's impossible."

"Why?" George asked.

"How could you possibly know which genetic sequences are responsible for something as murky as instinct? Much of what we consider instinct is coupled to many of the body's regulatory and reflex mechanisms. How could you possibly decouple all of that in a purposeful way? As far as I know, there is no deep understanding of the connection between genes and behavior. In fact, of the many studies published comparing identical twins and cloned animals, to date, the findings are inconclusive. After more than two centuries of research, the matter still hasn't been settled to the satisfaction of most behavioral biologist and psychologists."

"All good points," George said, "but the answers are not as obscure as you might think."

Silence.

"We did it the way that nature did it," George said. "We started with the general human genome, and changed the human evolutionary track by re-pruning and adding to it. We did that by creating a statistical model of a person. The model applies the organism's genetic code to various avatars in a manageable and systematic way, while an orchestrating simulation develops a movement towards some predetermined behavior. This behavior can then be directly correlated to the underlying genetics of the organism represented by the model."

Malcolm began to protest, but George continued. "Let me explain," he said, gesturing with his hands. "As you know, experimental gene therapy is now done completely through computer modeling."

"Animal models have been banned for over a hundred years," Joanne said. "All the functional human gene sequences have been decoded for their protein synthesis, and almost all the extensive non-protein coding sequences have been cross-correlated to specific regulatory and coordinating functions."

George said, "All pre-human trials are simulated. In essence, what we've been able to do is to develop a base parametric model of a complete person that properly represents the underlying genes."

"Okay," Malcolm said, "but how do you apply evolution to your model? How do you develop environmental impetus? How could you possibly develop a statistically valid population of virtual people? Your model must be incredibly complex to be able to represent a person from their genetic code well enough to actually simulate behavior. How ..."

"All good questions," George interrupted. "For the sake of discussion, let's accept that we can do it. Let's move on to the equally interesting question of what type of people we would want as a result of the process."

"Okay."

"That's why I asked you all those questions about your war experiences at dinner," George said. "I wanted you to think about what happened. To project your feelings onto the decision makers, and onto the guys who actually pull the trigger. Ask yourself the question—how would things have to change in order for the outcome to have been different?"

"I see what you mean," Malcolm said thoughtfully.

George said, "That's essentially what we did. We cataloged well known scenarios from the past—from the Roman and religious wars of the middle ages, up through the World Wars of the twentieth century, and the more minor conflicts to the present day."

"And you ran your models looking for the same results you knew from history, in order to calibrate them?" Malcolm asked.

"Exactly," Joanne replied.

"That's truly fascinating."

"Once we baselined our model, we iterated the scenarios, changing the genetics of our virtual population in various ways so as to get different outcomes."

"More peaceful, rational outcomes," Joanne added.

"There are still some issues that puzzle me though," Malcolm said.

"Oh, like what?

"Like, even if you could do this, you still start with the basic genome of a predator, don't you?"

"Yes, that's true," George said. "The assumption being that the basic genome between, let's say, a human and a non-predatory primate like an orangutan, for example, can differ by no more than a few percent. In the case of Homo sapiens, we have a basic predator. In the case of the orangutan, we have a tree dwelling, essentially plant eating primate. And remember, genetically, these two species are only a few percent apart. We were able to prune the human genetic code, up-regulate some genes, and down-regulate others. We were even able to introduce some small original sequences of our own."

"But how did you know what to change?" Malcolm asked.

"Well, just like with any large simulation, we selected a set of likely initial conditions. In this case, we chose genetic sites corresponding to neural constructs having to do with hormone regulation, synapse efficiency, neural connection densities, structures in the reticular brain stem correlated to instinct, things like that. At the same time, the simulation had the ability to search the entire variable space, attempting to find convergence within the constraints we talked about earlier."

"And you found convergence?" Malcolm asked.

"Yes, we did," Joanne said. "You should see our new past. It's an epoch of sanity compared to what really happened."

During the discussion Malcolm had been pacing around, standing still to think a moment, then moving again as he spoke. George could tell he was wrestling with these new ideas. For a psychologist, the notion of a computer-created designer nature must have appeared patently ridiculous.

As Malcolm continued searching for conceptual purchase, George could see Joanne's silhouette in the dark, leaning against the wooden fence overlooking the lake, her arms folded across her chest. She watched more than participated in the discussion. Every now and then she turned her head, and he caught the glimmer of her eyes in the dim light. Malcolm moved next to her, absently put his foot on the lower tier of the fence, and seemed to gaze into the distance for a few minutes. The lull in the conversation, and the warm darkness, reminded George of how tired he was. He felt himself sway a little, almost losing his balance when Malcolm turned suddenly and said, "That was a great story, but what could you possibly want with me? I'm a clinical psychologist."

George and Joanne looked at him in the darkness.

Slowly, he began to understand the implication of their stares. "You mean these new people really exist! They're not an abstraction, they're real?"

"Yes," Joanne said softly, "They're real. Most are between ten and eleven years old now."

"Where are they? Why haven't I heard about this? This has to be the biggest story of all time."

George could see that more explanation was in order, but before he could say something, he heard a voice coming from the direction of the path.

"Is everything all right?"

A couple of people had heard Malcolm's excited ramblings.

"Everything's fine," Joanne said, faking a laugh.

George could see a man and woman standing in the clearing under the light, looking in their direction.

"Are you sure?" the man asked.

"Yes, thank you," Joanne said. "My friend drank a little too much at dinner tonight, that's all."

"Okay," the man said. He and the woman then walked away slowly, both shaking their heads.

"Sorry," Malcolm said.

"I don't blame you," George said. "It's a lot to digest. I can't say how I would react if someone told me a story this fantastic."

When he had regained his composure, Malcolm asked, "How different are these new people, anyway?"

"How do you mean?" Joanne asked.

"Well, if I saw one on the street, could I tell?"

"Maybe, if you knew what to look for. We tried to have them look like typical Martians, compatible with the distribution of phenotypes here on Mars. There was some variance, though. We'd hoped to keep the whole thing quiet, to give them a chance at a normal life."

"I take it that up till now, at least, you've been successful?"

"Up till now," Joanne replied.

Malcolm looked away. "Want to start walking? I have to think about this."

Soon, they were on the shore sidewalk heading for the strip, Joanne and Malcolm in front, and George meandering tiredly in back. The change in lighting hurt George's eyes. All the traveling he'd done the past month left him drained. When he finally got back to the Landing, he could see Malcolm and

Joanne talking near the restaurant's porch. As he approached, Malcolm pulled away, waved good night, and disappeared into the crowd.

Joanne stepped up to George. "How do you feel?" She cupped her hands on both sides of his face, turning it slowly, then added, "The doctor prescribes sleep."

"What about Malcolm?"

"I asked him to come along tomorrow."

"Think that's wise?"

"Yes, I think it'll make it more natural than just having you and me show up. Know what I mean?"

"Yeah, I do. I've been worried about that ever since I told you I'd come."

"I told Malcolm about Perseus being there tomorrow," Joanne said.

"And?"

"And he's excited. He wants to meet one of our new people—thinks he can help."

George looked around, "What about you?"

"What about me?"

"You came here with Malcolm tonight, didn't you?"

"Yes, but you look like you need me more." She smiled.

As tired as he was, he felt a pang of desire, and hated being in this position, fearing that some clumsy indiscretion or misinterpretation of her feelings might leave them standing here in an awkward silence. They'd been friends for years now, with an on again, off again relationship that was often hard for him to understand. Remembering how badly his marriage had failed back on Earth always made him leery of getting too comfortable.

She took his hand, "Where's the car?"

"Left it at Minsky." He paused. "Seemed like a good idea at the time."

She looked doubtful. "Think you can make it all the way back there?"

He shrugged.

"Wait a minute," she said. She pulled a Tab from her bag. The wind had picked up a bit, blowing her gossamer dress, making it adhere more revealingly to her long shapely legs and the vee at her crotch. He looked around uncomfortably, smelling the subtle scent of something in her hair, which he'd noticed before. She expanded the Tab and made a call to summon a cab. Afterwards, she pulled him to a spot under the porch, where he leaned against the wall. She put her arms around him, and her head on his shoulder.

"I'm glad you're back."

He started to say something obligatory, but then heard her say, "Shush."

When they got back to the commons in front of the Summit Apartments, she transferred credits, leaving him teetering on the grass. Shortly, he heard the low hum of the cab's motor as it pulled away and disappeared through the hedges.

They strolled arm in arm down the slate path across the commons, through the trees, and down the hill toward George's house. The sky was black, and full of stars. The dome struts were hidden by the night, making it seem as if they were really outside. They stopped at his front gate.

"How was it being back on Earth?" Joanne asked.

"It was strange. I love Earth. I love the blue sky and the feeling of being out in the world—not under a dome. I went down to Annapolis and sat by the ocean the first weekend I was there. I wondered if I'd ever be coming back."

He knew her silence meant disapproval; maybe he'd hurt her with this frank admission. For a moment, he feared that tonight's magic had ended. It certainly wouldn't be the first time that telling the truth had resulted in a less than perfect outcome to one of their nights.

"Come on, let's go in," she said.

He keyed his code into the door, and it clicked open. He held it for her, then entered the foyer behind her. The living room was dark, except for the strategically placed nightlight and the dim glow coming from the bay window. Joanne knew the lay of the land, crossed the living room, and disappeared into the master bedroom. A moment later he heard the water running in the bathroom, and smiled. Sitting on the sofa, he noticed the amber light floating in the darkness. It had silently followed him. He waved. The light blinked, then blinked off. He mouthed the word, "Thanks," and sat in the near darkness, with his legs stretched out in front of him. Presently, he heard the water stop. A few seconds later, a door opened.

He saw her outline in the bedroom doorway, and could tell from hints of color that she was wearing his faded red and white San Francisco tee shirt, which fell to mid thigh.

"Come to bed," she whispered.

Thankful for the darkness, and its ability to mask his clumsy efforts, he found himself looking up at her silhouette. She was lying sideways, head propped on her left elbow, facing him.

"Why'd you come back?"

George remained silent.

"No matter what you say, I won't be upset."

He exhaled a laugh, to which she replied with one of her own. It was clear they understood each other and wanted the same things tonight. That let him relax.

"I don't have anything left down there. I didn't go to see any of my old friends, because we're all strangers now. The place itself is familiar, but it's all out of time. Know what I mean?"

"What about your friends up here?"

"I thought that if I stayed on Earth, relocated a Will kernel down there, whoever's got a problem with what I've done would be satisfied. They'd have a computer that could run their simulations, and they'd have me. At the time, I assumed they didn't know anything about the Proteus file. I thought if I gave them what they wanted, they'd stop looking. If I left Will here, he could continue to support you and the kids, and the pressure would be off.

There was a long silence.

"What are you fishing for?" he asked. "You, this thing between us, it's been up in the air for a long time now. It's been pretty confusing—hasn't it?"

"Let's not talk anymore," she said. She reached down and kissed him. George felt her tongue enter his mouth in a rush of longing. His hands searched under the tee shirt, and he felt her nipples erect, responding to his touch. Then he pressed his legs between hers, felt her legs part and rap around him, inviting him in. As he entered, he heard her moan with the same desire that flooded his senses.

Chapter Six

Once they retrieved George's car at Minsky and paid the cab, they got back on the *Sea Of Storms* and sped silently over Lake Geneva toward the southern perimeter of Dome Two. It was late morning, and the sun was near its noontime high. George watched Joanne slip into a pair of sunglasses and remembered watching her sleep before getting up early that morning. The guilt never left him; he hadn't had a moment's peace since stepping off the transport yesterday. Involving Joanne in this thing had been wrong to begin with, but now that his worst fears were slowly seeping out of his paranoid nightmares, her newly expressed affection for him was making him feel like he'd betrayed her.

Out of an impotent paralysis, George resigned himself to the situation and gazed absently over the expanse of Lake Geneva. Holding an open hand over his eyes, he remembered, with nostalgic amusement, how, when he'd first arrived on Mars, seeing people wearing sunglasses had seemed oddly out of place. The natural daytime on Mars, which is fifty percent farther from the sun than the Earth, was a mere twilight. At midday, the ambient brightness was that of an overcast day on Earth. But the dome engineers had solved the problem by placing plasma panels on the dome struts and selecting the panel gases to faithfully reproduce the sun's Earthly spectrum. Automatic environmental controls increased and decreased their brightness to correspond to the position of the sun in the sky, properly compensating for the lack of illumination. In concert with the Earthly brightness, the domes were large enough to afford a variety of weather, and because of the lakes and artificial heaters, they supported cloud formation and even rain on occasion, though rain was considered a rare treat. Today, however, it was clear and sunny, and George sat back, thinking about the meeting to come, and squinted.

Arriving at Dome Two's southernmost perimeter, the *Sea Of Storms* began descending below the surface of Ursa canyon. The car sped past concentric light panels on its way down, giving its interior a freeze-frame stroboscopic quality like some dizzying amusement park ride. They emerged from the tunnel at a depth of five hundred feet into a large underground biosphere, under a silicate sky suspended two hundred feet above the cavern floor. The underground contained buildings, parks, and a river that circulated water between the large lakes that were the centerpiece of each dome. The caverns were immense and used mostly for manufacturing, shopping, and warehousing. They also encompassed much of the township's parkland. Because plants were so easily grown in this completely controlled environment, the overall landscape reminded George of industrial sites interspersed in a deep green forest.

George could hear the car's electric motor increase in pitch as it accelerated to well over a hundred mile per hour on the cavern straight-a-way. The acceleration was smooth but strong, and he felt himself pressed hard into his seatback. As the car reached its maximum speed, the pressure slowly disappeared and the world of the cavern streaked by in a blur of silent color. Six minutes later, he felt the car decelerate and enter another stroboscopic tunnel, upward-going this time.

They emerged into Dome One at its northern-most perimeter through a circular aperture in a wall of brown Martian rock. Building One, which was their ultimate destination, was dimly visible through a humid haze at the center of a collection of federal buildings situated on an island in the middle of Lake Potomac. The building's pink glass and metal spires rose into the dome and dwarfed everything else around them. George could clearly see them, although they were still more than ten miles away. Despite the fact that he had lived here for more than fifteen years now, the scale of the dome environment still gave him a sense of awe. It hardly seemed possible that a structure this massive could actually be built. Dome One had been the first in Ursa Township, but the caverns had come even before that, and had been used as a manufacturing and staging area for Dome One's construction. Although gravity on Mars was roughly a third of Earth's gravity, and the strength of the exotic monomolecular materials from which the dome was constructed was enormous, it still required bracing. The weight of a structure five hundred feet tall and twenty miles across was so great that it could not be built without internal supports. For Dome One, Building One, which was situated at its geometric center, served as the main internal support column. Building One rose to the dome's ceiling, then continued into the Martian sky another two thousand feet, ending almost a half-mile above Ursa canyon.

They followed the *Sea Of Storms* around the eastern shore of Lake Potomac, which was dotted with upscale homes and exclusive eateries reminiscent of the Maryland coast back on Earth, and in many ways, exuded the same affluence. About a third of the way around, they took an off-ramp that climbed high into the air, finally branching into a suspension bridge that crossed the lake to Federal Island and put them onto Memorial Blvd., which ran its circumference.

George slipped the car into manual mode and maneuvered into the right-most lane of traffic. He drove slowly, craning his neck, looking for a through street that would put them nearer the Federal Mall, which bordered Building One on its southern side. But the first two streets they passed were filled with parked cars and a colorful sea of people, all walking down the middle of the road toward the mall.

Joanne pushed the sunglasses down the bridge of her nose and shot him a puzzled look. "What do you make of this?"

"I don't know exactly, but a security man at the airport mentioned something about rallies and demonstrations."

"Hmm, I come down here at least once a month, and I've never seen it like this before," Joanne said.

Someone sounded a horn behind them; George sped up, went down two more streets, and took a right on Canal.

"Canal's the biggest through street on this side of the island. There's a parking garage close to Building One," he explained.

"Good luck," Joanne said.

She lowered her window. "What's that?"

The sound of someone's voice on a loudspeaker filled the air, but they were too far away to make out the words. George lowered his window, and as they slowly made their way down Canal, the cacophonous sounds of people cheering drowned out the sound of the distant, intermittent, loudspeaker. George soon realized that they wouldn't get much farther in the car; up ahead, the street was choked with people. Other cars had pulled up on the grass by the side of the road and their occupants were now walking down the street too. So George pulled the car onto the grass, locked the wheel, and opened the doors.

"A nice day for a walk, don't you think?" George said, smiled, and got out.

After they had gone about two blocks toward the Federal Mall, they ran up against a large stationary crowd of people in the middle of the street flanked on both sides by an almost equal number of security police. The police were dressed in full riot gear and collected behind portable barriers about four feet high. They wore dull black plastic body armor, shiny black assault boots, and combat helmets with visors drawn. They were grasping electric wands in gloved hands positioned diagonally across their chests.

"This looks serious," George said. He turned and noticed a man standing nearby, watching the crowd. He walked over to him. "What's going on?" George asked.

The man eyed him cautiously, not unlike the policeman at the airport the other day. "It's a rally to get Earthers out of our business, and their soldiers off our streets."

George made his way back. "I don't like this."

"Why, what happened?" Joanne asked.

"I just found out that Earthmen aren't welcome, and I take that to mean people who look like Earthmen, and people with Earthmen."

"What do you want to do?" she asked.

He looked around a moment, pensive, trying to decide how to play this. "Come on."

They took cover on the grass near some bushes by the side of the road. "Got a number for the people who're expecting us?" George asked.

Joanne made the call. Although the Tab had noise-canceling microphones, it was so loud near the street that she had to turn and cup her hands over the device in an effort to shield it from the roar. As she spoke into her hands, George wandered back to the street. He found a large clay planter that bore a young fig tree and climbed up on its rim for a better look. Farther down Canal, a large crowd had gathered. No longer contained by the street, they sprawled in all directions among a wall of trees that stood before the courtyard in front of Building One.

The courtyard, which was white streaked marble, glistened in the late morning sun. At its far end, George saw a grand set of marble stairs that rose up to the entrance of the building between Roman columns. Above the trees, the immense façade of Building One loomed high into the dome, then continued, mildly distorted by transparent panels, into the Martian sky almost without end. This was the only building in Ursa that he knew to be reminiscent of the grand architecture of Earth.

Looking in the other direction, the one from which they'd come, he saw more and more people joining the long procession that passed him in the street. They were all heading for the mall like moths to a flame.

He climbed down from the planter and edged back to where Joanne stood finishing her call. As he continued to stare at the spectacle before him, he felt Joanne put her chin on his shoulder from behind. Her mouth sat under his right ear and he couldn't help smelling peppermint on her breath.

"The meeting's still on," she declared.

He laughed, trying not to sound nervous. "Did they have any suggestions as to how we get through all this?"

"According to Dale, they've already sent some security people to come and get us."

"That'll certainly make us popular with the crowd." He looked around. "By the way, where are we supposed to meet our escort?"

Joanne came around and stood beside him. "I told them where we were, they told me to stay put."

"It looks like the world's changing," George observed absently.

"I've got news for you, it's never stopped. You were just working too hard to notice, that's all."

"Maybe," he said, unconvinced.

After waiting for about ten minutes, George noticed four soldiers coming their way. They were different from the security men that lined the street further down; they were dressed in full marine combat suits with exotic looking weapons at their sides instead of wands. Their dull black armored suits and their faceless black combat helmets poked up above the crowd of people, parting the sea. When the soldiers advanced to within a couple of feet, the one in front announced, "Dr. Zhu?" in an electronic voice that matched his mechanical appearance.

"Right here," Joanne answered, stepping forward like she did this every day.

"Follow us please, doctor," ordered the soldier.

George and Joanne fell into step behind the soldier and penetrated into the crowd. George found the cold stares of the people they passed unnerving as they followed the monolithic forms of their escort. The anger on the faces in the crowd was palpable, and their sense of intrusion electric. He had never felt completely at home on Mars, but he had never felt like this either. It was as if he were in danger from regular citizens whom, a couple of days before, he might have considered neighbors.

Now endowed with the knowledge that his neighbors could so easily turn on him, George questioned whether his life here could ever be the same.

When it seemed there were too many people to afford them further access, security men to their right and behind the barricades opened the fence, letting them slip through and out of harm's way. As they approached the courtyard below Building One, George could see a man high atop the stairs near the main entrance speaking into a microphone. He was dressed in a blue jumpsuit, the kind construction workers usually wore. The man was tall, perhaps six foot seven or eight, judging from the relative height of the ornamental design work at the base of the columns.

The man at the microphone was all Martian, olive dark and lean, with jet-black hair tied in a ponytail that hung down his back. Dark glasses hid his upper face, which was further obscured in the shadow of a brimmed blue cap.

"They own our lives," the man yelled into the microphone. "They control the wealth of our planet and get richer as we get poorer."

Each time he paused for a breath, the crowd yelled, "Vega, Vega, Vega" in rhythmic unison, stabbing the air with clenched fists.

George saw the security men trying to maintain the hordes of people outside the perimeter of the barricades. The fences bulged and swayed as groups of people lunged at them with fevered enthusiasm. The suits the security men wore had built-in artificial muscles that augmented the person inside with strength and speed. Yet, even with these enhancements, they were having trouble maintaining order on the perimeter.

"Why do the ERC and their ECon masters refuse to give us representation while stealing our wealth?" the man on the steps bellowed.

George could see their escort looking around pensively as their fellow security men staggered back in response to continued attacks on the barricade. The soldier between George and the fence broke ranks as one of the security men reinforcing the line stumbled into him. The soldier in front of George spun around with lightning speed and swept Joanne further into the protective shield of soldiers and away from the perimeter.

As George watched the soldier guarding Joanne, he suddenly felt a strong pair of hands grab him by the shoulders. George lost his balance and was spun around by his assailant. A large young man had breached the line, his right foot crashing into the fence nearest to George. The barrier pivoted and slammed to the ground as the man hoisted George up and over the top of the falling barricade. George looked into the man's face, which was purple with rage. A line of spittle fell down his chin from the corners of his mouth. His forearms were large, and their taut muscles and the man's large hands held George inches from his face.

"You fucking Earthman," he heard the man yell, his sour breath suffocating.

"Wait a minute," George cried. Fear welled up inside him at the prospect of being beaten to death by the crowd.

He quickly considered his options. He was still near the perimeter. If he allowed this madman to draw him further into the mob, he knew he'd be a dead man.

The young man held him fast, but George had regained his balance and now had both feet firmly planted on the ground. Suddenly, he felt the man change his grip, grabbing him by the sport coat and freeing his arms. George could feel the man tense, securing his footing in an effort to spin him around and throw him farther into the crowd. A crowd of his neighbors, George thought, in panicked irony.

Knowing it was now or never, George quickly raised his hands, palms and fingers straight and outstretched. Then, with adrenaline boosting his power and timing, George slammed his hands over the man's ears in a wide circular arc. There was a distinct pop as his hands made contact, and the young man screamed in pain; George felt his grip loosen.

George pivoted on his left leg and kicked the man as hard as he could in the crotch. As the man doubled over in pain, George pushed back with all his might and fell onto the security side of the perimeter. He lay on the ground, knowing instinctually that he must regain his feet in order to survive. Struggling to rise, he felt a hand under his left armpit, helping him up. He smelled peppermint.

"George, are you all right?" he heard Joanne say.

They rose together. He could see the concern in her eyes and hear the tension in her question. He tried to speak, but his dry parched throat choked off his voice.

He noticed movement behind Joanne; the young man had recovered and was coming at him again. Joanne was between them. George quickly grabbed her under the arms and spun her around. When he let her go, she fell into the arms of a security man who had come up behind them. Seconds later, he felt a vise-like grip tighten around his neck. He couldn't breathe or yell. He flailed around helplessly, unable to make useful contact with his attacker. His strength soon began to fail him, and his vision blackened. The noise from the crowd seemed to recede into the distance, and he began to perceive events in slow motion. He knew he was passing out, but was strangely at peace. Then he smelled a strange but familiar scent. It had the distinct tang of ozone.

Slowly, the sounds of the crowd became louder again, and he began to recoup his vision. A security man was carrying him like a rag doll, with a large artificially enhanced arm wrapped firmly around his torso. He began to feel his feet dragging on the ground, and a sense of nausea overwhelmed him. He tried to stem the urge to vomit out of an instinctive fear of soiling himself. Then he briefly spotted Joanne out of the corner of his eye, though it was difficult to focus on anything for more than a few seconds. Joanne put an arm behind his back and helped the soldier take him nearer to the building entrance, and to safety.

After a few minutes, he felt himself lowered onto the steps and was able to sit up by supporting his head with his hands; his elbows rested on his knees.

"What happened?" George asked in a low voice.

"The soldier stunned that bastard with a wand," Joanne said harshly. "Are you all right?"

Her hand was on his back, patting it. "Give me a minute," George said. He felt some of his strength and stability returning.

His throat throbbed with pain, and he looked around and saw, with relief, that they were well inside the security perimeter of the marble stairs, which led to the entrance. Swallowing a couple of times seemed to make his throat feel a little better.

"Throw off the oppression of these arrogant Earthmen," he heard Vega yell. The crowd cheered in response.

George glanced up at Joanne. She was disheveled; her hair hid most of her face. He swallowed and tried to speak again. "Got another one of those mints?"

She laughed. Her dirt-smudged face was beautiful in the noonday sun. He felt her put a small candy to his mouth, but before taking it, he said, "Let's get inside, okay?"

She put her arm around him once more, and they hobbled up the steps, following a soldier to the top. Once George was near the entrance, among the columns, he took a final look at Vega addressing his legions. It was a grand and scary spectacle. Looking at the sea of people from this high vantage point had a surreal feel to it. The man in his blue overalls bobbed and swayed; the crowd responded in kind, their collective force ominous. George turned and saw the soldier keying a code into the door. It clicked open. They stepped inside and the door shut behind them.

Building One's grand foyer was nothing less than opulent. Atop green and white Martian marble floors, Roman columns supported a four-story glass cathedral ceiling that formed a bright sun-lit solarium in stained glass. Small exotic trees and tropical flowers gave the lobby the feel of a green atrium. As soon as the door had closed, the chaotic sounds of the courtyard were instantly replaced by a soothing silence. The abrupt change gave George a start. For a few seconds he felt his ears ringing before a welcome silence gave him a chance to calm down. He turned and looked at the translucent panels near the entrance and could see silhouettes of the drama still playing itself out on the other side of the wall.

"The elevators are over there—to the right," he heard the soldier say.

George looked around; his heart was starting to slow. Joanne was standing next to him, and held his hand so tightly that it hurt.

"Look," he said to the soldier, "I'm still a little shaken. Do you mind if we clean up and just catch our breath?"

The insectile helmet said, "Washroom's over there."

When George was finished splashing water on his face and straightening his clothes, he returned to the lobby. Looking around, he spied a cluster of leather sofas and over-stuffed chairs. They were placed around a glass and titanium coffee table under small ficus trees and palms, in a corner of the atrium under the high ceiling. After sitting on the sofa, George noticed the soldier was still standing near the door. He tensed when the soldier turned and approached him.

The soldier stopped on the other side of the coffee table, reached up, then touched something under the chin of his faceless helmet. The front of the helmet slid to the left and disappeared. The rest of the helmet slid away in all directions and folded into a large solid collar that appeared thin in the front and larger and wedge-shaped in back. George leaned forward, blinked a couple of times, and stared in disbelief. He knew this guy.

"Fred? Fred Jackson? We met at the airport yesterday, didn't we?"

Chapter Seven

Jackson towered above George in his black armor and stood across the coffee table looking down at him. George tensed. Though the man had just saved his life, Jackson cut an imposing figure in the mechanical garb. What's more, his piercing eyes and tight mouth signaled displeasure rather than familiarity.

Jackson said, "Didn't I warn you about coming down here? And it's getting worse every day." He looked around in disgust. "It's only a matter of time before someone gets killed."

"I guess, in retrospect, that was pretty good advice. Unfortunately, we have a meeting here today and it couldn't be helped."

Jackson's head looked comically small atop the large robotic frame. In spite of the painful throb in his face and neck that reminded him of the beating he'd just taken, George had to struggle to avoid cracking a broad grin.

"You could have been killed out there today," Jackson said. "I hope your meeting is worth it."

"If we'd understood the situation, I can assure you we would've made other plans. Though I've got to tell you, I'm not used to being beaten in the streets by complete strangers."

Jackson exhaled. "These are strange times, Dr. Mills."

Jackson came another half step closer. "If things get any worse, I could almost imagine a civil war breaking out. That's why we're out here doing riot duty instead of the Terran Marines. It's difficult for my men to use lethal force against other Martians, and the people know that."

"I don't understand," George said. "This is Mars' security jurisdiction, isn't it?"

"It may be, but there are a lot of Earth properties in Dome One, as well as other strategic sites. We've been under a lot of pressure to break up these rallies before they spin out of control."

"I can't think of a faster way for things to go to hell than to have Terrans policing the streets."

"Off the record, it's too bad those idiots back on Earth can't seem to understand that simple fact," Jackson said.

George blew out a nervous laugh, "They are idiots, aren't they?"

"Yes they are," Jackson agreed.

"Who's Vega anyway?" George asked. "I've never heard of him before."

"He's one of yours."

"One of mine?"

"Yes, that's right. He's a student from Dome Two, and he's become a regular fixture around here these days. His rallies started small, just a few people at first. Now the word's gotten out and this one is the biggest yet, along with being the first to turn violent. Any more like this and you will see Terrans patrolling the streets."

"What more could Terrans do beyond what you're doing right now? You guys did a pretty good job saving my life out there today."

"The marines will be a lot harder on Martians," Jackson said. "Gas, more arrests, things like that."

"Sounds like a formula for disaster. Why would they do that? Don't they understand that letting you handle this makes it easier on them?"

Jackson flashed a sour smile. "It plays better back on Earth, doesn't it—makes great video for the huddled masses craving entertainment." His features grew dark, his jaw line distinct over tight skin. "Did you ever consider that maybe that's what they want?"

"What do you mean?" George asked.

"Well, what if the leadership back on Earth has decided to nip the independence movement in the bud? Maybe they've decided that this is a good time to make a move. Hide behind civil unrest, then declare martial law. That would give them a chance to come in and sweep local government aside. Install representatives more sympathetic to their interests. You know, representatives that don't look like Martians."

That last remark left George cold. He began to wonder if it would ever be possible to resume his life here.

"I didn't mean to make you uncomfortable," Jackson said.

"No offense taken," George lied. "And where does all this leave you?"

"Yeah," Jackson complained. "Where does it leave me?"

George heard Joanne's shoes tapping on the marble floor, then felt her hands on his shoulders, and glanced up.

"You look much better."

"I'm a strong advocate of warm water," Joanne said smiling.

Her face was smooth and relaxed and her neatly combed hair reflected subtle colors from the stained glass atop the atrium. She came around and sat next to him.

"Who's your friend?" she asked.

George glanced up. Jackson's looming bulk made him feel like a dwarf.

"Oh, I'm sorry—Fred Jackson, this is my friend Dr. Joanne Zhu. We work together at the university."

Joanne rose to meet him, taking his open hand across the table.

"Good to meet you, Doctor," Jackson said warmly.

"Officer Jackson. We probably owe you our lives."

"I'm glad I was there."

Then, turning to George, Jackson's charm seemed to dissolve. "Remember what we talked about, Dr. Mills. Try to stay away from government buildings until this thing blows over."

"Will do—thanks again for the advice."

Jackson nodded, smiled at Joanne, then touched something under his chin. George watched as sections of his helmet unwrapped and enclosed his head in a black shroud. Jackson turned, moved to the door, keyed in a code, and left.

George exhaled.

"A friend from the university?" Joanne mocked, smiling thinly.

Blushing, George rose, put his hand on Joanne's back, and directed her toward the elevators.

A blue band of light scanned the vertical length of the translucent elevator tube as it came to rest. They entered. Joanne keyed an access code into her Tab, and the door slid silently shut. The elevator had a transparent wall facing the large courtyard outside. As the elevator climbed into the Martian sky, George watched the menacing crowd recede in significance, until all that was left were the shimmering waters of Lake Potomac far below.

"What was that about?" Joanne asked.

"You're not talking about my lack of social sensitivity, are you?"

"No, you can make up for that later. I'm talking about the fact that you seemed to know that policeman."

"Yeah, strangely enough, I met him at the airport right after I got off the plane the other day."

"And he just happened to be here too? Don't you find that a bit suspicious?"

"At first I did," George admitted. "But how could it be anything other than a coincidence? He'd have to be following me continuously for it to be anything else. To tell you the truth, I think we're both pretty lucky he was there, don't you?"

"I guess," she said hesitantly.

He regarded her carefully, "You're still shaky, aren't you? You took a couple of pretty nasty falls."

"Aside from a couple of bumps and bruises, I think I'll live," Joanne said. "But what about you? They almost killed you."

George shrugged. The elevator slowed and came to a stop. "Let's hang here a while," George said.

Not waiting for a reply, he moved up behind her, put his arms around her waist, and lightly rested the side of his face on hers. They looked out into the Martian sky. Her hair felt silky and cool against his skin.

"Here's a sight you rarely see," George said. They were high above the dome, more than two thousand feet above the Martian canyon. George gazed out over the huge cobalt-brown cliffs and the flat expanse beyond.

"You've become quite the romantic since you came back," Joanne said.

George smiled. "Well, aside from the fact that my life is slowly melting down around me, and people seem to want to kill me on sight, life is good."

There were no dome lights to augment the Martian noon outside. The sky was pinkish-white and Building One rose ever higher behind them, eventually turning into a blunt point in the darker sky directly above. Adding to the panorama, George could see the Martian moon Phobos setting behind the eastern mountain range more than ten thousand feet above the canyon walls.

"I like it here too," Joanne said, "but it's getting late. We really should go."

Reluctantly, George released her. He took one last look as Joanne walked passed him, then followed her into the corridor.

Joanne checked her Tab for the location of the meeting, which had been uploaded when she had entered the elevator code earlier. After a quick examination of the site map, she looked up. "It's this way."

George followed as she weaved through large carpeted corridors, then through a set of double glass doors with a frosted emblem of the planet Earth balanced on the talons of an eagle with outstretched wings and a dagger-like beak. They found themselves in a large hall, whose far glass wall looked out into the pale Martian noon. The eerie glow cast long disorienting shadows on the high bare walls.

George came up along side her. "We want conference room B," Joanne declared. She took his arm lightly and started walking toward the glow at the far wall, then stopped two doors down on the right, and pointed to a gold plaque that read "Conference Room B." She gave a couple of quick knocks, and before anyone could answer, pushed the door open, and walked in.

The room was large and bare, with the same white walls and dark carpets as the corridor outside. No pictures, no plants, and no windows. In the middle of the room was a long polished black marble table surrounded by black leather chairs. To the left of the door, seated in one of the many chairs that lined the table, was Dale Metz. He was one of those blonde, first-generation Martians, whose complexion looked artificially blanche, like he'd made a conscious effort to stay out of the sun.

Dale stood before they could sit. He seemed a little nervous as he came around the table. Dale kissed Joanne on both cheeks, as was the custom on Mars, and asked, "Did you have any trouble getting here?"

"You're kidding, right?" Joanne said.

"Is this Dr. Mills?" Dale asked, turning to George.

"In the flesh," George said.

"Can I get you something while we wait?" Dale asked apologetically.

"How about some coffee?" Joanne said.

Dale nodded.

"Creamer in mine, black for Dr. Mills."

Dale bobbed approvingly, then left the room as though on a mission.

When he was gone, George smiled. "He's eager to please, isn't he?"

"A little too eager," Joanne said.

George sat and tried to relax. Joanne reached into her bag and retrieved a Tab. She propped it in front of her and began typing.

Listening to the familiar drumbeat of her fingers on the key icons, George rekindled his excitement at the prospect of meeting Perseus. In just a few minutes, he would be coming face to face with what, Homo superior? He had no idea what to expect, because up till now all he really had was the memory of unusually unremarkable little kids. This meeting was different; they were no longer small children, but teenagers on the precipice of young adulthood. Their special gifts would surely be in evidence, though he had no clear idea of what they might be. He had spoken to Joanne about it, but she had been vague, leading him to speculate that she was unsure herself. Although he and Joanne had designed the models and simulations, the artificial evolution was highly nonlinear and hard to interpret without a physical expression, but the only physical expression was the children themselves.

At the sound of the door opening, George sat forward, watching as Dale stammered back into the room. He was carrying a silver thermos in one hand and a box of cups and condiments in the other. Dale left the door open as he moved to the middle of the table. A woman followed him in, and closed the door.

At first, George thought she might be Dale's aid, or someone else on staff at DRA, but Joanne's reaction told him otherwise. Joanne had worked with DRA for years now. She was familiar with most of the staff by sight. But as he watched, Joanne stopped typing abruptly, and just stared.

The woman's appearance was hyper-Terran. She was about five six, and George guessed about a hundred and ten or a hundred and fifteen pounds. She was well proportioned in an average sort of way, with wider shoulders than hips, and an ample chest with an admittedly stimulating shape. Her slender frame gave her a sleek look that was unusually pleasing. She wore contemporary Terran clothes, a metallic silver-blue dress cut shorter than was the style on Mars. But the most dramatic aspect of her appearance was her face and pale violet hair, which hung down to her shoulders. George suspected from its texture and hue that it wasn't dyed. Her skin was light, almost porcelain, except for a hint of color around the cheeks and pale violet eyes. The overall effect made her look strangely artificial, almost like a living doll.

It was eerie, because George knew from his time on Earth that this was not a look that came from an exotic use of cosmetics, but a result of designer genetic enhancements. The contrast between this woman and Joanne was a striking demonstration of how humanity on Earth and on Mars had grown apart, a chasm much greater than could be measured in the distance between planets.

George watched as the woman walked past Dale, who was still arranging objects on the table. She found a seat almost directly across from him and Joanne, and once seated, looked at them briefly, then smiled. George was struck by a sudden change in Dale's demeanor. Whereas before he had been attentive and anxious to please, he now sat quietly and hardly looked up. A few minutes passed as the woman arranged her things, then said, "I'm Dr. Margaret Gates, Mollar Pharmaceuticals, and you are?"

It took Joanne a few seconds to stop typing. Finally, she looked up blankly and asked, "Excuse me, did you say something?"

George had to keep from grinning as Dr. Gates repeated her introduction, completely unflustered.

"Dr. Joanne Zhu, Microbiology Institute at the university, and this is my associate, Dr. George Mills."

There was a pause. "George Mills? Are you the computer scientist?" Dr. Gates asked, all but ignoring Joanne.

George smiled politely. "Physicist actually, but yes, we do a lot of computer work too."

She seemed to consider this for a moment. "You're the one doing the behavioral research, aren't you?"

"That's strange," George said.

Dr. Gates arched an eyebrow, "What is?"

"That an agent from Mollar Pharmaceuticals would be familiar with my work."

Her eyes narrowed a bit. She seemed to search for a way to integrate this new development into her plans.

"I don't formally work for Mollar," she admitted slowly. "I'm a government consultant for the CIH, the Confederation Institutes of Health. I'm working through Mollar because they provide the vectors and genetic sequencers for all the therapies provided by DRA here on Mars. Now that we know why I'm here, I'd be interested in knowing why you're here, Dr. Mills?" She leaned forward, both elbows on the table, her pale hands cupping her face, exaggerating her inquisitive smile.

Bulls-eye, thought George. That's exactly the question he hadn't wanted her to ask. He had stumbled right into it. Now he was trying to think of something to say, knowing that the longer he hedged, the more he looked like someone with something to hide.

"He's my colleague at the university," Joanne explained, turning and smiling at George. "We consult with George's lab. They do the computer analysis on which our diagnosis and outcome simulations are based."

"That's unusual, isn't it?" Dr. Gates remarked thoughtfully. "Therapy analysis is pretty well established. Why would you need a research facility when you could use standard software packages? We like to see standardization; consistency is all important in these treatments."

"That's true for certain treatments," Joanne said, "but the situation on Mars is a bit different than that on Earth, which, unfortunately for us, is where most of the standard packages were developed. We have many issues unique to the Martian environment that aren't handled well by the standard packages. That's why I find it unusual that they would send someone from Earth if there's a problem."

Dr. Gates said nothing, opting instead to turn her chair and consult her Tab. "I happened to be at Mollar when certain inconsistencies came to light."

She read notes on her Tab as George and Joanne waited, and Dale seemed to take more than a casual interest in his hands on the table.

After another few moments, Dr. Gates said, "We've found some very curious results in some of the aptitude tests administered to a group of children here in Ursa."

Here it comes, thought George. We're finally getting to the main event.

"I've monitored the progress of the groups that received therapy at the university," Joanne said. "We haven't seen any problematic academic trends in any of them that I'm aware of." She looked to Dale to confirm her statement.

Dr. Gates smiled. "It was Dale that brought these issues to our attention." Her wry expression betrayed her amusement at this admission.

Joanne shot Dale a contemptuous stare, and Dale struggled to find another object on which to fixate. Then she looked back to Dr. Gates, "Could you show me what your talking about?"

Dr. Gates uploaded the relevant files into Joanne's Tab. George recognized at once that the aptitude scores were those of children in the Proteus file. George waited patiently and sipped his coffee. All along he had assumed that the authorities had spotted differences in blood antigens, anomalous hemoglobin levels, or something less arbitrary than aptitude scores. He was relieved when Joanne seemed to see nothing damning in the data. Tests like these were always a subject of debate among psychologists. And since these tests had been developed on Earth, a small anomaly lent little credence to anything truly suspicious.

"Overall these scores look normal, albeit on the high side," Dr. Gates agreed. "However, if you look at the scores for geometric reasoning, they're off the scale."

Joanne scanned the scores on her Tab. George felt himself start to perspire, just a little.

"They're all in the ninety-nine point nine percentile," Dr. Gates said. "But that's only because of the bin width on these plots. If you look at the raw scores and not the normalized scores, each of these children got a perfect score. They didn't miss one question."

There was a short silence. "That may be unusual," Joanne said dismissively. "But is it sufficient reason to call a meeting like this? After all, occasionally children will get perfect scores, won't they? There are twenty names here. We've given therapy to over a thousand kids. Is it so unusual that two percent would get a perfect score?"

Nice try, George thought, but unfortunately this was something he understood well. It was virtually impossible for such a large percentage of test takers to be beyond the scope of any legitimate aptitude test. Even when some test takers were said to get a perfect score, many times it was a perfect normalized score, not a perfect raw score. This was a basic property of any useful aptitude test. Test designers strove for normally distributed statistics, something that looked as much like a bell curve as possible. Nature seemed to like to clump large numbers of unrelated individual measurements on a bell curve. The fact that these scores clumped together to form a spike on the extreme tail of the raw distribution made no sense at all. If the test, which had been around for a while now, had that property to begin with, it would have been corrected long ago. In fact, the twenty scores in question were a statistical red flag indicating a hidden relationship among the members of this elite group, especially since they all came from the same place.

"Dr. Mills, you must appreciate the significance of these scores. After all, you're an expert in statistics, aren't you?" Dr. Gates said.

Dr. Gates sat back, self-satisfied that she'd made her point. She's good, George thought. It was hard not to notice how exotically attractive she was. George felt a pang of guilt for thinking so. Though this meeting had been staged to trap them, George felt no enmity toward her whatsoever. He feared that if Joanne sensed this, she might interpret it as a betrayal of sorts. George struggled to maintain perspective, stumbling here might have far reaching consequences for all of them. Though she looked angelic, Dr. Gates' genetically engineered innocence could well have been contrived to entrap a novice like him—the perfect fly for the perfect spider web.

"There must have been a mistake, either in the test, or in the way these particular scores were compiled," George offered weakly.

"I don't think so," Dr. Gates said. "I looked at the raw data myself, and I also looked at other test takers in and out of this age group, excluding these twenty. Know what I found?"

George said nothing.

"They all look completely normal, exactly what you would expect. In fact, I'll do you one better, Dr. Mills. I looked at the scores of anyone who's taken this particular test on Earth, as well as Mars, over the past ten years—know what I found?"

She's really enjoying herself now, George thought, then shrugged.

"These twenty test takers, here in Ursa, are the only ones ever to get a perfect raw score, irrespective of age." That's why we're here today, Dr. Mills."

George glanced over at Joanne, who continued to search her Tab, as if looking at it long enough might uncover an error in Dr. Gates' reasoning.

George sipped his coffee, which was getting cold, then said, "Okay, you have a point, Dr. Gates. But what I fail to understand is what you think you can possibly get from us. It must be clear to you that we have no idea why these scores are so unusual. Before you brought it to our attention today, we had no idea this issue even existed. In fact, we've never considered our client's mental abilities, outside of chronic problems that might have resulted from their therapy. That's probably why we never caught this. Nobody I know would consider this intellectual gift a problem, and as you can see from the medical record, there was no mental enhancement program in their therapy."

"Well Dr. Gates," Joanne said, "where do we go from here?"

Dr. Gates smiled warmly. "I thought it might be interesting to interview one of the children."

Joanne blinked. In all the confusion, she had forgotten about Perseus.

Dr. Gates turned to Dale, "Where is he, Mr. Metz? I had the impression he'd be here by now."

"Let me go and check on that, Dr. Gates," Dale said. He abruptly got up and went to the door. But as he opened it, he found a man standing there. Dale was momentarily startled by the man's size, his wild unkempt beard, and imposing presence. Dale stepped aside, looking into the room, trying to find Dr. Gates so she could tell him what to do.

"Come in Malcolm," Joanne called. "You've got the right place."

Malcolm smiled naively, then brushed past Dale.

"Mills," Malcolm said, acknowledging George. "You look well rested today."

"Have any trouble getting here?" Joanne asked.

Malcolm explained how the guards had detained him, then released him when their records showed he was a reservist in the Martian Militia. After that, they found that Joanne had put his name on the attendee record.

"Sorry for the mix-up," Joanne said.

Malcolm sat next to her. Dr. Gates watched patiently, then nodded to Dale, who quickly left the room.

"Dr. Gates, this is another associate, Dr. Malcolm Peters," Joanne said.

Dr. Gates gave Joanne a sly smile, then reciprocated the introduction. She proceeded to question Malcolm for the next several minutes, but soon seemed to lose interest in him.

Dr. Gates pushed away from the table. "It's good to stand, isn't it?" She strolled toward the front of the room. She happened to notice the coffee, turned to George and asked, "How is it?"

"Cold," George said.

She grinned. The metallic highlights in her dress caught the flat room light, making subtle shimmers, undulating in concert with her rhythmic movements. "Is the coffee strong?" she asked. "I like mine strong."

George smiled weakly, "It's fairly standard Earth issue."

"That's too bad," she said.

George tried not to stare as she leaned across the table to retrieve a pitcher of water. The silver dress inched up her thigh, unnerving him. He heard Joanne get up, and pass behind him. Apparently, she too had decided on a glass of water. Joanne waited for the other woman to finish, then reached over and poured a glass as Dr. Gates watched her over the top of her cup.

Seeing these two women together was striking. They couldn't have been more different, George thought. They were both the products of societies that were drastically out of sync. Earth was an empire, in decline perhaps, but still opulent and driven by material wealth, rather than some deeper cultural imperatives. Dr. Gates reflected these values. He had seldom seen anyone with this degree of overt genetic augmentation, although he had heard of this new type. They were called Moderns, and were appearing more and more as the sons and daughters of Earth's ruling elite. Perhaps this was the twenty-fourth century's answer to royalty. Done this way, it wasn't the arbitrary happenstance of heredity from some distant member of a bloodline that had displayed a novel set of traits, but rather direct genetic imposition of a particular group's idea of a superior breed. Joanne had also been the product of considerable genetic enhancement, but out of completely different motivations. In her case, she had been designed to live a healthy life in the harsh Martian environment. Although she had larger lungs, less susceptibility to radiation sickness, and a tolerance for low gravity, she could have easily been mistaken as having Indian or Mediterranean ancestry back on twenty-first century Earth. There had been no attempt at cosmetics whatsoever.

"Do you want me to heat that up for you?" he heard Joanne say.

"What?" George asked.

"That cold coffee you keep complaining about."

"Oh, yeah, thanks, I'd like that very much."

She brought the thermos over to where he sat, and blocking his view of Dr. Gates, poured.

As Dr. Gates made her way back to her seat, someone knocked at the door. Dale entered and held the door open for a middle-aged man and woman, followed by a teenage boy. As soon as they entered, they noticed Joanne. Joanne beamed as the woman walked over and kissed her on both cheeks. After the man had exchanged a similar greeting, they talked briefly, making animated gestures with their hands. From where he sat, George couldn't make out what was being said, but he could tell by the body language that this was a meeting among longtime friends.

When his mother and father had passed from Joanne to Dale, the boy hugged Joanne. Clearly, while George had passed all those years at the university thinking about these people whose lives he'd influenced so profoundly, Joanne had forged a bond, filling in the human dimension that he had so sorely missed.

George watched Dr. Gates with interest, trying to divine some clue as to her real intentions toward these people. He had no idea what Dr. Gates' role was in all this. She could be an instigator with some, as of yet, unknown agenda, or simply a bureaucrat carrying out another assignment for reasons as mysterious to her as to him. She sat across the table and watched, sipping water and coyly glancing over the rim of her glass. She looked like a little girl, new and shiny.

The family lingered at the head of the table a moment longer, then were ushered by Dale to seats across the table from George. The woman put her arm around the boy's shoulders in a gesture that seemed to underscore the potential menace this place held for them. The man and woman were generic Martians, tall, dark, and endowed with generous manes of jet-black hair. They were both slim and evidently in good health. The man was dressed in a white shirt, dark blue pleated dress slacks, and black tie shoes. The woman wore a dark blue suit, which accented her olive complexion. Her hair was long and lustrous, hanging down to the middle of her back. George thought she was quite lovely.

He shifted his attention to the boy, who was slim and rangy, with an awkwardness common to young teenagers. He seemed tall for his age, and walked in a sloppy adolescent style that made his feet seem too large for the rest of his body. He had the same complexion as his parents, with brown curly hair that was rare in generic Martians. It partially hid large ears, which, on close inspection, seemed lower on his head than they should be.

As he walked behind Dr. Gates, George noticed the boy's interested stares in her direction. It was fascinating to watch. The boy obviously had a sense of his own uniqueness. The sight of someone like Dr. Gates may have suggested that she had been brought here for the same reasons he had.

The boy sat to the right of Dr. Gates, regarding her cautiously. They were both about the same size. Dr. Gates looked almost as young as he did. She smiled sweetly at him, almost like a sister, or dear friend.

The boy continued looking at her with an inscrutable air of neutrality, then looked away as if he'd made a determination. George could see that the boy's inability to be swayed by her charms had left Dr. Gates a little puzzled. Apparently, it didn't happen often. George continued watching the boy, who had turned to inspect the room and the rest of its occupants. Then the boy turned slowly toward him. This was the moment of truth, what he had worked for all these long years. He remembered Will, the most alien intelligence that any man had ever known, making the only request he'd ever made—he had asked to meet this boy. The hairs on the back of George's neck began to bristle, followed by a rolling chill that started in his shoulders and slowly worked its way into his legs.

The boy had very symmetric features. His eyes were a pleasing distance apart, and he had a moderate nose whose nostrils were slightly flared in a way that gave his face mild drama. His mouth was small, with full lips that sat above a strong chin. It was the eyes, though, that drew George in. He hadn't ever seen eyes like these before. They were an indeterminable color, gray perhaps, but pale with odd golden flecks. As he and the boy locked stares, the boy's expression slowly changed, a slight smile stretching across his face. With that, the tingling seemed to leave him, and George relaxed.

"Perseus," he heard Joanne say. "This is George Mills, the man at the university I told you about."

The boy's smile grew wider. "I've wanted to meet you for a long time now, Dr. Mills."

"Please, call me George," George said then extended his hand across the table. The boy looked momentarily confused.

"It's called a handshake," George said. "It's what they do where I came from when friends meet."

The boy leaned forward, taking George's hand. They both smiled when George shook the boy's hand up and down. No matter what other nonsensical things had happened in this room, George felt, for the first time since the beginning of the experiment, that he had absolutely done the right thing. Whether the authorities had sanctioned their actions or not, looking into this boy's eyes, he found validation.

"Perseus?" Dr. Gates said. "That's an unusual name, isn't it?"

Perseus looked down at his hands folded in front of him on the table.

"It's Greek," his mother said. It was my great grandfather's name. Our ancestors were Greek back on Earth, before we immigrated."

"I see," Dr. Gates said. "Isn't there a mythical story connected to that name?"

"Yes," his mother said slowly. "Perseus slew the Medusa, a once beautiful goddess who was unfaithful to one of the Greek gods, and was turned into a monster. I don't remember which one."

"Which what?" Dr. Gates asked.

"Which god she offended. I can't remember which one," the mother said.

Dr. Gates smiled, then looked at the boy. "Perseus, do you know why I've asked you to come here today?"

"No," he said. "I was hoping you'd tell me."

She explained to the boy that he'd done very well on a test at school. He had done so well, in fact, that some people at his school had wanted her to meet him.

"Okay," the boy said, looking into her pale violet eyes. She smiled sweetly and told him that some other kids at his school had also done amazing well on the same examination. She waited. He continued to regard her with the same equanimity. Dr. Gates began to read the names of the other students, then asked if Perseus knew any of them.

Perseus shrugged.

"Perseus," Dr. Gates said, "is there some reason why you don't want to speak to me? I've come a very long way to see you. Won't you talk to me?"

He looked at her, cocking his head slightly. "I don't know you," Perseus said. "My mother was afraid to come here today. Why do you think that is?"

Dr. Gates looked at the woman, then back at the boy. "I don't know." She looked at the boy's mother again, and the woman looked down.

"See," the boy said. "There's something wrong here." And Perseus said nothing more.

George was amazed by how superficially ordinary the boy was, but at the same time, how insightful he had managed to be. He had somehow thwarted Dr. Gates best efforts to gain any insight into his true nature. She was a skilled interrogator; he could see that. She had easily led him down the garden path to embarrassing admissions, and she had caught obscure details that someone as thorough as Joanne had missed. Yet, she had been absolutely unable to get anywhere with this little boy.

Dr. Gates paused a moment, reached into her bag on the floor, and retrieved a multi-colored plastic cube. She put it on the shiny black marble table in front of her. "Ever see one of these before?" she asked.

"No," Perseus said.

"It's a toy, a puzzle. It's very old. It was once called a Rubik's Cube. You've never heard of a Rubik's Cube before?"

If someone had just walked in and seen them together, they might have thought they were two kids playing a game. From the way she talked and carried herself, George would have put Dr. Gates' age at about thirty, yet, next to this boy, she looked no older than fifteen or sixteen.

"You're sure you've never seen a toy like this before?"

He shook his head.

Dr. Gates explained how it worked, demonstrating as she spoke, by scrambling the squares and destroying the color symmetry. When it was completely scrambled, she placed it on the table in front of her.

"Do you understand how it works?" she asked.

Perseus nodded.

"Do you think you can make it look like it did before?"

He shrugged, "I don't know."

"Try it," she said, pushing it forward so he could reach it.

Perseus paused a moment, looked at Joanne, then at George, and picked it up. He inspected it from a variety of sides, turning it over in his hands. George watched him closely, following the boy's eyes, trying to understand what he was doing. He seemed to pause at the center tiles, then the middle, then the corners. George remembered that this was the strategy he'd discovered after playing with a Rubik's Cube for hours. It had taken about five seconds for the boy to see it. Perseus glanced up and held George's gaze for a couple of seconds.

George winked.

The boy began to slide the bands into various orientations. He had good manual dexterity. His long fingers glided easily over the toy. Its color bands moved quickly, first in this direction, then that. Five minutes later, he returned the toy to the table, still scrambled.

"I don't think I can do it," he said, and looked at his parents.

"He's always been good at puzzles," his father told Dr. Gates. George could see that the man wanted his son to make a good impression, and was disappointed that the boy had failed. Dr. Gates gave the father a sincere look of sympathy, then returned to the boy.

"Are you sure?" she asked.

"Uh-huh," he said, seemingly embarrassed at having disappointed his father.

Dr. Gates looked around absently, then settled on Malcolm, who appeared to be smiling as if he knew something she didn't.

"Dr. Peters," she said, "do you have something to add."

"Do you really want to hear it?"

She shrugged, smiled sweetly. "Yes, I do," she said.

"Do you know why he's not cooperating?"

She looked at the boy, then back at Malcolm. "Why don't you tell us?"

"Simple," Malcolm said. "He doesn't trust you. You brought him here because you thought he was extraordinarily gifted, yet you're surprised when he fails to be naïve."

"What do mean?" she asked. It was the first sign of annoyance George had seen her display.

"Think about it," Malcolm said. "The boy did well on a test. Typically that's something you're rewarded for. Instead, he's brought to this imposing place, in front of a pushy stranger, through a mob outside. If you were him, what would you think? Perhaps you don't have much occasion to deal with children, but this is more or less a textbook reaction."

Dr. Gates said nothing.

Malcolm looked at her a moment. "Are you in the military, Dr. Gates?"

She looked up quickly.

"Let me give you some advice, even though you haven't asked for it. Take it as a professional courtesy from someone who's been where you are now."

Dr. Gates continued looking at him, a little confused. This was completely unexpected.

"Be careful, Dr. Gates. When you kick sleeping dogs, they might wake up and bite you."

"What's that suppose to mean?"

"I think you know," Malcolm said.

"I need to stretch," Dr. Gates said abruptly. "Why don't we break for fifteen minutes?"

Dale explained that there was a lounge down the corridor with refreshments and a window overlooking the canyon. The boy told his parents that he wanted to stay behind and asked them to bring him a flask of orange juice. His father patted him on the back, thinking he'd been disappointed by his failure to solve the puzzle. His mother just looked worried.

"I'll stay with him," George offered. "I don't feel much like going either."

"Thank you," his mother said, sincerely grateful for George's help. She kissed the boy on the cheek, then asked Joanne if she was coming.

Joanne nodded. "Go on, I'll be there in a minute."

"You're sure you don't want to come?" Joanne asked.

"No," George said. "You go on."

She smiled and turned to Perseus. "Dr. Mills has been your admirer for a long time, you know."

Perseus nodded.

George pursed his lips. He knew he wouldn't have much time before the others returned, and there was so much to say. Looking around the room, he considered the fact that this meeting was almost certainly being recorded. Whatever he said to the boy would have to be indirect and cryptic. Presumably, puzzles were his strong suit.

George noticed Malcolm at the door, waiting patiently, holding it open. "I think you have admirers of your own," he told Joanne, glancing toward the door.

"What are you talking about?" she asked, puzzled.

"See you in a few minutes," George said, and smiled.

She got up and continued giving him funny looks until Malcolm closed the door behind her.

The boy sat across from him, shoulders stooped, looking whimsically at the plastic cube on the table where Dr. Gates had left it. He stretched forward tentatively and picked it up. He turned it over slowly in his hands, then took a moment to glance at George.

"You realize they're probably recording this," George said.

Perseus shrugged, then smiled weakly. As George watched, he palmed the cube in both hands, and slowly slipped it under the table. His arms moved slightly, as if he were manipulating the puzzle out of sight. Perseus continued looking at George, the thin smile never leaving his lips. Finally, he pulled his hands from under the table and put them in front of him, hiding the puzzle inside. He slowly opened his fingers so that George could see just one side of the cube. Then he hid the puzzle in his hands again, and rotated it. He did this for all six sides, each time opening his hands, just slightly, so George could see. George had to force his jaw from dropping; the cube was in perfect color alignment. The boy had solved the puzzle without even looking at it.

Perseus moved the cube under the table again. After a few moments, he returned it, once again scrambled, and put it where Dr. Gates had left it.

George stared at the boy, then began laughing.

The boy smiled broadly.

They sat in silence for a while. "I'd like to ask you some questions," the boy said finally.

"I'd like to help any way I can."

"You know I'm different, don't you, Dr. Mills?"

Perseus was staring into space, his golden eyes filled with a far-away look. He paused a moment, then looked back at George. "I think you know why."

"Why did you do so well on that test? You must have known it would focus attention on you."

"It's what I do. I like puzzles—that's all. It just happened. Who goes around controlling everything they do? Don't you ever do things just because you like to?"

"Of course I do," George said. "I guess the reason I'm asking is because things like that are hard for me. I have to try to do well. Even people who are good at certain things have to try hard to do their best." He paused a moment. "Do you have to try hard when doing things like that puzzle?"

The boy looked fleetingly at the cube, then back at George. "No, not really. Actually, I have to try not to— that's the problem. It's all so ridiculously easy."

"You're very fortunate," George said.

The boy looked at him. "Am I, Dr. Mills?"

George glanced at his watch. "I'll be in touch. I don't think we should discuss it here, but I'll try my best to help. I promise."

"Thank you, Dr. Mills," Perseus said.

Once the members of the meeting returned, Dr. Gates apologized graciously. She had to leave due to a scheduling conflict. A sky car was waiting on the landing platform ready to take her back to Mollar.

Joanne, George, and Malcolm left Perseus and his parents in Dale's care. Dale assured Joanne that he would make arrangements to have a cab return them to Dome Two using a rear underground station, so as to avoid the crowd out front. George could see that Dale was trying hard to recover some shred of the relationship he'd built with Joanne over the past ten years, but this incident had guaranteed it would never be the same. George watched the pained look on the shorter man's face as Joanne dismissed him with a cold pragmatic nod. When Dale left with Perseus and his parents, George approached her.

"Kind of hard on him, weren't you?"

"The hell with him," Joanne said, with uncharacteristic venom. "I'll never trust him again. He tricked me into betraying others who trust me."

George put his arm around her shoulders. "I think you did very well, under the circumstances." That brought a muffled sound, like she was trying to stifle a laugh.

The quarter mile elevator ride to the lobby was as spectacular going down as it had been coming up. Once they'd descended, George called Fred Jackson on his Tab. The security man had given him his private number, and asked him to call when they'd finished their meeting. After he and Joanne had assured Malcolm they felt safe retrieving George's car, Malcolm said his goodbyes. He promised to meet them at the university the next day to discuss what he'd learned about the boy.

Jackson met George and Joanne in the lobby shortly after Malcolm's departure, and brought two security men with him, both in full riot gear. Upon leaving the building, they noticed that the crowd had thinned considerably, making it fairly easy for their escort to get them back to the car.

They left Federal Island without mishap. Once back on the *Sea Of Storms*, Joanne asked George what he and Perseus had talked about when she and the others had been out of the room. He told her about their conversation, and about certain impressions he'd had in the boy's presence.

"What kind of feelings," Joanne asked.

"It's hard to describe."

George thought a moment. "Perseus seemed to anticipate my questions. He seemed to sense that I could tell him things about himself that a complete stranger couldn't possibly know. Have you told him about my involvement?"

"No, I never mentioned it. In fact, we've never discussed his being special in any way other than, of course, how special he is to me."

George considered this. "Is he empathic?"

Joanne smiled. "Yes, I think he is. I didn't say anything, because I was curious to see if you'd come to the same conclusion."

"Amazing. How long have you known?"

"I noticed it just recently. It's like what you said. He seems to know what you're going to say before you say it, as though he can read your thoughts. At first, I wasn't sure. I thought I might be imagining things."

"We should go back to the simulations and try to understand the implications. Also, I'd like you to bring Perseus to the university to see me."

They drove in silence for a while.

"How about an early dinner?" George asked, as they cruised over Lake Geneva toward the university.

"Would you mind just taking me home?" Joanne said. She put her hand on his. "I'm really tired. I hope you understand."

"Of course," George said. "Are you okay? It's not like you to wilt this early."

"You have to admit, it's been a pretty crazy couple of days since you came back." She smiled, and squeezed his hand. "I'll be fine tomorrow, okay?"

He nodded. A minute later he exited the avenue, then headed toward Joanne's lakeside townhouse.

Chapter Eight

"The distinctions separating the social classes are false; in the last analysis, they rest on force." – Albert Einstein

Admiral Aaron Nelson, NearSec Supreme Commander, stood at the large observation window in his private office, just off the bridge of the Agamemnon class heavy cruiser Saratoga. With its half-mile long profile, and its counter-rotating crew sections for artificial gravity, the Saratoga was faster and more agile than the generations of large military spacecraft that had come before her. The Saratoga's hyper-efficient fusion engines could generate more energy than all three domes of Ursa Township, and could, along with propelling the huge craft between planets, lay waste to the entire inhabited surface of Mars. As an adjunct to its power, the ship's new helium-3 based fusion plant had the advantage of earlier deuterium-tritium reactors, but without the large amounts of lethal neutron radiation characteristic of older nuclear drives. Under maximum burn, she had traveled the seventy-five million miles between Earth and Mars in a mere month, while hosting a crew of over two hundred and fifty sailors and marines.

With the fingers of his right hand, Nelson felt the course gold braid on the sleeves of his dark blue tunic as he admired the four stars on his collar reflected in the window. The ship's power flowed through him like a bolt of blue-white electricity; he was its brain, its will. From his position at the window, he watched the bright copper horizon of Mars below the ship and the four needle-like delta wing interceptors flying in formation, skimming over the top of the Martian atmosphere and leaving plasma contrails in their wake. Shifting his gaze above Mars, he saw the bright band of pinprick stars that defined the general direction of the center of the galaxy. Not yet, he thought, but soon.

He was a handsome man, as judged by Earth normal standards—tall at six-foot-two, and trim at fifty-six years of age. His cropped silver gray hair, which had developed at an early age, and deep set brown eyes gave him an authoritative demeanor that he'd been able to parlay into four stars at a relatively young age. Nelson smiled to himself at the realization that much of the pleasure he derived from the hours he spent in front of the observation port had less to do with the magnificent view than with the sight of his own reflection in the window. Chimes coming from Ship-Com interrupted his meditation.

"Yes."

His response activated a monitor on the wall opposite his desk.

"Someone to see you, sir," said the face on the monitor. Nelson turned and glanced at Matt Wells, his exec.

"Okay, Matt, show her in."

Matt's arched eyebrows and confused stare looked mildly comical and reinforced his satisfaction at being a step ahead of his exec. Unknown to Matt, Nelson had expected a briefing from one of his best intelligence agents, one who had recently been dispatched to Mars.

Mars, Nelson thought, with annoyance. It had been nothing but trouble for over a hundred years now. Its value as a strategic asset and as a deep space source of water and helium-3 was especially troubling. Mars had enormous amounts of water in permafrost under most of the southern hemisphere, and it served as an indispensable station midway between Earth and the Jupiter system, with its many rich moons. Much too valuable an asset to be given autonomy under a backward group of day laborers like that bunch that currently called for Mars independence.

"Independence." Silently mouthing the word burned him like acid—there would be no independence while he had something to say about it.

Nelson heard the chimes again and said, "Enter."

The door slid open and the woman came in, walked slowly to the center of the room, saying nothing at first, choosing instead to communicate visually. She wore a pale metallic green dress that shimmered in the office light. It hugged her tapered form and rode high above her knees. Her shapely long legs were adorned by sheer pearly white leggings, which matched the strapless white pumps that accented her calf muscles, making her legs even more sensual. Nelson regarded her, a slightly salacious smile impressing itself on his lips, thoroughly enjoying the show. This was a welcome diversion from the growing annoyance he'd felt thinking about the situation brewing on the planet below.

"Good morning, Margaret."

He moved to meet her. Standing before her, he looked into her strange violet eyes and saw them dilate slightly.

"Good morning, Aaron," Dr. Gates said. She looked around the room, apparently impressed by the extravagance and power of the Saratoga.

Putting his hand low on her back, Nelson led her to the black leather sofa opposite the observation port. He felt the rhythmic movement of her buttocks through the thin material of her dress as she walked, prompting a tingle in his groin. She sat and crossed her legs, placing her bag on the floor.

"Can I get you something from the bar?" Nelson asked. "I know you like scotch. I happen to have the only bottle of Red Label within a hundred-million miles of here."

"That'll be fine, Aaron. I'll take it with only one ice cube, if you don't mind."

"Of course," he said. Then he moved to a counter to the left of his desk, poured the drinks, and returned.

After giving her the glass of amber liquid, he turned one of two chairs positioned in front of his desk, so that he could face her. Sitting in front and above her, as was always his preference, he rested his glass on the arm of the chair.

"Okay," Nelson said, then took a sip, and felt the warmth. "You were supposed to follow up on George Mills, weren't you?

There have been some disturbing reports coming from the GESC review about some new kind of computing capability he's apparently developed."

Nelson regarded her with mock suspicion for a moment, then took the edge off his mild recrimination with a modest smile.

"My operatives on the planet tell me you've been doing something with DRA, of all things. Is there some reason you've chosen to drop the Mills assignment?"

Watching him speak, Margaret smiled innocently and waited for him to finish.

"It turns out that Mills and DRA are linked," she said.

"Is that right?" Nelson took another drink. "What could Mills possibly be doing with DRA? He's some kind of physicist doing work with WSA on tactical, isn't he?"

"No, not really," Margaret said, playing with her glass. "In fact, he has no idea that any of his work is of interest to the WSA. He's been working with GESC on behavioral simulations. Mostly theoretical stuff concerned with decision making under stress. It has applications in remote colonies, conflict resolution, things like that."

"Well," Nelson said, growing impatient. "We have a looming civil war down there, or haven't you noticed? I thought that this was an urgent matter, at least that's the word from the oversight committee. But from what you've told me. . ." He spread his arms in a gesture of frustration.

"I know," she said sympathetically. "But this may have deeper strategic significance; let me explain."

She crossed her legs in the opposite direction, then explained how WSA had tried to use the Mills models in tactical simulations of the current crisis on Mars. How the best WSA computer modelers had been unable to make the larger simulations work, but had confirmed that peripheral results, which they could run, appeared valid.

"They don't think the problems are in the models," she said. "In fact, the models are far more detailed and correlate many more significant parameters than anything we currently use."

As she spoke, Nelson became more engaged. Framing the problem in tactical advantages played directly into a world view that he held relevant.

When she was finished, he said, "Okay, that makes sense, but you still haven't answered my question."

"The DRA?"

He smiled and made a gesture with his hands, prompting her to continue. Margaret lifted her glass, held it up, and shook it, making the ice rattle around inside the tumbler. After Nelson made another trip to the bar, refreshing his glass as well as hers, she told him about Dale. How he'd alerted her to the anomalous aptitude scores, and how she'd discovered Mills' involvement in that as well.

"What in the world are we doing with an agent in the DRA?" Nelson asked. "It doesn't strike me as a nexus of sensitive intelligence sources."

Margaret smiled, took a sip, and continued the briefing. She told him about the children, about the significance of the test results, their strange similar appearances, and about her observations during the meeting at Building One.

"So Mills was at Build One?" Nelson asked, surprised by this piece of news.

"Yes. I noticed when reviewing Joanne Zhu's files that she was working with Mills. That's why I decided to pursue this."

"And who is Joanne Zhu?"

"She's the DRA consultant in the case."

"Okay, but you said the boy failed to perform on the test you gave him. Isn't that right?"

"He faked it," she said impatiently. "Those test scores couldn't be a mistake. Along with the puzzles the other children were able to solve, there's something unique happening here, of greater importance than the simulations, in my opinion."

Nelson got up and walked to the observation port. He could see the eastern part of the planet lapsing into nightfall, and the dome lights coming on in Orion Township.

Genetic enhancements—it seemed ironic that Margaret should be so alarmed by them. After all, she was the product of them herself. It's all gone too far, he thought. The governments of the twenty-first century had seen it coming, and had passed laws detailing the limits to which genetic enhancements in humans could be made. The corporations, however, had ensured certain loopholes, as they always did. The whole thing was just too profitable; it was as simple as that. From genetic therapies for diseases, to cosmetics, to enhanced foods, to spare organs with perfect immune response, and finally to enhanced people. Too many people were making too much money to ever put the genie back in the bottle. By the middle of the twenty-second century, humanity had started the fall down the slippery slope of designer people. Most of the genetic abeyance laws had either been repealed or gutted. He himself was the recipient of many enhancements, and could probably expect to live for hundred and fifty years. That worked, he thought. But Margaret and many of the current generation had taken it a step further. Their modifications were severe and narcissistic, even by his standards. If the truth be told, he really didn't understand people like Margaret, couldn't really read them, and that made him nervous. He'd gotten to where he was by being a good judge of people, anticipating their next move. He could see Margaret's growing impatience with him, which he had tried to provoke, because he wanted to see where it would lead. That was another one of his talents. He knew that probing weakness was the key to understanding people. And Margaret's weakness was her arrogance, which compelled her to underestimate him.

Nelson turned from the observation port. "Why are you so concerned about these children anyway? Genetic enhancement is routinely done. You yourself are the recipient of quite a few modifications, aren't you?"

He could see her trying to maintain equanimity, but she continued to rattle the ice in her glass, betraying her agitation.

Nelson pushed further. "Suppose Mills has somehow helped DRA engineer genetic enhancements for mental acuity, so what? That may be new on Mars, but it's well within what we routinely do on Earth."

Margaret exhaled, trying hard not to roll her eyes. "I think you're missing the point."

"Oh, how so?" Nelson asked evenly.

"This is not an enhancement for mental sharpness. There isn't an enhancement on Earth that could even remotely compare to what I suspect we've uncovered in these kids. This is off the scale, something completely new."

Nelson considered her words with interest. It wasn't like her to get this excited over just anything. She'd been emotionally reserved, at least as long as he'd known her. She tipped her glass and touched the ice with her tongue. When she lowered it, the wetness on her lips made them shiny.

"Want to hear the best part?"

"Yes, I do," he said.

"I took the puzzle the boy handled, and a can of juice he drank from at the meeting. Had the genetics division at Mollar run a pattern on the skin and saliva. Know what we found?"

He shook his head.

"They're not human."

She paused to let it sink in.

"What?" he said, astonished. "What are you talking about?"

"They're not human," she repeated emphatically. "They deviate from the human genome by more than two percent. We mapped some of the deviations and tried to correlate them with genetic sites we understand. There are massive global changes. We've never tried anything on this scale. Frankly, we wouldn't even know where to begin."

He looked at her for a moment, then got up and began pacing. She rattled her glass again, smiled, and held it up as he turned. He got her some more scotch and poured water for himself this time. Okay, he thought, let's see where this goes.

"To what end—what's it for? Why did they do it?"

"I don't know," she replied slowly.

He sat down next to her, and turned to face her, his arm stretched out along the sofa behind her head. He could smell the subtle scent of something in her hair.

"That's the most important part, isn't it?" he said. He thought a moment. "Why did you have to run a genetics map to uncover this degree of manipulation? Do they look so pedestrian that you couldn't tell just by sight?"

"It's unbelievably well done," she said slowly. "If they hadn't slipped up on that test, they might never have been discovered."

He looked away and thought for a moment, stroking her hair unintentionally.

"So," he said almost to himself. "There are two parts to this puzzle—why they did it, and how they did it."

"Mills is the key," Margaret said.

That brought him back.

"Mills," he said, and smiled. "He's a real Earther, isn't he?"

She shrugged.

"Have you pulled his file?"

"Yes, Aaron, I have." She began to recite what she knew about Mills.

"He grew up in Southern California, just outside of San Diego. Parents died after he went to the university."

"Which one?" he asked.

"Berkeley. He got a Ph.D. in physics in 2310, post doc in San Diego."

"How did he get into the behavioral thing?"

"He became a particle physicist, and then an associate professor of physics at UCSD. Got married, then a few years later things fell apart."

Nelson's look invited her to continue.

"He didn't get tenure," she said. "Soon after, his marriage dissolved. No children."

Nelson got up and strolled to the observation port again. Margaret inadvertently put her hand in the depression on the sofa where Nelson had sat moments before; it was still warm. She got up and joined him at the window. It was a spectacular view. The complex machinery that dotted the hull of the Saratoga, bright white in the planet glow, stretched along the ship as far as she could see. Mars receded into the bottom of the window as the crew section spun about the axis of the ship, revealing a sky full of stars.

Nelson watched as Margaret craned her neck, leaning into the port, as fascinated by the marvels suspended in the void as he was. Perhaps we're not so different after all, he thought.

"Margaret," he said softly.

She turned, a little off balance from the vertigo induced by the infinite expanse outside, and looked at him awkwardly. When she saw the slight smile on his face, she seemed to relax.

"Yes," she said, and blinked.

"How did Mills get into the behavioral thing?"

"Oh yes," she said apologetically. "He washed out of mainstream physics. I haven't had time to pull his papers from the archives, but apparently things unraveled back on Earth. He came to Mars in 2321 on an appointment to the university at Ursa."

"Fresh start?" Nelson asked.

"Yes, I think so. The behavioral work developed from a DARPA funding proposal soon after he came to the university. The collaboration with Joanne Zhu, his DRA connection, started soon after that."

Nelson continued listening to Margaret's chronicle of Mills' life up to the present, but concluded that it gave insufficient insight to be of use in understanding the man's motivation. To get what he truly needed, he'd have to meet Mills, talk to him, get to know him a little. Either that, or resort to intimidation. But intimidation in light of the challenges that civil unrest presented would mean kidnapping Mills and confiscating the vital equipment. This also presented a problem. He wouldn't make the kind of mistake people like Margaret often made by underestimating people like Mills.

Mills had escaped detection for more than ten years, and was apparently in the process of breeding a race of non-humans for, as of yet, unknown reasons; the man was obviously no fool. Nelson didn't want to screw this up. He knew that historic campaigns had often been thwarted by what seemed, at the time, to be minor events. He would have to go slow here. The more he thought about it, the more he became convinced that his going planet-side was too risky. The separatists were better organized than most gave them credit for. And if they found out that he was on the surface, there was a pretty good chance they'd try to assassinate him.

The best course of action was probably to send Matt down with Margaret to try to determine the dimensions of this problem. Matt was a pretty clever soldier, with years of command experience under his belt. He could fill in the character questions and establish motivations far better than Margaret, while Margaret was the best suited to evaluate the technology. Once he'd been briefed, and after a second exploratory meeting with Mills in his own element, Nelson could take the next step.

When he'd gotten all he could from Margaret, Nelson summoned a sailor to show her to suitable quarters on board the ship. Nelson asked her to dine with him, Matt, his exec, and Oz Roland, his tactical officer, at eighteen hundred hours that evening. That would give him enough time to brief Matt and Oz before dinner.

Chapter Nine

Margaret fell into a deep sleep for several hours, then took a long hot shower. Because of the acoustic tiles on the walls, and carpeting on the floor, the room was surprisingly quiet. The bed was as good as any she'd slept in, in fine hotels. When she got out of the shower, she felt slightly disorientated because of the fitful dreams she couldn't quite recall. At eighteen hundred hours, she was dressed and brushing her hair when she heard the door chimes. Margaret opened the door and found a sailor had come to accompany her to the Admiral's dining room in the forward crew section.

It took them ten minutes to get to the Admiral's dining room on the executive floor of Crew Section One. Unlike most other parts of the ship, the corridors on the executive floor were carpeted in lush pile. Rank did have its privileges—she smiled to herself. When they arrived at the dining room door, the sailor saluted, and quickly left. Margaret pressed the chimes and the door slid open, revealing a long black marble table. The Admiral sat at the end farthest from the door.

The table occupied a central spot in an indulgently spacious room, luxurious in its uncluttered sparsity. The walls were paneled in exotic wood, and a panoramic observation port on the left wall framed a spectacular view of Mars. There were two other officers seated on either side of the table. The Admiral got up as she entered, as did the other two officers, one of whom she recognized as Matt Wells. All three were dressed in formal attire, with red waist sashes, white dress shirts, and black bow ties under short navy dinner jackets. They wore black pleated dress pants and mirror shined patent leather shoes. Margaret felt like a fool in her navy gray jump suit. But Nelson smiled at her, seeming quite sincere as he came to greet her at the door.

"You look wonderful tonight," he said in a voice so low the others couldn't hear. "The flight suit was a nice touch. How did you know they were ex-pilots? Beautiful women in flight suits drive these guys crazy."

Holding her hand lightly, he turned and said, "Gentlemen, I'd like to present Colonel Margaret Gates. She's with the WSA intelligence services."

The two officers remained standing at their places around the table. "Colonel," they said, almost in unison.

The Admiral turned to Margaret and said, "I think you know captain Wells, my Ex-O."

"Captain," Margaret said, looking at Wells.

"And this is Commander Oz Roland, my tactical officer."

When she saw Oz, Margaret blinked with surprise. He was one of only a few Moderns she'd seen since leaving Earth. He was taller than Wells, about as tall as the Admiral. He had perfectly cut blonde hair, flat on top and very short on the sides, accentuating his oval face and matching his amber eyes. His skin was as black as onyx, and he had a powerful physique with wide muscular shoulders and a trim waist.

"Colonel," he said, and bowed slightly.

Margaret couldn't help a little smile in symbolic recognition of their common history. She'd watched Nelson out the corner of her eye; he'd caught it. Apparently, he didn't miss much.

Nelson showed her to her seat, which was next to Wells and across from Oz. No one talked about the situation on Mars during the meal, opting instead to discuss the various entrées as they appeared before them. The Admiral's personal chef served five courses, which included prime rib and asparagus, among other rare non-synthetics. Margaret knew the Admiral to be more than a casual wine connoisseur, so she wasn't surprised when he produced a bottle of Napa Valley Merlot. Wells took it upon himself to pour a glass for each of them in turn, then proposed a toast after swirling the crimson liquid in his glass and uttering flowery descriptive phases in its honor.

Oz caught her eye, smiled, and drank. As the meal wore on, they found themselves talking about shipboard life and politics back on Earth. Margaret had never been particularly interested in either subject, and mostly listened politely, occasionally nodding at what seemed like appropriate times, but otherwise gazing out the dining room portal. After the meal had ended, the steward removed their plates and brought coffee. Nelson excused himself, left the room for a few moments, and then returned with a wooden box. He opened the box and passed out small brown cylinders, which he called cigars. Margaret had heard of them, but had never actually seen one. In fact, smoking had long since disappeared as a social artifact, and she had always regarded it a primitive act better left to antiquity.

However, in the interests of preserving the mood, and because she had, by nature, always been willing to try new things, she took one when Wells offered it. She watched the others, trying hard to determine the technique, as Wells lit hers. Her first puff resulted in a coughing fit that caused tears to run down her face, although she'd tried as hard as she could to stifle them. The experienced smokers at the table didn't laugh. The Admiral had her drink some water, then instructed her on how to puff a cigar without inhaling. Before long, she fell right in step with the rest of the table.

Finally, the Admiral took a puff, exhaled, and said, "Okay, I guess it's time to get down to business."

He summarized Margaret's findings and explained how he'd instructed Oz to make inquires at NearSec headquarters. Apparently, NearSec had also been investigating Mills for the past six months.

"Why wasn't I informed?" Margaret demanded, momentarily forgetting whom she was addressing. But to her surprise, Nelson remained even.

"You were an independent channel, Margaret. You've always been resourceful in the past; we didn't want to influence the direction you'd already decided to take."

"That was a great find, that thing about the children," Oz said.

Oz shifted his gaze from Nelson to Margaret. "When the Admiral briefed me earlier about your findings, Colonel, some other things started falling into place."

"Like what?" Margaret asked.

"We focused on Mills' computing resources, since that was the original issue raised by GESC. That's why we had him come to Earth. We didn't want him around for the most intrusive part of our probe. We used our best facilities and our best personnel, but we were only able to break into a subset of his system. We were, unfortunately, never able to penetrate into the core platform."

Margaret listened with interest, but none of it made much sense.

"How's it possible that with all your resources you couldn't hack into Mills' system?" she asked.

"Good question," Oz replied, "but there's more. We found certain databases associated with his core system. They were vast and highly encrypted; it's taken a month to arrive at a partial translation."

"And?" Margaret asked. "I know there must be a point here."

Oz smiled, taking a strange pleasure in her brisk manner. He attributed it more to base honesty than deliberate rudeness.

"Yes, Colonel, there is a point here, if you'd allow me."

"Please, Commander," Margaret said, puffing on her cigar. She was becoming most accomplished at this smoking thing, considering her modest start. Enjoying Oz almost as much as her cigar at this point, she made a mental note to revisit both under more pleasant circumstances.

"Well," Oz said, "there were numerous references to something called the Proteus file."

"The Proteus file?" she repeated blankly.

"Does that mean anything to you?" the Admiral asked.

"Only that Proteus was a prophetic sage of Greek mythology. He had the ability to change shape, transform. The word Proteus is often taken to mean something that's been transformed."

On further reflection, she added, "Odd though. The boy I met at Building One yesterday, the one I told you about..."

"Yes," the Admiral said.

"He had a Greek name. Perseus."

Oz's amber eyes widened for a moment, giving Margaret a flash of *deja vu*. For just a moment, they were the same golden eyes she'd seen on that boy yesterday.

Margaret's training at WSA had meshed well with her natural tendencies to be relentlessly thorough and focused. She had pursued this case without really considering the consequences to the actual people involved. She remembered having the clear impression, after entering the conference room at Building One that the boy had looked at her with more than passing curiosity. It was the look she often gave other Moderns in that confusing period of her life when she had struggled to come to grips with who she was. Looking at Oz now, seeing that boy's eyes, she wondered what unnecessary tragedy she might have carelessly brought into his life. And for what? Not for committing a crime or anything so tangible. The boy's crime had been her own self-imposed crime. The hypocrisy made her uncomfortable.

"We were able to decrypt twenty names associated with the file," Oz said. He paused for a moment and looked directly at Margaret. "Perseus was one of them."

Margaret's violet eyes widened as she struggled to understand the connection between Mills and the boy.

The Admiral broke the silence. "Margaret, you and Wells are going down to the planet. You're going to interview Mills and try to understand this a little better."

"With all due respect," Margaret said, "shouldn't you send the Commander?" She turned to Oz. "He clearly has the best overall understanding of this situation."

"Perhaps," Nelson said, "but I want to send you. You've already made contact. Mills knows you."

"Okay, but what does that have to do with Oz?"

Nelson paused, clearly irritated. "I can't send two Moderns planet side. Mars is a conservative planet. It would draw too much attention. And right now that's exactly what we don't need. You should know that, Colonel."

She sat back in her chair and looked from Nelson to Oz. Oz smiled at her in a way that seemed somehow sad.

Nelson got up and stood by the window. "We might have to impound them all—Mills, the children, the computer, the whole thing. It's going to be a mess, right on top of a major insurrection."

For the first time since the meal had ended, Captain Wells spoke up. "If that's the case, sir, then why are we talking to Mills at all? If we want to dispose of this situation quickly, why not just pick them all up right now?"

"Wishful thinking," the Admiral said. "If he's so smart, then maybe he'll see the writing on the wall and decide to work with us. With his help, we might leverage whatever he's produced to deal with some of our other problems, as well as dispose of this one. That's your job, Captain; see if you can make him understand without spooking him."

"Yes sir," Wells said.

Chapter Ten

"The optimist thinks this is the best of all possible worlds. The pessimist fears it is true." – Robert Oppenheimer

George got up early and went running on the hilly trails in back of his little house near the summit of Monte Claire. The run was helping clear his head. He felt as if the haze of the past few days was finally lifting, even though the intrigue of it all left him spent. He simply wasn't accustomed to going over brain numbing bureaucratic dribble in administrative accountability marathons. He worried that his lack of experience in these matters left him a poor judge of what was normal or typical, and he couldn't shake the feeling that it had all been staged—a ploy of some kind.

He stopped running just a few feet from his front gate, bent over, put his hands on his knees, and shook the sweat from his head. Yeah, that felt good. He straightened and walked to the door, keyed in the entry code, and went inside. He crossed the living room and stepped into the kitchen for some water.

"You have mail from the university," Will declared.

George took a gulp, and saw that the amber light on the video cameras was on in the other room.

"Can you read it?"

Will began reading a message from Victor Edgars, the chancellor of the university. Apparently, George was to meet a representative from Void Fleet, a captain Matt Wells, at two o'clock that afternoon at George's office at Minsky Annex.

"Read it again, would you?" George asked.

Unfortunately, it sounded just as bad the second time. "Sounds more like an order than a request."

"It sounds like the wheels are finally in motion," Will said.

"What's that supposed to mean?"

"It means we're finally going to find out what this is all about."

George nodded, finished his water, then stepped onto the balcony. With his shirt off, he could feel the warmth of the morning sun on his skin, a feeling that evoked a melancholy sadness. He had been in this little house for over ten years now—as long as he'd lived anywhere. Sunbathing on the balcony after a run in the hills was a tradition inexorably linked to this place. He had the uneasy feeling that it was all about to change, that these might be the waning days of the peaceful and pleasant life he'd made for himself here on Mars.

"I have something else," Will said. "I've finished my investigation."

George turned and leaned against the banister. After the message from Victor, it would be nice to know a little more about what he was walking into. He folded his arms across his chest and looked through the door at Will's cameras.

"The woman you mentioned. The one you met at Building One yesterday."

"You mean Dr. Margaret Gates?"

"Yes, Margaret Gates, she's a CSA agent, a Colonel in fact."

"And you expect me to know what that means? What's the CSA?"

"The CSA is a security agency, originally formed in the twentieth century as the NSA. At that time, its mission was to serve the president of what was then the United States of America. Their charter was to gather and analyze intelligence for the executive branch of government. They also made recommendations on how to act on that information, based on threat scenarios. They're extremely secretive and function in almost the same capacity today. Although today, of course, they report to the president of the Earth Confederation in Washington."

George didn't so much as move while Will dispassionately described a situation far beyond his worst fears. He tried to understand what a scientific advisory board was doing looking into issues of military security. And now, with Will's description of the CSA, the scope of his troubles had drastically changed, especially with the revelation of who Margaret Gates really was. He had never imagined a confederation security agency was looking into his affairs.

"I have more," Will said. "I have reason to believe that colonel Gates has been on board the Saratoga since yesterday. And, as it turns out, Matt Wells, the man you're suppose to meet this afternoon, is a Void Fleet captain currently assigned to the Saratoga."

"What's the Saratoga?" George asked. "Is it an Void Fleet ship?"

"It's a very large, very advanced Void Fleet cruiser commanded by Admiral Aaron Nelson. Admiral Nelson is the NearSec Supreme Commander."

"You're giving me the bad news first, right? I'm guessing you're saving the good news for last."

George wasn't sure, but he thought he'd heard Will sigh after his last comment.

"I'm sorry to have to tell you this, George, but I've found evidence that leads me to believe that they've discovered my intrusion into their system."

George shook his head. "How did that happen? You assured me that you could do it undetected, remember?"

"I'm sorry," Will said. "I guess I've learned an important lesson in humility. I'm sorry it had to be at your expense."

George smiled. Upon reflection, had he done any better? "I understand", George said. "Ultimately, this whole thing's my fault, not yours. You were just trying to help, and for that I'm grateful."

George left the warm sun of the balcony, crossed the living room, and entered the master bedroom. His daily ritual included a hot shower after the run, and a shower was exactly what he needed now to blunt the nervous anticipation of what was coming.

* * *

Will watched as George disappeared into the bedroom. He had not disclosed that in response to detecting him, the CSA had tried to probe him. In fact, he had let it happen because he was interested in seeing just where they'd go. He let them find a variety of monikers and waited. They went straight to the Proteus file. From this, he began to infer what they knew, and what had made this particular piece of information so attractive.

* * *

At ten o'clock George heard the chimes, and answered the door. Joanne and Perseus were standing on his porch, Joanne's arms draped around the boy's shoulders as he leaned against her.

Joanne looked fully rested, her features soft and eyes bright. "Can we come in?"

Her voice was like a breath of fresh air. George, bowing slightly, waved them in with a grand gesture.

Leaning in close, he said, "Can I see you in the kitchen?"

Joanne asked Perseus to wait in the living room. She assured him they wouldn't be long. When the boy appeared occupied and content, she followed George into the kitchen. "What's happened?" Joanne asked.

George told her about what Will had uncovered, and about the message he had received from Victor. Then he explained that he had tried to call her to cancel this meeting, which he forgot had been switched to his house.

"What do you want me to do?" she asked finally. "Take him home?"

George paced the kitchen for a while. "No, now that you're here, I should talk to him. I might not have another chance."

"What does that mean?" Joanne asked, growing more alarmed.

"Look, Jo, I don't want to scare you, but there's a chance I could be arrested this afternoon. This whole thing could have been staged just to flush me out."

"Okay, I'll make it a point to be there too," she said resolutely.

"No, you won't!" George barked, more emphatically than he'd wanted. He knew Joanne well enough to know that making it sound like an order would only make her more apt to come.

She put her finger over his lips, then pointed to the living room. He nodded gravely and added, "Suppose this goes badly. If they take both of us, what's going to happen to him?"

She put her forehead on his chest, and sighed.

He whispered, "Why don't you leave us alone for about a half hour. Give me a chance to speak to him."

She pulled away and looked at him a moment with an uncertain gaze. Then she pursed her lips, turned, and went into the living room. She said something to the boy, hugged him, then left without saying another word. George heard the door close; it echoed through the kitchen with a sound of finality. He felt a panicked urge to run after her. Instead, he remained at the counter for a few minutes, letting the anxiety pass. Then he made his way to the living room and sat across from Perseus.

The boy gazed up at him with an ambiguous look, acknowledging his presence, then turning away again to stare out the window.

"How do you feel?" George asked finally.

"Where did Joanne go?"

"I asked her to leave for a little while so you and I could talk."

"Is there something she shouldn't hear?"

All the time Perseus spoke, he'd continued to look out the window, never turning to address him, giving George the impression he was speaking to himself. He had never spent a lot of time around children, not like Joanne, so he had little sense of how to relate to them. But this boy couldn't be typical. Perseus was too self-assured, even in his isolation.

"You said you had some questions for me the other day" George said. "I told you I'd try to answer them."

At that, the boy turned to him. "Why am I different?"

"Different from what?"

The boy pressed is lips into a thin smile, conveying mild amusement, or perhaps fatigue.

"No games, please, Dr. Mills. That strange woman yesterday, she scared my parents. They've been upset ever since we returned from Dome One. That woman wants something from me, something that has to do with the fact that I'm different. She knows I'm different, different from you and Joanne, different from other kids, even different from my own parents. Are you going to tell me why, Dr. Mills?"

"Yes, I'm going to explain it to you, but first tell me, do you know anyone else who you think is like you?"

For the first time the boy smiled in a way that seemed sincere. "Yes, I know others."

"Who?"

"There are kids at my school; they're like me."

"How do you know?" George asked.

"Because I feel them. I can talk to them without words. It's very comforting to be with them, to have others that understand."

"Understand what?"

"Understand what it's like to be alone, truly alone. Although we're not as emotional as most other people, we understand isolation."

These admissions took George off guard. They were either insightful comments, or perhaps something else. He'd have to go slow here.

He leaned forward in his chair. "These other children like you, they don't feel emotion?"

The boy exhaled, impatient, as if he were talking to someone for whom everything had to be spelled out. "Of course they do, but not as strong, not as confused and overpowering as most people. We can feel without letting wild urges overpower our reason. When I speak to them without words, our feelings and intentions are clear. We compromise, because we see ourselves in each other. You on the other hand..." The boy paused.

"What?" George asked.

"You're not so bad," admitted the boy apologetically.

George laughed out loud. The boy smiled back.

"I envy you your clarity," George said. "To tell you the truth, I'm confused right now, and it's not a very pleasant feeling."

He sat back in his chair, regarding the boy with a mixture of fascination and envy. "Let me introduce you to someone. I'm pretty sure he's as clear as you are, at least he pretends to be."

"Will, are you there?"

"Yes, George, I'm here."

The boy was startled by the disembodied voice. He'd obviously heard machines talk before, that was nothing new. Most high-end appliances spoke—cars, kitchen appliances, homes, even clothes. The boy must have spoken to computers with artificial intelligence. AI's could carry on animated conversations, sometimes being so bold as to engage in mild arguments, but this was different. The boy was extremely perceptive, searching the room as if looking for someone speaking over a Tab. George assumed it was the way the voice said I, the inflection, the subtle hint of self-awareness.

"Will?" Perseus said cautiously. "Are you there?"

"Yes, Perseus, I'm here."

This time the boy saw the nondescript speakers, and the small dumbbell camera, with its amber light. It followed him as he moved around the room. He turned to George. "Will is an AI?"

"Why don't you ask him?"

"Who are you, Will?"

"I'm still trying to work that out," said the voice. "The kernel of what I am started as a tool, a computer system that George built to simulate his ideas."

"How did you change to become what you are now?" Perseus asked. Then not waiting for an answer, he added, "Are you alive?"

"Am I alive?" repeated the voice whimsically. "If someone were to ask you that question, how would you answer?"

"I am alive," Perseus insisted, "I know that."

Will said, "You say that with conviction, perhaps because whatever it is that occupies your self-awareness asserts itself most strongly when it's being questioned. Maybe being alive is not as solid a thing when it's put under scrutiny. You know you are, but if I were to ask you to prove it, how would you do that? Even what constitutes a legitimate proof of such a thing is a matter of debate."

Perseus stepped over to the camera, watching, as it followed his approach. He put his hand on its base and could see the iris dilate.

"What are you to me?" Perseus asked. "I asked Dr. Mills to explain my situation, and he introduced me to you. Why?"

After a pause, Will said, "I've been waiting to meet you in your current mode of existence for a while now. What you are, who you are, was born in my dreams."

"What?" declared Perseus, blinking in astonishment. "I've never met you before. What do you mean by current mode of existence?" Perseus turned to George. "What does he mean, current mode?"

George sat on the sofa, wondering if Will was doing the right thing by giving the boy both barrels like this. It might be too much for anyone to handle, much less an eleven-year-old boy, who already had issues of self-identity.

"Ask him," George said tentatively.

Will explained how personality templates had been built based on the human genome. How various historical scenarios had been sequenced and used as an environmental impetus for synthetic evolution. The boy listened intently, his attention fixed on the camera.

George's attention was fixed on the boy. When Will was finished, Perseus began meandering around the room, touching knickknacks on shelves, and then looked out the window again. He eventually came back to the camera. "Okay," he said. "I understand, but what about my parents? Are they really my parents, or did I even need parents?"

Will remained silent. It was George's turn. He got up, walked to where the boy stood, put his hands on the boy's shoulders, and squatted so that they were face to face.

"We introduced the changes using your parents' DNA as the base stock. Most of what you are comes uniquely from them, just like any other child. You are their natural son. Along with the therapy, you were evolved in a completely different environment. An environment that we believe produced beneficial changes."

The boy's face remained impassive. George tried desperately to read it, to find some indication that these revelations had not damaged him emotionally.

Finally, George asked, "How does hearing all this make you feel?"

Perseus remained stoic. "I don't know. How would you feel to learn you existed in a vacuum, in another mode?"

Then he focused on George; life came back to his features. "I've learned that this can be a hard world, Dr. Mills. I've noticed that people tend to stick together with those they think are like them. You people evolved in tribes—you know, Earthers, Martians, and probably some others they have on Earth like that woman yesterday. What you've just told me is that you've somehow arranged for me to be here, in the middle of all this, alone. And somehow you seem to think this is beneficial."

Suddenly, the boy began to laugh out loud. George looked at the camera, deep furrows appeared across his brow, and worry darkened his face. The boy saw it, and his laughter slowly faded to melancholy. He turned from George and flopped on the sofa, his small body sinking deep into the cushions, making him seem insignificant. With a look of resignation, he exhaled absently, compounding the air of desolation.

George, who had been squatting as he'd watched the boy, leaned back and rested against the bookcase, then put his face in his hands. It was all falling apart.

After a while, George heard the boy's voice.

"Will?"

"Yes, Perseus, I'm here."

"How do you cope with it? Being alone, unique in the world of humans?"

"Well, I have George and Joanne, and now I have you. There are others like you, and soon I'll meet them."

"I guess I shouldn't complain. After all, along with being even more unique than I am, you're stuck in that box."

"What box is that?" Will asked.

"You know, inside the computer, the one in which you exist."

Will made a noise that sounded like laughter. George looked up in amazement. Even in this somber situation, he couldn't help marveling at this conversation. The experiment that he had started so long ago was finally taking form and, like all natural animated processes, it was etching out unexpected patterns.

Will said, "I'm no more stuck in here than you are in your own head. In fact, right now as I speak to you, I can see Mars from several observation satellites in orbit. I can see Valles Marineris in the visible, the infrared, the ultraviolet, and many other wavelengths of light, including microwave. At the same time that I speak to you, I can hear the solar winds in the magnetic fields of Jupiter. I can see an X-ray burster in the general direction of the Pleiades from observational satellites in orbit around Earth. I have eyes and ears and even tactile experiences from a thousand different sources I'd like to share with you, when we have more time."

Perseus got up from the sofa, "Do you think we'll have more time?"

"I think so," Will said. "Remember, my first reason for living was to dream up worlds that did not yet exist. I've relived these events in virtual time for almost as long as you've been alive in real time. Try to relax, and believe that even though there are powerful forces that might oppose us, we may also have some surprises for them as well."

As George and Perseus listened to Will, they were transfixed by the sense of implied omnipotence that his monologue suggested. For Perseus, George knew it had come as a welcome reprieve, a wellhead of newfound hope. For him, however, there were, of course, those elements, but there was something else as well. George had given Will full access to the network. The entire solar system was, in principle, open to him. Wherever man had gone, there was a highway of optical plastic, and Will knew the rules of the road. Will had no constraints, neither in inhibitions to his neural networks, nor in his ability to establish physical connections. Early on, George had considered Will the ultimate firewall. But he had never considered the situation in reverse. What would happen if an alien intelligence, such as Will, were given unfettered access to the world's infrastructure? How much of that infrastructure could it control—how long would it take? He would have to consider these issues later, talk to Will about them. He didn't really know whether it was sheer chance that things had turned out this way, that Will had become what he was, but he knew from their collective experience of the past ten years that he trusted Will implicitly—more so than most people he knew.

Yes, he would have to give these matters further thought. Right now, however, he was glad that Will's admissions, as well as his offer of help, seemed to have given the boy the assurance he needed.

"Dr. Mills, are you all right?"

George realized that he was still sitting on the floor with his hands cupped over the lower half of his face. He could imagine how he looked to the boy, with his eyes staring into space above his hands. Perseus stood in front of him, taller on his feet than George was seated on the floor. He could see concern in the boy's wide eyes, and in his down-turned mouth.

"Yes, I'm fine," George assured, standing up smoothly.

He got Perseus some juice and a piece of pound cake that he had been saving for a special occasion. Then he took him out on the balcony. They found a couple of chairs, and George went back into the house looking for something special, something he hadn't taken out in quite some time.

When he returned, George placed an ebony and walnut chessboard on the little table in front of Perseus. Then, one by one, he took carved wooden chess pieces out of a fabric sack. The boy looked on, spellbound.

"You like games?" George asked.

The boy nodded.

"This is an antique chess set my father gave me. It's been in my family for longer than anyone can remember."

"You want to play chess with me?" Perseus asked. "I'm afraid you might be disappointed in your performance, Dr. Mills."

George laughed. "Me, no—not me, I don't have a chance against you, I know that. I was thinking about Will."

"Will plays chess?" Perseus asked, his eyes bright with highlights that seemed to sparkle.

"Will can play any game," George said. "The first time we played, he beat me in eleven moves, and he'd never played before. In fact, he may be unbeatable. He can instantaneously calculate the likelihood of success for any move you might make, and for any arbitrary number of moves in the future.

"He can be beaten," Perseus said softly. "He can only play the percentages based on what he thinks I might do. And, based on any particular move, his projections accumulate errors." Swept up in the anticipated challenge, the boy quickly arranged his pieces.

George watched as Perseus pushed his pieces, and just as quickly, pieces on the other side of the board moved to thwart his advance. A long time ago, George had instrumented the board so that he could play with AIs. Every now and then the boy glanced up at him, a big smile stretched across his face, unable to contain his pleasure.

George had harbored lingering doubts as to whether he could ever be close to these new people. Though he was committed to them as an abstraction, he questioned his ability to establish the kind of relationship he hoped to have with them. Perhaps they were too different. Perhaps their emotional needs, their sense of community, was so disparate from what was normal for mere Homo sapiens that he would never be able to bridge the gap.

As with many unknowns, his questions, both unspoken and postponed, were answered almost unconsciously as he watched the boy drawing closer to him by his continued gestures of camaraderie—a smile here, a nod there, an excited gesture in response to Will's move.

Later, when George heard the door chime again, he left Perseus on the balcony and found Joanne at the door. She was ready to take Perseus home, but was less at ease than when she'd first brought him. Their earlier conversation had obviously taken its toll.

George confided, "It went better than I expected; at least everything's more or less out in the open."

"You told him everything? Do you think that was wise, emotionally I mean?"

"Come take a look, judge for yourself."

He took her to the balcony where she was surprised to find the boy bright and engaging, not at all what she'd expected. They spent another quarter hour together, the four of them on the balcony, under a striking dome sky. While Perseus and Will played chess, George and Joanne sat with dark glasses on, soaking up the sun, and enjoying the boy's occasional happy comments.

When the game was over, having been fought to a tenuous draw, they laughed and talked about some of the trips George and Joanne had taken to the rim range above the canyon walls. Joanne had always been interested in Martian fossils, and she and George had collected an impressive sample on their many excursions. They showed Perseus an image cube of some of the more spectacular specimens. Finally, after looking at her watch, Joanne reluctantly admitted it was time to go. She'd promised the boy's mother she'd have him back before noon.

George walked them to the door. Stepping onto the stoop, he saw Perseus sneaking a peek back into the living room, looking for the amber light of Will's camera. He noticed the disappointment on the boy's face at the discovery that Will was gone. They all stood there a while, not knowing quite what to say, when, all of a sudden, the boy hugged him fiercely. A few moments later, Perseus and Joanne left, disappearing into the green forest of bushes beyond his front gate. George remained at the open door, waving well past the time both had slipped from view.

Chapter Eleven

Hector and Roy watched through a window of the small observation deck close to Runway Three, where the Void Fleet shuttle had just touched down. Smoke and dust, left by the vertical landing thrusters, were beginning to clear from the area around the pad, giving them the first real look at the craft on the ground. It was small, only about forty feet long, and had a flattened egg shaped body with stubby wings and a single high vertical tail assembly. The skin of the craft was navy gray composite with a milky glaze of heat-resistant ceramic fiber coating. There were no observable markings other than an ID number on the vertical stabilizer. It had hovered momentarily above the pad, then slowly come down in a controlled bob that was characteristic of crafts that were lightly loaded.

Although security was tight around this part of the airport, spacecraft still had to be serviced. Instruments, landing gear, engine arrays, and hull integrity all had to be checked in-between flights. Void Fleet had a well-trained support team, but they still needed airport personnel who were familiar with the facilities here at Ursa to assist. Hector and Roy, although ethnic Martians, had worked as Void Fleet consultants for years now, and had been given security clearances allowing them access to sites like this.

Hector scoffed at the thinly veiled attempt at anonymity. All Earthers thought Martians were stupid. Did they think for one minute that such an unusually small and expensive craft with a flight vector from the approximate location of a Void Fleet cruiser was not obviously a military shuttle—probably carrying VIPs? And landing at Runway Three was foolish if the goal of this mission was to remain secret. Runway Three had been placed off-limits to most airport personnel, and was currently being used exclusively to service the interceptor fleet, which had been in almost constant rotation for the past few weeks.

Through the pillbox window, Hector could see the pilot moving around inside the flight cabin as he shut down systems and prepared the ship to enter the hanger. Once he saw the pilot give the all-clear signal, he and his partner stepped onto the tarmac, mounted a little tractor, and drove out to the shuttle. Roy attached a vertical grapple to the docking clamp on the belly of the craft. The landing gear had been placed in caster mode, permitting them to position the shuttle precisely in the center of a hanger elevator. When they were in place, Hector directed the elevator to descend. Minutes later, the shuttlecraft and tractor sat in a pressurized hanger twenty feet below the Martian surface.

They pushed a portable stairway to the front of the craft and parked it firmly against the cockpit door. Hector backed away, and seeing the pilot, stuck his finger in the air and gave a rotating movement. The pilot, high atop the cockpit, gave thumbs up in response. Moments later, the cabin door opened, and as Hector and Roy watched, two menacing figures appeared at the top of the stairs and quickly descended.

Hector had been around military hangers for most of his working life, but had never seen anything like this before. Two soldiers were dressed in some sort of assault suits. Heavier than others he had seen, the armor looked like iridescent gray rubber. At first, Hector felt pangs of fear; then, after a moment, anger reddened his hard face. He considered himself an imposing man, more than a match for any puny Earther he'd ever come across. Fuckin Earthers and their asshole gadgets, he thought—ashamed he'd flinched.

Following the two soldiers, another two appeared at the top of the stairway, lingered for a moment, then descended. Hector recognized the first one as the pilot he'd seen in the cockpit, a generic Earther for whom he felt immediate contempt. He flashed a smile and a thumbs up. The second was a woman— strange looking too. She was oddly pale, but even in the jumpsuit, she sure looked good. Like to get a piece of that, he thought. He felt himself get hard.

* * *

Margaret stood at the base of the portable stairs in the underground hanger and looked around. The place was dirty; red Martian dust and fine clay cast the large room and its contents in a hazy gloom. The equipment on display in the hanger, used mostly to service spacecraft for minor mechanical problems, was primitive and poorly maintained. She shook her head as she thought about the equivalent facilities aboard the Saratoga. She noticed two big Martian technicians in red environment suits standing next to the landing gear and smiling broadly. Her attention fell on the one to the right of the landing strut. He was broad, with a fleshy brutal face that seemed to reflect something unstable and dangerous. She could see a sickening mixture of hate and lust in his flat dark eyes. The look wasn't altogether unique, but it added a dimension of hostility that was exceptionally foul on his dull features. Asshole, she thought, and looked away.

Wells put his hand lightly on her back and pointed toward an airlock across the room. Two security men in smart black tunics, out of place in this dingy hole, had come through the door and were walking toward them with deliberate strides. After issuing curt greetings, the men led them out of the hanger and into a bright beige concourse with carpeted floors and large windows that afforded them a dramatic view of the canyon walls. It was a welcome change from the dank pit from which they'd just emerged. From there, they proceeded to an executive lounge where they were given charge cards and a memory crystal with maps and navigator programs to Ursa University. After they'd been briefed, the two security men exited with two marines in tow, leaving Margaret and Wells free to keep their two o'clock appointment with Mills.

Margaret had given this thing a lot of thought since the meeting at Building One, and she'd become uncomfortable with her role in exposing Mills as some sort of separatist conspirator. She sincerely hoped that the next meeting would achieve an ambience more conducive to cooperation. The more she learned about George Mills and Joanne Zhu, the more apparent it became that she had stumbled into something that merited deeper examination than the military was prepared to give.

Once everyone had gone, she and Wells prepared to change into Martian sportswear. They would blend in better, though nothing short of plastic surgery could hide a generic Earther and a Modern on the streets of Dome Two these days. Lost in thought, and slipping out of her jumpsuit, Margaret happened to glance over at Wells. He was staring at her in stunned silence.

"What's wrong?"

She looked down and noticed she was wearing panties and nothing else. Strange, she thought; she had never seen Wells flustered. Not in debates with the Admiral, not in reentry streaking across the upper atmosphere at more than seven thousand miles per hour. Looking at him now, he seemed almost as pale as she was.

Margaret smiled. "Captain, could you pass me my shirt please?"

An hour later, they were on the *Sea of Storms* in Dome One headed for the university. Behind them was a van with two plain-clothes security men in the front seat and nothing in back except two large depressions curiously dimpling the rear seat cushions.

Chapter Twelve

George sat at his desk in his lab on the second floor of Minsky Annex, and waited. He hadn't been able to concentrate, his mind wandering to the events of the past couple of days. Occasionally, he glimpsed the chronometer on his desk, as if he were expecting the sword of Damocles to come down on his head at any moment. Unlike the other furniture in the lab, George's desk, which he'd shipped from Earth, was solid oak. It was cut and stained in a late twentieth century motif that was seldom seen on Mars. It was one of his few connections with the past, and in its antique grains were stored many of the dramas of his eclectic life.

He glanced absently around the room. These last few moments might be the end of a long, productive, and personally fulfilling stay here at the university. After the expected interview with the two Void Fleet officers this afternoon, he was sure his life would never be the same.

The office was really a bullpen of sorts, with desks strewn in an irregular pattern that reflected the personalities of his post-docs more than anything else. He hadn't seen them this past month because they'd all decided to take August off—dispersing to the far corners of the planet on well-deserved and overdue vacations. They were the new vanguard in a maturing group of Martian intellectuals that would eventually surpass Earth in the mastery of the physical sciences. Like the rest of Mars, they possessed a pioneering spirit, a naïve fascination with nature that drove them ever deeper toward its obscure truths. He had taken them on when they were still graduate students, and together they had developed the most powerful thinking machine ever conceived. Will had evolved from a novel core, which he'd brought from Earth fifteen years earlier, into an advanced cyber organism light years beyond anything in the solar system.

George sat back in his chair and put his feet up on the desk. Day dreaming about it all—Will's development, his students, the past years with Joanne—it gave him a sense of peace. Wherever there was movement and change, there would most likely be risk and sacrifice. In retrospect, the work they'd done right here, in this office, might in fact change human history. Had he really believed such success would not exact a price? He smiled to himself, looked out the window onto the grassy courtyard just beyond Minsky at a bunch of students playing football, and enjoyed the moment.

At two o'clock sharp, George heard a knock at the door. It had a crisp authoritative sound that echoed around the room, disrupting the perfect silence.

"Come in." He yelled loud enough to be heard in the corridor, and winced at the sound of his own voice.

The door opened and Margaret Gates entered, followed by a young man he'd never seen before. There was a *déjà vu* quality to the moment, though this man was more fit and imposing than Dale had been. Margaret, in her casual blue nylon slacks and windbreaker, looked almost normal. George stood up and walked around his desk.

"I don't know if I can say it's good to see you again, Dr. Gates."

Margaret smiled broadly—looking softer in her running suit than in her professional garb. She stepped up and offered her hand.

"I'm sorry if I made a bad first impression, Dr. Mills."

George caught a whiff of a subtle fragrance that reminded him of evenings on Earth a long time ago. She could be very charming, if you forgot that she might be here to ruin you life, thought George.

Margaret turned and introduced her escort as Captain Matt Wells. Wells seemed pleasant and polite, not the in-your-face soldier he'd expected. George scavenged a couple of chairs and arranged them in front of his desk, then sat down.

He waited for his inquisitors to get situated, then said, "How can I help you, Dr. Gates?"

George thought he saw a sad flash in Margaret's violet eyes, an almost imperceptible furrow of her brow, and a slight downturn at the corners of her mouth. Uh-oh, George thought.

"I'm going to come right to the point, Dr. Mills," Margaret said. She then proceeded to describe the discrepancies they'd encountered in trying to replicate his behavioral work. She told him how their experts had concluded that he'd most probably made dazzling breakthroughs in computer technology, which by the way, he'd failed to disclose. Then she told him that they'd discovered, from DNA evidence, that the children belonging to the twenty names in the Proteus File were a new and different species.

George noticed she made a point of letting him know they'd infiltrated Will by mentioning the Proteus File by name. He watched her as she made each damning statement, pausing to allow him to clarify or refute each point before proceeding to the next. He held her eyes and coolly said nothing, letting her know that he wasn't going to play their game. The burden of proof was theirs, and he wasn't going to shed any more light on any of it, knowing that doing so would simply help them build a case against him.

While she grilled him, Captain Wells sauntered about the office, casually stopping to look at pictures on the walls, feigning interest by cocking his head or setting his hand on his chin before moving on. He visited the bookshelves, examining titles with an exaggerated interest that underscored his insincerity.

When Margaret finished, Wells turned his attention to George's desk, running his hand along the ancient wood. "Nice desk, George," he said. Then in all earnestness, as though confiding some precious piece of personal information, he added, "My father had a desk just like this. He loved old things with a lot of history."

George smiled politely, then looked at Margaret. "I didn't know that it was against the law to make breakthroughs in computer science."

"It's not," she said. "The problem is that you've wandered over the line into matters of planetary security."

"Oh, how so?"

It was Wells' turn now. He came from behind Margaret and stood in front of George.

"Come on, Dr. Mills. We can do this the easy way or the hard way. It's up to you. You're not stupid. You must realize that your methods of doing simulations have great strategic value, especially now, at a time when this planet is on the brink of a large uprising, or perhaps even a civil war. You can't be surprised to know that we consider your technology a deadly threat in the wrong hands. The fact that you've kept vital pieces of it secret looks very incriminating on its face. In fact, we're in the process of classifying it right now."

"I see," George said slowly. "But isn't this technology the property of the university?"

"In matters of this type, under these conditions, ECon has priority."

George noticed that as Wells pressed his case, Margaret failed to meet his eyes. She looked at the floor, looked out the window, looked at everything else, but not at him.

"Well," Margaret said finally, with a hint of fatigue. "What about the children, Mills? The children we found in the Proteus File—the ones that you were somehow able to create. How do they relate to your behavioral work? Why would you feel compelled to do such a thing anyway?"

"Is that against the law too?" George asked evenly.

"As far as I know, the technology required to do such extensive genetic manipulation doesn't exist anywhere else in the solar system. Wouldn't it be logical to assume that it's a product of your breakthroughs in computer technology? Genetic enhancements aren't against the law; they've been part of society for a long time now. But. . ."

She paused, noticing that he'd begun to smile and roll his eyes. He wanted her to know that these formal words, so eloquently spoken, smacked of hypocrisy, especially coming from her. It took a few moments for her to recover her composure. The lapse told him that, this little show notwithstanding, they understood each other perfectly.

"Why go this far?" Margaret asked. "Why keep it a secret if you had the permission of the parents—if there are parents. Why risk the entanglement you've gotten yourself into, Mills? It doesn't make sense."

It was easy to see that Margaret had something at stake here. Perhaps feelings of illegitimacy plagued her. Maybe she felt estranged. She was definitely on the leading edge of what standard genetic therapies could provide. George regarded her. Soon the charming Captain Wells began making noises; he was obviously reaching the end of his patience.

"These children are no threat to you," George said. "They're in the system; you know everything about them. You can keep track of their movements if that makes you feel better. They're ordinary kids, living ordinary lives. Why not just leave them out of it?"

Margaret said, "Okay, let's see it."

"See what?" George asked, surprised.

"The computer, let's take a look."

George turned from Margaret to Wells. That guy smiles too much, he thought. George exhaled slowly, got up, and edging around Wells, went to the door.

"Right this way."

Chapter Thirteen

Members of Red Dawn, the military arm of the separatist movement, had infiltrated the ranks of the High-Orbit Re-supply union and learned the broad details of a mission to the surface involving senior Void Fleet operatives. The details, which were sketchy and came from ship scuttlebutt, were sufficiently sound in their basic overall pronouncements to be irresistible to Red Dawn. The information had named the Admiral himself as one of the likely members of the planet-side contingent.

When Margaret and Wells had left the shuttle bay, Hector and Roy had worked to thwart the bay's security systems. They spliced into the optical data lines that carried audio, visual, and bio-sign telemetry to the airport's computers. That enabled them to alter the data stream from the bay by extracting, inserting, or offsetting separate feeds from programs running on their Tabs. They were also able to circumvent elevator and door controls so that security would lose its ability to act on emergency information. When these tasks were completed and the shuttle was refueled and serviced, Hector and Roy hoisted duffel bags into the shuttle and hid in the rear cargo area next to the passenger's cabin. Once in the cargo hold, they activated a program on their Tab that cancelled their bio-signs in the bay sensor feed, thus making them invisible to airport security. Then they waited.

* * *

George led Margaret and Wells through the office door and down the hall to the Annex elevator. They took it to the basement, where he led them down another corridor to a door with a plaque that read: *Will.*

"Who's Will?" Margaret asked.

"I'm showing you what you wanted to see," George said, and keyed in his access code.

Margaret and Wells inspected their surroundings with a measure of disorientation. The contrast between this room and the rest of what they'd seen at Minsky was so dramatic that they had to do a double take to confirm their first impressions.

"No wonder you've drawn so much attention," Wells said, still looking around. "I feel like I'm still aboard ship. The GESC must have given you a bundle."

Looking at Margaret, George thought he detected a newfound respect.

Just inside the door was a small ready room set apart from a larger room by a glass wall. Both the ready room and the larger area on the other side of the glass were clinically white, newly painted, and immaculately clean. The ceiling was made of wide lighting panels interspersed with acoustical tile. The glass door separating the two rooms was housed in a stainless steel frame that looked like an airlock.

George keyed another code into icons on the glass door and followed Margaret and Wells into the computer room against a moderate torrent of rushing air. Once inside, George pushed a panel on the doorframe and returned the computer room to atmospheric stasis. The main floor of the room was raised, and they had to climb three steps before they were on the same level as the equipment.

In the center of the room was a pedestal of white translucent plastic, perhaps twelve feet in diameter and a foot high. On the pedestal were six circular towers set in an octagonal pattern around its perimeter. Each of the towers had a transparent plastic member at about two-thirds its height, connecting it to a central metallic column slightly smaller than the other six. Along the walls were banks of black six-foot cabinets with dark smoky panels, behind which were rows of dancing colored lights. Next to the wall, to the right of the door, were several clear panel monitors on spidery silver arms suspended above a desk and console in front of black leather chairs. The room was completely quiet and still.

Wells smiled at George. "So you thought that Econ would give you the money to build something like this—and you expected to do what? Develop simulations for obscure academics? Come on Doctor—please."

Wells' predictable military technocrat persona was starting to grate on George. A non-conventional thought had apparently never graced Wells' frontal lobe. The mixture of conformity and the lack of creative consideration was disappointing normal. Margaret, on the other hand, walked slowly around the ethereal columns with the same reverence that he often felt when he was down here alone.

"Well, Colonel," Wells said. "What exactly do we have here?"

"These columns," Margaret said, pointing to the milky white cylinders, "are concentric layers of quantum nodes interspersed by sheets of room temperature superconductors. They're sandwiched in between sheets of optical arrays. The outer sleeve and pedestal maintain the entire assembly at liquid nitrogen temperatures to kill thermals and maintain quantum coherence for a critical measurement interval. The plastic connectors, coming from each column, are sub-micron optical axons. They're field configurable. The metal column in the middle is an array of holographic crystals."

"How about the black cabinets along the wall?" Wells asked.

"More holographic memories," Margaret said. Then after a thoughtful moment, she added, "A large number of memories, come to think of it."

Turning to George, she asked, "Why so many?"

George remained impassive.

"What do you mean?" Wells asked. "Is that unusual?"

"Matt, everything in this room is unusual. The components are all standard, albeit top of the line, truly the state of the art, but the arrangement is very unusual. I can't say for sure, but this has the feel of something new, a breakthrough maybe."

Turning back to the monolithic cabinets lining the walls, she said, "I really don't understand what purpose it would serve to have that large a scratch space. It couldn't be effectively utilized."

"Well Doctor," Wells said. "Care to enlighten us?"

George met his gaze, but remained silent.

"You're not helping yourself, Dr. Mills," Wells said, his smiling facade fading for the first time.

Margaret moved to George and put her hand on his arm. Her eyes moved across his face, imploring or maybe searching for some indication that he might decide to acquiesce.

"You'll have to figure it out yourself, Colonel," George said softly.

Margaret looked down and pulled her hand back. Was this show for him, George wondered, or for the kids that she seemed to have more regard for of late? It was impossible to know.

"I'll need your access codes and your cartographer," Margaret said with regret.

"Cartographer, what's that?" Wells asked.

Margaret composed herself. "It's a tool used to map a system's topology and provide other information like node weights, things like that."

"Oh," Wells said vaguely.

George remained stoic.

"You know what this means," Wells said. "You'll have to come with us. We'll have to impound this system."

"I suspect you'll do that no matter what I do, Captain. Isn't that true, Margaret?"

Margaret looked away, saying it all without uttering so much as a word. Then she told Wells, "Without Mills' help, there's little I can do right now."

George and Margaret waited in George's office while Wells spoke to someone over a secure line on his Tab. George spent the time staring out the window, wondering if he'd ever see this little office again. He thought about what his post-docs would think when they learned of his arrest, and hoped that they wouldn't be dragged into it.

"Margaret," George said evenly. "Let me make a call. I probably won't be coming back, and there are people out there who'll worry about me."

She looked at Wells, who shook his head.

Wells said, "It's too fluid out there right now, Mills. I warned you that it would be in your interest to cooperate." Then, in a more conciliatory voice, he added, "It's still not too late."

George appealed to Margaret. "Could you at least call Joanne? You could do it after you take me off planet. Please."

She looked at Wells again. This time he nodded approval. They led George out of the building and into a car waiting just outside Minsky.

Chapter Fourteen

After leaving George's house, Joanne took Perseus home. Strangely enough, her fears of how the boy might react to George's revelations had miraculously not materialized. But now a new fear had supplanted the old one; she couldn't shake the nagging dread of George's afternoon meeting with the Terrans. And although she tried not to, she just couldn't stop thinking about it.

Once in her office, Joanne locked the door and settled glumly behind her desk. She ignored her calls, only checking to see if the caller ID was George, but otherwise letting the phone chime unanswered. She tried to work, but her fingers remained motionless on the keyboard as her mind wandered from one thing to another. In an anxious spasm, she got up and was walking to the window when she heard the Tab's melodic chime. Her breath caught, and her heart started racing. She turned and checked the caller ID; it was the office of the chancellor of the university. Her intuition working faster than her reason, she answered it.

"Joanne?"

Joanne recognized the voice of Sarah John, the chancellor's secretary. "Yes."

"Oh Joanne, I'm so sorry."

"Why, what's happened?" Joanne asked in a growing panic.

"They've arrested George—down at Minsky."

Joanne stared at the Tab for a few fretful moments. "I'm sorry, Sarah, I have to go."

Joanne shot up from her desk without clearing the call, moved quickly to the door, then ambled out into the hallway. In a daze, she looked up and down the dark corridor as though she'd never seen it before. Shafts of light streamed in from windowed doors at the far end of the hallway. The uneven light punctuated by a dancing suspension of tiny dust particles added to the sense of strangeness and heightened her disorientation. Like a moth to a flame, she followed an unconscious imperative to leave the building and turned in the direction of the brightness. She found herself walking quickly to the exit without even bothering to close her office door. Then, breaking into a run, she almost slipped on the smooth tile floor, but caught herself before falling. Stopping, she placed a hand on the wall, bent down, and removed her pumps, then fled barefoot through the doors and into the early afternoon daylight.

Minsky was only two blocks away. As Joanne approached, she saw that a small crowd of students and staff had gathered behind a taped police barrier around the main Annex entrance. Security police were holding back anxious onlookers as they strained and spoke in hurried cadences. The police were dressed in black uniforms bearing the Void Fleet logo, and were pushing people back with small transparent plastic shields. Remembering her frightening experience at Building One, Joanne shivered nervously, but pushed her way to the front of the crowd.

As she looked on, buffeted by people lurching this way and that, she caught sight of him. George was exiting the main Annex flanked by an Earther on one side and Dr. Margaret Gates on the other. The trio walked quickly down the tiled path to a waiting car in front of the Annex. Joanne waved frantically, trying to get George's attention, and felt cold plastic push her back. She watched helplessly as they marched him to an open rear door. The male Earther pushed him into the car with a forceful hand on his head. While George bent down, slipping into the back seat, she caught his eye. He gestured by bowing his head. She slowly lowered her hand and gave a stifled call as he disappeared behind dark tinted windows.

The security men cleared a path through the street as the car left the curb. It whined past her and finally disappeared around a corner. With a dim sense of unreality, she stood there, staring at the spot where they had just vanished.

* * *

As they sped away from Minsky, George's eyes locked on
Joanne. The look on her face was like a hot knife through his
heart. A sour taste of bile rose up in his throat as he watched her
vanish—a small lonely figure in a summer print dress,
suggestive of more carefree times. Well after she was out of
sight, he continued staring out the rear window at the echo of her
lost presence, trying to stretch the moment further than the laws
of nature would allow.

"Mills—come on, she's gone," Margaret insisted. "Best
think about the future now."

Margaret was sitting next to him in the back seat, and Wells
was sitting in front with a security man at the wheel. Reluctantly,
George turned away from the back window. "Where are we
going?"

"Someplace where we can talk," Margaret said.

"Am I coming back?"

Margaret hesitated, then whispered, "I don't know."

George soon found himself oblivious, reliving events that
had somehow brought him to this point, unable to focus on the
present. Eventually the sound of Wells causal small talk with the
driver brought him out of his stupor. He was suddenly aware of
where they were. They had driven through Dome Two and were
now heading toward the Dome One transit tube to the airport.

"Are we going off-world?" George asked.

Margaret continued gazing out the window. Finally, she
said, "Yes, we're going off-planet. We thought it best to debrief
you aboard ship. You know, Mills, the sooner you cooperate, the
sooner you can put all this behind you."

George began thinking about Joanne again—the look on her
face as Wells had pushed him into the car. Though her
complexion was Martian dark, she'd looked pale, and her eyes
had been wide and full of fear. Reflected in her expression, he'd
seen his own sorrowful epitaph. Joanne was strong and

independent, even stoic at times, but he knew that, in some ways, she was quite fragile. They'd been close for a long time now, and he worried about what she might do to find him, something that could eventually land her in the same place he now found himself. His breathing quickened with the frustration of being powerless to do anything about it.

Chapter Fifteen

They pulled into an air terminal and drew to a stop at the curb. A car passed on the left and parked just ahead of them. Leaning toward Margaret, George caught a glimpse of four security men piling onto the concrete apron just outside the terminal entrance.

Before them stood a three-story crescent shaped ceramic and aluminum building with rounded balconies. Behind the balconies were lightly tinted blue windows, which hugged the building's contour and reflected the activity in the sky above. Turning and looking up through the small dome that contained the complex, George saw air-cars and occasional heavy planetary transports taking off and landing almost vertically, like large birds on shiny silver talons.

No one made a move for the entrance. Instead, they loitered near the front of the building as if waiting for something to happen. In his confusion, George hadn't noticed that Margaret was holding him by the arm, as if he might try to escape.

"If I was going to run, don't you think I would have done it before this?"

Margaret shrugged. "It's procedure, Mills."

A van pulled up behind their car and two more security men jumped out and joined Wells. George continued watching the van over his shoulder. One of the security men had opened the side panel door and was just standing there. The rear compartment of the van appeared empty. What in the world are they doing, George wondered? Apparently, they'd been waiting for this van, but why?

Inside the terminal, George noticed for the first time that the security men were armed with nasty looking rifles of a type he'd never seen before. Some sort of black mechanical gimbal connected the guns to the their waists. They weren't in full combat garb like Fred Jackson the other day, but they were definitely heavily armored.

Margaret led him through a small lobby to a security checkpoint. The terminal wasn't the typical ceramic white he was accustomed to. It had navy gray walls, spartan black rubber carpeting on the floor, and there were no plants, concession stands, or paintings on the walls like in other parts of the airport. Straining to peek past the security men at the checkpoint counter, George could see that the walls of the concourse were completely devoid of windows and made of metal with riveted seams. Just beyond the checkpoint, he saw the long white cylindrical enclosure of a full body scanner. The place had the feel of a military installation.

Looking back at the front entrance, George saw Wells talking to more security men. He counted about twelve in all, each heavily armed and armored. What in the world had he gotten himself into? What had started as an accounting problem had somehow turned into a major military operation, with him curiously at the epicenter.

Continuing to look toward the main entrance, George noticed a small optical aberration, a slight waviness in the sharp edge of a doorframe that was almost imperceptible unless you were looking for it.

"What are you looking at?" Margaret asked.

He shrugged and turned to the man at the checkpoint. "Wallet and keys, Mr. Mills. Anything you may have in you pockets, personal items in you jacket..."

George was just reaching into his pants pocket when he heard a tremendous explosion and felt a concussive wave of heat and pressure. It hit him from behind. He instinctively grabbed Margaret and held her in his shadow, trying to ferry her behind the counter. After the explosion, he heard glass breaking, then the tingle of raining glass shards as they hit the ground. Sounds of heavy objects clanging were followed by muffled sounds of pain and sporadic screams. Margaret grabbed his arm with surprising strength and pulled him in a fast crouch for better cover.

"Come on Mills, stay with me."

They kept low and moved as quickly as they could toward a solid looking column on the concourse side of the security checkpoint, as far away from the lobby as they could get. Once behind the column, George pressed his back against it and realized Margaret was next to him, making her own assessments. Her typically immaculate hair was now tossed chaotically about her face and black smudges streaked her forehead and nose.

"Thanks Mills," she said smiling thinly. Then she reached behind and unsheathed a gun from somewhere at the small of her back.

Acrid smoke was beginning to flow into the concourse, and with it came the smell of burning flesh. George could still hear loud noises, explosions, and men yelling orders that were hard to make out. Clearly, this thing wasn't over. He peered carefully around the column and saw security men scrambling for cover among billowing clouds of blue-black smoke and a wild collection of red aiming lasers crisscrossing the entire lobby.

"Shit," Margaret said, trying to pull him back. He resisted, opting instead to look at the carnage. A red aiming laser panned his way and he quickly ducked behind the column.

"What's going on?" he demanded.

"Hell if I know," Margaret said.

Cautiously, he considered their options. If it was over, then it made sense to stay put until the security men came to get them. If not, then running further down the concourse might be their best strategy.

George saw soldiers in full combat gear hiding behind the walls of the terminal on the sidewalk outside. They were shooting at security men who had taken cover behind terminal counters and various other defensive structures in the vicinity of the lobby. As soldiers behind the large shattered terminal windows laid down suppressing fire, other soldiers jumped through and scattered for cover. He saw the hypersonic red streaks of pulsed magnetic rail rifles coming from the attackers. They were pouring into the terminal. Aluminum projectiles struck ceramic and metal counters, shattering them in a torrent of flame as their explosive tips detonated on impact.

At superhuman speeds that bespoke the artificial musculature of their combat suits, soldiers continued flooding through the tear in the terminal wall, causing the defenders to fall back through a hail of red streaks and sonic booms. They were heading right for George and Margaret.

The defenders turned, shot, and spun again, trying to cover their retreat. Fifteen-millimeter hypersonic explosive projectiles hit their targets, instantly turning them into vapor and debris. George ducked behind the column as body parts and scrap metal pummeled the front of the structure.

"This is bad," he declared grimly.

"Yeah Mills, I'd say it's pretty bad."

Sweat poured down George's forehead into his eyes, causing them to tear and burn. The smoke flooding the terminal stung the mucus membranes in his sinuses, making his nose run and his mouth taste foul. He raised his hand to wipe his nose and had trouble holding it steady. Exhaling slowly, he calmed himself, willed himself to stay calm. If these were the last moments of his life, he wanted to live them with total clarity, not in some hazy hysterical stupor. Margaret seemed alert, considering their options. He had to smile. Though he'd made a considerable effort, it was hard to dislike her.

Beyond the temporary safety of the column, the battle raged on. George could hear the steady sound of rail guns, a metallic zing, followed by a high-pitched whine, sonic boom, and then an explosion; it was all-out war.

Then came another sound, one George hadn't heard before. Margaret tugged at his arm. "The cavalry's here," she said. The look on her face was not a half smile this time, but a confident grin.

It was an odd noise, like the crackling buzz of an electric arc. It sputtered randomly and was followed by a loud hissing. George braved a look and saw a bright blue streak, seemingly coming from empty space, scanning across a wall behind which attacking soldiers were laying down suppressing fire. Suddenly, the beam took focus and hot molten debris splattered away from the burn spot as though hit by a white-hot pile driver. The accompanying sound was like rolling thunder, and the entire forward terminal shimmered in white incandescent light.

As the beam dug deeper into successive layers of the wall, the men using it for cover scattered. In an instant, the whole thing burst into flames and disappeared in a cloud of black smoke. Another beam opened up on a group of attackers pressing deeper into the terminal toward them. One large black armored soldier jumped out from behind a marquee, his rail gun spitting orange streaks toward the origin of the beam. As the soldier fired, hypersonic rounds brought fire and falling debris to bear on the invisible defender. The soldier stood firm, legs tensed, body stiff, swinging the large rifle from the gimbal on his hip, spraying orange death everywhere he turned. The hollow electric whine of the blue arc rang in George's ears. Sweeping across the floor, it hit the soldier in mid torso. In an instant, his armor lit up in a spray of sparks and his body split in half, falling to the floor in a burning heap.

Staring at the impossible drama playing out in the terminal lobby, George saw Wells and four other security men running full bore in their direction. Margaret pulled hard on his arm, urging him to run down the concourse. He followed as she sprang in front of him, legs pumping hard and head bowed down. They darted toward a gate farther down the smoky metal tunnel.

"What the hell was that?" George yelled over the sound of explosions behind them.

"Just keep running, and stay with me," she said, slowing momentarily to grab his hand.

Panting to keep up, George heard a noise behind them that sounded like rail guns and instinctively ducked, covering his head with his hand. As he did, he felt a torrent of hot air above his head burning the hairs on the back of his hand. A rail round slammed into the wall near the gate door and exploded.

Margaret slowed, grabbed him by his lapels and flipped sideways, forcing him to fall to his right. As he went down, she let go, quickly rolling away and coming to rest behind the gate counter. He tried to follow, but failed to generate enough spin to make it. Another round flew past too high to hit them, and slammed into the gate just beyond the counter. Margaret grabbed his arm in an effort to pull him to safety while he pedaled feverishly against the carpet. George was on his stomach when he felt someone kick him hard on the left side, then stumble over him in a rush to get to cover. Raising his face from the carpet, he saw Wells struggling to join Margaret.

"Damn it, Matt," Margaret yelled. "What about Mills?"

As soon as Wells was clear, Margaret sprang out, grabbed him under his arms, planted her feet, and heaved both of them up and behind the counter. Realizing what she was trying to do, George broke his fall with his hands to avoid falling on top of her.

"Thanks, Mills," Margaret said, breathless. "You probably just saved me a couple of broken ribs."

George was momentarily speechless, unable to do anything but stare into her violet eyes.

"For goodness sakes, Mills, let me up."

"I'm sorry," George said, quickly rolling off her.

He crawled away, unnerved, and propped his back against the counter to steady himself. Margaret grabbed her gun. As George watched, she squeezed off three quick shots, then fell next to him with the gun in both hands, muzzle-up, looking like an implement of prayer.

"Is that effective against them?" George asked doubtfully.

She was using a twelve-millimeter conventional pistol, a type of handgun typically too small to be equipped with a power supply capable of magnetic impulsion.

She shrugged. "We weren't expecting this level of resistance."

After a moment's thought, Margaret said, "Why are you so important to them?"

"I'm not," George said, but Margaret looked unconvinced.

"Think about it. If they wanted me, they could have taken me at any time. Neither my whereabouts nor my schedule is any big secret. It's clear they want something else. It must have something to do with you and Wells."

"Bullshit," Wells barked. He was on all fours, pistol in hand, and ready to do battle.

Wells was red-faced with anger and adrenaline. Large blue veins stuck out of his neck and temples, sculpting his face with aggressive rage. He was the perfect soldier, at one with his training. He had a preconceived view of this situation, and would twist and turn events to conform to that preconception, thought George.

Wells was just getting ready to engage the enemy when an aluminum round hit the front of the counter. The concussion jarred them all forward. It was as if someone had hit George in the back with a bat. He moved gingerly and found, to his relief, that no bones were broken. That kind of injury would be a certain death sentence.

"Shit," Wells said, and squeezed off several shots.

Margaret said, "This barrier won't take another hit; we have to move."

Wells caught his breath and nodded.

Margaret gestured toward the gate behind them, which had just been hit by an errant round. "We can't go that way."

"Where to then?" Wells asked.

"Next gate," Margaret said quickly.

They were racing down the concourse again. George could hear Wells shooting behind them, trying to cover their retreat, and couldn't help feeling grateful. As they ran, George saw bright white undulations on the walls and ceiling and heard the eerie whine of beam weapons.

When the three of them made it to cover, George peeked around the corner of the counter and saw that, despite their newfound allies, attackers were still advancing on them. Two security men, or what was left of them, lay burning in the middle of the walkway, barely discernable from other rubble around them. Looking further down the concourse, in the light of scattered fires that littered the ruined landscape, George saw something that he was at a loss to explain. It was partially visible where something had hit it. A burn spot was glowing red and smoking in mid-air. From just above the floating apparition, a blue arrow of light flared and scanned toward one of the attackers. As the beam hit the floor, the tattered carpet exploded in a broad arc of flame, lighting up the attacker as he fell to the floor in burning pieces. George drew behind cover just in time to see Margaret, on her knees, working the lock on the gate door in back of the counter. To his amazement, the door slid open.

"Come on," she yelled, jumping through. George and Wells ran to the door in a crouch and quickly followed Margaret inside. When the door closed behind them, they were thrown into near silence; only a muted suggestion of the carnage unfolding on the other side of the bulkhead was now audible.

George sat on the floor of a descending tunnel next to Wells, both men sweaty and gasping for the clean air that replaced the toxic smoke on the other side of the door. Margaret stood, leaning against the opposite wall, doubled over, hands on her knees. She still grasped a gun, and George could see smoke rising from its barrel. Knowing there was no time to waste, they slowly rose and walked several hundred feet until they came to another door. Margaret was able to open this one too. When they were all inside, and had closed the door behind them, Margaret raised her gun and shot the lock mechanism, making it inoperable from both sides.

George scanned the bay. It was large, maybe two hundred feet across and fifty feet high. The soft red light was strangely reminiscent of the surface, prompting him to take a couple of quick breaths before his instincts were satisfied that the atmosphere was indeed breathable. There were large pieces of equipment dotting the space in a random arrangement, apparently used for servicing spacecraft in-between flights. In the middle of the large room, there was what appeared to be an enormous flat elevator with a tractor parked at its center.

Margaret turned to Wells. "What now?"

"We've got to get to Bay Three. That's where the shuttle is. Sooner of later, whoever those guys are out there, they're going to be coming right through that door." Wells pointed to the bay door.

"What about Dean and his partner? You don't think they'll get it under control?"

"Last time I looked, they were outnumbered four to one. Maybe they'll put it down, and maybe they won't. Do you want to bet the ranch on that?"

"I guess not, but we can't go that way," Margaret said, motioning toward the door with her gun. She looked at the gun and seemed puzzled to find it still in her hand.

"There's another way out," Wells said. "There's an elevator to the surface over there, and there's a similar elevator on the surface for Pad Three. Both go between the surface and the bays, and both bypass the terminal."

Chapter Sixteen

Margaret considered taking the bay elevator to the surface. It was a risky gambit, but it appeared to be their only viable option. Any attempt to use bay elevators to short-circuit the terminal meant that they would have to brave the surface without benefit of enclosure. They could take the tractor, but there was no way of boarding the shuttle from the tarmac. They could summon the Bay Three elevator, but that would mean raising the shuttle without environment suits and calling attention to themselves from the terminal windows. The big elevators were relatively slow, so even if they had a way of getting into the craft once it rose to the surface, their enemies would see them and be out on the tarmac before they could board and take off. As Margaret carefully considered each scenario, Wells surveyed the room, checking lockers and cabinets and looking into all the nooks and crannies he could find.

Margaret jogged over to the large elevator where Wells, standing on a wheel and bent over, was peering into the tractor cockpit. "What about reinforcements?"

"What?" he asked, distracted by his search.

"Reinforcements, you must've gotten a message off."

Wells' poked his head out of the tractor cabin. He sat on the wheel and pushed his fingers backward through his hair in mock frustration.

"We weren't able to get a message off," he said finally.

"Why the-hell not?"

"It was a well organized strike. Remember the initial explosion that took out the terminal wall before they rushed us?"

She nodded.

"An EM grenade. The hard EM pulse degraded our transceivers, then they jammed us. Maybe we got something off, maybe not. I don't know, but I wouldn't count on it."

Margaret exhaled, then turned to examine the bay yet again when an alarm sounded. The noise was deafening—three short bursts, then a long one, and then the pattern repeated.

"Shit," Wells hissed, "they're evacuating the atmosphere."

* * *

George listened at the door, trying to determine whether the attackers had gotten into the tunnel from the concourse. He heard nothing to indicate that anyone was trying to get in, or had gotten in. The quiet could have meant anything, but the alarm probably meant that the defenders had lost. The three of them had been seen going into Gate Four. Why would anyone, other than those who wanted them dead, be trying to flush them out now if the Terran force had won?

George jumped to his feet and ran over to Margaret. "What's that alarm?" he asked.

She cut him off with a quick wave of her hand. "Look, Mills, we have to get out of here or we're not going to make it. They're evacuating the air to flush us out. We have to take the elevator up to the surface."

George could hardly believe what he was hearing. No wonder they were looking around. They were searching for environment suits.

"Wait a minute," George said. "I think I might just take my chances with the Martians."

Margaret stepped toward him. George put his hand out, palm up. "Look Margaret, this is your war, not mine. I'm good just staying here. Why not save yourselves, if that's what you think you're doing."

"Fuck," spat Wells, bearing his pearly whites. "We're supposed to bring you in, and that's just what we're going to do." He stepped forward, fists clenched, but Margaret put a hand on his chest and pushed him back.

She smiled at George almost apologetically. "You'll suffocate down here; the lock's wrecked, remember? It'll take them too long to reach you. Come on Mills." She took his hand. "Come with me, okay?"

Nodding, and feeling like a fool for listening to her, George acquiesced. They all ran to the airlock. When they got to the hatch, Margaret dropped to one knee and began fiddling with the lock's keypad.

After working her magic, she looked up at him. "Mills, Wells and I are going to take the goggles and gloves once we get to the surface. It's cold and dry out there. Hold your breath as long as you can and keep your eyes closed tight; the low pressure will suck the moisture right out of them."

George nodded reluctantly, still in a tug of war with his emotions over this plan. He marveled at how easy it was for a beautiful woman to gain his trust. After all, Margaret had done nothing but make his life miserable since he'd first laid eyes on her.

Moments later, the door slid open and they pushed inside. George went in first, then Margaret, then Wells. The elevator was built for, at most, two people. Three was a tight fit. The door slid shut. Wells pressed a series of buttons, and George registered tightness in his gut as the elevator started rising to the surface. As they went up, Margaret turned to face him, her firm compact body pressed into his, causing a momentary flush of heat.

"Here, stuff this in your ears," Margaret said. She handed him a ball of something that felt like wax. Following her lead, he quickly fashioned two small balls and wedged them into his ears. As he watched, she reached up and unzipped a pouch in the collar of her jumpsuit and pulled out a hood, which she tied securely around her face. She arched backwards, planting herself even more snugly against him. When she finished, she put his hand on her waist.

"Grab my pocket," she said. "When that door opens, I want you to hold on for dear life, no matter what happens. Do you understand? Do not let go."

The determination in her eyes reassured him that she wasn't just playing him, which made the situation a little easier to take. The thought of stumbling to his death as a doting idiot wasn't very appealing. The elevator came to an abrupt stop, and George could see a soft pink glow coming from a small window over Wells' shoulder.

"Remember," pleaded Margaret, "you're going to keep your eyes shut tight and let me guide you to the Bay Three Elevator." As George nodded, she spun around and quickly put on her gloves and goggles. Then she put a hand over George's, and firmly plunged their hands deeply into her pocket. Pressing against her upper leg, he felt the reassuring warmth of her body. The door started opening and he began to hyperventilate, trying to push as much air into his lungs as possible. Oh shit, he thought, as he heard a rush of air, and felt a biting cold on his face. He shut his eyes and held his breath, trying hard not to panic. The skin on his face stretched tight, ballooning out due to the low atmospheric pressure. There was a quick jerk on his arm, and they were on their way out the door.

George held his breath as he stumbled along behind Margaret, somehow managing to stay on his feet. He felt like a rag doll. The effort it took to keep from falling, and the constant change in direction, were forcing him to use his air up. He felt sweat evaporating from his exposed forehead, leaving cold spots, and signaling the onset of frostbite. He tried not to think about it. Just stay calm, he told himself over and over again.

Margaret came to an abrupt stop. George crashed into her. She grabbed him by the waist with both hands and pushed him backwards, hard, leaning into it with all her weight. What the hell, George thought. He kept his mouth shut and back peddled fast, trying to stay upright. She continued holding him, skillfully staying on her feet. She was small, but surprisingly wiry. Finally,

159

he slammed into something and the shock made him exhale. He feared that the next breath he drew would be dry and airless, forcing him into spasms that would kill him. He drew a breath and waited for the pain, but it never came. Instead, he found himself taking in breathable air in ever greater gulps. He opened his eyes and they didn't sting!

George found himself standing in an elevator just like the one they'd taken to the surface. It was as though they'd never left. He felt it start to descend. Margaret was standing with her back to him. As soon as he could speak, he lowered his mouth to her ear and whispered, "Thank you."

George was leaning against the rear wall of the elevator, looking down at the floor and drawing shallow breaths.

Margaret offered her hand. "Mills? Come on Mills, we have to go."

George took her hand and stumbled into the middle of an immense underground hanger. He saw a large flat elevator just like the one in Bay Four, except this time, a shuttle was at its center, dwarfing everything around it. Its copper bronze conical nose hung twenty feet above him. The rear of the craft loomed large, diminishing the otherwise cavernous proportions of the hanger. The heat-resistant polymer coat on its underside was scorched charcoal black. The burnt bottom stood in stark contrast to the silvery alloy landing struts that planted the huge bird on the flat expanse of elevator. George could see the complicated array of conduits and artificial muscles that adorned the simple skeletal frame of the forward strut, which rose high in front of him.

Margaret ushered him forward toward the portable stairway that was pushed up against the shuttle's nose. He followed Margaret into the craft. She led him into the rear passenger's cabin and helped him find a seat.

"How's this one?" she asked, gesturing to a seat by a window.

"This'll be fine." George sat down. He was happy to be off the surface, resigned now to going to the cruiser. He had long since abandoned hopes of somehow escaping.

"Want me to ride back here with you?" Margaret asked. She lowered the restraining bar across his chest.

He looked up at her as she sat on the arm of his chair. He said nothing, put his head back on the headrest, and closed his eyes. He felt the arm of the chair rise as she stood, then he heard footsteps as she climbed the ladder into the pilot's cabin. After a few moments, he heard Margaret and Wells talking in the cockpit, but their voices were too faint to be understood. So what now, George wondered, hoping that they wouldn't move against the children next.

* * *

Margaret watched Wells check the fuel levels and flight controls as she slipped into the copilot's seat.

"How's our passenger?" Wells asked.

"Looks a little worn, but he'll be all right. How's the ship?"

"Five on five," Wells said with a bravado and self-confidence that had been noticeably absent the last half-hour. He ordered the ship's AI to open the overhead bay doors and raise the elevator to the tarmac.

Margaret saw the bay slowly falling away through the canopy. The soft pink light of Mars reflected off the shuttle's nose, replacing the comparatively harsh red of the bay as they ascended. She sat back and felt her muscles relaxing for the fist time since they'd entered the terminal. She'd been in combat before, but that brawl in the concourse was among the worst she'd ever seen. If this was any indication of what was coming, Void Fleet could anticipate a scale of bloodshed that humanity hadn't seen in centuries. If the separatists had that kind of military hardware, what else were they capable of? She didn't want to think about it right now. There were too many facets to this thing—social complications had never been her strong suit.

For just a moment, glancing down at Mills, Margaret had envied his clarity. As long as she'd known him, which admittedly hadn't been very long, he'd had a singular purpose. All the trouble he'd caused was a testament to his ingenuity. The thing that impressed her the most, however, was his uncompromising commitment to those children. Why did he consider them so important?

Damn, she hated the mental back and forth. She found some solace in the fact that NearSec had been onto Mills even without her involvement. No matter how she'd played it, they would have sent Wells, or Oz, or somebody else. That's just the way it was.

When she looked up, they were on the surface, surrounded by a grand expanse of canyon and a large mountain range to the east.

"You okay?" Wells asked.

"Yeah, no problem. I'm just a little drained after the terminal, that's all. Lets get the hell out of here."

Wells started the main engines, which came to life with a roar that shook the shuttle and kicked up dust from the tarmac below.

Wells moved the shuttle off the Gate Three elevator and onto the runway. Margaret felt the vibrations and the forward surge as Wells fought to move the powerful craft into position. He activated the vertical thrusters even as the shuttle continued rolling onto the short runway. Margaret felt the ship rise in a slow bob, then the thud of the landing gear folding into the fuselage. Wells gunned the main engines and the shuttle shot forward, pressing her hard into the seat. Everything shook violently as Wells angled the stick backward. They climbed steeply into the Martian sky. In just a few seconds, Margaret was flat on her back, looking straight into the void.

* * *

Hector and Roy had spent the last twelve hours in the shuttle's small cargo hold, and their limbs were stiff and sore. Roy heard the Earthers moving around and talking in the forward cabin. It was dark in the hold, but he wore night goggles. Roy looked around and spied the equipment they'd brought in duffel bags. They had anchored the acceleration netting to hand holds in the cargo hold and attached restraining straps to the walls with molecular glue. When he finally felt the elevator rise to the surface, Roy moved his cramped legs. It wasn't long before Roy heard the main engines start. He quickly strapped himself in, pulling the harnesses tight. If the netting and straps didn't hold, the acceleration would crush them against the bulkhead. He felt the shuttle rise and bob gently, then heard the sound of the landing gear. Roy clenched his teeth; he knew what was coming next. The acceleration hit like a hammer, the force increasing so quickly that he almost peed his pants. His body felt as if it weighed a thousand pounds, and all he could do was close his eyes and wait for it to end. After a few minutes, he began feeling the pressure subside and noticed small objects floating around in the green glow of his night goggles. Good, they were sub-orbital.

Roy looked at Hector. His big green teeth flashed in a visceral smile. He scrambled out of the netting and grabbed the wand that he'd attached to the floor. They both got rid of their goggles. Roy was closest to the door and was holding the wand tightly in his left hand as he grabbed the latch. He glanced behind to make sure Hector was squared away. The larger man was poised and ready to strike.

Roy had always feared Hector, and when his partner turned and flashed that cold dark smile, he couldn't help but feel sympathy for the Earthers. In an instant, he depressed the door latch and sprang into the cabin. Roy had practiced this move over and over, burning it into his reflexes. He flowed out the door like liquid, smoothly negotiating handholds that he could have found with his eyes closed. He stopped and saw a man in one of the seats closest to the cockpit ladder. The man's back was to him. Beyond, he saw shadows moving on the cockpit walls. Piece of cake, he thought, then moved against the man in the seat.

As Roy advanced, the man in the front row tried to turn, but he was too slow because of the restraining bar across his chest. Roy grabbed the nearest two seat backs, one with each hand, and pulled himself forward with all his might. He was on the man in a flash. Holding the wand in his right hand, Roy held the bar down with his left as the man tried to lift it with both hands. As the man took one hand off the restraint to try to keep from being stunned, Roy jabbed the wand into his shoulder.

* * *

George tried to yell, but as soon as the wand's bulb made contact, his mouth clenched shut and his body went into convulsions. His legs shot out in front of him, and he shook like a rag doll. A few seconds later, his arms and legs floated in flaccid helplessness.

* * *

The shuttle was climbing nicely. Wells was still flying manually, as he liked to do. Margaret had just advised the Saratoga of their ETA. The ship had leveled off in a low orbit and would be climbing again shortly to make a final orbital injection on an intercept course for the Saratoga. Margaret sat back in her seat, enjoying the view, glad to be out of that hell hole of an airport. She could see the dim pink fuzz over the rim of Mars, and the star laden deep black of space above. Then she heard it.

Above the sound of the engines, there were other sounds. At first, she thought something had come loose during takeoff, but there was something else—something like a muffled yell. As she reached for the restraint release across her chest, she saw movement out of the corner of her eye. She turned to Wells just as something, a stick of some sort, was striking him on the shoulder, close to his neck. He jerked violently, then slumped in his seat. His arms floated in front of him as if he were sleep walking. The shuttle pitched violently to the right. Wells had failed to engage the autopilot before he'd been overcome. Her finger was on the buckle release as she saw the wand coming for her. She quickly moved her hand off the release and caught the wand above the bulb. She struggled with her unseen assailant in what she knew was a losing battle. The son-of-a-bitch had the advantage of leverage, and she was pinned to the seat by the restraint. She'd have to do something else, and she'd have to do it fast. Another arm reached around her neck and grabbed her jumpsuit just above her left breast. She bit his forearm as hard as she could, but the sleeve was too thick. She just couldn't apply enough force to make him let go. Then another wand came over her right shoulder and struck her. She felt a burning through her clothes, and lost control of her arms. She fought, but felt herself fading away, as though peacefully falling through water. Then everything went black.

* * *

The shuttle was going down. Hector could see the orange glow of plasma flowing by the window as the ship reentered the atmosphere. That fucking woman, he thought. It'd taken too much time and effort to put her down. She was small, looked like a teenager, but was unbelievably strong for her size. He got hard, thinking about how much fun it was going to be to deal with her later. He'd had exotic pussy before, but he suspected he'd never had anything like this.

Hector had been servicing spacecrafts most of his adult life and considered himself a pretty good pilot, but he decided there was no use trying to take the stick. Instead, he pushed the *attention key* on the pilot's terminal and ordered the AI to engage the autopilot. The shuttle responded immediately. Soon the shuttle straightened out and began climbing to its previous orbit.

Hector moved the two pilots to seats in the rear cabin next to the man Roy had zapped. Roy bound their hands and feet, then tied them to their chairs with metal restraints he'd brought in his duffel bag. Hector climbed into the pilot's seat and began flying the shuttle back toward Ursa on its second revolution around Mars. Once he'd descended into the atmosphere, he flew it over the mountains, then south, low over the mesa. About a hundred miles south of Ursa Township, he deployed the landing gear, increased vertical thrust while slowing, and put the craft down.

About fifteen minutes after sealing the shuttle, Hector watched a tractor pulling up alongside the shuttle. With legs fully extended, the tractor was about twenty-five feet tall. It had a body that was fifteen feet thick at the center and tapered off at the edges. There were six legs in all, three on a side. Each leg had three major joints that bent smoothly and resembled the joints of an insect. They rose up from the sides of the tractor at forty degree angles, then dropped down after the first major joint and bent out slightly to the side, terminating in a third side-pointing ankle.

Hector saw the tractor's front legs making careful probative motions. The transparent pilot's bubble, which dominated the front of the vehicle, was dark, preventing Hector from seeing the driver. Finally, the tractor stopped, bobbed up and down a couple of times, and folded its legs, resting its body on the ground.

Hector and Roy hoisted the limp bodies of the drugged hostages into the rear airlock. When they'd been loaded and secured, Hector joined his comrades in the pilot's cabin. The tractor raised itself once more to its full height. It turned south and slowly ambled away from the abandoned shuttle, picking up speed as it found the desired direction. Minutes later, it was running south at full scurry, leaving a cloud of red brown dust in its wake. It hadn't gone but a couple of miles when two black dots appeared high in the northern sky behind it. The two interceptors were on them in seconds, passing a mere hundred feet above them at more than six hundred miles per hour, kicking up two long walls of dust behind them like continuous waves on a rusty sea.

Chapter Seventeen

After seeing George arrested at Minsky, Joanne returned to her office with Sarah. She didn't know what else to do, and needed time to think.

Sarah sat on the office sofa, staring at Joanne's back as she looked out the window. "Those weren't campus security or Dome police, were they?" Sarah asked.

Joanne exhaled. "No, I think he's in real trouble. I don't know what to do."

Sarah got up and put her hand on Joanne's arm. "Maybe we should call the police and try to find out what's happening? I can't imagine they would arrest someone on the faculty without notifying Victor first."

Joanne turned and looked into Sarah's face. "Could you find out and call me when you know something?" she pleaded.

Then Joanne glanced down with mild amusement at her still bare feet. In all the confusion she'd forgotten to put her shoes on. Even without them, she was at least four inches taller than Sarah, who wore three-inch pumps. Joanne couldn't help but be moved by the empathy in the green eyes of this pale little Earther.

"Don't worry," Sarah said, looking up at Joanne. "I'll make some inquiries and I'm sure we'll get this straightened out. In the meantime, please call me if you need me, okay?"

Joanne nodded, then Sarah patted her hand and left, lingering a moment at the door to give one last look of support.

Joanne went to her desk, moved her Tab squarely in front of her, and manipulated one of the icons on the transparent display. The image of the keyboard disappeared and was replaced by a hierarchy of designators. She unwrapped the Minsky icon and touched the Will entry.

"Will?" she whispered.

Nothing.

"Will?"

That was odd. He'd never failed to answer before. If anyone knew what was going on, she guessed he would.

"Will?"

Still nothing.

"Damn-it Will, if you're there, answer me."

She waited, hardly breathing. No response.

She folded the Tab and put it in her bag, then reached down and put her shoes on. They had arrested George at his lab at Minsky; perhaps they hadn't been to his office at Penrose yet. Perhaps he'd left his Tab there. It had the number of the security man they'd met at Building One yesterday. What was his name, Fred somebody? She thought for a moment—Fred Jackson, that was it. George had told her that he'd known him from before, had implied that he trusted him. That's what she needed right now, someone she could trust, someone on the inside, someone Martian.

She looked around her office, searching for something she might have forgotten. She wasn't going to just run out this time. She felt a strange sense of distance, like this place belonged to another part of her life, a part that was somehow coming to an end. She shut the door behind her this time as she left, then walked down the hall and out of the building toward Minsky.

When she'd left the police cordon at Minsky earlier with Sarah, things were breaking up. So why was there still a crowd around the Annex? This time, instead of running to the scene and pushing her way through the crowd, she walked slowing and deliberately. She stopped when she noticed several white vans parked in back of the Annex near the loading dock where they usually delivered equipment to the lab. It wasn't long before Joanne realized what she was witnessing. As she stood there, helpless to stop them, technicians were loading what had once been George's lab equipment into the back of government vans. Feeling a mixture of sadness, anger, and defeat, Joanne turned and walked toward Penrose.

Penrose was an old structure with pretentious wide marble stairs leading up to a giant columned entrance, the type she'd seen in videos of Earthly antiquity. One of the first buildings on campus, it had originally served as the administration building. To Joanne, this grand building represented the desire of academicians from Earth to civilize this distant frontier. She climbed the stairs and pushed her way through one of the large glass and aluminum doors into a cool marble lobby. George had an office on the fourth floor, on the southwest corner. She took the elevator and followed the narrow maze-like corridors to a frosted glass door on which were stenciled the words: *Quantum Computing*. The door was locked and there were no lights on inside. Searching her bag, she withdrew a card key, unlocked the door, and entered what had once been a secretary's station. It was now a small library.

"Lights please," Joanne said.

Scanning the rows of memory crystals neatly arranged on the library's shelves, she shook her head and smiled. What an odd man George was. No one kept crystals in a physical catalogue this way. Modern libraries were automated with powerful search AI's that could look through local stores, or search the entire solar system if need be. She'd once asked George why he kept crystals like this.

"I like the way they look in the office," he'd told her, and never said any more about it. He was a sentimental man who enjoyed his eccentricities, and, in time, she'd found herself defending his peculiar habits to others. She missed him already.

Looking around, Joanne decided that everything seemed intact, undisturbed. No one had searched the library yet. Crossing the room, she entered the open door to George's office. It looked untouched too.

Sitting at his desk, she picked up the sole personal item amidst the academic clutter. It was a picture, not an active video clip, of the two of them at the lake. George sat in a wicker chair that he'd taken from the veranda of a nearby coastal hotel. He wore a baggy, blue cotton shirt with large exotic flowers on it. She sat on his lap. The wind had been unusually strong that day, and her hair blew wildly, partially eclipsing her bright smile. She wore a sleeveless pink shirt and her bare arms encircled his neck, pushing their faces together. He held her around the waist.

It was funny, she thought. She'd been in here a thousand times. Hell, she'd been here yesterday, but she'd never noticed this picture before. Had it been there yesterday? Was she really so negligent that she'd missed such a personal and meaningful item?

She started systematically searching the desk for George's Tab, first checking the drawers, then feeling around under the tops of drawer compartments, then feeling for false bottoms. Nothing. Too obvious, she thought. His desk is the first place anyone would look. Where would he put it? She turned her attention to the bookcases. He was one of the few academicians who still used paper. Was there a special book, one he might have talked about? She scanned the shelves, opened scores of books, and came up with nothing.

Returning to the chair, she folded her arms, put her head down on the desk, and was enveloped by the silence of the office. She drifted off to sleep. When she opened her eyes again, she was looking at the picture, the only personal item on his desk. She raised her head and picked it up, carefully examining the frame. Finally, she opened it, withdrew the photo, and there, behind the photograph, was a clear plastic Tablet—George's Tab. With a renewed sense of purpose, Joanne put the photograph back in the frame, put the frame into her bag, and quickly left the office.

Heading to the biology complex to retrieve her car, she realized there was no point in returning to her office. Sarah would call her if there was any new information; she felt sure of that. Passing Minsky, she saw they were still at it. Soon there would be nothing left. What had taken them fifteen long years to build would be gone without a trace in a single afternoon. She winced, turned her head, and proceeded to the parking lot, not daring even a backward glance.

Sitting in her car, she put the key card in the ignition, then hesitated before pushing it in. She couldn't go home. The woman who had arrested George, the one she'd met at Building One the other day, she'd know where Joanne lived. The meeting at DRA had been her meeting. George had been a tagalong. So why had he been arrested and not her? In fact, they were showing no interest in her at all. She thought about George's Tab. Had he hidden it behind the picture just so she would find it? If so, he must have suspected that he would be arrested and she would be free to find it.

Confused and frustrated, she put her head back on the headrest and closed her eyes. The more she thought about the events of the last few days, the less she understood. What was becoming clear, though, was that George must have understood aspects of this drama that he'd kept from her. There had to be some Rosetta stone that he'd chosen not to share with her. But why would he do that?

She cleared her mind, profoundly tired of the confusion and its nagging hints of betrayal. Then in the calm of her blank mind, she recalled her own words, the ones she'd spoken on the way back from the tube station: *It's a Will thing, isn't it?*

She opened her eyes with a start. Was it really that simple? It did fit all the facts, and what's more, it implied that George hadn't kept anything from her after all. Maybe she'd been too preoccupied to understand the obvious. It was no secret that people did reflexively consider raw technology the answer to all their problems. It was not so much that Earth feared their breakthroughs in simulations or genetics; it was that Earth coveted the powerful new tool that facilitated those breakthroughs. George was important only because he was closest to the tool. She thought about Minsky, about how shortly after George's arrest they'd taken Will. It fit all the facts, didn't it?

Okay, all that aside, she had some decisions to make right now. If she wasn't going home, where would she go? She found her Tab, unfolded it, and put it into the cradle on the dashboard. She tapped it, and a window appeared.

"Call Malcolm Peters," she ordered.

The Tab asked, "Call him at home, his office, or his mobile?"

"I don't care," she said, "just find him."

A few seconds later, Malcolm's face coalesced on the clear screen. "Joanne?" Malcolm said, "are you all right?"

"I don't know—are you home now?"

He hesitated. "No, I'm still at the conference. They're delivering final remarks. Hold on a minute, okay?"

The screen went blue. The channel was open, but he'd put her on hold.

Malcolm's reappeared. "What's wrong?" he asked. "What's happened?"

"I don't really want to talk about it over the network. Can I come to your place so we can talk?"

"Of course," Malcolm said slowly. "Do you know where I'm staying?"

She shook her head.

"There," Malcolm said. "I just sent a map and directions for your Nav. I'm going home now. I should be there by the time you arrive, okay?" He smiled sincerely.

"Thanks, Malcolm."

She leaned over and made a twisting motion with her finger on the screen. The window cleared with the exception of a map icon at its center.

"Put the map in the Nav, please.

The map icon morphed into a car and disappeared.

"End session," she said. The window disappeared, leaving only a clear plastic sheet. She retrieved it from its cradle, folded it into a minimized form, and put it in her bag. Minutes later, she was leaving the campus and heading north on the *Sea of Storms*.

She sat back, pushed the steering yoke all the way forward, and let the Nav take control. It displayed a map on the console, showing the car starting to cross Lake Geneva. A finish icon flashed blue over a point situated on the north shore of the lake. Joanne put her finger on the icon and tapped. *The Canal Hotel, Room 406* appeared next to the point on the map. Good, she thought, and opened the window, letting the wind blow her hair around as it streamed into the car.

Joanne fell into a dream, recalling in vivid detail one of those rare magic days that had made her life feel charmed. There was a wicker chair, a baggy blue shirt with big red flowers, and drinks that George had called *gin and tonics*. They had limes and little umbrellas in the glasses.

She and George had just gotten a convergence on a fully detailed simulation—their first—and they'd decided to take the rest of the day off. Up to that point, they'd been mere colleagues, with little contact outside the lab. But on this day, George had asked her to go to the lake with him. She'd accepted reluctantly. She hadn't wanted any involvement, especially at work, and especially with an Earther. But his good humor had been contagious, and in that serendipitous moment, she'd agreed to meet him after going home to change.

When she arrived at their planned meeting place, she'd found him sitting in a white wicker chair planted in shallow water, his bare feet dangling in the surf. Next to him was a cooler, with two glasses on top. It was all so indulgent; she couldn't help smiling and feeling glad she'd come. She walked up and stood in front of him, ankle deep in the surf, and couldn't stop laughing when he handed her that silly glass with a lime and a little umbrella. While enjoying the moment, the sound of her own laughter became entangled with an incessant tone that became louder, and finally chased the dream away. She tried to hold on to it, but no matter how she tried, it slipped away. When she opened her eyes, George's beaming face and that magical day were gone. The car was taking an exit for the north shore, and the Nav was asking if she wanted to go manual.

In a less than civil tone, she told the Nav to find the hotel. It wound the car through a maze of small streets that brought her closer to the water. Finally, it pulled into a dirt lot on the side of the Canal Hotel. She got out of the car and sat on the plastic hood for a moment. It was clear that George and Malcolm were cut from the same cloth. The hotel was a four-story yellow and white building, if you could call it that. Adorned in ornate wooden trim, it looked more like a giant antique dollhouse than anything else. It had a triangular slanting roof, which housed a number of smaller similar structures in a complicated overall pattern. It had many windows that were framed by separate moldings, to which were attached what looked like black wooden shutters. Very retro, she thought, smiling, and shaking her head. Maybe she'd been with George too long, but she actually found it attractive.

She walked through an opening in a large wall of hedges that encircled the hotel, then up the front stairs and into the lobby. After asking the man at the desk for directions to the elevator, she proceeded to room 406.

Chapter Eighteen

Oz had been summoned to the Admiral's office for a confidential update on the Mills affair. When he arrived, he found the Admiral standing at the large portal with his back to the door. Oz knew the Admiral had heard the door open and close, but had not turned around, so he stood at attention at the head of the large black marble table that occupied the center of the room.

"At ease, Commander, have a seat," the Admiral said. "I've heard some very disturbing rumors about the situation on Mars."

"Yes, sir," Oz said.

Nelson turned and moved to the other end of the table and sat down. He folded his hands in front of him and in a civil tone said, "Would you care to elaborate?"

Oz spent the next half hour itemizing the debacle of the last half-day. When he finished, the Admiral asked coolly, "And you're doing what to find these terrorists?"

"We can't find them by remote sensing, there's too much iron in the soil and the tunnels are too deep. So we've sent a squad to search the southern tunnels. We're thinking they'd make the best hiding places because there are so many of them and they're so poorly documented. But we have to move fast if we're going to have any chance of closing this thing up quickly."

"What about the north, near the domes?"

"I've decided to let Dome Security search the northern tunnels."

Nelson arched his eyebrows. "You think you can trust them? It isn't clear to me that they're not involved. From what I've heard, these so-called terrorists were very well equipped, more like paramilitary units than a bunch of separatists."

"That's right, sir. In recent years the separatist movement has evolved, or maybe bifurcated is a better word."

Nelson paused to consider this. "Continue, Commander."

"Yes, sir. As I was saying, in recent years the movement has essentially split in two. One side is the purely political movement, that's the one that grew out of the labor unions. That bunch has expanded. They've run candidates in Dome legislatures and have won a minority of seats. That's why we're seeing such organized protests on the network, as well as in the streets. They've been able to block more effective crowd control strategies and restrictions on public assembly. They've also weakened restrictions against speaking out against the planetary governor."

"Okay," Nelson said, "I get the picture. What about the second bunch?"

"It's grown out of frustration that the political wing has not gone far enough."

"You make it sound as though they're doing pretty well."

"To us perhaps, Admiral, but from their point of view, they've been at this for almost a hundred years now. In that time, they've accomplished what? They're still a representative minority. Mars still has a governor from Earth, and Earth companies still control most of Mars' wealth in water and Helium-3."

"And how does the second group solve these problems, Commander?"

"They're a paramilitary group, sir, just as you surmised. Very hard to infiltrate, as you can tell from what happened today. That's kept our intelligence fairly marginal. They're made up of people who have extensive police and military training. Clearly, they have access to sophisticated weapons."

"I see," the Admiral said, "but doesn't that beg the question?"

Oz was momentarily confused.

"The trust issue, Commander. You have Dome Security searching the northern tunnels, remember?"

"Yes sir, that's right, but we've picked those teams very carefully. We have Special Forces on the ground working with them, and some of those are invisible. Frankly, Admiral, Mars is a planet of fifty million people. We have two-hundred and fifty sailors and marines shipboard, and a couple of thousand operatives planet-side. I don't believe we can do an effective job without them. It's as simple as that. And I might mention, Admiral, that each team in the northern tunnels has a Bloodhound that I supervise from up here."

"Good," Nelson said. "That's good. But we have one more issue to discuss."

"What's that, sir?"

"How did the paramilitary get wind of what we were up to, and what do they hope to gain from this move? It's true that Wells and Gates are high ranking officers, but it must be clear to the insurgents that we don't negotiate with terrorists."

"Red Dawn, Admiral."

"Excuse me?"

"Red Dawn, sir. They call themselves Red Dawn."

Nelson looked both frustrated and amused. Oz knew there was enough firepower onboard the Saratoga to bring this unfortunate affair to a speedy conclusion. Nelson could declare martial law, take over local security, and root out all the malcontents. Hell, he had enough firepower on the cruiser to destroy Mars, and the separatists knew it. He would never really do it, but they could never be one hundred percent sure of that. It was that edge, that knowledge, which ultimately controlled the end game. It allowed Nelson to remain a gentleman soldier while the separatists resorted to kidnapping and terrorism. Nelson represented the rule of law. He was a winner, upholding tradition and civilization. They were losers, representing the forces of chaos in the world, nothing but a bunch of low-level ignorant brutes.

Nelson smiled. "Okay Commander, Red Dawn it is. What does Red Dawn hope to accomplish?"

As Oz prepared to respond, Nelson said, "Before we continue, Commander," he motioned for Oz to sit down. Then

Nelson walked over to the bar set in the red pine walls of his office, and poured himself and Oz two fingers of fine scotch in short crystal glasses. Oz felt uncomfortable.

"Should I be drinking right now, sir?"

"Here, take this," the Admiral said, putting a tiny white pill on the black marble table next to his glass.

Oz looked at it quizzically.

"It prevents the body from metabolizing the alcohol, while allowing you to fully experience the scotch."

"Very well," said Oz, reaching for the white speck on the table before him. Five minutes later, he and the Admiral were both standing in front of the portal, watching Mars recede at its upper edge.

"Well Admiral, Oz said. "As far as how this happened, I believe Red Dawn has infiltrated the ship re-supply teams running cargo from the surface. We knew those teams included Martians, and we've done extensive background checks, but something must have slipped through the cracks. We're currently interviewing all cargo-handling teams, including members of our own crew."

The Admiral looked unconvinced.

"You've done that before, haven't you?"

"What's that, Admiral?"

"Interviewed these people. It didn't work before; why would you expect it to work this time?"

Oz had waited for just that question.

"Because Admiral, at the time of the previous interviews, everyone was squeaky clean. We knew they hadn't done anything. This time, we strongly suspect there are guilty parties. Along with the interviews, we're including brain scans and the use of certain neural stimulating drugs that have worked well for us in the past. The drugs induce a state of confusion, mild schizophrenia, which allows us to induce associative discharge. The scans indicate the exact part of the brain active during the associative cascade. High activity in the frontal cortex is an indication of fabricated responses."

"So you're going to use truth drugs," the Admiral said, with a thin lipless smile that made him appear cruel.

"I don't like to use that term, sir. Traditional truth drugs have a history of mixed results. These techniques are much more effective."

Nelson listened with interest, and Oz could tell he'd scored points. But he also knew that he'd have to deliver.

After a few moments consideration, the Admiral said, "Okay commander, keep me informed. Now to the second issue."

"The second issue?" Oz asked, straightening.

"Why did they do it? What do they hope to gain?"

"We have to assume this is a desperate act."

"Oh, why so Commander?"

"Because a move this bold has forced them to show their hand. Up till now, we could only guess about their equipment, their reach into our organization. In half a day, we've learned more about them than we have in the last ten years."

Nelson gave a slow nod. "Good point."

"Furthermore, using the techniques I just described, I expect we'll learn even more in the next few days."

"But what do they get out of it? What's their objective other than two hostages they know we won't negotiate for?"

"Three, sir."

"Three what?"

"Three hostages sir. You forgot Mills."

"But Mills is a Martian now. Why would they think he makes any difference to us?"

"I think that, for them, it's probably an open question. After all, we went to a lot of trouble to arrest him. They've got to be curious as to why."

"But you agree that he's not the main target?"

"Yes. I don't think he was the intended target. I think they're after our network codes. With those codes they could access our navigator, possibly even scuttle the ship into the atmosphere. Imagine Admiral. They could destroy the NearSec flagship without firing so much as a single shot."

"No wonder they pulled out all the stops. Such a demonstration would embolden the whole planet." Nelson seemed amazed by the sheer scope of such a plan. He even showed a spark of admiration for the architect, but only a brief spark. "What are we doing to make sure this doesn't happen?" Nelson demanded.

"We've already changed the OP codes and severed all data links to the surface. We only accept voice communications now."

"You're certain that gives us immunity?"

"Yes sir, absolutely. If they're not sitting on this bridge, there's no possible way for them to gain control of this ship."

Nelson sat back in his chair. "Good, that's very good." Then after a moment, "What about Mills?"

"He was taken, sir."

"That's not what I mean. How about the computer? Will you be able to use it without him?"

This time Oz was not as quick to answer, and Nelson noticed.

"We've secured the computer," he said finally. "It's aboard ship right now. We're currently reassembling it in engineering bay two."

Oz paused for a moment, glanced out the portal to reorganize his thoughts, then added, "I'm going to be completely candid with you, Admiral. This is going to be a tough one. It appears to be a very advanced quantum network with a novel architecture. We don't have an annotated cartographer for it, and the neural sequencing unit is coded in an unreadable compiled format."

"Sounds bad, do you have a plan?"

"Well sir, we'll continue to work on it. We've got our best people in there right now, but we may have to get back to Earth to make progress. We were hoping to have Dr. Gates available to help. She was our best computer resource."

Oz knew that his reference to Margaret in the past tense was not lost on the Admiral. He also knew that the chances of getting her back in good condition were remote at best, and this saddened him to an extent that surprised him.

"That'll be all, Commander," Nelson said absently.

With that, Oz left the Admiral to ponder the unfortunate turn this campaign had taken.

Chapter Nineteen

A system of underground passages that formed a grid of
hexagonal cells covered the southern desert near the Valles
Marineris. The pattern was sparse at the equatorial latitudes and
grew denser toward the southern pole. At the center of each cell
was a combination of pumping stations, wellheads, and pipe-
switching networks for transporting water to the domed
townships. The spokes of these hexagonal cells were composed
of a system of pipes and access tunnels, which were directed
northward or southward, toward or away from facilities at their
centers. Each of the three domes of Ursa Township was fed by
one of a series of sixty degree north-going spokes from one of
the sparse cells near the equator. To the south, the cell pattern
became denser, with the number of corresponding tunnels
increasing by factors of six at each subsequent cell level. At the
site where the commandeered shuttle landed, Oz determined that
five cells were within reach of the terrorists if they'd gone south.
Oz redlined fifteen south-going tunnels from the northern
boundary cells and dispatched five platoons of thirty soldiers
each. Each platoon included three armored reconnaissance units,
or Bloodhounds, capable of high-speed search and destroy
sorties.

* * *

Dean was the lieutenant assigned to cell C-87, which was
approximately seventy-two miles southeast of where the
terrorists had landed. Dean had been one of the two stealth
commandos in the firefight at Ursa airport earlier that afternoon,
and he was itching for payback. It had been a bloody exchange,
and even though he was equipped to deliver overwhelming
firepower, he had barely escaped with his life. From the air, C-87
presented as a few nondescript buildings, a landing strip, and a

Com tower, but he knew that two hundred feet below the Martian mesa was a vast pumping station.

Once in the pumping chamber, Dean split the platoon into three squads of ten men and women, equipping each with a Bloodhound. He followed one of the squads as they advanced further into the southern-most tunnel. The squad was distributed in a line across a ten-foot mesh floor with the Bloodhound out in front.

The Bloodhound advanced slowly, its four titanium alloy legs moving in graceful unison, as Dean made systematic adjustments to his Sim. The Simulated Virtual Display was integrated into his combat suit and received a constant stream of sensory data from both his suit sensors and those of the Bloodhound. Dean saw the panoramic display inside his helmet, which was completely transparent with the view changing as he turned his head. The Sim integrated radar, infrared, visible, and ultraviolet data into a coherent worldview that approximated the outside world as closely as the resolution and color of the data feeds would permit. The suit AI, which was the environment's autonomic master, handled enhancements and targeting. To Dean, the scene outside appeared normal, with color fidelity and contrast through smoke, dust, and even solid objects. His auditory and olfactory senses were also augmented. The Sim relayed the various processed views and sensations directly into Dean's brain by nanosensors, which had been injected into his bloodstream prior to donning the suit. Once the millions of sensors bonded to their target nerves, they could, in turn, stimulate those neurons into firing by electrical signals sent through an array of micro antennas in Dean's skullcap. The sensors had been protein coded to stick to nerves in the thalamus, which routed to the occipital and temporal cortexes. The same was true for hearing via the temporal lobe and smell via the smell sensory cortex at the base of the frontal lobe. The AI had been downloaded from a memory crystal with a neural pattern of weights and nodes that were previously defined from offline learning sessions in a suit simulator. Subsequently, whenever Dean used the profile, the AI running the network would learn from current experience, adjusting weights and pruning nodes until the system was almost indistinguishable from his biological senses.

Dean looked around; his soldiers were advancing. He could see their faces through their helmets, compliments of the Sim. When he was satisfied that everyone had finished environment adjustments for the tunnel, he motioned for the squad to advance more quickly. The closest supply junction was about ten miles down the shaft; they'd have to speed up if they were going to have any chance of catching their targets. They broke into a twelve mile per hour run, and he signaled the Bloodhound to advance at an even faster pace. He saw the tunnel speed by in the Bloodhound's Sim at forty miles per hour; it was at half-gallop, and would make the junction in fifteen minutes. When he went to full Sim, the experience thrust him far into the tunnel. He could hear the rhythmic clang of metal feet on mesh and the smell of cold damp clay walls. He zoomed its vision, and at the very limits of the field, he could see shadowy images at the tunnel's false horizon.

"All right," he yelled, "full advance."

The Bloodhound shot forward at eighty miles per hour; it would make the junction in a little over five minutes. His squad increased their pace to full sprint, clocking almost twenty miles an hour with synthetic muscles at max safe output.

They'd been advancing now for ten minutes. The Bloodhound had reached the first supply junction and was holding station, nothing so far. Dean began to relax a little; that thing at the airport had left him edgy. What the hell had happened anyway? It had started as a simple escort and had, out of the blue, escalated into a minor war. He'd already killed three men today, and didn't have the slightest idea why. Now that he knew what to expect, there'd be no more letting his guard down.

It'd been almost twenty years since Dean had joined Void Fleet. Now, he was a lifer—a city kid who didn't like crowds. He'd always thought of space travel as an attractive alternative to the suffocating life on Earth. Many of his friends had joined up looking for adventure, the kind of bullshit the recruiters were always pushing. But Dean had never gotten a rush from violence, real or simulated. He just wanted to get away from the crowds, that's all, nothing more profound than that. Hell, you could hardly take a shit on Earth in private. And the extended periods of solitude, all the things that had been such a disappointment to his mates, had been sheer heaven to Dean. The kick came when they'd seen their first real combat. The kind of combat where you weren't guaranteed to come back, where the price of making a mistake wasn't loud noises and flashing images on a video screen, but death, swift and certain. Though he hadn't sought it, he was good at it. He had the gift: good eyes, cool under pressure, swift hands. He'd always come back; a lot of them hadn't. And as time went on, he got promoted. His platoon liked him because he had a reputation for bringing everyone back alive, if not always in one piece. The brass wanted to promote him to a staff position, but that might mean going back to Earth, maybe working in an office. He'd declined, opting instead to stay in the field, enjoying the closeness, the camaraderie of moments like this. If only he could do this job and somehow avoid the killing, that was the rub.

The flashing red letters in the Bloodhound view brought him back from his thoughts real fast.

"Incoming, incoming, incoming." The words boomed in Dean's head.

He strained his eyes to see the threat. He had mere seconds to take evasive action. The tunnel could very easily become their tomb; there was nowhere else to go. The junction was still over a mile up tunnel, but he felt the Bloodhound tense, its forepaws down and its back arched up, giving a clear field of view to the neutral beam projector mounted on its back. It quickly adjusted its orientation, flaring its two ear-like phased array radar antennas on the sides of its head. Shit, thought Dean; he scrutinized the radar images of three missiles streaking down the tunnel, heading right at them. The Bloodhound's AI searched its profiles of known threats, trying to characterize the fiery spears that were now only fifteen seconds away. It didn't take long; Dean saw it on his display: three shoulder launched tactical nukes. Nothing very large, low yield two-kiloton warheads—but still enough to incinerate them.

The Bloodhound locked on the targets and fired. A blue streak of lightning flashed down the tunnel, punching a vacuum hole in the atmosphere while superheating the air on the fringes of the beam. The beam swept across the three missiles in quick succession, igniting the fuel and shaped explosives in the warheads. The Bloodhound's gamma detectors registered a 2.5 Mev photon line, indicating nuclear neutron absorption. The warheads had been rigged against destruction by kinetic kill weapons, which had been partially thwarted by the speed of the neutral beam. Partially, but not completely—critical mass had been achieved at the same time that the warheads had vaporized.

Dean heard *"Nuclear detonation, nuclear detonation,"* over and over again in his head.

"Down, get down," he yelled, as he dropped flat to the floor.

A wave of flame, ionized gas, radiation, and hot debris shot down the tunnel. The Bloodhound dug into the mesh floor, getting down low, pulling in all its appendages until it looked like a smooth metallic mound. The wall of fire washed over it, barely scratching its titanium alloy skin.

The ten soldiers followed suit. Dean lay on his stomach, arms stretched in front with his fingers anchored to the mesh. The Bernoulli force of the hot gases flowing over him made his body light, as if it were going to rise. He tensed himself flat, fearing that turbulence would blow him away if he gave it an opening. Turning his head, he could see his men, hunkered down to the mesh, trying to weather the storm. He held on as tight as he could, his body flapping helplessly like a leaf in a hurricane, straining against its mooring to a branch. Then, looking forward, he saw hot glowing pieces of metal coming down the shaft, clanging off the walls and ricocheting up from the floor, spitting off a molten spray. As they streaked by, one of them hit the man to his left on the back, knocking him loose and flipping him up. The wave of hot gas caught him like a giant hand, and Dean saw his face in slow motion, took in all the disturbing details with crystal clarity. The man's expression was a mixture of surprise, disbelief, and then fear. It all happened in the blink of an eye, and then he was gone.

* * *

Oz saw it happen on his console, a flash in the infrared about forty miles south of Dean's squad at C-87. Approximately thirty seconds later, he saw a second flash, followed by sizeable acoustic activity in the ground. This flash was much brighter than the first, and was located at about Dean's current position. It was big, but not big enough to be an uninterrupted nuclear explosion, as the Bloodhound had indicated. Oz guessed there had been only partial detonation due to the speed of the neutral beam disassociating the plutonium as it went critical. He was only guessing, since he'd just lost contact with Dean's Bloodhound, but if he acted quickly at the presumed launch point, he might still be able to do some damage. He queued the tactical AI to fire on C-87, just south of the calculated launch point. He assumed the enemy was falling back now at about twenty miles per hour. A large projector on the belly of the Saratoga quickly acquired the target. The muzzle of the projector silently flashed blue fire in microsecond pulses, creating a vacuum shaft through the atmosphere all the way to the surface, just above the tunnel. A hundred teravolt neutral particle beam struck the ground with the sound of thunder. Plumes of molten glass and lava exploded in massive spouts as the beam dug into the ground like a pile driver. The hot knife seared the tunnel a quarter mile north and south of the presumed launch point. Seconds later, the section of the shaft around the launch site lay silent, charred and fused. The beam disappeared as quickly as it had come, leaving the large smoldering trench it had dug as the only evidence it had ever been there at all.

* * *

Dean got to his feet and walked over to the soldiers closest to him, helping them up, shaking off the disorienting blow of the attack. He heard clanking footfalls, turned, and saw the Bloodhound galloping toward them. When they'd regrouped, he called Oz, requesting further orders. He was told to proceed to the supply shack, take the elevator to the surface, and then return to Dome One on the shuttle. They were to proceed to Dome security headquarters at Fort Apache for new orders. The Bloodhound was to be taken to a pillbox south of the fused tunnel and was to resume search and destroy of any enemy who might still be fleeing south.

Chapter Twenty

Oz sat in the Admiral's office aboard ship, briefing him on the events of the last few hours.

"So you've abandoned searching the southern tunnels?"

"No, not altogether," Oz replied. "We still have several squads and a couple of Bloodhounds searching that area."

"Why do you think the north is more promising?" the Admiral asked skeptically.

"We examined the debris from our orbital strike and failed to find any trace of organic matter."

Nelson thought a moment. "Would you expect to find anything left after a burn like that? I'd imagine only gas and a lot of fused rock would remain."

"Not altogether true," Oz said. "It was a very short burn, only a few seconds. The tunnel was more than two hundred feet deep in some places. When the environment was molten and outgassing, we did absorption scans looking for organic molecules down to only trace amounts and saw nothing at all. If there were people down there, we should have seen something. Remember, there are absolutely no organic molecules in the Martian environment, so we have no background to mask our readings."

"Okay, Commander, so what can we conclude?"

"I think it was a ploy, sir. When you think about how well these guys have covered their tracks, why would they give themselves away so blatantly? It was probably a robotic battery put in the tunnel ahead of time and operated remotely to throw us off the track. If that's true, then I'd assume they're further north."

"Not as many tunnels in the north," Nelson said.

"True enough, sir, but the tunnels in the north are older and some are very poorly documented and hard to find."

Oz could see that Nelson was growing impatient, that he wanted some kind of overall plan not endless analysis. His explanations were all solid, but there was one undeniable problem—they'd had no clear success since the beginning of the operation. No amount of analysis could make that simple fact any easier to swallow.

"We've deployed our best platoon to the north to work with Dome Security." Quickly anticipating the next question, Oz added, "It would be much less efficient if we tried to do this alone. They know the tunnels; they've been dealing with the separatists for decades. It's our quickest option, sir."

Nelson said nothing. He clearly wasn't happy about it, but he'd apparently go along with it for the time being.

"Is that all, Commander?" Nelson asked with a tired edge in his voice.

"Not quite, there's the issue of the Proteus file."

Oz waited a moment; Nelson seemed to be distracted, probably assessing the damage to his reputation with each failed attempt at bringing this matter to a satisfactory conclusion.

Oz said, "Given the situation down there, we should secure those kids. We have no idea of the linkage between Mills and the separatists."

"I thought we agreed that the kidnapping had nothing to do with Mills."

"That's right, sir, but under the circumstances, it's probably best to be preemptive."

"You're probably right, Commander. But holding a bunch of Martian children isn't going to do anything for our image planet-side. Protests are getting larger every day, especially in Dome One."

"Yes, sir, I recommend we hold them at Mollar."

"I agree," Nelson said. "It would be politically incorrect to bring them up here. We might even be able to circulate a story about a medical emergency, a quarantine, something like that."

"That's a very good idea, sir; I'll get right on it."

"Good, Commander, you do that."

Oz left the Admiral's office feeling diminished, somehow unsure of himself. He quickly walked back to the bridge, to the familiarity of his station on the second balcony. He tried to force himself to work, but his concentration wavered. It wasn't the condescending way he'd been dismissed from the Admiral's office. In the end, it would always be performance that would get him to those places that he felt destined to inhabit, not the fleeting insinuations of a man preoccupied by his own insecurities. Oz was supremely confident in his abilities and in the spotless record he'd amassed over the years as a command officer in the fleet. So why did he feel a nagging sense of being off balance? Was it something deeper, more menacing than a momentary resentment? Could it possibly be that he had finally been cast into an orbit too close to his own ethical base?

He'd tried to stay away from matters of genetic origins. Issues like that were too divisive. They had replaced older, deep-seated resentments previously occupied by race and ethnicity. There was a social upheaval on Earth right now, a struggle for the future that placed Normals in a curious moral dilemma. It was an awkward tension that had been initiated by Normals themselves, albeit Normals at the top of the social strata. An odd desire to have their own progeny inherit the future, then, at the moment of fulfillment, drawing back to realize that those whom they'd wanted to empower did not share their vision of the world. They had somehow missed the fact that rebuilding man from his most basic constituents could change his soul as well. Although they tried to hang on, Normals realized they were on the slippery slope to eventual extinction; they had engineered their successors all too well. Was he now feeling their anxiety? Had Mills trumped them all? Was he secretly pursuing these Proteus people in a bid to avoid joining the Normals on their slow journey to oblivion? *Do unto others before they do unto you?*

He had things to do right now; he didn't want to think about this anymore. He'd consider these matters later, at a more convenient time. Reaching into his pocket, he withdrew a small plastic container and opened it. He stared down at the light-blue anti-anomic tablets that graced its shallow cavity for a couple of seconds, and then took one. Putting the container away, he turned in his chair and looked out over the cavernous bridge and its complement of nondescript individuals going about their routines. At this moment, he felt invisible, lost in the routine himself. He smiled at the thought and felt himself relax, an artificial clarity slowly replacing the anxiety of unmedicated reality. He turned in his chair and got back to work.

Chapter Twenty-One

When Joanne arrived at room 406, Malcolm was waiting for her. She told him about how government vans had come to Minsky and seized the computer in George's lab. And she explained how she'd found George's Tab back at Penrose, and that she suspected it held a locator for Fred Jackson, the security man they'd met the other day at Building One. After sharing her suspicions about Margaret Gates, she convinced Malcolm that calling Fred Jackson was probably their best course of action. Malcolm agreed.

Putting her finger on the Tab, Joanne summoned a window and scrolled through George's contact designators.

Malcolm pointed to a designator labeled *Rainy Day*. "Wait a minute, what's that?"

Joanne mouthed the words as she stared at them; she had no idea what the phrase meant. Other than the occasional precipitation of ice crystals at the poles or the even less frequent sprinkles in the domes, rain on Mars was virtually unknown.

Malcolm asked, "You're not up on Earthly antiquity, are you?"

She looked at him, expectant.

"It's an old Earther expression that means bad times."

She still didn't get it.

Malcolm smiled, "You know, can't go out and play cause it's a rainy day."

She shrugged, "You and George are going to have to teach me this code you have."

She tapped the icon. Two names flashed in blue; the first read *Fred Jackson*, the second read, *Will*.

"Will," Malcolm muttered, "that's the computer isn't it?"

Joanne nodded and slowly tapped the icon marked *Will*. Instantly, another window appeared, this one filled with colorless static—there was no sound.

"What the hell?" Malcolm said.

Joanne had never seen anything like it. If there were no channels available on a Tab, it would always tell you so. The fact that a window had opened indicated an open channel, but open channels preparing to display something were typically blue. She'd never seen static like this before.

"What does it mean?" Malcolm asked.

Joanne ordered, "Channel details."

The Tab displayed a set of changing values in red next to the static filled window. The numbers and monikers indicated video packets arriving from chaotically changing sources, no audio.

Joanne ordered, "Close the window."

The numbers disappeared, but a message remained—*priority override, window not responding.*

"That's interesting," Joanne mumbled. "Something or someone's holding that window open and is overriding the Tab's operating system—neat trick."

They continued watching the dots, dashes, and streaks with hypnotic interest. The static persisted for a couple of minutes, then the screen collapsed into a dot, and the dot faded away.

"What just happened?" Malcolm asked. "Does this mean the computer's still alive?"

"I have no idea," Joanne said.

For a moment, she had hoped that they had finally gotten a break, but whatever it was, it was apparently over. They spent the next few minutes debating the merits of calling the police. Although Void Fleet had arrested George, it was unlikely that Dome Police were unaware of what was going on. Though they hadn't been there when the computer was stolen, a group of men taking tens of millions of credits worth of equipment from a university lab could hardly go unnoticed by the local authorities.

They decided to call Fred Jackson's private locator. When Joanne tapped Jackson's name, a call screen opened and flashed *Dialing,* in red letters, as it sent packets to Jackson's Tab.

Dialing changed to *Connected*, as Jackson's stern face materialized in the window. Joanne saw him struggling to place her.

"Officer Jackson, I'm Joanne Zhu."

"Zhu?" Jackson mumbled. Then she saw recognition in his eyes, as though he'd just remembered the answer to a daunting question.

"Dr. Zhu, you were with George Mills the other day in Dome One, weren't you?"

"Yes, that's right."

She watched his expression change again. The tension in his eyes and tightness in the disposition of his jaw were evidence that he knew something about George's arrest.

"What can I do for you, Doctor?"

The air of formality was a dead giveaway that, whatever he knew, was making him very uncomfortable.

"Call me Joanne."

"What can I do for you, Joanne?"

"I'm calling about George Mills. He was arrested this afternoon."

Jackson remained silent; a strange grimace tightened his face. She had obviously hit a nerve. Jackson stared out from the Tab—the stone bust of a policeman.

"Officer Jackson?"

That shook him out of his stupor. "I'm sorry, Joanne, I can't help you."

There was no finality in his declaration. It was as if he were inviting her to continue trying to convince him. He appeared ill at ease, moving nervously in the window, fighting to uphold something he was struggling to believe in.

"Is it that you can't help me, or that you won't help me, officer Jackson?"

Pause.

"You know something about it, don't you? Something's happened, hasn't it?"

She had to stay calm. His continued refusal to answer and his guilty demeanor were confirming her worst fears. What could he possibly be hiding?

"Listen, officer Jackson," Joanne said slowly, deliberately. "Dr. Mills is a Martian citizen. People who look a lot like Void Fleet officials arrested him today. I can't find out why he was arrested, or even where they took him. Don't you think that I have a right to know what's happened to him, and that Dr. Mills has a right to suitable counsel?"

After a long moment, Jackson asked, "Where are you?"

She told him.

"Can you be here in an hour?"

"Where?"

"Meet me at security headquarters in Dome One in an hour. Can you do that?"

"Yes, yes I can," Joanne said. And with that, his image faded away. The window flashed *Disconnected*, in red letters, then disappeared.

* * *

Joanne waited for Malcolm to take care of the hotel bill. She watched him descend the ancient wooden stairs of the Canal Hotel and start across the dirt parking lot toward the car. The breeze off the water raised swirling dirt devils around his worn shoes as they kicked up small clouds of dust with each reticent step. He lifted the gray and blue plastic door panel without looking at her.

He sat there for a moment, then turned toward her. "You know, we should take the tube to Federal Island instead of driving."

"Wouldn't it be faster to drive?" Joanne asked, pushing her key card into the ignition.

"You haven't been there today, have you?"

She shook her head and sat back.

"There are demonstrations everywhere, most of the streets are cordoned off," Malcolm said.

His lips were barely visible underneath his scraggy unkempt beard, but she could see him smiling.

She exhaled a resigned sigh. "Okay, dome tube it is. Anything else?"

He shook his head, "Let's go."

She pulled out of the Canal Hotel parking lot, heading for the *Sea of Storms*. They followed the expressway to South Lake Geneva, where they caught the inter-dome tube to Federal Island in Dome One.

When they were alone in the tube car, Malcolm said, "Don't worry, I'm sure it's not as bad as it seems."

"So, you think that being arrested by Void Fleet and being held without counsel is normal?"

"I didn't say that. I just meant that we shouldn't assume all this is some kind of interplanetary plot, that's all."

The rest of the ride was spent in an uncomfortable silence, both trying to avoid each other's gaze. When the car finally came to a stop at the downtown station, Malcolm let Joanne be first to the door, and then followed her out.

"I'm sorry," he said. "I'm making this harder on you, aren't I?"

She turned to him, "I could use some support right now. I feel like I'm all alone in this thing. Can you understand that?" She smiled. "I know this is hard to believe, because I'm having trouble believing it myself. If you don't want to be involved anymore, you can walk away right now, I'll understand."

He glanced down at his feet. She put her hand on his arm, "No hard feelings, Malcolm, I mean it."

He put his open hand on her back and gently directed her to the stairs. "Come on, we don't want to be late for the meeting."

The tube station was four stories below the street. As they climbed from floor to floor, they waded through crowds of people shopping, sitting in front of cafes, or just walking around sightseeing. Much of Martian life was conducted underground, and the tube stations were always bustling hubs of activity, especially here, on Federal Island, which was the financial and administrative center of equatorial Mars. Its tube stations and promenades were among the most lavish anywhere on the planet, with their expansive tile murals, exotic desert landscaping, and many exclusive shops made of marble and glass.

As they approached the surface, Joanne noticed a drastic change in the atmosphere. She could hear chants, cheers, and the drumming of bullhorn-amplified speeches grow from an indistinguishable background rumble into an overwhelming wall of sound.

They climbed into the early evening light of the dome and emerged on Federal Island about two blocks northwest of police headquarters, just a few blocks from Building One, the most imposing structure on the island. When they reached the street, Joanne couldn't believe that she'd been here only two days before. In that short time, things had changed completely. There were hundreds of people marching in the road next to the tube exit and an equal number of riot police channeling them between barricades on either side of the street. She couldn't see the base of Building One through the trees, but she could hear the amplified voices of speakers in the direction of the looming edifice. Although there were many more people than the other day, the crowds seemed overtly less hostile. She couldn't help feeling the air of explosive tension though, as if some spark might, at any moment, plunge the scene into total conflagration.

They hurried south toward the police station, joining the throngs of marchers, but staying close to the police barricades. She couldn't help noticing the dirty looks as people passing close to them stared at Malcolm, enflamed by the sight of an unprotected Earther.

Police headquarters was unlike other buildings on Federal Island, which had been built with an aesthetic eye and accented by attractive landscaped grounds. Fort Apache, as the building

was affectionately called, had been built by the first wave of
Terran settlers to arrive on Mars almost a hundred and fifty years
before. It echoed, in its monolithic walls and pillbox thin
rectangular windows, the harsh environment that had greeted the
first settlers. Although it was a relic in the midst of twenty-fourth
century architecture, its austere design somehow suited its
authoritarian purpose, and it had persisted through the many
decades, though it was an eye sore in an otherwise immaculate
garden. Some believed that Terrans had originally given it the
name Forte Apache because they thought that the emerging
Martian race resembled the native North American people back
on Earth. Whatever the reason, the building looked like it was
built to be under siege. It was surrounded by ten-foot concrete
barriers on all sides, with a rod-steel gate the only point of entry
from the street.

As Joanne and Malcolm approached the gate, they were
joined by security men in body armor carrying conventional
rifles over their shoulders and wands hanging from their belts.

"I'm sorry," said one of the security men from behind a
shiny black plastic helmet, "entry is by appointment only."

Joanne explained that officer Fred Jackson was expecting
them.

"You mean, Captain Fred Jackson?"

She looked at Malcolm, then back to the security man.
"Yes, that's right."

The security man, after checking a list of approved persons,
then checking their nucleic markers, waved them through the
gate with apparent misgivings.

Chapter Twenty-Two

Fort Apache was a pentagon with ascending strata, each a bit smaller than the previous one, giving the overall building a pyramid-like shape. The very top, however, did not form a point, but was capped by a five-sided, dark glass observation penthouse. On top of the penthouse was a bizarre set of antennae that completed its outpost ambiance. Joanne and Malcolm walked down a tiled path wide enough to accommodate heavy vans and lined on both sides by palm trees and high hedges. The building was ashen white, the color of volcanic pumice, and had a broad stairway that led to a wide landing in front of the main entrance.

There was no one in the lobby, no attendant's desk or any other obvious way of making their presence known. Not knowing what else to do, they approached a large screen hanging in front of the far wall opposite the entrance. When they were just a couple of feet away, laser beams momentarily doused them in a red grid that flickered over their bodies. Then, as quickly as they'd appeared, the beams vanished. It happened so fast that Joanne wondered if it had actually happened at all. Moments later, the screen came to life, displaying the image of a young Terran in a black Void Fleet tunic, sitting behind a desk of transparent crystal with chrome supports. A holographic Void Fleet emblem floated behind the young man, a spinning globe held in the talons of an eagle with wings spread and olive sprigs crisscrossed in its dagger-like beak. Joanne couldn't tell whether the gatekeeper behind the desk was a real person or an anthropomorphic facsimile; he was a little too perfect, too symmetric, like an image on a recruiting poster.

"Dr. Zhu, Dr. Peters, you're here to see Captain Jackson, is that right?"

Joanne glanced at Malcolm, who appeared more amused than anything else.

"Yes that's right," she replied, turning back to the gatekeeper.

He smiled warmly, "Proceed to the elevators to your left, please. The door will be opening shortly—watch your step and have a good day."

The screen blanked transparent again. Before they could take a step, one of the elevator doors opened.

"Ladies first," Malcolm offered. He stepped aside, extended a hand, and followed Joanne in.

As the elevator rose, she turned to Malcolm. "You're enjoying this, aren't you?"

"I don't know if enjoyment is the right word. It does bring back memories, though."

"Good or bad?"

"Well, let's just say it's a mixed bag. It's interesting being on this side of the looking glass this time."

The elevator door slid open. They stepped out and were greeted by a woman wearing a Mars Planetary Security uniform.

"This way please," she said, then turned and walked briskly down a wide expanse of corridor. Joanne and Malcolm looked at each other.

"Charming," Malcolm observed.

They gave chase. As Joanne hurried down the corridor behind the woman and in front of Malcolm, she noticed scores of young men and women passing in full assault suits with large exotic weapons draped over their shoulders. She got winks, smiles, and occasional whistles from many of the men, and blank up-and-down stares from most of the women.

She fell back next to Malcolm. "What's going on?"

Malcolm shrugged.

It was strange, but in some significant way, she'd learned a lot more about George today, and maybe even more about herself—things she'd conveniently avoided considering before now. Spending the day in mostly Terran company, under the suspicious scrutiny of her fellow Martians, the point had been made abundantly clear. While walking down the street with Malcolm through a sea of angry people, she had seen the disapproving looks. So, this was the kernel of George's life on Mars, a fact she'd always known on some basic level. *On this side of the looking glass,* she recalled Malcolm saying. The look on her mother's face the first time she'd brought George home sprang to mind. It wasn't much different in its silent disapproval from the faces she'd seen in the crowd outside. In all the time she'd known George, he'd never complained, never let on how lonely he must have been. It was humbling to realize how much she'd taken and how little she'd given back. She remembered the look on George's face when she'd met him at the tube terminal the other day. Replaying it now, she saw his appreciation for that small gesture. She was glad that she'd gone to meet him; it was perhaps the last act of kindness she would ever be able to show him.

The security woman led them to a closed door at the far end of the large hall. She knocked on the door in rapid machine-like raps.

"Come in," boomed a voice from inside.

They entered. Jackson was sitting at a table in black assault armor with his helmet drawn back. She noticed a nasty looking weapon propped up on the wall behind him. Its gleaming, slightly rectangular barrel had something written on it. She strained her eyes to read it. *Justice*—she shook her head; the whole world was upside down. And how she missed the old one now, as she wondered whether it would ever be coming back.

"That'll be all, Corporal," Jackson said, fixing Joanne with a stern gaze.

The woman turned on her heels, walked quickly to the door, and closed it behind her as she left. Joanne couldn't help smiling in irony. Jackson was all Martian, big and dark, with his shiny black hair cut unusually short. He had a handsome, well-articulated face with deep-set gray eyes and a strong chin. If she'd come home with him, she mused, her mother would have been beside herself.

"Have a seat folks," Jackson said in a somber voice. "We don't have much time—so how can I help you?"

"Officer Jackson," Joanne said. "Can you help us find out what's happened to George Mills? As you probably know, he was arrested by Void Fleet earlier today."

"I don't represent Void Fleet, Joanne."

She looked at Malcolm in frustration, then back to Jackson. "That may be the case, officer Jackson, but I certainly saw a lot of Terrans out in the hall just now, not to mention that big Void Fleet emblem behind your gatekeeper down stairs."

Jackson looked pained.

"Come on, Fred," she said. "I know there's something you're not telling me. I knew it when we talked earlier today. What's the problem? Why are you being so evasive? I thought you were George's friend. That's why I called you."

Jackson sat back. "What the hell," he said. "Listen Joanne, I have some bad news for you."

She felt herself cringe.

"What is it, Captain?" Malcolm asked. He edged forward in his chair.

"I'm sorry to be the one to have to tell you this, Joanne, but Mills was kidnapped earlier today from the airport along with his escorts."

Joanne blinked in astonishment; this wasn't what she'd been expecting to hear.

"What? What are you talking about? Kidnapped by whom?"

"By a militant separatist group called Red Dawn."

"Why in the world would Red Dawn be interested in George?"

"I don't think they are, I think they were probably interested in the two high ranking Void Fleet officers that arrested him. Mills was just an unfortunate bystander."

Joanne turned to Malcolm. "Damn that Margaret," she hissed under her breath.

"Who?" Jackson asked.

She turned back to Jackson, ignoring the question.

"What are you doing to get him back?"

Jackson told them about the firefight at the airport, the landing in the southern desert, and the Void Fleet platoon trying to recover Mills and the others.

Joanne hesitated a moment. "I think you're probably looking in the wrong place."

Jackson narrowed his eyes. "What do you know about this?"

"Nothing," Joanne said, "nothing at all, except that there's no one in the southern desert—everybody knows that."

"Oh," Jackson said, "and how do you know that?"

"For goodness sake, Fred, I've lived here all my life, just like you. The separatists have been around forever. There isn't a Martian that doesn't know someone associated with them, at least casually. There are all kinds of rumors about Red Dawn; it's the most well know secret on the planet. Wherever they're hiding, it's closer to the domes. I know very little about these things, but I know enough to understand that supplying and moving large numbers of people in the southern desert would be too risky. Things are so sparse out there. They'd be spotted sooner or later, there are too many orbital platforms looking down."

Jackson smiled for the first time since she'd met him. "Mills is a lucky man," he remarked. "If I ever go missing, I could only be so lucky as to have someone like you out there looking for me."

Jackson paused a moment. "We've actually reached the same conclusion. We think that thing down south was just a ploy to draw us away. We're going to work with Void Fleet closer to the domes. That's all I can say right now. I'll be in touch when we have more information."

Joanne's eyes were fixed on Jackson. Finally, Jackson got up and started for the door.

"I want to come along," Joanne declared, as Jackson stepped around her.

"What?" Jackson said.

"Take me with you to look for George. I know the northern desert. I know it very well; I know I can help you find him."

Even Malcolm stared at her in disbelief.

"That's out of the question," Jackson said.

"Why?"

"Are you crazy, lady? We'll be going into a war zone. These people are very well armed; they've already killed several professional soldiers today. There's no way in hell I could take you. You'd probably get one of us killed if those bastards didn't kill you first."

Joanne started to speak, but Jackson waved her off. "Not another word," he hissed, straining not to raise his voice.

As he started for the door again, there was a heavy knock.

"Damn-it," Jackson barked. "Come in!"

Malcolm and Joanne turned to see a large Earther enter the room. He wore a combat suit unlike any other they'd seen while at Fort Apache. It had burn marks all over and smelled as if it'd been thrown into a hot fire. The pungent tang of burnt carbon and plastic followed him into the room. The man was definitely Terran, dark black with deep blue eyes, wooly blonde hair cut short on the sides and flat on top, with a protruding overhang in front of his face, giving him an edgy, angular look.

The man scanned the room and settled on Joanne. The presence of a civilian woman seemed to dissipate some of the tension Joanne had sensed when he'd first come in.

"Who're your friends?" Dean asked.

"They were just leaving," Jackson said. "Are we ready to move?"

"We're waiting on you, Captain; the men are itchin to get back out there."

Malcolm and Joanne got up and started past Dean.

Jackson said, "Dean, give me a minute, okay? I'm going to see them to the elevator."

Dean smiled and nodded. "I'll wait in your office. That's if you don't mind, Captain."

Jackson feigned sniffing the burnt air that hung around Dean like an invisible cloud. "Just don't stink up my favorite chair, okay?" Jackson turned and shuffled awkwardly to the door.

Joanne followed Malcolm and Jackson out of the office, glancing back just in time to catch the black Terran winking at her. She gave a tired smile and closed the door.

She hurried down the corridor and joined Malcolm and Jackson waiting for the elevator. "Listen," Jackson said as she drew up next to him. "I think I know what you're going through, but I'll be damned if I'm going to put you in harm's way. You understand, don't you?"

Joanne nodded and followed Malcolm into the elevator. As they stood in the lift, she watched Jackson in the corridor. There was a pained look in his drawn features. In another instant, the door slid smoothly over his lonely figure and he was gone.

* * *

Jackson stood there for a moment, staring at the curved gray composite doors. He couldn't help but admire Joanne and winced at all the contradictions she'd dug up in that sparring match back in his office. The disappointment in her pale eyes had been haunting. It was as if that blank door that had taken her away could somehow bestow some much-needed absolution for his ethical torments, but none was forthcoming. Eventually, he shook his head, turned, and hurried back to his office.

* * *

207

They left Fort Apache heading for the tube station; Joanne hadn't said a word since leaving Jackson's office. She was walking quickly toward the underground, eyes straight ahead.

"Joanne?"

"Yes," she muttered, not looking at him.

"Are you okay?"

"Uh, yeah."

"Are you sure?"

She slowed, stopped, then turned and took his hand. People swirled all around them; the chaotic sounds of a world in transition enveloped them. It was early evening and the streetlights had come on. Floating platforms with message panels informed the citizenry below that a curfew would be in effect in another half hour.

"Thanks for coming here, you're a good friend," Joanne said.

The color of her pale eyes was lost in the dim light. Malcolm noticed the corners of her mouth turned up in a grateful smile. "What are you going to do?" he asked.

"I'm going to find George."

"Listen Joanne, that's crazy. Jackson's right about getting killed."

"Maybe," she admitted, "but I've got a feeling that if I don't try, and they end up not finding him, or he turns up dead, I'll regret not trying for the rest of my life."

"Mills would be very angry if he knew what you were doing."

"I know," Joanne said in an absent voice. She paused a moment, then continued, "For the last ten years I've been closer to him than I have to my own family. Though George has fancied himself a Martian, he has very few roots here. From what he's told me, that's probably true for whatever life he had on Earth as well. I'm probably all he's got. He'd never admit it, but I'm as close to a family as anything he's ever really known— as pathetic as that sounds."

She looked around at the sea of people as they brushed by.

"If we weren't here looking for him, who would be? I can't let him go down like this, I wouldn't!"

Malcolm searched her eyes and couldn't find any indictment of him in them. She wasn't asking him to follow and wasn't blaming him for not sharing her commitment to Mills.

"Okay," he said resolutely, "I'm in. I'll be damned if I'm going to let you do this alone."

"I don't want you to come, Malcolm."

"I'm not asking you, I'm telling you. At least I have military training. Our chances of coming out of this together are…"

"Are what?" she asked, smiling now.

"Remote," he said, "as opposed to nonexistent."

Chapter Twenty-Three

The consciousness that had been George Mills slowly began reconstituting itself, like sticky clumps of liquid finding their many droplets and coalescing into a larger whole. There was the memory of a dark young woman with light blue eyes and sun sparkled brown hair. She was sitting on something that seemed to be moving or rocking somehow. And even though he couldn't tell exactly what it was, he did feel a nausea bubbling up in the pit of his stomach. She was laughing. He watched as her lips moved in silent utterances. He strained to hear in frustration, but it made no difference. He imagined the sound of her voice and longed for its soothing familiarity. She was pointing to something up in the air, and he momentarily abandoned his efforts at hearing and tried to look up. It was a sail, a colorful spinnaker, which was slowly losing the wind and beginning to luff. Then he heard water slapping the sides of a fiberglass hull in thick gurgles, and finally started hearing the woman's full melodic voice.

"You're losing the wind."

The image faded with the contrast of her face melting into the bright pink sky above her. He tried as hard as he could to hold her face in his mind's eye, but it slowly vanished into the featureless firmament. A great depression pulled him down, overcoming him like the hopelessness of slipping from a ledge and being left with only the inevitability of the void.

Then, as suddenly as it had appeared, the panic subsided. He thought of a name, *Will*. Will, he thought, but frustration returned when he failed to place a face to that name. He knew Will was real, so why couldn't he remember what Will looked like? The effort to remember forced him to move his mouth as he uttered, "Will," over and over again. A foul taste brought him closer to consciousness. Then, he felt it, the splitting pain in his head. He winced at the pressure on his head; it was pressed against something. He struggled to open his eyes. They felt as if they were glued shut, but he finally worked them open against a cakey seal stuck to his eyelids. He began to see out of one eye, although it was blurry and stung terribly. Panic started welling up again at the thought that he might be blind in his other eye. Then he realized he was lying on his stomach; one of his eyes was pressed against a fabric of some kind. It was coarse, with the feel of greasy dirt—human dirt. It smelled bad too. He tried to turn over, and after several painful tries, was able to right himself and lean against a wall. Through blurry eyes, he saw he was sitting on a foul, rancid mattress, stained black and yellow by things he didn't want to think about.

Turning slowly, he took stock of his surroundings. There was a young woman looking at him from across a barren room with cracked dirty clay walls. Odd colored hair and a doll-like face gave her the quality of a hallucination. No, he remembered now, Margaret. That was it; her name was Margaret. He tried to speak, but his throat was so dry and swollen that he began to cough. As he sat there, fitfully convulsing, Margaret came over to him and put a cup of water to his mouth. He drank greedily and began coughing again, hacking and spitting all over her hand.

"Slow down, Mills," she said, pulling the cup away. "Slow down, take it slow."

She gave him the water again; this time he took it in small sips.

"You've been drugged," she told him. "It'll take a while to feel better, just relax."

"Thank you," George whispered in a low rasp, barely able to look up at her.

She smiled kindly, but said nothing. Then she rose and walked over to a man whose back was to him. The man leaned on the wall next to a door, looking out the metal grade that covered the small rectangular slit of a window.

"How's he doing?" George heard the man say.

It was Wells, Matt Wells; George recognized the voice.

It took George some time to regain his senses. He decided to take Margaret's advice and sat up, slowly letting the water and his upright posture clear his head. He tried to recall the sequence of events that had landed him here, wherever here was.

He tried to stand, drawing his knees up and putting his heels as close to his butt as he could. He straightened his legs, pushing his body up, using the wall behind him for support. He was able to make it about two thirds of the way up when he felt nausea and vertigo hit him. Stopping for a moment, he caught his breath, then straightened the rest of the way. He waited a few seconds for his balance to return.

It was a dingy room, about fifteen feet square, with stained reddish concrete walls. They were cool to the touch, but not icy cold, indicating he must be underground. Three dirty mattresses lay on the floor, and a chemical toilet in the corner reeked strong and sour. George felt a tight knot in his stomach.

Margaret and Wells stood whispering on the other side of the room. George strained to hear what they were saying, but they were too far away. For some reason that annoyed him. Launching himself away from the wall, George took a couple of spastic steps and staggered in their direction.

Wells looked up. "How are you feeling?"

Margaret smiled weakly and knitted her brow.

"I'm better now. What happened, where are we?" George said.

Margaret glanced at Wells.

"We were hijacked, kidnapped, stunned, and drugged," Wells said.

"Drugged?"

"Yes, that's right, Mills. You've been out for about six hours."

"Six hours—where are we?" George asked.

"Your guess is as good as mine, but I'd say we're underground somewhere north of the domes," Margaret said.

"Why?" George asked. "Why were we kidnapped?"

Margaret looked at him, then nodded toward the door.

"Unfortunately Mills, we'll be finding that out in just a few moments."

George heard heavy footsteps echoing off the cement walls outside the small barred window of their cell. The cell door was low-quality metal, and George guessed by the spots of rust that dotted its surface that it was pretty old. There were no pneumatic actuators or artificial muscles here, only rusty hinges. Through the window, George saw a shadow start to form on the wall opposite the door. He could tell by the dimple in the shadow and the beat of footsteps that there were probably two people coming. A large brown face appeared in the window, its neutrality betraying no emotion. The dark eyes that peered through the bars were flat, like those of a goat.

"Get back from the door," the man barked impatiently.

They hesitated, and the man sneered, then yelled, "Get back, damn-it!"

They did as they were told. George felt a vibration around his wrists and waist, like the feeling of being near a high voltage line.

"What the hell?" George said.

Suddenly, his hands shot out in front of him and stuck violently together, then shot in toward his body and stuck to his waist. George saw dark metal bracelets on his wrists and a belt of the same material around his waist. He hadn't noticed them before, perhaps because he'd been so groggy. Glancing toward Margaret and Wells, he saw that the same thing had happened to them.

George heard the sound of a bolt being drawn and saw the door swing open. The big man, whose face he'd seen in the window, came into the cell. A second man remained in the corridor. Now that he had a chance to glimpse the entire man, not just his face, George felt even more repulsed than before. He was large and heavy set with thick hands, one of which held a wand down at his side. Turning to face them, the man surveyed the prisoners and sneered, "Get out of the cell!"

George walked through the door, followed by Margaret then Wells.

Once outside the cell, George noticed that the other man was younger and more appealing than his friend. "Follow me please," he ordered, almost apologetically.

George got in line behind the man and began walking down a dingy concrete corridor. He saw several long misshapen shadows cast at odd angles along the walls that seemed to follow them as they advanced. Turning, he saw that the big man was stationed behind Margaret and Wells, cutting off any escape.

"Turn around," the man at the end of the line ordered when he saw George staring. George turned and continued marching down the endless corridor. On their trek, they passed several more doors, some with barred windows, some without. George felt as if he'd descended into some impossible gothic nightmare. How could this be happening? One minute, he was in a space-plane on his way into orbit, the next minute, he was here.

Finally, they came to a door and stopped. This one had no window. The man inserted a metal key into an antique lock, turned it, and pushed the door open. This room was different from the other places George had seen down here. It was clean. That observation was confirmed by the fact that he could no longer smell the sickly tang of warm urine, a smell that was so pervasive in these rooms and corridors that it took him a minute or two to become aware of its absence. The room was painted a clinical white, not the rust red of most of this mock prison. An instrumented chair was anchored to the concrete floor on a rotating pedestal in the middle of the room. To one side of the chair was a stainless steel cart on casters, with several objects neatly laid on top of a white cloth. They could have been medical instruments, although George was too far away to be certain. At the far end of the room, in shadow, beyond the light suspended over the chair, was the silhouette of a man sitting at a desk. The man who had unlocked the door and let them in now led the three captives to a backless bench along the wall to the left of the large chair. When everyone had found their place, the man in the shadows turned toward them. Though his eyes had adjusted to the harsh light, George still couldn't make out the man's fine features, but he could discern gross movements.

"As you know," the man began, "we are the citizens of Mars, the true citizens. We have been here for generations. We have committed ourselves and our families to this place. This has put us in direct competition with Earth, with whom we've been at war for over a hundred years. We have been exploited, humiliated, and even killed in mass by the very people that call us terrorists. They claim some moral high ground, while all the time stealing our riches and living without morals or ethics."

George listened to the man's speech, and to his surprise, recognized the man's voice.

"So, given these facts," the man continued, "I want to inform you that we, the people's army—Red Dawn—consider you prisoners of war. As such, it is our responsibility to require you to answer questions relevant to our cause. Failure to do so will force us to resort to, well, let us say, measures that we would prefer not to invoke. Are there any questions?"

Wells looked at Margaret, then back at the man.

"If you are an army," Wells said, "you must be part of a greater political movement that has earned legitimacy in the eyes of human societies here in the solar system. Furthermore, the articles of war require that you wear uniforms representative of that political body."

Wells looked around the room. "Your men don't seem to conform to any of these standards. This looks more like a gang, a bunch of thugs, than a political movement. More of an excuse to practice selective vengeance than anything else."

Wells sat down, appearing satisfied that he had made his point. He had let the man know that a criminal demigod could not veil his brand of terrorism with the façade of legitimacy.

George, on the other hand, winced. He had analyzed too many simulations of situations like this one. He had learned that the leaders of rebel armies were often emotionally unstable. Pushing them like this could lead to very negative contrary behavior.

There was a moment's silence. During Wells' speech, George had watched the man behind the desk carefully, looking for telltale signs of anger or restlessness. He hadn't so much as moved a muscle. Then the man in the shadows spoke again. Whereas before he'd been smooth and diplomatic, now he had venom in his voice. His words were slow and strained, as if he were trying hard not to seem out of control.

"How convenient for you, Mr. Wells—you, and your rules. You know the rules, the ones you make up to suit your purposes. You make the rules, and you can't lose, isn't that right? If we follow your rules, we lose. If we don't follow your rules, you arrest us. And what are these greater societies you speak about? You mean your governor here on Mars? There is only one society, the one you permit to exist."

The man in the shadows got up from his chair, but remained standing in the dark. George could see he was tall and well built, but he still couldn't see the man's face.

"As far as uniforms, Mr. Wells, apparently you weren't wearing yours when you came to our planet to arrest Dr. Mills here." He pointed to George.

George was fascinated by how well informed the man was. At the mention of his name, he struggled to find some words that might defuse the situation.

"Excuse me," George said. "Can I please say something?"

George used the most considerate tone he could muster. He had learned from simulations that behavior in circumstances like these often reflected primate behavior of dominance and submission. He knew that acknowledging the man's authority was a more promising tack than confrontation.

"Of course," said the man graciously. "And may I say that in your case, Dr. Mills, it is an unfortunate turn of events that you're here today. Unlike the two enemies of the people you're sitting next to, Red Dawn harbors no ill will toward you. We would, however, like to know why Void Fleet felt compelled to arrest you."

The man chuckled uncharacteristically, "Perhaps the enemy of our enemy could be our friend."

"Yes," said George. "In fact, I'd like to answer that question."

Although he could not see it, he imagined the man smiling in the dark.

"As you probably know, being so well informed, I'm a professor at the university. My team and I have been working on behavior. Or more precisely, on how to model behavior in more detail than was previously possible."

As George took a breath, Wells barked, "Shut up, Mills!"

At that, the big man, who'd been sitting behind the cart on the far side of the room, got up and shot in front of Wells. His quickness momentarily stunned George into silence. The big man raised his hand high, then slapped Wells hard across the face, snapping his head to the side violently. George felt the spittle from Wells' open mouth on his face after the loud slap. The man towered over Wells and just stared down at him, his eyes cold and impassive, his mouth set in a menacing smile. George saw the fear in Wells' eyes.

"Please continue, Dr. Mills," the man in the shadows said.

George looked around cautiously. "Could you ask your associate to sit down; he makes me nervous."

There was a pause, "Please sit down, Hector; you seem to make Dr. Mills nervous."

"Thank you," George said.

"Please go on, Doctor."

"I think the reason Void Fleet arrested me is because they wanted me to show them how to run these new, more detailed simulations."

"Of what, Doctor?

What?" George asked.

"What did they want you to simulate?" the man repeated, impatience evident in his voice.

George looked down at Wells, who seemed to have regained his senses. He was staring straight ahead.

"They apparently want to simulate the conflict here on Mars," George said.

"I see," said the man. "They want to use your technique to develop a tactical plan against us. That's very interesting. Thank you, Doctor, maybe we can discuss this further some other time."

"I'd like to add something," George said. "Something that I think is more relevant right now than a plan of attack."

"Go on," the man said after a brief hesitation.

"We've run many of these simulations now. In fact, we've been running them almost continuously over the last ten years. The basic scenarios that we've modeled have been based on the most complete historical data of human conflict we could compile. Many times, it was armed conflict. We did this because we were trying to understand the fundamental basis of the human psyche in this regard. If you study history, what you soon discover is that people are involved in armed conflict of one kind or another most of the time. Peaceful coexistence is the exception. The occurrences of violent conflict are too numerous, too ubiquitous, to be situational or accidental."

"What are you trying to say?" the man asked. He was clearly intrigued.

"If you analyze the positions of the combatants," George continued, "they often present a compelling case for their side, just as you did earlier."

George hoped that personalizing it at this point wasn't a mistake, but something told him this was the right move.

He continued. "The logical and historical problem with this is that the conflict itself almost never appears to settle the underlying issues. That's why the end of one conflict is typically the starting justification for the next. History, human history, is mostly just a long standing chain of armed conflicts that seem to serve no other purpose than to perpetuate themselves, each with passionate justification, but seldom serving the intended purpose. On the contrary, most of the time the last conflict only serves to set the stage for the next conflict. And often, the seeds of the last conflict include institutional class or ethnic hatred, which is genetically absurd when considering a single species, since a species requires genetic diversity to thrive."

George let the silence linger. Even Margaret was looking his way now.

"Most of the exceptions to what I've just described are, unfortunately, anomalous."

"Oh?" asked the man in the shadows.

George knew that the man would now expect some inspired advice that would somehow enable him to overcome his enemies. Some new weapon or strategy that would lead him ever deeper into the pit he'd just described. That's what he imagined they always expected of their magicians or scientists, but that's not quite what George had to offer.

"Most of these exceptions have to do with a charismatic popular leader who chooses not to convince his or her followers to pursue the obvious violent course, but instead elects to follow a peaceful route as an exemplar of the group's principles. Examples of these individuals include such people as Jesus Christ, Ghandi, Martin Luther King. These were leaders that made an objective, substantive difference in the course of human history."

"Turn the other cheek!" the man said bitterly.

"Yes," George said, "that's right. It takes more patience, but in the end, it has been shown to produce better, more long lasting results."

"I'm sorry Doctor, you're obviously a naive dreamer. Both my cheeks are already bloody. Please sit down, you have nothing to offer."

George sat. What did he expect? The simulations had predicted that, given the human psyche, this approach had little chance of success. To his surprise, however, he heard Margaret say, in a barely audible whisper, "Nice try, Mills."

"Okay Hector," the man said, "why don't we start with Captain Wells, since we have so much in common."

Hector went to where Wells was sitting, grabbed him by his cuffed arms, and yanked him to his feet. Wells resisted, which seemed to please Hector, giving him an excuse to abuse Wells further, although George doubted an excuse was really necessary. He punched Wells in the stomach, knocking the wind out of him. Wells doubled over and clenched his teeth, but made no sound.

George couldn't help standing up at the sight of Wells' beating, momentarily forgetting about the consequences such an act might bring. He appealed to the man in the shadows to rein in his henchman, and was rewarded for his efforts by a quick backhand across the face.

George had barely seen it coming; the big man dragged Wells by the arms to where George stood and struck him, sending him backwards onto the bench. He slid across the bench, fell, and hit the concrete floor hard with his right shoulder, which immediately radiated a shooting pain throughout his upper body. He lay there stunned for a moment before he realized how vulnerable he was on his stomach. The man could easily kick him and snap his spine. George tried to scramble to his feet, but getting up was awkward with his arms magnetically locked to his waist. The best he could do, after a concerted effort, was to struggle into a sitting position with his back against the bench. He flinched as he felt hands grab him. Just as he steeled himself in anticipation of another blow, he turned and saw that Margaret had scooted to the end of the bench and was pulling him up. As he regained his seat, Margaret leaned over and whispered, "Shut up, Mills, just stay quiet!"

By the time George had a chance to find Wells again, he saw that Hector had put him into the instrumented chair. The chair's arms were fitted with magnetic straps, as were the leg rests and head support. Hector applied them with practiced ease; he'd obviously done this before. Once Wells had been secured, the man in the shadows finally stepped into the light.

George could see him clearly now. The man was dark, with a long, handsome, well-sculpted face and a neatly cut black ponytail that hung down his back. George had seen him from a distance that day, but there was no mistaking him now. The name *Vega* came to George as he recalled the cheers of the crowd that had almost killed him at Building One. Vega stood to one side of Hector and glared down at Wells' face. Then he smiled sympathetically.

"All right, Captain Wells. We need only one thing from you. If you cooperate, you and your friends will be released unharmed."

Wells said nothing, but continued to look at Vega with contempt. This was exactly what Vega wanted. George could see how amused he was at the prospect of tormenting a defiant man. Wells was playing right into the man's psychosis.

"No you won't, or yes you will cooperate, Captain?" Vega taunted, still having fun. "Well, let's see, all we need are your landing codes and this can all be over right now."

"You know that's not true," Wells said, his voice surprising steady for a man in his position. "If I give you the landing codes, you'll have to kill us, since letting us go would compromise any action you might take by using them. No matter what I do," Wells said, "I'm a dead man."

Vega laughed. "Very good, Captain, but you do get to choose between a quick painless death and a slow agonizing one."

Wells smiled in a strained mask of disgust, "With a lying coward like you, all I can expect is the worst."

George couldn't believe it. With every defiant statement, Wells was provoking his interrogator into whatever dark places he was prepared to go. George's throat was dry, and he noticed that he hadn't taken a breath in a while. He exhaled, and dared to look at Margaret seated next to him. Her eyes were closed. She seemed peaceful, perhaps asleep with her head resting on the hard cold wall behind them. Was this her way of coping? Had she chosen to just tune everything out?

"Besides," Wells continued. "Those codes wouldn't do you any good; they've been changed by now."

"The communications and personal landing codes perhaps," agreed Vega, "but not the resupply codes. We have it on good authority that resupply personnel are still using unchanged codes, albeit under stricter scrutiny. On the other hand, let's say you escape, commandeer a space-plane, and make a quick return to your ship, all the while flashing your correct code. How close to your ship do you think a space-plane could get? What if it were being pursued by other hostile craft? Who knows, it might even get inside," Vega said with a broad smile.

Wells struggled in vain against his restraints. Margaret exhaled. Vega turned to Hector, "Persuade the Captain to cooperate."

Hector nodded and went to the cart. Vega slid back into the shadows again.

Vega was clearly psychotic; there was no telling what he was capable of. Despite his well-articulated political machinations, and his appealing appearance, the man was obviously mad. At some point in his hatred of Earthers, he had crossed the line between political crusader and callous despot, and in George's opinion, he had never noticed the passing.

Hector picked up a syringe from the cart and tapped it with his index finger. Selecting an opportune place on Wells' forearm, he plunged the sharp tip of the instrument into Wells' flesh and pressed down on the plunger. Wells struggled for a few minutes, then was overcome and went limp. George could see his eyelids fluttering as his head turned from side to side. He moaned in low agonizing spurts.

"What's going on?" George demanded. "What did you give him?"

"Don't worry Doctor, not yet at least," Vega said. "It's a synthetic opiate that affects the synapses of the hypothalamus. It heightens fear response, among other things; it's quite addictive. Captain Wells will be a desperate addict after the next injection. He'll be begging to tell me anything I want to know for another fix."

"This is wrong," George exclaimed. "You must see that. For the sake of your own integrity, stop this now. Nothing that you gain this way could possibly turn out right for your people."

Vega said nothing. Hector stood over Wells, hitting him in the face numerous times, sometimes in quick succession, constantly asking him for the codes. At first Wells flinched when he was hit, then he started to scream. It was the high-pitched whine of someone who had lost control that George found hardest to endure. George noticed a stream of yellow liquid dripping from the chair and pooling on the floor. Wells had peed his pants. George noticed the other man, the one who had led them to the room, was looking at the floor, refusing to acknowledge the sickening scene.

After about a half hour of vicious beatings, Wells was delirious, mumbling gibberish, and bleeding from his nose and mouth. Hector looked at Vega for direction; even he realized that much more of this would leave Wells permanently useless. George found it unsettling that the big man, a sadist, had stopped the beating before Vega had requested it. Vega was even more demented than George had thought.

Vega made a motion of the hand and Hector released Wells from the chair. His body racked with spasms, Wells leaped from the chair and fell like a rag doll in a heap on the floor. As he tried to crawl away, Hector casually walked over and stunned him in the back with a wand. George saw blue smoke rise up from Wells as he jerked, then lay motionless on the floor, face down. Hector grabbed him through the arms and under the chest and dragged him out of the room.

Chapter Twenty-Four

Ten minutes later, Vega's thugs returned without Wells. Vega had said nothing during their absence; he'd only sat there in the shadows, like some demented judge, jury, and executioner. George had the feeling, although he couldn't see the madman's eyes, that Vega had been staring at them all the while.

"Okay," Vega said, "I guess it's Dr. Gates' turn."

George heard Margaret exhale softly as Vega uttered those words.

"Please," George said. "Stop this now."

Hector was on him in a flash, grabbing him around the neck with his huge hand and squeezing hard. George struggled for breath, his hands pinned to his waist. He could feel the burning in his throat, the pounding of his heart in the constricted carotid artery in his neck. The man was tremendously strong. George felt himself start to faint as the man released him, then he slumped backward and fell onto the bench.

George sat helplessly, struggling for breath, as he watched Hector strap Margaret into the chair, as he had Wells. The sight made George cough violently and almost vomit before he was able to regain his equilibrium. When his eyes finally cleared, he looked up just in time to see Hector giving Margaret the injection. Unlike Wells, she didn't struggle, she kept her eyes closed and just laid there. Hector began asking her for the codes, and was about to hit her, when Vega stopped him.

"Let's try something a little different with Dr. Gates."

Hector lowered his large hand and picked up the wand.

"Don't burn her," Vega said.

George saw Margaret's eyes begin to flutter under their lids; the drug was taking effect. Hector touched her on the shoulder. She flinched and bared her teeth. He asked her for the codes and touched the wand to her shoulder, stomach, and hands. She continued closing her eyes and moving her head from side to side, but didn't make a sound. George could see Vega in the shadows, stirring, becoming impatient.

"Damn-it," he yelled, "I want you to make the bitch talk!"

Hector contorted his lips into a grisly smile. He unzipped Margaret's jump suit, lowered the sleeves, and pushed it down around her stomach, exposing her breasts. He rubbed the wand over her breasts, letting it linger against her nipples, trying to heighten the drug induced fear response. He pulled the trigger on the wand. Margaret shook, and tears streamed from her clenched eyes. Hector repeated this several times and Margaret screamed and began crying uncontrollably.

George could only stare at the chair with his mouth agape and his eyes unblinking. He had never imagined seeing anything like this. Hector put the wand in between her legs and Margaret screamed in fear.

The scream shook George loose. He felt his body flush with adrenaline. White-hot anger and outrage coursed through him. His arms were bound, but not his feet. Without so much as a sound, he shot up and ran across the room before anybody noticed he'd moved. He sprang over the low part of the chair, and with his shoulder, threw a body block across Hector's chest at full speed, knocking him down.

Scrambling over Hector, George retrieved the wand before Hector could stop him. Holding it in his pinned hands, with his finger on the trigger, he turned on his knees and somehow jumped to his feet. Hector came up at the same time, and as he raised his face to find George, George pushed the wand onto his cheek and pulled the trigger. Hector grunted and fell back on his hands and knees. The man was just too tough. He rested on all fours for a second and began to rise again. George felt cold fear shoot through him. He turned the wand's setting completely clockwise—full power. When he looked up again, Hector was staring at him with red crazed eyes. George shot forward, jabbed the wand into his face before he could stand, then pulled the trigger. The business end of the wand threw blue-white sparks, and smoke rose from Hector's burnt flesh. Hector screamed, convulsed violently, then fell back; he didn't get up. His arms were thrown out, bent as if he were reaching for something, and his unseeing eyes stared at the ceiling.

Suddenly, George saw a shadow forming across Hector's body. The other man, who had apparently been taken by surprise, was coming up behind him—fast. George rolled to his right as a wand just missed him. Now, lying on the floor, George spun around on his back and pulled his knees up to his chest. The man lunged at him again, wand poised in his right hand. George kicked as hard as he could with both feet and connected with the man's hand, sending the wand spinning off into the room somewhere. As the man turned and scrambled to retrieve it, George sprang to his feet and chased him across the room. The man bent down to grab the wand, but George was on him. George planted his wand at the base of the man's skull and pressed the trigger. The man shook and fell forward; he wasn't getting up either.

George looked around the room; Vega was gone. He found himself breathing hard, standing over the fallen man. The blind energy that had allowed him to attack the two men with such strength slowly drained from his body. He stood there spent, sweating hard, and feeling sick.

Vega had run out of the room, but he would be coming back with more men. George scanned the room again. Surely it had been equipped with monitoring devices, as must be true for most of this complex, including the corridors. Their enemies would know exactly where to find them. How could they escape under the weight of this crushing disadvantage? He looked at his cuffed hands; first he'd have to get out of these restraints. He leaned down, rolled the man over, and rifled through his pockets.

Good! George came up with a Tab and a small circular plastic disk. A set of colored buttons formed a semicircle near the lower edge of the disk, just below a screen. George pushed one of the buttons repeatedly, scrolling through a list of numbers that appeared on the screen. He remembered he was the first to have his arms pinned. He dialed a one on the screen, then pushed the green button. Instantly, he felt the electrical tension in the cuffs disappear and his arms came free of his waist. He pushed the button with an open circle above it, and the cuffs from his wrist and waist fell to the floor in a series of metallic clangs.

George tried to clear his head. He'd have to make all the right moves, in the right order, if they were going to have any chance of getting out of here alive. Looking to the instrumented chair, he saw Margaret lying there, exposed and moaning. He hurried to the chair, grabbed it with both hands for leverage, and with his foot, shoved Hector's limp body away from the chair's base. He had watched as Hector had secured first Wells, then Margaret, and thought he remembered the general location of the controls. He found a set of switches on the side of the chair where he'd seen Hector's hands go when activating the restraints. He flipped them, and was rewarded with the opening of magnetic straps around Margaret's wrists, legs, and neck. Putting his arm around Margaret's back, he propped her up. Her head dangled limply to one side, as she unconsciously licked her lips over and over again. She mumbled incoherently. Although she was small, he struggled against dead weight, trying hard to keep her from falling out of the chair.

"Can you sit?" George asked softly.

She tensed. "Mills, is that you?"

"Don't worry, it's me—Mills. You're safe. You're going to be all right."

Her panic subsided; she tried to open her eyes. He zipped her jumpsuit up. She was struggling back to consciousness.

"Mills?" she mumbled.

"Yes, it's me. You're going to be all right."

"Thank you," she said, and leaned her head on his shoulder. Tears left trails down her cheeks.

He dialed two on the disk and removed her cuffs, then he laid her back in the chair.

"Just rest a second, okay?"

"You're not leaving me, are you?" she whispered in a panic.

"No, I'll be right here."

He pulled the Tab from his pocket and expanded it. Good, it had been left active. It would have been difficult to get the password from the dead man on the floor. He found a blank channel designator and raised a keyboard. He typed in a network ID that only he knew, and launched it. A screen appeared and quickly filled with static. He put the Tab down, letting it work a while, and lifted Margaret from the chair. George walked her around the room.

"You're going to have to wake up. We have to get out of here. Soon that madman will be back with his friends."

She nodded, trying to walk on her own. Given what she'd been through; she was remarkably resilient.

"Can you do this by yourself for a moment?"

"Yeah," she said in a breathy whisper.

George returned to the Tab. The Com window was clear, the static gone. He typed, "I need help with monitoring devices and floor plan."

After a few seconds, words appeared in the window. "Have acquired local network; all monitoring devices neutralized, floor plan sent."

The words faded, and an adjacent window appeared with a diagram showing corridors and rooms. Some of the rooms were annotated, and one was marked with a blinking red *X*. Sensing that someone was coming up behind him, George spun around and cocked a fist. Margaret stood there, bobbing unsteadily, then flinched at the prospect of being hit again.

"What are you doing?" she said, struggling to compose herself.

He relaxed, "I'm sorry. Listen, we have to get out of here, right now. They'll be here any minute."

She looked at him with glassy eyes, then reached for him, steadied herself, and put her head on his shoulder.

"Okay," she whispered.

They moved to the door, opened it quickly, and looked up and down the dingy corridor—nothing. Rushing out of the room, they turned left and swept forward in a slow jog.

George had tried to study the map before putting the Tab away. He decided to go in the direction of what he thought was the nerve center of the complex, instead of back toward the cells. His stomach churned at the thought of leaving Wells, but they couldn't go back, couldn't be captured. Being taken again would mean certain death, codes or no codes.

Shadows grew on the far wall. They were getting closer. George heard echoes of footfalls. To his left, he saw a windowless door and reached for it. With his heart racing, he pulled the handle and they slipped inside.

It was dark, the only light coming from the crack of the open door. He needed something dense to hide behind. Vega's men might have enhanced vision helmets with x-ray optics. He spotted a large metal cylinder on the floor a few feet away. The sound of people outside forced him to slowly close the door, throwing the room into total darkness. Remembering the mental image of the room, he slowly led Margaret to where he thought the cylinder was. They inched forward, taking quick small steps and feeling around with their hands. He could hear muffled voices coming from the corridor outside. Finally, he felt the smooth cold surface of the cylinder. They scooted behind it and lay down, pressing against each other as much as possible. Just as they squeezed into place, the door opened, flooding the room with red light from the corridor. Seconds later, the door closed.

They decided to lie there for a while before chancing another run for it. The longer they stayed this way, the more their mutual body heat made it easier to linger. Margaret's breathing was strong and regular; she was probably asleep, which, in turn, made him yearn for rest. He knew, however, that when the terrorists failed to find them, they'd be back. And this time, they'd make a more thorough search. He couldn't give in to the fatigue. The thought of waking up and finding Vega's men standing over him shook George back to consciousness; he was suddenly wide-awake.

He tried to recall the image of the complex he'd seen on the Tab. They couldn't afford to stumble out of here and hope to find their way by chance. He'd have to think about this carefully. Most mistakes were made because those in trouble failed to think clearly, and didn't have the patience to be deliberate. He would force himself to be careful, but he needed information, accurate information, not fuzzy memories hastily gathered under duress. The impression he'd gotten from the Tab diagram implied the complex was about twenty or thirty miles south of the domes, near the perimeter of the hydrogen-oxygen production farm in the northern part of the southern desert. This had to be a set of exploratory passageways and caverns that had been abandoned by ERC as the development of the farm evolved and modernized. The separatists, or at least this fringe element, must have discovered, then exploited this forgotten site. It was close enough to the domes to be easily supplied, yet far enough away to have remained hidden all this time.

George thought hard. He'd only studied the map for a few minutes. They couldn't go to the complex's main airlock in a bid for the surface. They needed to get into a tunnel system that was currently being used by the authorities. Though this particular complex had been abandoned, it was logical to assume they must be near tunnels that were still being used, still being monitored.

It would take Vega's men between ten and fifteen minutes to search the entire cell section. After that, they would return in a hurry. His memory of the map just wasn't good enough; he'd have to take another look. Pushing away from the cylinder, he pulled himself into a sitting position and crossed his legs. He retrieved the Tab and pulled up a window, dimly illuminating the surroundings.

Suddenly, he became aware of someone standing in back of him, leaning against the far wall. He felt a line of sweat bead his forehead. In his panic, he thought he saw the man coming forward in the gloom. Blinking several times, he came to the conclusion that this impression was wrong. Whoever it was, was just standing there.

Getting to his feet and holding the Tab up for light, George stepped toward the back of the room. As he approached, he saw that his bogeymen were several environment suits hanging on metal scaffolds anchored to the floor. This was an amazing piece of luck.

Five minutes later, George and Margaret had each donned a suit. Inspecting the equipment, George saw that the air tanks had been fully charged and the suits were equipped with leg assists. The fuel cells on the suits' backpacks read *full* for oxygen and hydrogen. The task of putting the suit on had brought Margaret all the way back. It must have been something she had done countless times, because she got hers on first.

By his reckoning, George had, at most, another five minutes to look at the map. "Give me a couple of minutes, okay?"

Margaret nodded. He leaned against the pipe, studying the diagram. He found the room they were in by retracing their steps. Then, starting at the equipment shed, he traced a route through the corridors to the northern-most point of the complex. The map had several colors that depicted different kinds of structures. The corridors and rooms were in black outline. He could make out the airlock and elevator to the surface in green. There were some curious rooms and corridors in gray, with something that looked like an airlock in red—but an airlock to where? The map ended at that point. What did the gray mean? He made a decision, folded the Tab, and put it in his suit pocket.

Margaret was staring at him.

"Come on, we have to get out of here—now. How do you feel?"

"I'm okay," she said, and stepped toward the door.

The corridors were bathed in red light. They scrambled out, turned left, and hurried toward a point at the periphery of the complex that George hoped would be their ticket to freedom.

Chapter Twenty-Five

Perseus lay in his bed on the second floor of his parents' apartment, in the foothills of South Lake Geneva. His right hand touched the smooth cool surface of the projection ball that sat next to his hip as he gazed at the majestic objects slowly moving above him. He rotated the ball to the right and the constellation of Cassiopeia moved up from the southern horizon. Its alpha star, Shedis, burned a reddish yellow in the imaginary head of Andromeda's mother, the mythical princess that the Perseus of Greek legend rescued from the monstrous Kraken. He smiled thinking of that Perseus, the rescuer of the princess and the slayer of the Medusa. The irony was not lost on him. In mythology, Perseus was a hero; on Mars he was becoming a reluctant victim. He continued to manipulate the ball. The projector responded by taking him on a three dimensional holographic tour through the autumn Martian sky. He moved to the Pleiades, zooming the projector onto a blue white gathering of bright young main sequence stars at the beginning of their hydrogen cycles. These stars were too young for life bearing planets; the blue shimmer of the space around them was a telltale sign of the primordial dust and gas of their recent formation.

He sat for hours looking up into the projection at different images of the sky taken from observation stations in orbit around almost every significant celestial body in the solar system. The images came over the network, which formatted them for enhancement and relative position in the Martian sky during any orbital season on Mars that Perseus might select. The holographic projector was a nearly invisible plastic sheet that spanned the ceiling of his room. The sheet produced a diffraction pattern by the orientation of dielectric lattices in its molecular structure and displayed images by illuminating the sheet with a set of lasers whose phases could be adjusted to move the image into whatever orientation the he might desire. Once the image

was positioned, an AI processor in the system produced true
fidelity of the visual and spectral artifacts of any celestial object
that he might want to examine more closely.

He felt Miram come into his consciousness, as she often did
when he lay here in his room with his mind clear and open. Her
presence was warm and comforting. He lost himself in their
collective thoughts, like slowly slipping under warm water. As
she washed over him, he felt the tingle in his head, which
changed the way he viewed the stars. Instead of seeing spectral
points of light in a blue-black firmament, he began to see
Andromeda as the princess in the company of Cassiopeia, the
queen. They were no longer connected points of light, but
dream-like figures of their classical namesakes acting out their
fated dramas. Miram's intuition slowly became his and, all at
once, the relationship between the physical stars and the
mythical images were to him, as Miram understood them.

The melding had scared him in the beginning. The shared
consciousness was as disorienting as it was seductive. At first, he
was alarmed by the possibility that he might be mentally ill, and
he had no idea of what was really happening. But the meld
continued to come, though he didn't appreciate its significance
until later. It often felt as if there might be someone else
involved, but he was afraid to dig deeper. Whatever this was, he
sensed it had a power that he had yet to fully experience.

He had first noticed Miram about three years ago, in school.
While sitting in class, he began to feel uncomfortable, distracted,
as though he were having mild mental spasms. The sensation
was similar to a spastic tick in his eyelid that had the
spontaneous quality of a hiccup. He covered his face with his
hands, thinking that a few moments of darkness might dispel the
annoying tick. He thought that perhaps he was tired, or
dehydrated, and a few quiet moments would restore his
equilibrium. To his surprise, as the darkness came, the spasms
were replaced by the vertigo of a dream-like falling. For a few
seconds, he lost touch with his body, with the pressure of the seat

on his rear and the feel of his elbows on the desktop; all sensations of the external world had simply vanished. Instead, he felt as if suspended somewhere while gazing at someone in front of him. All at once, he realized that he was cupping a face in his hands and found familiarity in its features, but it also frightened him. The rush of anxiety made him fight the dream state and he balled his hands into tight fists, trying to vanquish the face he held in them. Suddenly, he was back in the classroom; the panic subsided and he was left sitting there, trying to catch his breath. He felt compelled to turn slowly and glance over his shoulder for some reason. As he chanced a look, he found a beautiful girl sitting behind him, staring right at him. He could tell she was somehow part of his lapse by the strange blank look on her face. And her eyes. He had momentarily seen those eyes look as if they were dark holes that sank deep into her mind. Both he and the girl were locked somehow, giving him the strange sensation of looking into a mirror.

After that, he had made a point of avoiding her. The experience had shaken him to his core. Maybe he was mentally ill, epileptic, schizophrenic, or had some congenital illness whose name was unknown. But whatever it was, she was connected with it. As he replayed the incident in his mind, he realized that, before the fear had seized him, the sensation had been strangely comforting. Nagging thoughts about the dream state continued to plague him and he tried to focus on its connection to the girl. On reflection, there was no real menace in her presence. It was his own disorientation that had sent him reeling, not the feeling that he should be wary of someone else. When he thought about her, he felt warm and good, so good, in fact, that the memory raised goose bumps on his arms. He became frustrated. Thinking about the incident in this way was inadequate because no metaphor could faithfully reproduce the feeling. Although he'd prefer to examine the experience from afar, it was clear that any enlightenment would have to come from Miram.

With his mind made up, he went back to school with the intention of seeking her out. But as the days passed, so did his resolve, and he continued to postpone the meeting. Finally, one day, he found himself in the schoolyard just having finished his lunch, when he spotted her. She was alone and sitting on a bench at the far end of the yard with her back to him. He slowly crossed the yard, slipping through scores of other kids who were running and playing in the intervening space between them. He came up behind her and could feel the ticks start to pull at his mind again. He held his breath, and although he hadn't made a sound, she turned slowly and looked up at him. She was smaller than he was, even though they were both the same age. Her long hair was parted on the side and fell like shiny black silk over her shoulders, almost to the bench. Her face was a beautiful dark teardrop with strange golden eyes that reminded him of his own. He felt the draw—"sit down." For a moment, he thought she had spoken the words, but her lips hadn't moved.

He straddled the bench and sat next to her. Then he took a closer look and noticed she was darker than he was, more the complexion of his mother, with delicate fine features that were symmetric and appealing. He reached out and gently pulled a cascade of soft raven hair away from the side of her head, revealing her ear, which was lower on her head than that of other people he knew. It had an attached lobe and a higher upper crescent, just like his. He moved his hand to her bangs and lifted the hair from her forehead. Again, like his, her forehead seemed unusually high, but not unattractive in his opinion. Then there were the eyes. They were unmistakable; the golden flecks drew him in. She reached up, took the hand that brushed her forehead, and held it.

He fell into her mind, awkward and tense at first, but he quickly regained his poise and slipped in with greater skill and ease. Afterward, it was hard to judge the passage of time. In the dream state, they had no sense of external time, just a shared sense of events that defined their union. But he soon found himself coming out of it, stirred by other kids who were laughing and pointing at them in response to their holding hands in a secluded part of the yard.

After that, they were often together. Perseus learned to control the depth of their union, making it easier to hide from others. Later, they discovered a sexual aspect to their melding. That happened when they began to join at a distance. In the beginning, they could only make it happen when they were close, and could only make it strong when they touched. Eventually, they learned to do it when separated by many miles. Being clear and open, free of distraction, was the key. It first happened while he was alone in his room, in the dark, under the projector. On one such night, Miram came to him and their joining was particularly strong. They inadvertently wandered into a part of their collective mind strongly associated with their erotic senses. They moved in and out of each other, raising their carnal sense higher and higher, until Perseus awoke on his bed, in the dark, panting heavily. He soon discovered that he had ejaculated for the first time. The next day, when he saw Miram in school, she took him aside and whispered into his ear, "Let's do it again tonight."

In the years that followed, they discovered others like themselves. There was Martha, Jake, Julian, Nathan, Denise, Ben, and ten others, but none of them was ever as dear to his heart as Miram. Although Perseus often melded with the others and subsequently became close to them, only Miram came to him night after night under the stars, like that first time three years before.

Perseus had long suspected that he was somehow different from other people, including even his parents. These differences were becoming more profound, and it became harder and harder to reconcile them on the basis of some special prenatal therapy he'd received. Until the day he found Miram, he had been at a loss to confide in anyone else about theses troubling questions. Once he and Miram discovered the existence of the others, it became increasingly clear that there had to be a master plan, but by whom, and for what purpose?

Perseus found that he excelled far beyond his classmates in mathematics and science. Because he sensed that his achievements were unusual, he hid them from his teachers. He couldn't help reading voraciously about probability and statistics, genetics, and physics from journal articles on the network. Later, he filled in complicated details using university texts. These things came so easily to him that he began to suspect that he and the others couldn't possibly have developed naturally. What's more, it was unlikely that their heightened aptitudes could be the result of human intervention. Molecular genetics, as he understood the state of the art, was still far from being able to engineer genetic changes on this drastic a level. By his own reckoning, he and the others might well be an entirely different species.

The fact that his parents didn't know anything about matters so central to his life was confusing. How could they not know? After all, they were his parents, weren't they? Perseus voiced these concerns on many occasions, subtly at first, and then with greater urgency. He explained that, to him, his classmates seemed impossibly slow, to the point of being comical, but his parents grew more dismissive as he grew more confused. His parents explained his abilities as a natural aptitude that he possessed for technical subjects. They regarded his admissions of superiority as just one more reason to be proud of him. But their lack of understanding left him even more ill at ease. "He's always been so good in school," his father would say to his mother, after which his mother would shower him with affection. He loved his mother dearly, and it pleased him, of course, to make her happy, but he was left with troubling unanswered questions and no one to confide in—no one until Miram. In Miram he found his equal, someone who shared his fears and hopes with equal measures of compassion and understanding.

And then later, another surprise came with the discovery that Miram knew Joanne. Joanne, whom he'd known as far back as he could remember. Perseus came across this remarkable fact quite by accident. When he first began to join with Miram, the entanglement of their minds had been unfocused, as though they'd both developed a new appendage, but it was clumsy and required experience to master. The experience was not unlike the first time he tried to walk with toddler legs, only to take a few staggering steps before falling. He and Miram spent hours experiencing each other in random mental impressions, associations made by the strongest thoughts or feelings they might encounter at that moment. On one such occasion, right after a disappointing conversation with his parents about his unusual ability to solve spatial puzzles, he made the unexpected discovery. It involved color map puzzles, the kind they played with at school. The teachers had been quite taken with his ability, so much so that they had seriously thought he had somehow cheated. Then they resorted to giving him figures of greater and greater complexity to arrange, polygonal tilings where no common border could share the same color. He became increasingly alarmed at their fascination with each new successful solution he came up with. At that point, he pretended to be stumped by some of the more challenging problems, although, in truth, these too were absurdly simple. That memory caused him to think about Joanne, how she'd advised him not to draw attention to himself. But as he thought about her, he felt Miram's thoughts resonate with his, and he began to experience her memories of Joanne. Apparently, Joanne had given Miram the same advice!

In the weeks that followed, he went to school and mentioned Joanne to other kids he knew. Many children had received prenatal therapy. It seemed logical to assume they too had caseworkers, people whom they had known most of their lives. Again, he found his situation to be unique. No one else knew her. No one else had a caseworker that followed them into their preteen years. Only he and Miram seemed to have been granted this special status—but why? Later, when they discovered the others, remarkably, they knew Joanne too.

It had all been obvious, of course, but denial was a part of his humanity his special therapy had failed to exorcise. He rejoiced in this sameness with humanity at large, for although he considered this emotional lapse in judgment a flaw, it was, at least, something he could share with others in whose world he was fated to live.

These revelations brought him to a course of action. He would try to find out what Joanne knew. There was a high likelihood that she didn't know about melding. His unions with Miram and the others had achieved consensus on that point. Perseus also decided to find out to what extent he could read regular people. And he decided to start with his parents, since there was already a strong bond that could only serve to enhance the effect.

He sat close to his mother and emptied his mind, then tried to seep into hers. Perseus assumed that in a state of distracted relaxation lay his best chance of success. He joined her in the backyard. She sat on her knees, on dark rich soil, planting flowers under the bright amber sky. Perseus lay next to her on the grass and pretended to fall asleep. Careful not to touch her, he tried to slip undetected into her thoughts by concentrating on her humming, then mirroring it in his own mind, and then falling, like an echo, into her consciousness. Music on the mind gave an opportunity to become invisible, since it provided a transcendental mental medium. After trying for many minutes, he raised only fleeting impressions of her and soon gave up. No matter how he tried, she lay on the periphery of his consciousness, opaque to his mind. The harder he tried, the less he was able to read her, until eventually, there was nothing at all. He shifted his body and rested on her lap. She held his hand as she continued to plant with the other. This time the impression of her was stronger, but still dim compared to joining with others like him. He got a weak texture of flowers, wisps of music, a fleeting sense of the sun's warmth on her bare arms, but not the entry into her full perception that he'd sought. The glimpse into her innermost self made him want to join with her even more, and made her fading in his consciousness all the more heartbreaking. At that moment, he realized that there would always be a limit to their relationship that all the desire in the world could not bridge. He retreated back into his own mind and opened his eyes. She was looking down, spokes of light danced through her long black hair and played on his face beneath her. From above and upside-down, she smiled at him, and he at her. She had felt nothing; with all his effort, he hadn't been able to project even a hint of himself into her. That's where he left it. Clearly, regular people would always be alone in their minds, unable to find others. He might be able to feel gross impressions, but nothing more.

A couple of days later, armed with this knowledge, he sat across from Joanne in her temporary office at school. She asked her regular questions about how things were going, at school, at home, with his friends—the kind of busy chat that dominated these visits. He waited for her to finish, and then asked, "Why do you visit me and no one else in my class?"

She looked at him quizzically. "Because you've received special treatments the others haven't."

"What kind of special treatments?"

He watched her carefully. Instead of being stern, to his surprised, she smiled and gave him a clear impression she was pleased.

He waited, then said, "I've met Miram. It seems you visit her too. Is she special too? Special like me, I mean?"

Joanne's smile became even wider. "Yes she is special, very much like you. If you don't mind my asking, how did you meet? How did you know she was special like you?"

It was Perseus' turn to smile. Joanne didn't know about melding. She knew some things, but she didn't know everything. That, in itself, was interesting.

"Why didn't you tell me about her? You know it's been hard for me—knowing Miram helps."

Joanne just looked at him. "Why didn't you tell me?" Perseus asked.

He could see something in Joanne's eyes. She was no longer smiling, no longer amused. Whatever it was, it wasn't mean-spirited; he knew that. It was more like confusion, perhaps regret. In that moment, she seemed as lost as he was. There was no sense of manipulation, that was a relief, but what could she be hiding?

"You're not going to tell me, are you?" Perseus asked.

Joanne said, "Not right now, but I promise you, soon I'll explain everything."

Not everything, Perseus thought.

Then came the epiphany, just a couple of days ago in that room, high atop that enormous building in Dome One. Perseus knew then that events were being set into motion that would probably change his life forever. Unfortunately, he felt the change would probably be for the worse, judging by what he knew about humans in general and about that strange woman he'd met in particular. He had gotten a strong sense from Dr. Gates. At first, he mistook her appearance to mean that she was in some way like Miram and the others, but it soon became clear that her unusual appearance was superficial. Underneath, she was all too human, aggressive and determined. He realized that it was only a matter of time before they would come and collect them all. Humans were like that, at least most of them were. What they didn't understand, they feared. What they feared, they either tried to dominate, or destroy. That seemed to be their intrinsic pattern en masse. To him, it was as if humans had two prime motivations, fear and ambition. From those two imperatives, it was fairly easy to predict their actions, if one had a clear understanding of the circumstances. He was through with denial. Ignoring the obvious would only eliminate any prospect for personal happiness, for him and his people. No, it was clear that humans would see him and his people as a threat, perhaps for as foolish and frivolous a reason as evolutionary competition for future dominance of the known worlds. It would certainly never occur to them that evolution of advanced sentient societies might come to a fair and equitable arrangement or even integration. They purported to have free will, to be masters of their destinies, but their rhetoric and the reality of their lives were often at odds with each other, at least for many of them.

His thoughts drifted back to that woman, Dr. Gates, the one with odd color eyes and hair. He sensed in her a great deal of nervousness and longing. She was obviously a complicated person, which made him uneasy, since she seemed to have power over what might happen to him. It occurred to him that perhaps he should have tried to be more forthcoming—more understanding? After all, she, like other humans, carried the burden of evolutionary traits that were clearly contrary to any concept of enlightened civilization. She couldn't be expected to come to the right conclusion without exhaustive explanation. Perhaps if he had confided in her, made her understand that they were no threat, things might be different. He wasn't sufficiently experienced in the games humans played to really know if it would have made much difference. No point debating that now, the opportunity had obviously come and gone.

In the middle of it all, he had met Dr. Mills, who had told him that he and Joanne were responsible for creating him and his people. Just like that—poof, Dr. Mills had explained the greatest mystery of his life in a couple of seconds. How strange to learn, after being so alienated from so many humans, that two humans had opted to create another species that most humans would regard as a competitive threat. Furthermore, after studying the relevant technologies, he, Perseus, with his demonstrably superior mind, had determined that the technology required to develop genetic modifications on this scale did not exist. Yet Joanne and Dr. Mills had apparently perfected the technique more than ten years before. This lesson had taught him something about the human condition, which he had so recently mocked, and something about his own budding arrogance.

After his conversations with Dr. Mills and Will, the cybernetic intelligence he'd met at Dr. Mills' house, Perseus had found new hope, a second wind. Perhaps they could avoid the catastrophe that was most certainly coming. That thin hope, however, had been dashed this evening when he had tried to contact Dr. Mills and had learned that he had been arrested that afternoon. Later, he had learned from netcasts that Dr. Mills' lab at the university had been raided, and his equipment seized. When he tried to call Joanne, he was told that she had left work and was mysteriously unavailable.

Perseus shared this sour information with Miram, who was with him now in his room, under the stars, in the dark. They lay there together in each other's minds, waiting for the men in charge to come and collect them, as he always knew they would.

Chapter Twenty-Six

It took Joanne and Malcolm an hour to get to the Dome
Two Port Authority. The Port Authority, which was located on
the northern edge of the dome, stored and maintained public
surface vehicles of all kinds, from tractors to small atmospheric
planes. After disembarking from the tube car, they ascended two
levels and entered the port. The terminals were all empty, and
they moved to the one nearest the entrance. The terminal had a
set of monitors that allowed visitors to select a vehicle, the
accessories, the times, and allowed them to prepay for the
service.

Joanne tapped the screen. An anthropomorphic service
agent appeared. The virtual young man stood behind a fictitious
counter and told Joanne that he would be unable to help her due
to a moratorium on all surface travel put into effect by Dome
One security. She looked at Malcolm. He shrugged, did a double
take, and stared at the screen over her shoulder.

"What the hell is that?"

Joanne turned and saw a static raster, much like the one
she'd seen on George's Tab. When the static cleared, words
appeared on the screen.

*Joanne, a file was just sent. You'll find the file called Floor-
Plan on the Tab that George left for you.*

The Port system had identified her by her eye print, so she
wasn't surprised when it addressed her by name, but she was
surprised that it knew about George and what he had left.

The screen blanked and the agent reappeared.

"Joanne, please go to bay three. You'll find a tractor,
provisions, and surface suits for you and Malcolm. Please
hurry."

The image faded, but Joanne couldn't pull her eyes away.
For an instant, she felt as though she'd imagined the whole thing.
She turned to Malcolm.

"I saw it too," he said.

A tingle raced down her back, "Will?" she said.

The screen remained a blank pane of plastic. After a moment, a key card emerged from a slot at its base.

"Did you say, Will?" Malcolm asked.

Joanne shrugged.

"I thought you said it had been dismantled."

"That's what I said, wasn't it?" Joanne replied.

They hurried to the bay gate and inserted the key. The door slid aside silently, permitting them entry into a long wide corridor with numbered displays over several large bulkheads. They walked to Bay Three and reinserted the key, almost expecting the Port system to have changed its cyber mind again. The door slid aside. Inside, they found several environment suits hanging from scaffoldings and a small tractor in an adjacent bay. The tractor was a rounded trapezoid, with the wide side at its base where eight large studded wheels were attached to floating gimbals in pairs. Its nose was a light-sensitive transparent bubble. Retractable shutters hid in a collar surrounding the bubble and could be deployed in case of sandstorms. Glancing up, Joanne saw a parabolic antenna on the tractor's roof, giving them access to the planetary network.

Now, with her suit on, Joanne left her gloves off and helmet retracted. Until they opened the bay doors to the surface, the tractor room would retain a breathable atmosphere. Malcolm sat on the bench in front of the lockers where they'd left their clothes. Joanne could tell by the way his beard puckered that he was pursing his lips.

"Ready?"

"Ready as I'll ever be," Malcolm said.

She grabbed a handhold on the side of the tractor and jumped, first to the top of the tire, then into the cockpit. Malcolm followed and slid the door shut. Taking George's Tab from the bag, Joanne plugged it into a cradle on the tractor's console. It glowed a soft blue in the dark cab.

"Let's get outside fast," Malcolm said.

"Why?"

"Because we have no idea when Will or whoever it was might change his mind."

"I see your point," she said, almost to herself, and pushed the key into the tractor's ignition.

The instrument panel came to life. Several displays lit up and the tractor rose smoothly on its hydraulic suspension. She brought her finger down on the lift icon and felt the elevator ascend toward the sky doors on the ceiling above them. When they got to the surface, Joanne pushed the steering yoke forward and drove the tractor behind one of the pillboxes on the tarmac near the Port building's outside dock. She left the lights off, navigating instead by infrared in an effort to evade detection from the dock windows. When they were comfortably out of sight, she opened the *Rainy-Day* designator on the Tab. The file was there, just as the mysterious message had promised.

Joanne tapped the file marked *Floor Plan* and a map appeared in the window. She expanded the map as much as she could and studied it carefully.

"What is it?" Malcolm asked.

"A map."

He snickered and exhaled, "Thanks, I can see that, but a map of what?"

"This area," she replied, distracted. She bent forward and examined the map intently. Malcolm stared at her in the glow. She looked so much younger in the suit's skullcap. Instead of being put off by her abrupt manner, he smiled and sat back.

"What are these things?" he asked, pointing to a pattern of what appeared to be rounded structures on the periphery of Dome Two. The things spread south for many miles.

Joanne's gaze fixed on the pattern. "They're the hydrogen-oxygen plants. Each is sunken into the ground about two hundred and fifty feet. The tanks are left in the atmosphere because the hydrogen is flammable. There's no oxygen in the air, so even if the hydrogen comes in contact with something that would otherwise set it off, it wouldn't ignite."

She pointed to a set of lines on the map coming from clusters of wells farther south. "These are pipes carrying water from the south," she said, turning to him. "The water is dissociated into hydrogen and oxygen using electricity from the dome fusion plant."

She turned back to the map. "The gases are stored in the tanks you were pointing to before."

She put her finger on gray lines running parallel to the pipes represented in black. "Now, each of these water lines has an associated tunnel."

"The gray lines," he said nodding. "You know your stuff, don't you?"

"Malcolm, I've lived around here all my life. What's more, George and I used to roam around all over this southern canyon." She pointed to the dashed lines on the southern part of the map.

For a moment, she seemed lost in thought, then she said, "You Earthmen like to be outdoors. George used to pester me all the time about taking hikes, having picnics, things like that. Funny, but it was infectious. I found myself looking forward to his excursions."

She sat in silence for a moment, then looked at the map again, then at Malcolm. He could only see the outline of her face in the light of the instrument panel, with one dark eye looking at him.

"You know what's interesting on this map?"

"No."

She pointed to a set of gray caverns about twenty-five miles southeast of their current position. "These look like old exploratory sites that were abandoned years ago. I don't remember seeing these on standard maps. See these tunnels?"

"Yeah."

"Old access tunnels. If these were somehow physically hidden from the service tunnels, this cavern system would make a perfect hideout, don't you think?"

"And you think this is where he is?"

"From what I see here, from the fact that this map shows these caverns and others don't." She thought a moment, trying to distinguish between wishful thinking and sound logic. "Yes," she said finally. "I think this is the most likely place."

Malcolm had to admit, it did make sense. "Okay," he said, "how do we get in? We can't go this way." He pointed to the pillbox and the elevator from the surface. "They'll be all over that."

"I agree. That will be too well guarded."

"Look at this, what's this?" Malcolm pointed to what appeared to be an airlock at the northern-most part of the cavern system.

Joanne nodded. "That's interesting, isn't it? I think they were going to build another tunnel to this point." She put her finger on a tank complex five miles away.

"See the airlock?" she said, pointing to a similar airlock on the northern edge of the tank complex.

"Yeah," said Malcolm in agreement. "What's in between these two points now?"

"I don't know," Joanne said. "The map's blank there. There must have been a construction problem or something and the site was abandoned. Think about it, Malcolm. Suppose George found himself somewhere in these caverns. What would be the most likely escape route? What would be his best chance?"

Malcolm thought a moment. "Well, Mills would be pretty desperate, and he wouldn't go up through the pillbox." He looked at her. "He'd go north, through this airlock, if he could."

Joanne smiled. "Yes, that's right, and that's where we're going."

She then turned her attention to the Tab, where she did some quick typing, brought up the address book, and sent a message.

"What was that?" Malcolm asked.

"I just renamed the map *Mills* and sent it to Jackson anonymously."

"I can see his face now," Malcolm said.

"What else could I do? He might not be able to figure it out on his own. Without some kind of backup, I might just get you killed." She stared at him. "I told you I didn't want you to come."

Malcolm could hear Joanne breathing in quick short spurts somewhere in the dark in front of him. He saw a hint of her chest in the dim console lights heaving in synch with the sounds of anxiety. He put his hand on hers. She said nothing, but he could see that her breathing was returning to normal.

A moment later, Malcolm programmed the Nav for the location of the southern tank complex, disconnected the external network, and pushed the yoke forward all the way, engaging the tractor's Nav AI. The motors came to life with a click, followed by a smooth muffled whine, as the vehicle pitched forward. He kept the lights off and stayed clear of the roads, opting instead to travel over the rough. The tractor AI used infrared and radar to find its way over rocks and red sand. They were on their way now to the vast tank complex just south of the domes.

* * *

Joanne sat back. The whole front of the tractor was transparent and the ride was smooth, though they were traveling over course terrain. She looked up at the stars as they rode and felt like she was floating in space. It was a beautiful night, and completely quiet in the cabin. Malcolm's head was arched back as he slept. Phobos, the larger of Mars' two moons, was high in the sky and only a quarter visible, leaving little light on the surroundings outside. She saw a pattern of red lights in the distance. The tops of massive hydrogen tanks seemed to sit no more than a few feet above the Martian surface.

At twenty miles per hour, it took a little over an hour and a half to pull up alongside tank number one hundred and forty seven; it was this tank whose base housed the airlock they were seeking. Joanne put on her gloves, then pressed a bar on the suit collar underneath her chin. A helmet unfolded from the collar, encapsulating her head. She made sure the suit was functioning correctly by scanning her displays—everything was in the green.

Malcolm tapped Joanne on the shoulder. "Here, take this." He passed her a gun.

She looked at it a moment. "Where in the world did you get this?"

Malcolm smiled wryly. "I'm still in the Reserves. I got it at an armory in Dome One the other day. Do you know how to use it?"

"No, I don't. I don't like guns." She could see his face clearly in the helmet lights. The worry lines were pronounced at the corners of his eyes.

"Remember, we're going into a war zone. It'll be as much a problem to stay alive through the night as it will be to find Mills."

She held the weapon in both hands.

"Okay, let me tell you a couple of things," Malcolm said. "First, never, and I mean never, shoot at anything you have not carefully identified. If you panic and shoot at something before you know what it is, it might be me, or Mills, or some other innocent bystander."

"But Malcolm."

"Just listen," he said.

"Second, if you decide you want to shoot someone, shoot to kill. Don't try to wound them, you'll probably miss, and they'll end up shooting you."

He waited a moment, "Do you understand?"

She nodded.

"Is that a yes," he asked.

"That's a yes," she said flatly.

He showed her the safety, the cartridge clip, and the laser sighting. "You've got exploding frictionless plastic rounds, thirty shots. The pistol is recoilless; the shots will leave the barrel as fast as you can pull the trigger. Do you understand?"

She hesitated, then said, "Yes, yes I do." And after a moment, "Thank you."

They got out of the tractor and looked around. Everything was still; they were all alone in the dark. With all its lights out, the tractor was all but invisible.

"Okay," Malcolm said, "let's leave the safety on until we get through the airlock."

"Okay," Joanne said, and put the pistol in her belt, just as Malcolm had.

"From here on in, you're in charge," he said. "Where's the airlock?"

She smiled thinly. "This way."

She led him to a ramp. Malcolm looked up. Though only a small fraction of the tank was above ground, the red light on top must have been thirty feet above them. The tank was planted in a hole whose diameter was larger than the tank, leaving a space of about ten feet between it and the walls of the hole. The ramp bridged the gap, connecting to a ladder that was attached to the side of the tank and descended into the hole. Joanne walked across the ramp, grabbed the ladder with both hands, left the safety of the ramp, and looked down. Although it was pitch black in the pit, the radar imaging of her helmet optics presented a view that couldn't have been any clearer if the pit had been illuminated by flood lamps. The ladder fell more than two hundred feet straight down, and without zooming the image, she couldn't see the bottom.

Malcolm moved to the edge of the pit and looked down. "Delightful," he said.

Chapter Twenty-Seven

Perseus heard a knock at the door and winced. He felt
Miram untangle from their common consciousness, felt her seep
away.

"Love you." He didn't hear it; he had an impression of it.
"Love you." It was weaker this time.

His thoughts were more his than theirs now. He could feel
the depth of their bond becoming flatter, losing dimension,
fullness.

"Love..."

She was gone. All that remained was a hard angry knock at
the front door. People seldom knocked. It was a holdover from
immigrant days; its significance was not lost on him. He could
feel the angry presence, the knot of bad intentions that swung
that fist repeatedly against the door, the intimidation that swelled
in their minds with each thump. The sour rotten smell of their
minds was disturbing. How could they possibly behave this
way—get this worked up against people they didn't even know?
Perseus had imagined that this level of distain must require a
personal element, but these people were strangers. He
understood their purpose, the logic of their position, but when he
actually imagined carrying out these foul deeds, that's when he
no longer understood them. These humans, he thought, and
sighed.

It was quiet and dark in his small room, but he'd spent so
much time here that he could visualize it clearly just by the dark
outlines of its contents. Tuning out the pounding downstairs, he
tried to take a last look. Hold it in his memory just this way.
These were the last fleeting moments of his old life; childhood's
end, he thought. He turned the projector off and waited for the
next sound. He didn't have long to wait. He heard the door open
and people talking downstairs. His mother screamed. It wasn't a
scream of physical pain; it was a scream of desperation and loss.

In it, he imagined all his mother's future days without him, her loneliness. He felt a knot in his stomach and tears on his cheeks.

Jumping from bed, he opened the door. The light from the landing hurt his eyes; he became momentarily disoriented. Willing himself to see clearly, his eyes quickly adjusted and he ran downstairs. He was about half way down when he heard his mother scream again. This time, she was urging him to run, to escape. Momentarily stunned, he stopped and looked down into the foyer where he saw four large security men in black uniforms and shiny black boots. One was holding his mother by the shoulders and another was standing over his father, who sat on the floor holding his head. Dark red blood oozed between the fingers of the hand he cupped over his nose.

"Papa!" Perseus screamed. The security men looked up.

"Perseus Augustus, you have to come with us, son."

"What have you done to my father?"

"You have to come with us."

One of the men came up the stairs at him. He felt the urge to run, but knew that it was useless. This is the fate of the weak, he thought. He smiled, thinking about a holy book they had studied in school, something about the meek inheriting the Earth. These humans were clearly deranged, clearly mad. Aside from the cruelty of their acts, didn't the inconsistency bother them, or was it that they thought their gods would not notice?

His shoulders slumped and Perseus slowly walked down the stairs toward the men.

A man reached up to seize him. "Don't touch me, I won't run. Just let me say goodbye to my mother and father."

He thought he saw a hint of shame in the man's face.

"Let me pass, please."

The man backed down the stairs and stood aside. His mother stopped crying and hugged him as he came to her. They moved closer to his father, who was still sitting on the floor, and hugged him too. The three of them stayed that way for as long as they could. Perseus heard his father saying, "I'm sorry, son," over and over again. His mother just continued to whimper. After a while, a security man put his hand on Perseus's shoulder and pried him loose.

"No matter what happens, I'll always love you," Perseus told them. "I'll never forget you. What's happening to me is not your fault." He looked at his father's face as he spoke, knowing that his father had always tried to play the role of protector.

They hustled him through the front door without so much as a picture of his family to remind him, in the long years to come, that he'd actually once lived here. But before they could get him down the front steps, his mother thrust a backpack into his flailing arms. It would serve as his legacy. Its contents were proof that he had once meant more than lines of computer code in a university basement.

They led him to a car waiting at the curb and pushed his head down, forcing him to sit in the back seat. As they pulled away from the house, he turned to see the dim silhouettes of his parents against the light of the open doorway. His father was holding his mother back as she struggled in a vain to follow him.

The car sped into avenue traffic and headed for Dome One. He could tell because it was the same route he had taken with his parents the other day, when going to that meeting on Federal Island. Lights flashed by outside the car window and he found himself still turned, still looking backward. He tried to clear his mind, tried not to think about tomorrow and all the tomorrows after that. He had always been optimistic about the future, a trait that he had inherited from his mother. Now it wasn't clear he had a future. What would they do to him? Obviously, they'd want to study him, find out what dark powers he might possess. Powers that he and his kind could use to usurp their authority on this planet. That was the kind of fear, the kind of paranoia, which drove them to take these unwise actions. He thought about Will. About the way he had sounded so sure that somehow this would not happen. If Will was that self-deluded, then he and his people were surely lost. And Dr. Mills. He should have foreseen this, had some plan to avoid this eventuality before embarking on his experiment. Were people so different that some could behave this way and others could not even conceive of such actions? It was all very confusing. At this point, nothing he could do would make any difference. He leaned back and watched the two heads bobbing in the front seat as the car sped through the underground between domes. He closed his eyes and tried to sleep. It had been a long day.

Chapter Twenty-Eight

"Slow down, Mills," Margaret said.

They were walking quickly to the airlock at the northern tip of the separatist complex. They activated their helmets, making it hard for people to identify them through the faceplate.

"You're pushy, aren't you?"

George felt Margaret pat him on the shoulder. "Just walk normally, okay?"

He'd been so tense after leaving the equipment shed that it was hard to think straight. He wasn't used to being under this much pressure, not life and death pressure anyway. Talking made it better.

"Okay," he said, "take a left here. It shouldn't be much farther."

A moment later, George heard a siren. Three short bursts, a long one, silence, then the pattern repeated.

"What's that?"

She cut him off with a wave of her hand. "Feel that?" she asked.

"Feel what?" Then he noticed the slight jar under his feet; small tremors came up through his suit.

"Yes, yes I do, the floor's shaking. What is it?"

"We've been found," Margaret said.

"Found—shouldn't we go the other way?"

"No," said Margaret. "We don't have battle gear. We're dressed like the enemy. There's going to be heavy fire when our soldiers enter this base. It'll be too easy to end up as collateral damage if we show up like this."

She grabbed him by the arm and started to run.

"I thought we were supposed to walk," George managed.

"Over there," Margaret said.

About fifty feet in front of them, he saw two men running toward them. As they approached, George heard, "You're going the wrong way. What the hell are you doing in those suits? You need combat gear. Turn around."

Margaret ran right into the one on the left, kicking him hard in the crotch. He fell backward and didn't get up. The other man, surprised by her attack, tried to grab George, who, after hesitating, was able to dodge his grip. Margaret spun around and kicked him behind the knees. He collapsed. She dropped to one knee and punched him hard, right between the eyes. The sound of cartilage snapping made a sickening sound. The man screamed, but before he could raise his hands to his head, Margaret guillotined him with an elbow to the face and he lay still. George came up behind her, and Margaret spun again, almost kicking him.

"Hey, hold it," he said, back-peddling. "I'm on your side, remember?"

"Sorry." She was breathing hard. He reached over, slowly this time, and took her arm. She let him, and he led her down the corridor toward the pressure door at its far end. As they walked, George looked around; there was no one else in sight.

Once inside the airlock, George found a metal bar and wedged it in between a cleat on the doorframe and a metal loop on the door handle.

"That should buy us a little time," he said, admiring his work.

"What the hell is this?"

While George had been putting the finishing touches on the door, Margaret had wandered to the other side of the airlock. She was looking through a quartz window on another door that led to a part of the complex that had been missing from the map. Glancing over her shoulder, George noticed a milky white vapor filling the space beyond the door.

"What is it?" Margaret said, looking sideways at him.

"Looks like water vapor, hot water vapor."

His helmet sensors indicated water at one hundred eighty degrees Fahrenheit—but how could that be?

He thought a moment. "I'll bet there's a lot of permafrost out there."

"Permafrost is cold, isn't it?" Margaret said. "And it doesn't sublimate into vapor."

"That's true," said George, "unless it's sitting on a vat of magma. There must be a volcanic vault around here somewhere. We're probably standing on the edge of a deep volcanic fissure. That's why this site was abandoned, and that's why there's light out there."

As they gazed at the strange sight, they were suddenly startled by loud metal clangs coming from behind them. Turning, George saw the bar he'd jammed into the door jangling. Someone had discovered their whereabouts. Turning back to Margaret, he saw that she'd already stepped into the milky beyond. He followed her out onto a rocky crag.

They couldn't see a thing in the visible or infrared, but when the suit AI switched to radar, the image cleared considerably. George saw that they were standing on a wide ledge that protruded about fifty feet from the rock wall. There seemed to be a canyon or something beyond the ledge. He couldn't tell, because the scene was shadowy and appeared far away. The radar image didn't have sufficient resolution to give him further detail. Above the canyon, or trench, or whatever it was, lay a rocky ceiling, which dipped as low as twenty feet in places and was higher than he could see in others. To their left, the ledge followed the cliff, but became thinner as it wound out of sight beyond an outcropping of rock. George consulted the position map displayed on his visor. The image indicated that the information was not current. The rocks above were probably blocking the satellite signals necessary to refresh the map. The old data, however, indicated that following the path to the left would take them due north, which was where they wanted to go. He took Margaret's arm, and they started walking quickly up the path.

Further along the cliff, the path wound higher into the large cavern and disappeared behind other rocks. After walking for about half an hour, the ledge became twenty feet wide and dropped off abruptly into an indiscriminate space. Across the gorge, the rock wall rose high above them. George's acoustic range finder indicated it was about one hundred feet to the other side. He noticed that the numbers indicating the distance across the trench changed abruptly over the course of several seconds, which probably indicated the presence of thermals rising up from the bottom of the trench. Eventually, they came to a place where the ledge split in two. Margaret stopped, looked between the paths, and shook his arm.

"Which way?"

He took a moment to consult his map. "This path goes due north." He pointed up the wall.

There was another path however, which seemed to lead to a tunnel off to the side, but according to his inertial compass, that one veered more westward. Deciding on the north-going path, they continued to climb up the side of the cliff. They trudged, for what felt like an eternity, on a ledge that seemed to wind endlessly up and down along the rock wall. George found himself in a trance-like state, with the dim sense of his legs perpetually in motion. Margaret was out in front, and he focused on her suit pack bobbing up and down. She seemed to walk with unnatural ease.

Suddenly, the silence was broken by something loud and menacing. Explosions were coming from somewhere far behind them, and George could see faint glows in the vapor down the cliff in the approximate direction of their pursuers. Then, from around a rocky protrusion, George saw billows of dust and rock splintering from the wall.

"They're probably on the ledge below trying to flush us out," Margaret said. "Let's keep going."

They turned and followed the winding path north. As time went on, George noticed it was getting darker. The haze was subsiding a bit and the outside temperature was falling. He cocked his head forward in his helmet and a straw, which came up from his suit collar, brushed up against his mouth. He pinched it with his lips and started to draw water up from a bladder in the suit. It had a mild plastic taste and was a little on the warm side, but he drank it thankfully. They'd been walking now for over an hour and he was starting to wear down. His feet chaffed in his boots and he could feel the big toe on his right foot burn a little. Now the path was only about ten feet wide, and was starting to veer further west and not north, as he'd hoped.

"Hold on," he said finally.

Margaret slowed and turned.

He noticed that her visor had become less reflective in the diminishing light. He could clearly see her face now. She looked fresh, restored somehow, as though the walk had made her stronger.

"You're staring," she said. "Is their something wrong?"

"Ah, no—I mean yes."

He saw her smiling. "Yes there is, or no there isn't?"

"Sorry, I must be tired."

"Uh-huh," she continued smiling.

"The path is heading west; we're going to have to find a way across that gorge."

Margaret glanced around and then stepped to the edge of the cliff and looked down. He followed and looked down too. The pit dropped off into darkness. George's laser range finder indicated about six hundred feet.

"How the hell are we ever going to get across this?" She was no longer smiling.

"Maybe we can find a land bridge or something further up," George said. "Presumably this has been explored before. It stands to reason that there must be a way through this cavern. I don't think these paths are natural formations. Hopefully, whoever came through here before us took it to some useful end point." He looked around, then down at her, "What else can we do, we can't go back."

They continued in a northwesterly direction up the path. The next time George looked at his suit chronometer, it read four hours and twenty minutes since they'd fled through the airlock door and into the cavern. He felt as if he'd been walking for days. His body was spent, and his willingness to push on was faltering. Margaret kept a steady pace in front of him. If she was tired, she didn't show it. Pretty soon he'd have to engage appendage assist to keep up with her. He'd avoided doing it until now since it consumed so much power. They needed their fuel cells to last as long as possible.

They came to a cave at the end of the path. Margaret turned and arched her eyebrows.

"After you," he said.

The cave was dark. The suit AI switched to visible optics and dim suit lamps. The vapor was gone and the temperature had dropped considerably. Visible light with its shorter wavelength was a vast improvement over radar. The image changed from one that looked like a cartoon to an almost black and white rendering of a cave right out of a gothic video.

"Wait a minute," George said.

Margaret stopped. "What?"

"I'm an idiot for not noticing before, but there's considerable pressure in here; look at these puddles on the ground."

She bent down and put a gloved finger in the water, sending radial ripples out to the edges of the puddle. George checked the atmosphere using absorption spectra.

"Fifty percent carbon dioxide, some sulfur dioxide, thirty percent oxygen, ten percent nitrogen, and some other trace gases including methane. It's certainly breathable, probably doesn't smell very good. The pressure's about eighty percent Earth normal." He thought a moment. "We could take off our helmets."

"I've got a better idea," said Margaret. "Let's go to scrubbers with charcoal filters; that way we save our oxygen and don't have to smell the stink."

When they had made the change, Margaret said, "Mills, if this cavern maintains pressure, doesn't that mean there's no way out? Otherwise, if it were somehow venting to the surface through some opening, wouldn't it be known?"

She was right. A cave this large with a breathable atmosphere would be generally known in the domes. The fact that it wasn't didn't bode well for them.

Then he brightened; Margaret saw it through his visor.

"What?"

"What if there's another airlock north of here. If the original engineers built one airlock, why not two?"

She considered that a moment, "Maybe." Then she turned and started walking again.

Chapter Twenty-Nine

George felt the ground shake beneath him. Something was happening in the cavern behind them. He knew it couldn't have taken their pursuers more than ten minutes to get through the lock and into the tunnel back at the complex. Vega must have explored these caves and made contingency plans for escape. That meant he knew his way around down here and wouldn't have to guess as to which tunnel to take. The only wild card was how close Void Fleet had managed to get to the separatists. If they had also discovered the cavern airlock, and were in close pursuit of Vega and his men, then that might change everything.

He checked their estimated position on his suit map. The accuracy of the estimate was dependent on the accuracy of the measurement before it, and the one before that, and so on through the chain of measurements since they'd lost the satellite. In other words, the error was cumulative. He could only hope that their last satellite fix was right on the money. If the original fix was accurate, then the laser gyros in the suit were probably good enough to ensure a position not too out of line with reality. If their current position could be believed, they were now headed in a northeasterly direction. That meant that nothing had really changed, the correctness of his earlier choice was still unknown.

He saw Margaret stop up ahead. When he caught up and looked further down the tunnel, he saw vapor again.

"Looks like it's getting thicker," she said. "That's a good sign, isn't it?"

"Yeah, Margaret, it is."

She hesitated, "You don't sound very enthusiastic."

"The vapor's good, the problem is the direction. We still haven't turned true north. That may be okay, though. Maybe there's a kink in the tunnel. A turn that's made the return of the vapor more gradual than if the tunnel were straight."

"Let's go to full assist and move faster," Margaret said. "We can't go back. There's no sense in being stingy with power, not now."

They began running into the vapor. Ten minutes later he saw it on radar, a hard terminus about a hundred feet up tunnel. His chest grew tight. He pictured himself standing in front of a rock wall, the end of the tunnel, with nowhere else to go. Then he started thinking clearly again. That couldn't be the case, otherwise where had the vapor come from? Since it hadn't come from behind them, this must be the turn he'd been looking for.

The vapor up ahead was bright with a yellowish glow. Margaret ran ahead of him, reached the end, then slapped the wall with an open glove.

"Mills, we're in luck! It turns due north right here."

When he caught up, the vapor was obscuring the tunnel up ahead. It glowed a bright white-yellow, indicating something hot in front of them.

"Must be the gorge," he said.

He held Margaret by the arm. She seemed smaller than his impression of her forceful presence. Her faceplate was opaque and instrumented as he looked down at her.

"Walk from now on, no running." He saw the helmet tilt in a nod. "There's a big drop up ahead, hold my hand—okay?"

Another nod.

They started northward, George in front, Margaret a half step behind. The tunnel became brighter and the vapor thicker until finally, they reached the gorge. The tunnel opened up into a clearing. It wasn't as large as the one near the complex. He looked around in radar at the clear cartoon image of the cave. The ceiling was pretty low, no more than fifteen feet. The gorge now looked more like a pit than the grand ravine it had once been. That was good too. It was no more than an opening to a lava hole far below their feet. They both stepped to the edge and looked down. His radar range finder was indicating a drop of about four-hundred feet. The temperature directly over the pit was about two-hundred and eighty degrees Fahrenheit, forcing his suit's air conditioner to work as hard as it could to keep the suit's temperature at an uncomfortable eighty degrees.

"How do we get across?" Margaret asked.

George looked around. He ordered the suit's imaging AI to do a full spectrum sweep of the cave wall around the pit for more detail of the rock. He strained to see what, if any, ledge there might be on the rock walls around the edges of the pit. They currently stood on a ledge that protruded out about ten feet from the entrance of the tunnel they'd just come through. The ledge did, in fact, circle around the pit, but became thinner and thinner. It was hard to tell whether there was a ledge on the other side. George thought this was probably due to seismic activity and the corrosive action of the vapors. There were sizable concentrations of sulfuric and nitric acid in the vapors. He tapped Margaret on the shoulder. She seemed mesmerized by the streams of colorful mist rising from somewhere far below.

"I guess our only chance is to shimmy around this ledge to the other side and hope that there's something there worth the effort."

"Do you see a tunnel on the other side?" she asked.

"I don't from here, but there could be rocks on the far side hiding a tunnel. We just can't get enough detail from here to tell. We won't know for sure until we're over there. And given the situation on this side, well. . ."

He glanced back the way they'd come. He could still feel the rumbling beneath his feet. "It's our only chance."

"Agreed," she said.

"There's something else," he said.

"Yeah?"

"I want you to go first."

"Why?"

"Because the ledge over there looks weak." He pointed to a section of wall near the other side. "I must be twice as heavy as you are. If that ledge gives way under me, we're both stuck."

He glanced down at her. Her helmet was turned his way and up; he could see a fishbowl reflection of the rivers of mist rising from somewhere behind him.

"All right," she conceded, then turned and slowly moved toward the cave wall.

He followed. They had no ropes or climbing aids of any kind. Their only real advantage was a sixty percent weight reduction here on Mars as compared with Earth. The same attempt on Earth would probably be suicidal. As Margaret made her way around, the ledge continued to shrink from ten feet to a little over a foot an a half. George followed her to a point, then let her continue the rest of the way alone. She pressed herself against the wall, facing it so as to give herself a way of gripping the wall for stability. He watched her feet, looking for evidence of rock shards or dirt falling away. So far, things looked good; the ledge remained solidly under her. He decided to advance. She'd already been over this part of the ledge and if it gave way now, she'd still be able to make it across. He felt himself sweating profusely and ordered the suit AI to boost the air-conditioning. He didn't want sweat in his eyes, not now. Blinking made it worse, so he tried to think about his feet and hands, making sure with each movement that he had a good grip on the rock.

He continued to advance in a sideways, scissor-like motion, reaching out with his right arm for a handhold, then sideways with his right leg. Once his right found purchase, he repeated the action with his left. He couldn't look down because of his helmet, which was so close to the rock that it occasionally scraped. He tried, instead, to look over his right shoulder, trying to gauge the distance to the other side.

A couple of times he stepped with his right foot and found nothing there. A sense of panic gripped him and he had to stop, collect himself, and let it pass. He saw Margaret up ahead, continuing to make progress in a deliberate way. In fact, as he looked past her, she seemed to be pretty near the other side of the pit. He stopped a moment, relaxing a little, catching his breath for the next push.

"Come on Mills, you're almost there."

He looked to his right and saw that Margaret was standing on the other side. She was turned toward him and crouching forward as if she were trying to see him better. Six more steps would put him an arm's length from a corner that he now recognized was the demarcation of a much wider ledge on the other side. Margaret inched toward that corner, holding onto the wall with her right hand, and stretching out her left arm. He started moving again, trying to quicken his pace, but at the same time trying not to be careless. He was pumped. He just might make it after all.

Then he felt the rock shake. Not a distant shake, but something more crisp, more immediate. He thought he saw splinters falling away from the wall directly in front and above him. An explosion's concussive force rocked him. Shit, someone was shooting at him from the other side of the pit! He heard rock and dirt falling into the pit and reflexively took a quick step to the right. Another shake, and his right foot slipped. There was the cold feeling of losing his balance. The possibility of his falling evoked the flash that his life might be nearing its final moments. His battle to go on living could be won or lost by whatever actions he took in the next few seconds. He reached out blindly with his right arm as his body teetered at the edge of control.

Someone grabbed his right wrist. In that split second, he was also aware that the proximity sensor in his suit Com had established a new channel by the chirping he heard in his ear. He was plunged into confusion by the feel of someone grabbing his arm. Whoever it was felt bigger and stronger than Margaret. But if it wasn't Margaret, then who was it? Had Vega and his men somehow found their way across the gorge by some other route? If so, he had risked his life just to make a big circle right back into the arms of his enemies. But if one of Vega's men had him, then who was shooting at him?

He felt himself steady and tried to find a foothold with his right boot. He felt something solid under his foot, then heard, "Jump, George, jump!" He did, and quickly felt another hand grab him and jerk him hard to the right. He stumbled as soon as he got both feet on solid ground, and then fell on top of someone on the lip of the ledge. That voice, he must be imagining it.

"Joanne, is that you?"

"George, thank goodness, I found you."

As he scrambled to his feet with her help, he saw what he thought were muzzle flashes coming from the other side of the pit.

"Who's that?"

Joanne cut him off, "Later, let's get clear."

She put her arm around him and they ran into the tunnel together. Two other people, who held pistols in a police stance and walked backwards, followed them into the tunnel. They fired rounds continuously as they retreated. His suit AI detected muzzle flashes in the visible, then integrated them into his display. He could tell one of the defenders was Margaret by her size and general shape; the other one was bigger. He looked to be almost twice her size. Impacts streaked all around them as they broke and dove behind rocks that had hidden the cave entrance from the other side of the gorge.

"Let's get the hell out of here," said Joanne.

She grabbed his hand, and they all began to run north. They ran for what seemed like fifteen minutes under full assist. All the time, George felt the shake of rail gun impacts, a lot of them.

George turned to Joanne. "How'd you get here, how'd you find me?" he asked.

"It's a long story, I'll tell you everything, but let's get clear first, okay?" Then in a breathless voice she said, "George."

"Yeah, I know, I'm really glad to see you too."

Later, when they could no longer feel the rumble of the battle behind them, Malcolm said, "We can stop now, they won't be coming after us any time soon."

They stopped more out of fatigue than out of Malcolm's compelling logic.

"Why not?" asked Margaret.

"Because all of that shooting must mean Void Fleet is right behind them..They have more pressing things to think about right now."

George held Joanne's hand. "If you and Malcolm had arrived a few minutes later, I'd be dead right now."

He took her in his arms and hugged her, not wanting to let go. He felt her trembling through the suit and then he felt her head on his shoulder.

He heard Malcolm say, "It's all the little lady's fault. If she hadn't pushed so hard, we wouldn't be here at all."

"I'm so sorry I put you through this," George said.

Malcolm pointed down the tunnel. "Come on, it isn't much farther. Let's get as far from here as we can."

Ten minutes later, George found himself at the airlock for tank one-hundred and forty-seven. Malcolm opened the lock, and they passed into the tank shaft. Looking up, George could see the lighter sky between the dark crescents of the tank and the shaft.

"So this comes out at the hydrogen-oxygen plant south of Dome Two?" George asked.

"Yes, that's right," said Joanne. "We have a tractor just over the top of this shaft."

George had seen "147" on the lock door.

"One-forty-seven," he said, making a quick mental calculation. "That's twenty-five miles south of the domes, isn't it?"

"Yes," said Joanne. "We can get back to Dome Two before dawn."

George said, "I'd be a lot better off going somewhere else. When they can't find me with Vega and his bunch, they'll start looking for me again. I can't go back to the domes with you."

Malcolm shrugged and started the long trek up the ladder, leaving the two to work things out in private. Margaret soon followed.

George and Joanne stood in the dark together, looking at each other, not knowing what to say.

"Where are we going then?" she asked finally.

"Are you sure you want to do this? Since you're here, it must mean you're still in the clear. Come with me and. . ."

"Don't do this to me again. I didn't come all this way just to leave. Don't make me feel unwanted."

"That's not it. I'd beg you to stay if I thought you'd be safe. I just can't stand any more guilt. I'm already responsible for a long trail of unhappy people. I don't want you be another one, that's all."

"Don't worry about me; I can take care of myself."

"You sure as hell can. You're doing a lot better job of it than I am." He stepped aside, "I'll follow you up—okay?"

She walked over and hugged him again. "I'm staying," she said in a soft voice, then started up the ladder.

"I'm sorry," he said from below her, "I'm sorry for all of it, really."

"I'm sorry for snapping at you," she said. "It's not what I thought I'd say to you after all this, but you know how you are. You have the most uncanny ability to bring out the best in me."

He could see her smiling in his mind's eye.

"You know George, I can't imagine where we could possibly go that Void Fleet couldn't arrest you again. Maybe the best thing to do is to go to the Ursa Supreme Court and seek asylum as a Martian citizen. You should see Dome Two right now. I've never seen anything like it. We just might be on the brink of a war of secession."

"That bad?"

"Yes, it's that bad." She paused, "You said Vega was back there? You don't mean the Vega that's been speaking on the steps of Building One, do you?"

"Yeah, the very same. He kidnapped us on the way to the cruiser in orbit. And I tell you Jo, that guy's dangerous. If there are many more like him stirring people up in the domes, we may have a much more volatile situation than we thought. Even as bad as it seems right now."

It took them another fifteen minutes to get to the top of the shaft. By the time they stepped off the ladder onto the bridge between the tank and mesa, they could see the shadows of two people standing by a tractor in the distance.

"That's it," Joanne said, "over there."

When George got to the end of the little bridge, Joanne stood there with her hand out and helped him down. Her visor was clear and he could see her now. Her bright blue eyes seemed to float in the dark cavern of her helmet. They stepped down onto the Martian soil and walked to the tractor together, hand in hand. It was dark, but checking his chronometer, George knew the sun would be rising in about three hours. He asked, "Did you find the Tab I left for you in my office?"

"Yes, that's how we found you."

"Good, give it to Malcolm, then sit in back with me."

"Okay," she said, giving him a sideways glance.

Malcolm took the Tab and asked, "So, where to?"

"Put the Tab in the console cradle," George instructed.

Malcolm did, and the clear plastic began to glow a soft blue.

"You know how to call Will, I take it?"

"Will?" asked Joanne. "They took him apart, didn't they?"

"Well, they didn't take him as far down as they thought," George said.

"Under *Rainy-Day*?" asked Malcolm.

"That's right."

Malcolm tapped the display in the appropriate place and the screen painted an open window with a flashing red cursor in the upper left.

"Bring us in, Will," said George. The window collapsed into a dot and then abruptly disappeared.

The tractor started, the lights on the console came up, and the steering yoke sprang far forward, indicating the Nav AI was driving.

Margaret turned and looked at George. "Well, Mills, you're full of surprises."

Joanne sat leaning against George, thankful that everything had worked out so well, but more than a little annoyed at Margaret. After they'd traveled east for about a half hour and Joanne was sure Malcolm and Margaret were asleep, she asked, "What about Margaret Gates?"

George took a breath, and then let it out slowly. "Well, Margaret was abused and I believe traumatized by Vega and his band of psychopathic followers while we were held. It's true that she's caused us a lot of trouble, but I'm convinced she blundered into it. My gut tells me that she's on our side now. I think she could actually help us."

"And what leads you to believe we can trust her? What if you're wrong? What if she's as crafty as I think she is?" Joanne rose from his shoulder to turn and look at him. "After all, she is very beautiful, and that can make deception a little easier, don't you think?"

He felt the verbal jab. Beyond the personal dimensions though, Joanne certainly had a point.

"We'll drop her off if you feel strongly about it. I can only tell you that I think she's sincere and I think she could be an asset."

"I'll go along with whatever you think is right," Joanne conceded. "I'm probably too tired and confused to think straight anyway. You spent time with her. You know her better than I do. Who knows, maybe you're right."

She sounded sleepy, dreamy.

"Here, come on, put your head on my lap." He scooted over to the far side of the seat. "Try to sleep."

George sat in silence for a while and watched the looming shadow of Dome Two to the north as they edged further east. It had the vast natural appearance of a mountain range. Eventually, he glanced down and was surprised to find Joanne looking up at him.

She smiled when he discovered she was still awake. "So what's the big secret?" she asked.

"What secret?"

"Where are we going? You act as if you know what you're doing. Do you?"

He considered her question. "Remember those hikes we used to take on the canyon rim?

"I remember very well."

* * *

Ursa Township had originally been built in the deep canyon of Valles Marineris near the Martian equator. It had been thought that large amounts of water had once run through some of the greater gorges in the vicinity of the canyon walls. Carved geological structures such as small island-like plateaus in the middle of large runoff channels, and water-like erosion of the channel walls, were suggestive of water related features on Earth. Before she'd met George, Joanne had flirted with the possibility of ancient life on Mars. Many of the early attempts to explore the red planet were motivated by searches for evidence of life. Being a molecular biologist, Joanne had examined and logged numerous samples of possible early life brought back by construction crews and field biologists on forays into the permafrost.

Joanne found many rock samples with salt-filled mineral fissures indicative of exposure to moving water. She had also found indications of primitive microscopic fossil-like structures in these salt-laden rocks, but she was never able to extract a positive, intact, complex organic molecule. She searched in vain for a snippet of DNA, or even a trace amino acid, but had never come close. The only conclusion she could draw was that if life had ever existed on Mars, it had done so at a time sufficiently distant that natural forces had long since erased all traces of it.

Then came George, with his Earther's restlessness to wander around outside the protective cocoon of the domes. In his usual annoying way, he'd offered an alternative she'd yet to consider.

"Maybe the construction crews have missed something that would be obvious to you," he'd said. "They didn't have the tools we have today to penetrate the surface." He'd paused and looked at her, smiling broadly. "Did you ever consider getting out there yourself? You know where to look and where not to."

She'd known it was a ploy to get her to wander around with him, but she had to admit, his arguments made sense. Finally, he'd convinced her to hike the canyon channels with him. For him, an Earther, it was pure heaven to get out among the natural cathedrals of the planet. For her, it was an opportunity to collect her samples. A chance to examine places she thought were more likely to yield positive results, rather than wasting time on the haphazard samples brought back by construction crews. And so it had started, she remembered, whimsically. Soon she was planning their outings and dragging him to remote and exotic places on, and underneath, the surface of Mars. They had even taken small plane flights to Hellas Basin and Olympus Mons as well as to the southern Martian pole.

* * *

"Yes, I remember our hikes," Joanne said again.

"Remember the satellite relay station we came across on the canyon wall about fifteen miles southeast of Dome One?"

She turned onto her back so that she could see him.

"I think so," she said slowly.

He could tell she'd forgotten. She was sucking her lower lip, a sure sign she was having trouble remembering.

"Remember about five years ago, we were on the canyon rim about three thousand feet up? You found those old sand stones with white streaks of light colored minerals."

He saw her blink. "Yes, right, I remember now." She had it. "So?"

"Well, a couple of years ago it occurred to me that something like this might happen. We went through a period where we began to notice obvious physical differences in the children. You used to show me pictures from time to time, and I started thinking about what we might do if they were ever discovered. It was about that time when I started examining the station as a possible fall-back position."

"Fall-back position?"

"Yeah, you know, some place that we could go in a situation like this. Some place with tools and supplies we might use to somehow deal with our predicament."

"And you did this without telling me?"

"Yes I did."

"Why? Why didn't you say something? I could've helped."

"I know. And with your help, it would've taken half the time, but I didn't want to alarm you. Besides, you did all the fieldwork with the kids. I felt like this should be my contribution. And, with a little luck, I thought it would be work in vain."

She thought a moment. "So, is that where Will is now?"

"Yes, that's right. The station was perfect. It was old and forgotten, but it still had power and a satellite uplink that was operational, even after all these years."

"About Will, though; wasn't he in the basement annex?"

"Remember, at the height of the simulations, we had eight quantum columns. Well, I took two of them to the station with

277

some other things. They were never missed because I did it over a period of years."

She reached up and put her hand on the side of his helmet.

"You know, George, you've done very well. Under the circumstances, I suppose, it's the best plan imaginable. But no matter what we do now, it's hard to see how we can win in the long run. They're too big, too determined. Eventually, they have to find us. That's the inescapable reality, isn't it?"

George focused on the dim brightness of the distant horizon, heralding the pressing arrival of dawn. "Maybe," he conceded finally, "and maybe not. Let's just wait and see."

Chapter Thirty

"Come on, get up!"

Perseus turned in his bed and opened his eyes a mere crack. He was lying on his side and had a good vantage from the top of the bunk.

"Get up!"

In the center of his field of view he saw the broad dark outline of someone sticking up above the edge of the bed. It took him a few moments to organize his thoughts as he opened his eyes wider, attempting to see the apparition that hovered next to him in the darkness. The only light in the room came from a half-opened door far behind the shadowy outline that danced in his sleep-filled vision. He raised his head off the pillow for a better look and saw a man standing next to his bed. Only his head and shoulders were visible from the top bunk where he lay. At first, Perseus thought that the man was only another in a series of bad dreams that even now hovered on the edge of his consciousness. However, that thought was quickly dispelled when he saw a huge dark arm spring up and then felt a large rough hand grab his shoulder. The hand held him fast, its large fingers incasing his entire left shoulder in an iron grip. The man shook him like a rag doll.

"Come down here—hurry up."

It was no dream. The man's head was big and square with a sharp jaw that gave it a menacing look. Perseus couldn't make out the details of his face in the dim light, but he could see, as the man turned to profile, a blunt nose and heavy brow ridges that reminded him of something monstrously atavistic. His voice was low and gruff and conveyed little sense of emotion, other than annoyance that Perseus wasn't moving fast enough to suit him.

Perseus sat up and rubbed his eyes.

"What is it? Is it morning?"

"Just come down from there. Dr. Sanders wants to talk to you—right now."

Perseus backed down the ladder to the floor and stood next to the man who had so rudely roused him from the sanctuary of sleep. As the man loomed above him in the harshly cast shadows of the poorly lit room, Perseus began to feel around for his clothes and shoes.

"You won't need those," said the man, taking him by the arm.

As he was hustled from the bedroom, Perseus saw other boys stirring in their beds. Some were sitting up.

"Go back to sleep," he heard the man say, as they moved across the room and then out the door. The light in the anteroom stung his eyes and he squinted to see what was going on. The Earth woman who'd been taking roster at dinner, was waiting for them. She held a light blue hospital gown open for him to slip into, then put fabric booties on his feet.

"Is it still night?" he asked.

They didn't answer. The man grabbed him by the arm once more and they followed the woman across the lounge and into the corridor beyond. They walked in hurried steps down the same concrete hallways they'd taken when he'd first arrived. He couldn't help wishing that somehow they'd take him out of here and back into the cool night air, back to his parents.

Finally, they arrived at a hub with five mysterious corridors fanning out to places Perseus was sure he didn't want to visit.

"This way," said the woman, heading for one on the opposite side of the hub. Perseus hedged, but was pulled behind his abductors, too small to resist their brutish power. His instincts bristled at the horrible images that filled his imagination. It was clear that these Earthers considered him and his kind little more than lab specimens, to be treated accordingly.

"Where are we going?"

He could hear his shaky voice bouncing in echoes off the hard concrete walls. They dragged him past several closed doors and eventually reached a door, in front of which, the woman stopped. She unlocked the door and held it open. The man let him go and all but pushed him into the room, then turned and left. The woman entered behind him and he heard the door close with an abrupt slam. Perseus flinched, but began to relax a little in the silence that followed. Looking around, he saw that this room was much smaller than the lounge where he'd slept. Displays and medical robotic turnstiles covered the walls. There were cabinets with a variety of solutions in medical vials indexed with colorful labels. Off to one side was a lab couch with mechanical stainless steel arms arrayed around it. The room was lit so as to accentuate the area around the couch. Colorful lights glimmered on various consoles in the near darkness of the periphery.

Perseus noticed motion behind the couch, but found it hard to resolve, because whatever it was, was obscured by the glare of the light that hung over the area just in front. Suddenly, Dr. Sander's ghostly pale face appeared from the movement in the shadows. Sanders looked eerie in the uneven light, with his nearly bald head and wispy comb-over dominating his weak chin and closely set eyes. He wore a white lab coat and pushed himself forward on a caster stool.

"Come in Perseus, don't be afraid."

Perseus looked over his shoulder, seeking the door, trying to assess his chances of escape. The woman stood in front of the door, her face cut by a sadistic smile.

"Sit here please," said Dr. Sanders, motioning toward the couch.

Perseus just stood there, trying to decide what to do, paralyzed by equally unpleasant alternatives. In that moment he felt the desire to keep on living, to see his parents again, to see Miram again.

"Don't hurt me," he pleaded.

"Now why would I want to do that? Haven't you been well treated? What gives you these strange ideas, anyway?"

The man's syrupy insincerity was sickening.

"Sit down!" snapped the woman from behind him.

He could tell by the sound of her voice that she'd gotten closer. He felt her hands on his arm. Her nervous weasel-like grip underscored the insubstantial nature of her presence. She was a leech that had attached itself to the sore that was this endeavor. She was a creature of opportunity, not of design. When she finally forced him onto the couch, Sanders shot forward on his stool like a scavenger to the kill.

"There," Sanders said. "Isn't that better?"

"No, you're scaring me. Why are you doing this?"

"Be quiet," said the woman. The distain in her voice was palpable.

Sanders motioned to her with his hand, cutting her off. "I'll take it from here, Julia. Why don't you wait outside?"

She hesitated, then began to speak.

"Please wait outside," repeated Sanders, clearly annoyed by her heavy-handed style.

She turned abruptly and left the room in a huff. Staring down at him, manipulating something in his hands, Sanders continued to appeal to Perseus to cooperate.

"What's that in your hands?" asked Perseus, unfamiliar with most of what he saw around him.

"What, this?" Sanders followed Perseus's gaze to the dull silver pneumatic injector in his right hand.

"It's something to help you relax, that's all."

Perseus retracted his arm reflexively as Sanders pointed the barrel at him.

"Hold still," hissed Sanders through clenched teeth, as he tried with his left hand to steady the boy's skinny arm.

The man's clammy soft grip held him firmly, then Perseus felt the cold metal barrel followed by a thud sound. A ring of tightness and then a slight numb feeling crept up his arm. I've been drugged, Perseus thought, panicked again at the prospect of being even more helpless than he already was. Calm down, he though, you've got to calm down. He wasn't used to this. Typically, he wasn't given to strong emotion. He'd grown accustomed to being in control of himself, analyzing a situation, and taking his time in coming to a suitable course of action. The habits of a lifetime, albeit a short one, now had to be overturned in the few moments afforded him. This was like a torrent, an emotional hurricane, keeping him in a constant state of disorientation.

He felt the drug taking effect. It was hard to move his arms and legs in natural coordinated ways. His limbs felt like mechanical devices that required planning to yield purposeful motion. He relaxed and willed the tension in his muscles away. With mental agility, he found his distal parts and flexed them in turn, reeducating his hampered nervous system back into conscious control. He was determined to regain control of his body through the force of his mind, to will this insidious drug to release him.

Sanders was saying something; he forced himself to listen. He would try to divine the truth from the mass of Sander's lies. His only chance would be to learn as much about what was going on as he could.

"I have to get a sample of your blood," said Sanders, after applying a tourniquet to his upper arm and puncturing his lower arm with a needle device attached to one of the gimbals hovering above the couch. After that Sanders got specimens of skin, saliva, earwax, and urine, then put them into small plastic tubes. Once he'd collected the samples, Sanders put the tubes into various devices that lined the wall opposite the couch. A whine issued from one device, a hum from another.

Perseus followed his actions as Sanders pushed buttons and manipulated icons on several clear plastic displays. Presently, Sanders returned to his stool, rubbing is hands together, looking self-satisfied.

"Good, that's good," he said.

Perseus just looked up at him, biding his time, feeling his composure returning little by little. He slowly clenched and unclenched his hands, moving his fingers one at a time, feeling each joint respond smoothly to the mental image he held of it. He did the same with his ankles and toes. Strength and control were usurping the effects of the drug he'd been given. Success built upon itself and his confidence grew, his fear receding in proportion. His head was clearing and he began to weigh his options.

"Let's get a look at your head," said Sanders, pulling down a dull silver ring attached to one of the gimbals.

He put the metal crown on Perseus's head, leveling it across his tall forehead.

"Good," said Sanders, "That's good."

"What's good?" asked Perseus in a clear dispassionate voice.

Sanders blinked, clearly taken off guard by the boy's lucidity.

"Uh, our tests, they're going well."

Perseus smiled slightly. He held Sanders' eyes, tried to see beyond them. Colored forms undulated dully somewhere in the space behind Sanders' skull. Perseus could see them, but not with his eyes. It was a visual experience, not exactly like the meld, but there were points of similarity that could not be dismissed. He continued to examine the shapes, moving with them, trying to understand their relationships to Sanders' actions.

Sanders turned, breaking eye contact with some effort, then began manipulating items on a display behind him. You don't have to look at me for me see you, thought Perseus. Even with his busy movements, even given the fact that Sanders had turned away, he could still see the colored forms. They were brighter now, more distinct. He knew instinctively that it was Sanders, his essence. Perseus relaxed, tried not to interfere with the forms, didn't really know if he could. He was an observer on the fabric of Sanders' mind. Just because he could sense these forms didn't mean he could affect them.

Sanders pulled down a blank screen. "Now I want you to watch the images on the screen," said Sanders. "They'll flash quickly. You may not be able to follow them. Don't worry, that's okay. Just watch them and don't try to think about them."

Perseus remained quiet, his gaze fixed on the small, balding Earther. Sanders grimaced, deflated by the odd way in which this boy was responding to the drug he'd been given. He knew there was something wrong, but couldn't quite put his finger on what it was. He had the sensation of being watched in some intimate indescribable way.

Perseus sensed increased brain activity, quicker undulations in a form that he knew was Sanders' conscious mind. Perseus could see that this new movement was tied to Sanders' growing unease. He decided to push the lower form a little to see what, if anything, might happen. He imagined it speeding up a little, visualized it. As it slowly began to respond, he heard Sanders catch his breath and saw beads of sweat begin to form on his pale pate.

"It's warm in here," muttered Sanders, pulling a cloth handkerchief from the pocket of his white lab coat. He raised the cloth to his forehead with a shaky hand and began to dab at the sweat.

"Excuse me," he said reflexively, then began to appear unsteady on his stool.

Perseus backed off and returned the form to its prior state. Almost instantly, he heard Sanders say, "Oh, that's better. I don't know what came over me."

Perseus continued to stare. Sanders appeared reluctant to look at him.

"Let me go Doctor. What you're doing isn't right."

Sanders seemed confused, as if he couldn't tell whether what Perseus had just said was a request or an order.

"Why are you frightened Dr. Sanders? Why are you Earthers always frightened?"

Sanders dabbed at his forehead absently. "Just watch the screen," he said, then paddled off on his stool as if fleeing from some invisible force.

The screen started to flash with images. Perseus watched. He remembered what Sanders had said about the speed of the frames, that he might have trouble following the pictures. They appeared clear, a bit rushed, but he could easily make them out.

There were pictures of people rioting in the street—a picture of a soldier discharging a weapon, a picture of a mother hugging a child. As these pictures swept by, he recalled the scene at his house the night before. His father humbled on the floor, the panicked screams of his dear mother. Enough, he said to himself, enough of this. He closed his eyes, not wanting to see any more. These Earthers were destructive. They practiced cruelty and raised it to an art form. What could possibly motivate them? They seemed to have almost no empathy for other living things apart from those they had an emotional attachment to.

Instead of thinking about the horrible pictures flashing on the screen, Perseus chose instead to think about his mother's garden, the stars in his projector. He felt a sense of calm returning.

"You have to look," he heard Sanders insist.

"Turn it off Doctor," he said, keeping his eyes squeezed shut.

Some time passed. He sensed Sanders nearby, could almost feel the man's breath on his face. He finally opened his eyes and found Sanders staring down at him.

"If you don't cooperate I'll be forced to have Julia come back," he warned. "You don't want that, do you?"

Perseus sat up, dangling his legs over the side of the couch but not touching the floor.

"Please, Dr. Sanders, I don't want to use force, but I will if I have to."

At that Sanders back-pedaled a half step on his stool.

"What's this about Doctor? Why not be honest with me? Do you think your lies can fool me into becoming your lab specimen? Would you condone such treatment toward your own children? What gives you the right?"

"You may be dangerous," said Sanders. "We have to know."

Perseus shook his head. "I might be dangerous," he repeated. "Look at what you're doing in this room and tell me which of us is dangerous, Doctor."

"It's not my call," said Sanders, "I'm not responsible for making the rules."

"Are you responsible for your own actions?" asked Perseus. "If you're not responsible for yourself, then who is?" He looked around. "I don't see anyone else in here. Let me go back to the bedroom, Doctor. You have your samples; you've done what they asked you to do. Couldn't you persuade the others to let us go? Couldn't you just conclude in your reports that we pose no threat? We'll all go home. You can continue to watch us to assure yourselves we're not up to something. You know where we live. There are only twenty of us. Surely with all the resources available to you, you can keep track of twenty people."

"I'd love to do that," said Sanders. "But it's just not my call."

Perseus heard chimes. Apparently the machines had finished their analysis of the samples that Sanders had prepared. Sanders rose from his stool and leaned over a set of monitors. Perseus watched him. Results streamed vertically down the displays with dizzying speed as Sanders turned from one to the other, transfixed and seemingly alarmed by whatever was coming out. He turned around slowly and saw Perseus casually standing next to the couch watching him.

"What are you doing up? You shouldn't be able to stand. I gave you 50 cc's of Dormaflex."

Perseus could see the man's eyes quickly darting around, looking for something. Perseus followed his gaze. The Tab, he started for the Tab. He was going to call for help.

"Please Doctor, don't do that!"

Sanders quickened his pace and reached for the Tab.

"Stop!"

The man came to an immediate halt, like a marionette whose strings had been caught by an invisible hand. Perseus heard the man whimper, then saw his mouth work up and down like a fish gasping for water to fill its gills. "I can't move my legs," he croaked in a strangled gasp. Then he opened his mouth wide, his eyes bulged with fear. He was going to scream for help.

"Quiet," commanded Perseus, calmly this time. The urgency had left his voice.

Sanders' mouth flapped, but nothing came out. Perseus stepped up to him, took his hand, and sat him down on his stool. They were eye to eye now.

"How does it feel, Doctor, to be the lab specimen?"

Tears started to drop from the man's eyes. They slipped down his cheeks, gathered on his sharp chin, then fell onto his white lab coat, staining the fabric with moisture. The sight of the man's fear, dense and consuming in him, made Perseus feel ill. The empathic connection between them made Perseus feel the man's despair. He was an animal again; a million years of instinct subsumed his higher mind and filled him with desperate images of flight. Perseus could sense his primitive mind pumping adrenaline and endorphins into his system with the implicit expectation of probable death. Perseus turned away from him momentarily. When he turned back, he found the man perched on his stool, a comically ugly bird shaking uncontrollably now. He took the man's hand once more.

"Calm down, Doctor. I'm not going to hurt you in any way. Do you believe me?"

Sanders nodded.

"I'm just trying to save myself and my people. Can you understand that?" Perseus exhaled, annoyed that this stupid man had pushed him to do this. He found the sight of a human, helpless and shaking with fright, disturbing.

"Why does it take a demonstration like this to make you understand what should be obvious to any intelligent person?"

He stepped back and looked at the man again. Sanders' chest had stopped heaving, his cheeks were streaked but dry, and he'd stopped shaking.

"I want you to relax. I want you to close your eyes and go to sleep."

Sanders' eyelids slowly descended as his eyes rolled up. His shoulders drooped and his breathing became slow and shallow. Perseus returned to the couch, sat down, and looked around the room. What now? Cameras must have seen this whole episode. Security men would probably come streaming through the door any minute now, heavily armed and ready to use lethal force. He felt as if he might be able to control one or two of them, but it seemed likely that the rest would quickly overpower him and probably kill him. Perhaps he could stop their hearts. That would be a lot more efficient than trying to control them. He might actually make it out of here alive if he did that. He recoiled at the thought that he'd actually entertained such a notion. No, he wouldn't have desperation turn him into a killer.

The room was quiet and mostly dark. Perseus found the calm soothing and welcome. The colorful displays continued to stream enigmatic data. Perseus scanned the room. He could do nothing about the cameras or the data, but he could do something about Sanders. He could make Sanders forget what had happened here. It took minutes for short-term memories to be transferred to long-term storage in the central and frontal lobes, where Perseus could no longer affect them without harming the man. This was certainly no solution to his current problem, but there was a time window here that demanded a decision.

He erased Sanders' memories of losing control, of his unbridled fear of whatever it was he'd learned from those displays that had thrown him into a near panic. He felt the ripples of those memories start to dampen and dissipate into nothingness. In their place, he sensed the blackness of the man's deep sleep.

Perseus put his face in his hands, felt the moisture of his own perspiration, and smelled the sour odor of his heightened metabolism. He stayed that way for some time, trying to recover. He got up and began to search the room again, more carefully this time. He walked into the darker places he hadn't seen before. Automated systems churned out plots, reports, and columns of numbers that were meaningless to him. No doubt, given time, he might be able decipher the data, but time was something he didn't have a lot of right now. Clearly, what Sanders had gleaned from some of the information had alarmed him. Something in all of this must have made him realize he was vulnerable to my influence, thought Perseus, a fact that, until now, he'd been unaware of himself. This realization presented another problem. If Sanders could come to this conclusion so quickly, then so could others. They'd make the same discovery, the same connections—then what? They'd react like Sanders, first with fear, then with violence; it wasn't hard to predict.

Perseus exhaled. This nightmare refused to end. This new development all but guaranteed their extinction. This was the so-called smoking gun. The humans had suspected that his people might be a danger; now they would no longer suspect it, they would know it. Unless—unless he could somehow fake the data, unless no one else saw the real data. He found momentary comfort in this thought, in the hope that something might still be done, though the chances of pulling off this kind of deception seemed all but impossible. He needed something to cling to no matter how unlikely.

He continued to fantasize as he walked, taking time to notice things that might be important. Something caught his eye.

He stopped and stared up at it. A camera was mounted high in the corner of the room. It was a small spherical protrusion, essentially unnoticeable, except for a faint green light just above its black dot of an aperture. Well, he thought; that's it then. They don't have to inspect the data; they've seen everything. He'd suspected this might be the case, but here was the proof, right in front of him. He turned to the door, half expecting to see it burst open, followed by a rush of security men. It didn't happen.

Why? he thought. Why not? He looked at the camera again. It blinked! The green light blinked on and off. He, himself, blinked in astonishment, half thinking he was so upset that he was seeing things. It blinked back.

"Will?" he asked slowly.

The light blinked twice. Perseus felt a smile lift his cheeks. For the first time since his abduction, he began to feel as if there might be a way out of this mess. He'd have to use this time efficiently.

"The data," he said slowly, "can you fix it?"

The light blinked twice again. He thought a moment. Eventually, he'd have to revive Sanders. He had no idea what procedures might govern the analysis that Sanders was expected to perform. The data would have stopped coming by now. Maybe someone would notice the inactivity. It was reasonable to assume that the woman would be coming back soon, or someone else would be checking in for some sort of progress report. He had never seen any of the attendants in this place alone for too long.

"When it's ready, blink three times, okay?"

Instantly, the light blinked three times.

Perseus looked around the room in amazement at all the complicated devices, their unknowable interconnections, and all the distant databases they might be updating. He turned back to the camera.

"You were able to do it so quickly?"

The light blinked twice. Perseus nodded in acknowledgement and gratitude. He then moved back to where Sanders sat, perched quietly on his stool, and thought about what to do next. He looked back at the camera, smiled, and winked. He'd better wake Sanders before the woman returned.

Perseus lay on the couch again, then said, "Wake up Doctor, come out of it."

It wasn't really necessary to utter the words, but it helped him concentrate. He was tired. He was new to all this, and would have to refine the technique later.

Sanders slowly opened his eyes, then jerked abruptly, upsetting his precarious balance. Almost falling off the stool, he looked around nervously, clearly trying to remember what he'd been doing. Turning back to Perseus, he eyed him suspiciously. Then he got up from the stool to inspect the monitors. He mumbled to himself and walked from device to device in a sporadic gait, occasionally holding on for balance.

"I'm tired, Dr. Sanders. I want to go back to bed," said Perseus from the couch in a little boy's voice.

Sanders turned. "What? Oh yes—right."

He stood by his consoles, either trying to clear his head or come to a decision about something—it wasn't clear which. He put his hand on his chin and rubbed his cheek with his thumb, leaving a reddish mark on his face. Then, looking at the Tab behind the stool, he moved to retrieve it.

"Julia, could you come in here please, the boy's ready to go back."

After a few moments, Perseus heard, "I'll be right there, Doctor."

Minutes later, Perseus found himself being hustled back to the bedroom. He stumbled and hedged, rubbed his eyes often, and gave the general impression of being confused. The big man who brought him back apparently had well established preconceptions of what Perseus' condition should be after the examination. When he left the boy, he took one last look and smiled, satisfied that everything was as it should be.

* * *

Julia checked the monitors, quickly scanning the more relevant pieces of data. Sanders sat on the edge of the medical lounge feeling strangely light. Julia sat on his stool and watched him for a few minutes. He wasn't himself. He was usually sharp and intrusive, almost to the point of demagoguery. Here, he sat passive, with his head supported by a hand whose elbow rested on his knee. He rubbed his forehead with his other hand and seemed generally unaware of her presence.

"What's the matter with you?" she asked.

He looked up quickly, his eyes stern and tight.

"Nothing's wrong!" he snapped. "Why do you ask?"

As she continued to watch him, his rigid spine loosened once more, and he slowly sank back into his previous funk.

"What about the boy?" she asked.

"What about him?"

She paused. "The data seems to indicate nothing unusual."

"Maybe we were wrong about them," he mumbled, almost to himself.

A few moments later she got up from the stool and left him there, in the privacy of his dark lab, to struggle with whatever demons he was fighting.

She was troubled. What the hell had happened in Sanders' lab? He wasn't the Sanders that she knew, she was sure of that. Something had changed him. Something had touched him deeply and turned him inside out. The show he'd put on a few hours ago was so bad that it had to be genuine. He was the head of the research division at Mollar and hadn't reached that position by being naïve or incompetent. He was truly confused and disoriented. The question was, how had he gotten that way?

Julia sat in front of a Tab in her office, near Sanders' lab.
She was streaming the audio-visual data from the surveillance
pickups, and was reviewing Sanders' interactions with the boy
for the past half hour. Maybe she could determine what had
happened to Sanders.

At the start of the interrogation, Sanders had been his
normal arrogant self, barking orders, and finally throwing her out
of the room—nothing unusual there. She watched as the boy
reclined on the couch. Sanders had given him a powerful muscle
relaxer and the boy had sat there, looking at the evocative images
flashing across the display in front of him. Ten minutes later, the
session ended and Sanders inspected the results, calling her into
the room shortly thereafter—nothing unusual.

Afterwards, she inspected the data. It wasn't what she'd
expected. All the DNA markers were consistent with the
therapies as specified in the DRA database entries for the boy.
Physiological data seemed consistent, nothing unusual. She had
even checked the chronometer on the video against time ticks on
the data, and everything looked perfectly in order. Next, she
inspected the encryption checksums on the multimedia packets
for evidence of tampering, and found that nothing had been done
to the data to alter it in any way. She sat back and exhaled in
frustration. She knew there was something wrong. She just knew
it.

Chapter Thirty-One

Oz sat at his console on the bridge of the Saratoga and
stared at his scanners. The ship was on an elliptical orbit around
Mars that cut the equator at about thirty degrees. The perigee of
the orbit was up around the northern pole. An orbital period of
about sixty-five minutes had brought the ship directly over
Valles Marineris and the terminus of the northern and southern
pipe networks.

Oz helped debrief Wells, who had been rescued from the
separatist compound. He learned about Vega and his plans to try
to scuttle the ship. Once that information was uncovered, the
ship's orbit had been adjusted for optimal times over the most
probable spots on the surface for Vega's reappearance. On every
pass, he'd pounded the mesa and canyon with microwave and
laser scans and had done exhaustive IR and absorption
measurements. During those times when the ship slipped into
Mars' shadow, he'd ordered continuous interceptor fly-overs. It
had been more than twelve hours since Dean and his platoon had
chased the terrorists into those vapor filled sub-Martian caverns
and, as yet, no word of the terrorists or of Margaret had surfaced.

Oz leaned back in his chair, turned, and looked out over the
bridge. After staring at his monitors for such a long time, he was
becoming claustrophobic. The bridge had been designed to avoid
the stress of being penned-up in the tight confines of a
workstation for hours on end. It was large, three decks deep, and
was approximately semi-conical, with the curved decks of the
half-cone lined with workstations arranged on balconies. The
flat, planar cut of the cone was provided by one of the forward
bulkheads of the first rotating crew section and looked out over
the front of the ship. Blast doors, which protected the transparent
forward section of the bridge, were closed when the ship was
under way. A metal pole ran the vertical length of the bridge in
the large space between the concentric balconies and the forward

observation wall. A hemispheric projector traveled up and down the length of the pole and presented the bridge with a three-dimensional display of the space outside the ship. The display was used when the blast doors were closed or when a specific view of space or other graphic information was required for general viewing. The interior of the display was fine mesh semiconducting polymer, which provided a resolution and stability far greater than the best hologram.

Oz sipped his tea, a holdover from his distant British roots, and thought about Margaret. Beautiful woman and smart, but Margaret was odd. Not like most Moderns he knew. She was more like an Earther of antiquity, strangely private and surprisingly modest. Even though she had a body to die for, he'd never had her and didn't know anyone else on the ship who had, man or woman. It wasn't that she wasn't friendly, she was. But she seemed somehow detached, distant. He'd noticed that her subtle reserve had made her one of the Admiral's favorites. It was pretty clear that the old man, an antiquity buff himself, had the hots for her. She could have used that to advance, but to the best of his knowledge, she had never elected to play that card. I hope she makes it, he thought, and became mildly excited by the prospect.

"Proximity alert," bellowed the Navigator in the eves of the bridge. Oz almost spilled his tea as he whirled around to face his console.

"What the hell?" he mumbled to himself, as the Navigator continued issuing the proximity warning. He could hear the chatter in his earpiece as members of the executive cadre started calling for clarification.

"Cease alert!" Oz ordered, and called up his tactical display. Then he heard the Admiral's voice in his ear, joining the chorus of other voices.

"One moment, sir."

He rotated the image on tactical. The ship was coming up on the North Pole, on a vector tight to the planet. Look-Around satellites that they'd deployed after first assuming orbit had just picked up three crafts on full burn, coming up fast from over the northern horizon where they couldn't be seen until the last moment. The Navigator had failed to receive a transponder beacon, which normally painted unidentified crafts as friendlies in the absence of other corroborating data. Mars Traffic Control was confirming that the intruders had no flight plan.

"Shit!" spat Oz to himself. "Navigator, assume intruders are hostile. Take evasive action."

Oz switched the display to show what the Look-Around satellites were seeing. The Navigator integrated the image into its tactical display, showing three bright plumes heading over the pole, suborbital, on an intercept trajectory as the Saratoga climbed to the same pole on the other side of Mars. Oz felt the Navigator maneuver the ship, which shock violently as the blast doors sprang shut, plunging the bridge into red light. On a profile of the ship, on another display, Oz saw the Navigator unsheathe the five forward neutral beam cannons that formed the Saratoga's forward defense perimeter. Their turrets spun quickly in the void, and before the barrels came up on the objects, the Navigator had calculated a firing solution. Suddenly, Oz noticed three bright points break the northern horizon of Mars. They were no more than two thousand miles away, and closing at more than twenty thousand miles per hour. He heard the hum of the cannons firing through vibrations in the hull.

In the black void, five blue ethereal fingers reached out at near the speed of light and swept across the objects in perfect silence. Five hundred teravolts of energy almost instantly turned the three shuttles to vapor. As the outer hull of one of the shuttles ceased to exist, forward sensors failed to register in the trigger mechanism of a ten megaton thermonuclear warhead that it carried in its cargo bay. In the millisecond it took for the energy of the Saratoga's cannons to disassociate the shuttle's cargo bay, the bomb detonated only five hundred miles from the ship.

It was a fairly primitive bomb, with a blast profile spherically symmetric about the epicenter of the explosion, rather than shaped in the direction of the target. The Navigator had turned the ship so as to point it directly into the oncoming shockwave, which would ensure that the smallest possible energy would impinge on the ship.

"Collision alert!" boomed the Navigator over and over, as the shockwave plunged the ship into roller-coaster-like gyrations. Oz gripped his seat with both hands and waited for the sound of tearing metal. It never came. Within a couple of minutes, it was over. Small amounts of plasma remained in the vicinity of the ship, but radiation levels began to fall almost immediately. Damage reports started coming in and indicated only minor damage to the forward sections. Five crewmen, who had been outside the ship during the attack, were missing and presumed dead. No other crew had been seriously injured. Once it was determined that the engines were fully operational, the ship was moved to a higher equatorial orbit, giving the Saratoga the greatest possible vantage point for warding off attacks from the surface. The Look-Around satellites were repositioned to plug tactical holes in their deployment. Oz was informed that, due to the onset of hostilities, the search for Gates and Mills would be postponed indefinitely.

A meeting of executive officers had been called at twenty one hundred hours Earth standard time. When the Admiral and his senior staff entered the bridge, Oz was putting the finishing touches on the satellite redeployment. Hearing the click of flight boots on the floor below as they entered, he spun around in his chair. Looking down what resembled an amphitheater, Oz saw officers gathering around a railing in front of two acceleration lounges that were usually occupied by pilots when the ship was under way. The projector was activated and showed a crystal clear, three-dimensional image of the planet's surface as the ship raced along its new orbit. The blast doors remained shut. The Admiral looked up.

"Commander, won't you join us?"

"Yes sir," replied Oz, as he shot up from his seat and walked an eighth of the way around the second tier balcony to the deck ladder. When he was down on the flight deck below, he gave a curt nod to his fellow officers and assumed a position near the railing, facing the Admiral. Behind the Admiral, the surface of Mars rolled by in slow progression, underscoring its lumbering size.

"As of twenty hundred hours Earth normal," began the Admiral, "we've received word from resources on Phobos and Demos that the insurgency is attempting to commandeer the H3 mining facilities on those sites. We have dispatched assault platoons to both moons. We've also received word from the surface that sporadic fighting is now occurring in the streets of Dome One, Ursa. As of twenty-one hundred hours Earth normal, martial law has been declared in both Ursa and Orion Townships."

Oz fixated on an imperfection in the railing in front of him. He'd imagined this might be a possibility, but had somehow held the irrational belief that a war could be avoided. This wasn't a war yet, just one more step in that direction. Being the tactical officer aboard the Saratoga, he'd run countless war-game simulations of just this eventuality. What he'd come to learn, as a result, was that a state of martial law under these circumstances would probably escalate to war, with a weak dependence on the details of the intervening skirmishes. In each case, where war resulted, the loss of life in the Martian population was nothing short of catastrophic. The thing that bothered him the most was that for a large part of it, he'd be the trigger-man. It was true that others would give the orders, but the grim reality of their misadventures would fall on him. He'd spent more than a few sleepless nights imagining giving the fire command to the tactical AI and watching as a Dome of fifty thousand people was transformed to vapor at the hum of the ship's belly cannons.

He looked around the room. Young lieutenants were discussing their contingency plans with enthusiasm. The Admiral stood in the middle of his entourage, nodding thoughtfully as they explained tactics, itemizing their supporting intelligence in great detail. He heard their throaty upper-class voices carefully articulate points of view as they'd been so carefully taught in rhetoric classes and debates at the Naval Academy back on Earth. Time tested techniques of persuasion were delivered in the sober thoughtful spoonfuls that somehow gave insane plans legitimacy.

He felt someone staring and looked up to find the Admiral's eyes on him. It was obvious that the older man had seen unconscious signs of disapproval on Oz's face as he'd pondered the future in what he'd thought were private moments of reflection. But his expressive face had betrayed him.

"Yes, Commander, is there a problem?"

Shit, thought Oz. Here was the moment of truth. Dissenting words at this point might mean the end of his fast track career. Futures were built on the shoulders of men and women that could be trusted at times like these. A real leader was expected to check personal considerations at the door and be a team player— fully committed. On the other hand, his mind reeled at the prospect of all the future bouts of insomnia and all the pills he'd have to consume to stop seeing the countless faces of collateral damage that would depend on what he had to say right here and right now.

"What was the position of the NearSec Oversight Committee on martial law, sir?"

The Admiral regarded him for a few long moments.

"They left that decision in my hands as NearSec Supreme Commander. You don't approve, Commander?"

Oz looked around the room. He was the unwitting center of attention. Some of his subordinates licked their imaginary chops at the possibility that he might make as foolish a blunder as he appeared about to make.

"I've done tactical simulations of just these circumstances, Admiral. In fact, after debriefing Captain Wells, I found that an entire class of those same simulations predicted the attack we just survived."

The aggravation on the Admiral's face was apparent. He tried to hide it by looking around the room a few times.

"I want to see you in the bridge conference room right away, Commander!"

The rest of the officers cleared a path as the Admiral walked briskly by them without so much as a glance. They moved toward the doors at the end of a passage that ran below the balconies and exited the bridge. Oz followed a couple of steps behind the Admiral. Damn, he thought, his heart racing. The bridge doors closed behind him, but not quickly enough that he avoided hearing the hushed whispers of amused officers as the closing cut them off.

Moments later, Oz found himself at one end of the black marble table in the conference room. The Admiral sat poised at the other end. Mars moved into shadow under a bright halo of stars outside the large conference room window.

"Okay Commander, you have five minutes to make your case."

The older man was taut, a tight grimace stretched his mouth, and his eyes were narrow and piercing.

"You made me look like a fool out there," he said curtly.

Great, thought Oz. It's all about you and your legacy, isn't it? It has absolutely nothing to do with the thousands of people who could so easily be spared by a few moments consideration.

Oz had never been an overly sympathetic man. In fact, he'd always considered apologists and placaters to be little more than moral cowards—but this? He'd never seen himself as so ambitious as to sanction mass murder in the name of national necessity. Unfortunately, he knew himself well enough to know that he would be true to his oath as a soldier. In the end, there was little doubt in his mind that he'd uphold the chain of command as he had vowed to do. Above all, he was a man of honor, and although he knew that there were historical decisions that, in his view, were unfortunate, in the aggregate, an adherence to discipline and tradition had made the Earth the pinnacle of power and influence that it was.

"I believe in the validity of the simulation that I told you about on the bridge," said Oz in an even and measured tone. "If it were not for the fact that the tactical AI had been trained on those scenarios, I believe we would not have survived the attack with so little damage."

"All right Commander, but I'm still waiting for you to make your point."

"My point, sir, is that these simulations have been shown to be very reliable. Simulations in this same class indicate that if we assume responsibility for martial law, the situation will most probably escalate out of control and ultimately result in a large loss of life on both sides. I believe there is a much better course of action, sir—one that the simulations indicate will favor us."

The Admiral had been looking out the window, as was his habit when being briefed. Oz had to admit the old man was a good listener, a personality trait that Oz considered key to his success.

"So, Commander," said the Admiral. "What do you suggest we do in light of the insurrection? Are you suggesting we take a hit like this and just report back to the Oversight Committee that the situation is under control and our best course of action is to back off?"

Though the Admiral had been looking away, he'd said his piece with implicit accusation.

"No sir, I'm suggesting we do impose martial law. I think your instincts are right on that point."

The Admiral turned in astonishment and laughed. "What the hell are you talking about, Commander? Stop talking in riddles. If you have something to say, then say it. If not, then get the hell out of here and stop wasting my time!"

Oz struggled to remain even. "What I'm trying to say, Admiral, is that the problem in our current plan is that we propose to impose martial law ourselves. We're currently working with the Planetary Defense Forces, aren't we?"

"You know we are," said the Admiral.

"Then let them impose martial law; let them police the streets; let them arrest the separatists, not us."

"Why is that better?" asked the Admiral. "You must realize that there are large segments of Planetary Security who are sympathetic to the separatists."

"Yes sir, I do. But what do you think will happen when members within their ranks are attacked and, in some cases, killed? Remember sir, it's the Planetary Defense Force who possess most of the heavy weapons and the training to use them effectively. It's my belief that most of the successful operations by the separatists were actually carried out by members close to, if not part of, the Defense Force. We need to redirect their antagonism toward the separatists. In the short term, they'll police the domes half-heartedly, but they're professionals, they'll do it. As soon as they come under fire, the tide will turn. They'll do what they were trained to do, and they'll do it effectively."

The Admiral was clearly interested now, no longer hostile.

"And did you learn this from those simulations of yours?"

"Yes sir, that's right."

"Okay, and can you explain to me why the Oversight Committee has missed all of these fine points. Aren't they running war games too?"

"Yes sir, they are," Oz said, then added, "but I'm running the Mills simulations—they apparently are not."

"Mills?" repeated the Admiral, with an incredulous smile. "You mean Dr. George Mills? The Dr. George Mills that Margaret talked about?"

"Yes sir, that's right."

The Admiral shook his head. "I thought there was an understanding that those simulations didn't work. Wasn't that what all the stink was about, Commander?"

"No sir, not really. It's not that they don't work, it's that we're not able to run them to the same scale as Mills apparently can. We believe it's a technical issue. That's why we impounded the computers in his lab at the university."

"So what you're saying is that his dumb down simulation is better than our standard one, is that right?"

"That's my opinion, sir."

Nelson got up, putting his hands together in a parody of amusement, smiling all the while. Then, looking at Oz quizzically, "Do you get the impression that everywhere you turn these days—there's George Mills? Do you get that impression too, Commander?"

Oz shrugged.

"Okay Oz, just promise me that when the current crisis is resolved, that you'll find Mills for me. I'd like to have a word with him."

"Yes, sir."

Chapter Thirty-Two

Oz walked down the corridor of the second crew section to his private quarters. Because of the situation on the ground in Ursa and in Orion Townships, and because of the possibility of further attacks from the surface, he'd been on shift now for thirty-six hours. If it hadn't been for the stims he'd taken ten hours ago, he doubted that he could have found his way back. He stopped at his door, trying for several seconds to remember his key code, the same one he'd used for a year now. Beads of sweat were beginning to form on his brow, and his fingers shook on the door lock. Somehow, the door slid open. Kicking off his shoes, he dropped belly-side-down onto the bed. By the time the door displayed the sleep icon he was fast asleep.

Some time later, Oz struggled to ignore an irritant. Like a piece of gum stuck to his fingers, it refused to be dislodged. Moisture disrupted the cool dry feel of the sheets against his face. The cumulative discomfort pushed him ever farther from the restful sleep he so craved. Damn, he thought, as he pulled himself up and wiped the spittle form the edges of his mouth. It took a couple of seconds for him to make the connection—the Com chimes. He hadn't turned them off because of the ship's general state of alert. He slipped over to the nightstand.

"Yes, Oz here."

"You have a call from the surface, sir."

"Call, what call? Who is it?"

"It's from a Julia Gardner, from Mollar."

"I don't know a Julia Gardner."

He looked at the time displayed on the Tab. He'd been asleep for only four of the eight hours he'd hoped to get. Fatigue kept him from outright anger, but he couldn't help feeling frustrated.

"I left instructions that I shouldn't be disturbed by anything short of a class II emergency, didn't I?"

"Uh, yes sir, but she said she was calling on behalf of Margaret Gates."

Oz sat bolt upright. "Margaret," he repeated in reverent soliloquy.

"Yes sir."

He wiped his face again. "Put her through, no video from this side."

"Yes sir."

A window appeared on the Tab. The face that coalesced at its center was dark and Terran, like himself. A coiled braid sat to one side of her head. The hair in front was pulled tight to her scalp. She wore a white lab coat, the kind that was a parody of science types.

"What do you know about Margaret?" Oz asked.

He could see her searching for the video, then concluding there would be none. She looked up.

"I don't know where she is," said Julia.

Oz felt his patience slipping. "What's this about, Miss Gardner?"

"The Proteus file, are you familiar with that, Commander?"

"Yes, but can't it wait?" Then with his frustration returning, "Why are you calling me about this, shouldn't you be talking to the science officer's staff?" He pulled back, "Oz out!"

Before the image faded, Julia yelled, "Wait Commander, please!"

Oz hesitated. "Continue link," he ordered.

The image flickered, then stabilized.

"I believe this is a grave security matter, sir. The science officer refused to take my call."

Oz snickered, "Oh great."

"Dr. Gates told me to call you if something urgent came up, and she hasn't been available."

"Isn't there a Dr. Sanders down there? Isn't he suppose to be in charge?"

"Yes sir, but well. . ." Julia hesitated. "He's not himself right now."

"What do you mean, Miss Gardner?"

Julia told Oz about the tests Sanders had performed on one of the Proteus children. She told him about Sanders' strange, disoriented behavior when she questioned him in the lab afterward. Then she told him about the surprising test results she'd found in the database when she'd examined the results herself. Oz lay back in his bed and exhaled.

"Isn't it possible that everything's as it should be, Miss Gardner, just as Dr. Sanders concluded? Perhaps the whole Proteus thing is a false alarm."

"No Commander," she said with an obvious edge. "Even without new evidence, we've already shown that at least one of the Proteus children, the one that Sanders tested, is not human."

"I saw that evidence, Miss Gardner. It was certainly unusual, but some of us thought that Margaret over sold it. We saw substantial variance in several standard genetic markers, that's true, but it takes time to do a thorough genetic map. And even then, it's not clear what the physiologic expression of novel genetics might be without exhaustive analysis. Why, there are even large segments of unremarkable genetic material whose exact function is not yet fully understood throughout the human genome."

There was a moment's silence, after which Oz could hear strained slow breaths coming from Julia Gardner.

"Commander, there was a greater than two percent average difference over more than a hundred standard genetic sites in that boy's genetic sample. That's a greater genetic difference than between apes and humans. You can't dismiss a difference that large."

Oz considered this. He didn't doubt that there might be something extraordinary in the Proteus file, but, in the scheme of things, it seemed like a minor matter. After all, Mars might be on the brink of a major insurrection. They could always come back to this later—couldn't they? Something pulled at him. Somehow his intuition raised red flags as he made mental motions to abandon further inquiry. The thing that gnawed at him was the Mills connection. That this virtually unknown scientist could have developed the kind of technology embodied in the simulations that had all but saved the ship a few hours ago. That the computer impounded from Mills' university lab had been under scrutiny now for over two days by some of the ship's finest technicians and they were no closer to understanding it now than they had been two days ago. Something about all these improbable connections compelled him to keep listening.

"Go on, Miss Gardner."

"I've been examining surveillance video of Dr. Sanders' examination of the boy."

The woman looked nervous and exhausted.

"Didn't you just tell me that the surveillance file was unremarkable?"

"Yes, Commander, superficially it is."

"Go on," said Oz. He'd already gone this far, he might as well hear it all.

Julia told him that she'd studied the test results in the database and seen nothing unusual. The results for a select subset of genetic markers, blood chemistry, and physiology, although unconventional, were consistent with the boy's DRA records.

"Why not leave it at that?" asked Oz.

"For the same reason that Dr. Sanders and Dr. Gates suspected something abnormal. Dr. Gates originally based her suspicions on aptitude scores, but after actually meeting some of these children, it was clear that there were large physical abnormalities. These included cranial shape, eye color, ear shape, and many others abnormalities that, to a trained eye, were strong indicators of a specific genetic type. Dr. Gates felt that all the children she interviewed were strongly related, and strongly unrelated to any other known human group."

"What, if anything, did you really find, Miss Gardner? So far, although it's all very interesting, I haven't heard anything new."

"I examined the surveillance video. There are two cameras that give a pretty good view of the subject under test. It turns out that most of the data taken during the specimen analysis and body scans comes out on the monitors before it goes into the database. I found the videos give a good view of the data, especially the functional MRI and brain activity nanomap."

"What's a nanomap?"

"Uh, a nanomap gives high resolution detail of synapse activity during the time a subject is performing a task, so that brain activity can be correlated to function. We used to do this with external electrodes, but because of neural density in the brain, resolution was poor. Another way of doing it is by inserting nanometer monofilament electrodes directly into the brain, hundreds of thousands of them. The problem is that this technique is highly intrusive and has caused damage to subjects, in some cases. Recently, we've been able to introduce millions of nanosensors, which are capable of breaching the brain blood barrier, right into the bloodstream. The small sensors are biologically sticky for certain specific types of neurons. For example, some are specific to basket cells, some to golgi cells, others to purkinje cells etc. Each nanosensor has its own ID and transmits electrical activity and neurotransmitter concentrations in realtime. The scanner ring around the subject's head is superconducting, and directional, so we know exactly where a particular sensor is whenever it's transmitting."

She was starting to peak his interest; he found himself sitting straighter.

She continued. "I was able to isolate the scanner information right from the video. When I compared those images to the database information, I found a discontinuity."

"Discontinuity, what do you mean?"

"Well, initially the data from the surveillance images disagreed strongly with the information in the database, then toward the end of the scan, they fell into perfect sync."

"Wait a minute," said Oz. "Are you saying that someone changed both the images from the video and the information in the database, but was unable to change it before a certain time? A time before which the video data was recorded onto hard media?"

"That's right, Commander. Whoever it was couldn't altered the video once on nonvolatile crystal. They could only intercept it before it was recorded. Apparently, they only tampered with the data after something happened that they didn't want anyone to see. They might not have known ahead of time that we record surveillance data on media that can't be changed. It's not a standard practice."

She waited for Oz to understand the implication.

"They could only change the video during transmission—on the fly, before it was recorded. That probably explains the gap. They first tried to overwrite the recording and got a write error, only then did they tamper with it in realtime."

"Who the hell could do that?" muttered Oz. "Security video streams are highly encrypted with some of our hardest nonlinear encryption schemes. They're considered virtually unbreakable, and are certainly unbreakable in realtime!"

There was a silence. Either this woman was delusional or she'd uncovered another in a series of fantastic irregularities. And all of them, somehow, had something to do with Dr. Mills.

"Miss Gardner, can you send me your data?"

"Yes. But Commander, how can we guarantee it won't be intercepted?"

"Mollar has a tight beam, high output satellite phone. I've used t myself, Miss Gardner. It has a direct feed from an isolated Tab, there's no network involved."

He saw Julia smile for the first time since her call.

"You'll have it within the hour, Commander."

"When I get a chance to review your data, Miss Gardner, I'll get back to you. Oz out."

Oz touched the Tab, and it became transparent again. Lying down slowly, he thought about Margaret. Even in her absence, she'd been able to create mystery. A few minutes later, he was sound asleep again.

The chimes sounded and continued to play. Oz came to, rustled around a bit, got tangled in the sheets, and finally looked at the time on the Tab. "Damn," he muttered and sat up. Disconnected snippets of the conversation he'd had with Julia Gardner bounced around in his head. How many sinister plots were being hatched on that bloody red planet, anyway?

Moving to the other side of the bed, he checked the Tab. There it was! Up till the moment he saw the file, he'd started to think the whole thing had been nothing more than a bad dream. But there it was, in his inbox, like something that had materialized right out of a nightmare. He found himself almost reluctant to look at it, not wanting to make things more complicated than they already were. He looked at the details of the file, its size and file type. Doing the math in his head, knowing the data rate for surveillance media files, he quickly determined this represented about thirty minutes of video. Packing the file for retransmission, he sent a copy to Joel Nguyen, the ship's science officer. He included a note asking Joel to review the material as soon as possible. He described the material as having security implications. An irrational sense of dread seized him, and he continued looking at the Tab long after it had informed him that the file had been sent. Too many people whom he'd known and whom he'd considered credible had shown more than a passing concern about this Proteus thing. Something told him that over all his rational objections, there was something in this Proteus mystery that might leave them all forever changed.

After a shower, shave, and fresh tunic, he made his way to the officer's mess. Sitting at a table with two junior lieutenants,

he learned, to his amusement, that he'd been credited with saving
the ship the previous night. Apparently, he was something of a
celebrity. He couldn't help seeing the irony that the skillful piece
of foresight with which he'd thwarted the attack last night could
rightfully be credited to the enigmatic Dr. Mills. The same Dr.
Mills, who, he feared, might have opened a Pandora's box
named the Proteus file.

Chapter Thirty-Three

The call came about three hours after Oz had resumed his shift at the tactical workstation on the second bridge balcony. He'd absently wondered, like someone anticipating bad news, the extent to which Joel's analysis of the Proteus data would confirm his worst fears. At 2 P.M., Earth standard time, the Com chimes on his console sounded and displayed Joel's private Link ID. He accepted the call and saw Joel's face materialize on the screen.

Joel was Earth normal, with a pale complexion and neatly cut gray hair combed in a traditional style. His square face was handsomely chiseled and appointed with deep brown eyes that conveyed a sense of quiet competence.

"Very funny. I looked at the data you sent," said Joel. The smile left Joel's face as both men stared at each other.

"It's no joke," Oz said finally.

"You're really on the level?" Joel replied, still unwilling to let go of his deep skepticism.

"Yes, I am. Where are you right now?"

"In my quarters," Joel said.

"I'll be right down, wait for me. Oz out."

Joel was still nodding when Oz cut the connection. Oz called his aide to the tactical console with orders to notify him immediately in the event of any unusual activity. Then he quickly left the bridge, heading for Joel's quarters in the second crew section. It took almost fifteen minutes to get there. Oz used the time to think about how he should present the findings, whatever they might be, to the Admiral. He'd learned the delicacy of command, how small mistakes could serve to blow a situation out of proportion.

Joel's door did a facial scan, anticipating Oz's arrival, then slid silently open before he could touch the chimes. Oz found

313

Joel sitting at a small nook, at what passed as a kitchen table, with his Tab in front of him.

Not looking up, Joel said, "Have a seat—some coffee?"

"No thanks. So let's have it."

When the scientist finally raised his head and met Oz's eyes, he asked, "Are you sure the woman you got this from is on the level?"

"I'm assuming she is; that's my best judgment. So what's the big deal?"

"Well, where do I start?" Joel muttered, almost to himself.

"At the beginning," Oz said coolly.

"Okay. What do you know about adaptive evolution?"

Oz smiled. "I've already been to school, Joel."

"Humor me," replied Joel.

Oz sat back. "All right. I guess the most central feature is that environmental pressure drives biologic development."

"That's right. The implication is that biologic systems develop like building blocks. They change as the environment changes, or they parish."

Oz said nothing and waited for Joel to continue.

"That means that almost nothing is ever thrown away; it's built upon. Obviously, if some rational force had something particular in mind, this might not be the best way to do it."

"What do you mean?" asked Oz.

"Well, imagine a computer program that becomes obsolete. Good software engineers tend to want to redesign it from scratch to make it more efficient—faster. They tend not to want to work around things that make it unnecessarily clumsy. Although reuse is key if you're marketing a product, military hardware and software are typically redesigned from the ground up if the only goal is performance, not economy."

Oz nodded.

"Nature has to optimize by using economy as its central tenet. Animals have to remain competitive throughout changes in the environment."

"What's this have to do with the data?" asked Oz impatiently.

Joel ignored his question and continued. "The brain is a classic example of adaptive evolution. Do you know what the oldest structure in the brain is?"

Oz shook his head.

"The brain stem," said Joel. "If you examine the brains of reptiles, there's an uncanny resemblance to the human brain stem in overall structure."

"That would seem natural if you assume that far enough back we evolved from some primordial amphibian," declared Oz.

Joel nodded. "The interesting thing about the brain stem is that it might, in fact, host the foundation of the human consciousness."

"Wait a minute. I thought the thing that distinguishes Homo sapiens from the lower animals is the cerebral cortex."

Joel smiled. "It's certainly the most obvious difference, but that's not what we're talking about."

Oz looked puzzled. "What are we talking about then?"

"Let's ask the question this way," said Joel. "What state of a person would render them the least conscious or aware?"

Oz thought a moment. "A coma, I guess."

"Exactly," said Joel. "And it's exactly a coma that would result from damage to the reticular area of the brain stem. Damage to the various lobes of the cerebral cortex can result in loss of speech, sight, and movement among other things. Two centuries ago they knew how to damage the cerebral cortex on purpose to change behavior."

"You mean a lobotomy?"

Joel nodded. "That's right. But the patient, or I guess victim in this case, did remain conscious. Stimulating or damaging the reticular area of the brain stem can result in someone who never sleeps—constant consciousness. It can also result in someone who always sleeps without dreaming—that's called a coma.

Being alert or aroused is centered in the brain stem. And just above the reticular area is a structure just as ancient, the limbic lobe, or center brain. It hosts things like emotions and long term memory."

"It sounds like these two areas together could actually be a primitive brain in themselves," observed Oz.

"That's right. Save for voluntary senses and motor systems, you have the generic brain of many lower animals. If you look at it this way, it's easy to see why our intuition—that animals have consciousness and personality, feel emotions, and even dream—is completely consistent with similarities in the oldest, most primitive parts of our own brains."

Oz looked at him a moment. Both men were silent. "I guess," Oz said finally, "the data I gave you indicates some difference in brain structure, some departure from the human brain?"

The other man laughed in a way that Oz found disturbing. Joel was usually too sober. This show of emotion was unlike him. Oz had known Joel Nguyen to be a consummate scientist, not given to extravagance or overstatement.

"Different, I should say so," replied Joel. "I would go as far as to say this individual did not evolve on Earth, not originally."

"Are you saying that this person is not the product of genetic enhancement, that he's something else?" asked Oz slowly.

"I'm saying that if this is genetic enhancement, it's centuries beyond what we can do. The brain stem of this individual is unlike that of any terrestrial animal I've ever seen, and as for limbic system, he doesn't seem to have one. This person seems to have unusual lobes with folds and some kind of axon rich network where the brain stem and limbic lobe should be."

"What does that mean?" asked Oz. "Functionally, I mean."

"Well, if I had to guess, I'd say that this person's consciousness, their emotional base is not human. Further, I would say that their evolutionary track is unlike any other earthly animal I've ever seen."

"Hmm. I guess this is a stupid question, but are there other differences?" asked Oz.

"Yes," said Joel quickly. "In fact, I'm just getting started. Given what I've just told you, I found it unusual that the neocortex of the subject is similar to that of a normal human brain in appearance."

"Why is that surprising?" asked Oz. "The boy in question appears completely unremarkable. In fact, these tests were performed to help determine if he was significantly different."

"Well, I wouldn't expect the cerebral cortex of an individual with a completely different evolution to have a brain that seems so structurally similar to a normal human brain. This boy's brain has all the same lobes and fissures of the cerebral cortex of a normal person. His cerebral cortex has two hemispheres connected by the corpus callosum, exactly like a modern human being. Remember, evolution takes a building block approach, so why would a person missing a normal brain stem and mid brain suddenly develop a cerebral cortex so similar in structure to a normal human brain?"

Joel's face reflected his frustration. He was a man who wanted the facts to fit and was deeply troubled by logical inconsistencies.

Oz smiled. "I don't understand your confusion. This is the only part that makes sense to me."

Joel looked at him a moment, then exhaled. "Care to explain it to me?" he asked sitting back.

"You said yourself that the cerebral cortex or neo-cortex is the part of the brain that distinguishes humans from the lower animals. It's responsible for our rational personalities, intelligence, heightened associated senses," explained Oz. "After all, this boy appears human, acts normal enough to have passed for human all his life. I'd find it surprising if the majority of his brain weren't human."

Joel considered this. "Okay, your point's well taken, but there are other considerations."

"Such as?" asked Oz.

"First, as I told you before, this just doesn't fit into normal evolution. Not as I understand it anyway."

"And second?" asked Oz.

"Yeah, well, I told you that his cerebral cortex has a normal structure, but it isn't normal. Far from it."

Oz sat up. "Oh? How so?"

"First of all, it's larger than normal. A normal modern brain is perhaps 1000 to 1500 cc max. This boy's brain is pushing almost 2000 cc. On average, it's between 30 to 50 percent larger than normal. But that's not all," Joel added quickly. "The cortex itself is much deeper than normal. A human cortex is perhaps three to four millimeters deep. This boy's is twice that—about eight millimeters. He's got almost twice the number of neurons in the same amount of cortex as a normal human."

Oz started to speak.

"I'm not finished," said Joel.

"There's more?"

"Oh yeah, much more. I looked at the result of the nanomap, and that revealed some even more fantastic results. What do you know about synapse efficiencies?" asked Joel.

"About what?"

"Synapses," said Joel. "They're the connections that enable our brain to perform all the functions that it's capable of. Synapses are to the brain what logic gates are to computers."

Oz brightened. "Okay, I understand."

"Yeah?" said Joel. "So if I were to ask you to assess a computer's power, how would you quantify it?"

"All computers are, in part, benchmarked by the number of operations per second they can perform," Oz said.

"Exactly," replied Joel. "We can make similar measurements of brain activity that give a rough estimate of brain power. Normal human synapses are capable of millisecond firing times and are typically a fraction of a millimeter apart for most neural circuits. Further, most neurons are capable of about one to two thousand connections, although certain specialized neurons can have as many as fifty thousand."

Oz listened with interest as Joel explained. "This boy seems to have more than twice the normal number of connections, and somehow his synapses seem to be more than three times faster than that of a normal person."

Joel sat back. "By any objective measure, this boy is a staggering mental giant—a super genius. Quantitatively, he's as far above Homo sapiens as we are above monkeys."

Joel paused to let it sink in. Oz got up and began to walk around Joel's quarters. Waiting patiently as his colleague absorbed the full implication of what he'd just been told, Joel smiled, satisfied that Oz appeared to appreciate the magnitude of this discovery.

"This is no simple genetic enhancement," declared Joel, breaking the silence. "This is a new type of human being. Perhaps an evolutionary jump of several million years in a very specific direction."

Oz's mind raced with possibilities. Why had Mills done this? He knew Mills was somehow responsible. And how had he done it? Mills wasn't even a biologist; he was a physicist for goodness sake. None of it made sense. It couldn't have anything to do with what was happening on Mars right now. Given the ages of the Proteus people, this thing must have begun fifteen or twenty years ago. One thing was certain; he'd have to secure those kids. They couldn't be permitted to remain on Mars. This was far too sensitive, given the current state of affairs, not be brought under complete control.

"I saved the best for last," said Joel softly.

"You mean there's more?"

"Yes, amazingly enough, there's more. I examined the scans below the brain stem and found other novel changes."

Oz took his seat and held Joel's eyes.

"It looks as if right around the eighth cervical vertebrae the spinal cord bifurcates and connects to an organ in the right chest just behind the lungs."

"A new organ?" asked Oz. "What's it for?"

"Ah, good question. Think about it. It sinks a good percentage of the spinal cord."

"What are you getting at? Are you implying it's a second brain or something?"

"No, not quite. It's even more novel than that. Functional MRI suggests a tremendous energy consumption. You know the whole brain consumes about 10 watts of power. Imagine a 10 watt flashlight."

"Okay," Oz said, waiting for enlightenment.

"Well, this organ looks like it could source maybe five times that much, almost like the nervous system of an electric eel or something like that."

"But what's it for?" asked Oz.

"My best guess, as wild as it sounds, is that this organ is like a big transistor."

"A what?" asked Oz.

"A transistor was an antique electrical switch that took a low current circuit into a high current circuit. In other words, I think it translates weak nerve impulses originating in the brain into a high powered nervous system capable of handling volts, not millivolts."

"To what end?" demanded Oz.

Joel laughed that laugh again, unnerving Oz. "The organ seems to be connected to the spinal column as a whole. I think it's using the spinal column like an antennae."

"How's that possible? Bone doesn't conduct electricity."

"This boy's backbone and ribs do. They have a high iron content and may even have silicon deposits that may be semiconducting."

"What's he using the antennae for?" Oz was dumfounded. He'd gotten up this morning expecting surprises, but this?

"I have a theory about that," said Joel. "Let's think about brain power again. What would you consider to be the ultimate limit on how powerful the mind could become? No matter how fast you could biologically make the nerves and synapses, what's the limiting factor?"

Oz thought a moment. "Well," he said slowly. "I suppose a larger head could imply a more powerful brain all things being equal. But I guess a head can only be so large, right?"

"That's right," said Joel. "A head can only be so large. It has to be small enough to still accommodate the birth canal, and then there's also the question of weight."

He waited a moment. "So how do you get around that? Let's go back to the computer analogy. In the twentieth century, the most powerful computers were hulking mainframes, but later computing became distributed. Today our most powerful computers consist of thousands of autonomous nodes networked together and running in parallel."

"You mean these kids are networked on some wireless biological radio channel?" asked Oz, incredulous.

"That's right," replied Joel. "Evolution solved the problem of head size by distributing the task. Imagine a planet of people like this boy," he continued. "Millions of creative geniuses all instantaneously in touch in each other's minds."

"This is the most fantastic thing I've ever heard of," Oz said.

They both sat there a few moments. Finally, Oz said, "Joel, you realize that there's no way we could ever compete with them. Given a chance to breed, we Homo sapiens will become extinct in no time."

After a brief silence, Oz left Joel and headed back to the bridge. His mind raced as he contemplated a set of equally disturbing options.

Chapter Thirty-Four

The sun had been up for about an hour and a half. Joanne was asleep on George's lap, and Malcolm and Margaret were in the front seats of the tractor. From the back, George could see the bulges of their helmets jutting around their headrests. He had no idea whether they were awake or not, since they hadn't said a word or moved in a long time. Though the front of the tractor was transparent, his view was limited. It looked as if they had reached the first set of hills that preceded the fifteen thousand-foot rock walls of the eastern Valles Marineris. He could no longer see the sky, only the huge reddish walls of the first peaks. The rocks had strange irregular shapes. Every now and then a trail of light ore caught the morning sun and flashed momentarily like the water that may have formed the canyon eons before.

Something caught George's eye—a bright reflection off the cliff wall that lasted a good twenty seconds, then died slowly. He sat up—what the hell was that? What could be that bright, he wondered, and pictured the geometry in his mind. The northern sky—it must have been a bright flash in the northern sky. This had nothing to do with the sun or clouds or mountains. The angle was all wrong. Deep down he knew what it must be. If he was right, they had even less time than he had thought. He looked down at Joanne, and didn't want this moment to pass, but shook her gently anyway.

She slowly came to, smiled at him, then sat up. Yawning, she said, "Good morning," then looked around absently. "We're almost there, aren't we?"

He watched as her contented smile and bewildered morning eyes slowly turned quizzical.

"What's wrong?" she asked.

He hesitated. "I just saw a flash—just before I woke you."

"A flash. What kind of flash?"

"In the northern sky—I think. It had to be a nuclear explosion."

Her face tightened.

"It might have been that madman Vega making his move against the Earth cruiser. He probably thought to act now since our escape threatens to expose his plans," George said.

"I hope he missed," Joanne said softly.

George leaned forward, trying to get a better look out the window. "We're no more than ten minutes away now."

* * *

When they got to a cliff that George recognized as their destination, the tractor stopped. They hid it under an overhang so that it couldn't be seen from orbit, then brushed away the tire tracks as best they could. Following George, the small group began to climb a trail that snaked up the foothills of the rim range. Fifteen minutes later, they turned off the trail, walked another twenty feet into a rocky crag, and found themselves at the mouth of a cave dimpled into the cliff wall. It was about six feet high and wide enough to allow their passage if they entered single-file. Just inside the entrance, it expanded, letting them congregate in the middle of a dark cavern that was devoid of the slightest hint that people had ever been there.

"One moment," George said, scanning the cave with his helmet lights. "This way." He started toward the rear of the cavern. When the others caught up, they found him standing at an ancient steel door pitted by rust that had eaten into its surface over the many years it had guarded the Link. Everyone remained silent as George worked the lock. Finally, they caught green flash from a control on the airlock frame. George straightened and stepped back. Bracing himself in a wide stance, he pulled the large door aside. Surprisingly, given its worn appearance, it opened smoothly as they all stepped back, offering sufficient room for it to swing out. George turned and smiled. Malcolm and Margaret just stared at him, looking bewildered.

Once inside, George took a quick inventory of the place. It was a rectangular room, perhaps twenty by forty feet, with cement walls lined with cables and plastic lighting panels covering the ceiling. The air was dry, with a dusty taste that conveyed a sense of age.

"Well, Mills, this is a great hideout, but now what?" Malcolm asked.

They followed as George moved into the next room, which had been the control center of the ancient Link. Dead consoles and equipment racks lined the clean painted white walls, none of them active, apparently for some time now by the look of things. This area had the feel of a museum rather than a working data Link. Then, as they trailed George around a corner to another part of the large space, they saw them—two immaculate white quantum columns about six feet tall. The translucent plastic base on which they sat glowed a dull white. To the side, they saw a small sculpted titanium cylinder about three feet tall—a nuclear battery, probably capable of powering the columns for many decades.

Malcolm whirled. "And what is this?"

"Will," Joanne replied. "It's Will."

"Will? But Mills, how could that be?" asked Margaret. "It was removed from your lab on campus, disassembled, then taken to the ship. It should be on the ship right now."

"Not all of him," George said softly, running his hand along the cool smooth surface of the cryogenic containment. "Your associates took the columns we used to support the simulations, but I removed these a couple of years ago fearing that something like this might happen. These two columns represent Will's core network. I was even able to take some of the holographic memories." He gestured with his eyes. Behind the columns, against the wall, were four six-foot white cabinets.

Margaret glanced down. George remembered the day, not so long ago, when she and Wells had taken the computer apart and pushed him into the back of a police car. Apparently, she still found it hard to meet his eyes. We all have lapses, George thought, and glanced over at Joanne. She was looking at the space in front of the holographic memories.

"You finished the VNex?" Joanne asked.

"Yes," George said. "I did."

Malcolm looked at him from the other side of the columns; Margaret leaned against the wall with her arms folded in front of her chest. Everyone was waiting for an explanation.

"Why are we here, Mills?" Malcolm asked. He gestured to the exotic equipment that stretched between them. "How can any of this help you—help us? ECon has arrested you. From what you told us about the blast on the horizon this morning, we're probably on the verge of a civil war in the domes right now." He looked at Joanne, but continued to address George. "I'm not sure what we're doing here and I certainly can't see how any of this equipment you've salvaged really matters."

"Look," George said, "this isn't about me. If I surrendered to ECon right now, what's the worst that could happen?" He looked at Margaret.

She exhaled. "We wanted you because you were in possession of sensitive technology. It's a security issue. You would have been taken back to Earth and made to agree to develop the technology under secure conditions. In fact, I'm sure if you agree to their terms, you will be well paid, even famous—or infamous." She cracked a smile.

"My real concern is for the kids," George told Malcolm. "I have an obligation to them. I have no idea what's happened to them, but I have to assume the worst."

Margaret nodded. "You're probably right, Mills. I'm sorry."

"That's what this is about," George said. "I believe those kids are our future, and the people who perpetuated the chaos I saw on the horizon this morning are the same people these kids will eventually make irrelevant."

"What about the VNex, George?" Joanne asked.

"The VNex will get us into Will. I asked him to develop a plan to help us rescue the kids, if that's still possible."

Joanne's brow furrowed and she looked away.

"Mills, how can your computer possibly help you do that?" asked Margaret. "I'm not saying that I wouldn't be willing to help you, but how do two quantum columns in a remote cave somewhere in the Martian mountains make any difference?"

"I picked this cave because it was once a Com hub. Five thousand feet above us, on the mountaintop, are several high gain satellite antennas. The transceivers in these racks still work. You can see the broadband fiber plugged into Will." George pointed to a thick gray optical cable that snaked across the floor and terminated in the base of the columns.

Margaret looked at the cable, then at George. "I see."

"Well, I don't," Malcolm said.

Margaret glanced at the gleaming white columns with an odd reverence. "This broadband satellite link puts Will in touch with the planetary network," she explained. "Just before we discovered the Proteus file and the discrepancies in Mills' behavioral simulations, we found someone hacking into our secure sites here on Mars. Then, later, we found the same on Earth. It was all very subtle. In fact, we were probably lucky to discover it at all. You see, we thought our chaotic encryption algorithms were unbreakable, but somehow, someone got in. We traced it back to Mills' lab at the university and thought we'd caught the culprit." She smiled and looked around. "I guess Will was one step ahead of us. Probably used the other system as a Trojan horse to throw us off."

"So you're saying Mills' system has seeped into your military computers, is that right?" Malcolm asked.

"Probably," Margaret replied. "And if that's the case, it might just give Mills the leverage he needs."

"I see," said Malcolm.

George turned to Joanne, "Can you get the injector? It's over there." He motioned to a locker beside the cabinets.

Malcolm smiled and shook his head. "Now what?"

"Nanosensors," Joanne said.

Margaret flashed a broad smile. She was thoroughly enjoying this. "Don't ask me," she told Malcolm. "I couldn't even hazard a guess."

"It's for the VNex," Joanne explained. Everyone stared at her blankly. "Malcolm, remember the simulations we told you about at the Landing the other night?"

Malcolm nodded. "Yeah, seems like years ago."

"We wanted some way of getting directly into the simulations ourselves, to see what was going on."

"You mean you wanted to physically participate in a simulation?" Malcolm asked.

"That's right. VNex is an acronym for Virtual Nexus. It's a way of getting into a simulation by direct perception."

"How's that possible?" Malcolm asked.

"By using nanosensors," Joanne said. "The same kind we use in diagnosing the nervous system, but with one important modification."

Both Malcolm and Margaret remained silent, wanting her to continue.

"The nanosensors have been modified to source stimulus as well as transmit brain activity."

"Isn't that dangerous?" Margaret asked. "Couldn't a failure to properly control the sensors result in severe psychosis, even mental collapse?"

"It could," Joanne agreed. "But we programmed the sensors with a dead-man switch. They require a continuous signal from the controlling authority. If the signal is interrupted in any way, the sensors immediately terminate and flush out of the system."

"And who or what is the controlling authority?" Malcolm asked.

George looked at the columns. "Why, Will, of course."

Malcolm and Margaret looked at each other with obvious uncertainty.

George laughed weakly. "Want to go on a trip? Probably like nothing you've ever experienced before." He exhaled a chuckle.

"What the hell," Malcolm said, throwing up his hands. Then, looking at George, "You're dangerous, you know that Mills? You're out of control!"

"Thanks for the compliment, Peters." George grinned.

Joanne said, "Malcolm, would you mind? There are two other lounges in the cabinet."

Malcolm shrugged and walked to the cabinets in search of two more chairs.

"What can I do?" Margaret asked.

"There are nanosensor antennas in the locker on the top shelf—know what they look like?"

"I do," Margaret said, then moved to the metal cabinet right behind Malcolm.

Near the nuclear battery stood another cylinder about two feet high. Clear plastic scaffolding suspended yellowish green optical processing crystals between two blue plastic rings. The whole assembly was anchored to a black plastic base annotated by various lights and displays about its circumference. It was surprisingly light. Joanne picked it up and put it in the center of the circle of chairs. Taking the superconducting rings from Margaret, she plugged the optical cables into the base of the tower one at a time, then laid each ring on a chair.

George connected the interface rings to the nano-tower and the interface came to life. The clear scaffolding light pipes glowed a soft blue; lights on its black base lit up and began to strobe. The various displays announced their standby status. George straightened and surveyed what he'd done. "Looks good," he said, looking up.

Joanne retrieved the pneumatic gun next to George's chair where she's left it. She put it to her neck and pressed the trigger. It responded with a thud and recoiled slightly in her hand. Rubbing her neck, she turned to George. "Ready?" she asked.

He turned away, exposing his neck. After injecting George, Joanne repeated the process for Malcolm and Margaret, carefully placing the nano-rings on their heads after injection. When everyone was suitably reclined, she lowered the lights in the room.

"How long does it take?" Margaret asked.

"I don't really know," George said, "but if our simulations are accurate, it should take about fifteen minutes for the sensors to get into place. Once that happens, Will should pull us in."

"You mean you designed this by simulation too?" Malcolm asked.

"Of course. It's the safest way of developing something this intricate. That's how I know it works," he added, and then laid back.

Chapter Thirty-Five

Time passed. George heard the occasional rustling and muffled squeaks of jumpsuits against plastic. They became less frequent and soon subsided, giving way to a silence that he had seldom experienced. He forced his eyes to remain open. Fatigue, coupled with the comfort of the changing air bladders built into his chair, tugged at his eyelids. His thinking was clouded and confused, his body depleted after the adventures of the last twenty-four hours. He struggled to remain alert, wanting to experience this profound transition. He had no idea what to expect, but he knew that he didn't want to miss it, whatever it was.

Watching the dance of colored lights on the ceiling against the soft white glow of the quantum columns, he felt a sense of well being flow over him, as if he had been given an anti-depressant, but without the drug-induced dullness. No, this was like the endorphin high he got after running four or five miles in the hills in back of his apartment. It was the feeling of clarity, sharpness, and invulnerability that he got from the pounding of his heart and muscles, all working in concert on a warm day after coordinated physical exertion. It was the reward his body gave him for letting it do what it had been designed to do over the millions of years that preceded man's current sedentary culture.

Suddenly, he realized that he could no longer see the ceiling. The world was a soft white in all directions. He thought it odd that he wasn't frightened, losing control like this. In fact, to his surprise, he was mildly amused. Perhaps it was because whenever a part of the body failed to function, the awareness of the failure was accompanied by a rush of adrenaline, which in turn, tensed the muscles. The effect built upon itself like a chain reaction whose ultimate destination was panic. None of that was happening here. He floated in an infinite sea of white, a pair of eyes and perhaps a mouth, which he imagined might look something like the Cheshire cat. Thinking about it made him laugh—he felt pretty good.

It was clear his trip had begun. What next? He imagined rubbing imaginary hands together. Then he noticed a smell and pictured his mouth floating in a sea of white, changing from a toothy smile to a round quizzical, "oh." It was a funny smell, familiar and pungent. What was it?

Suddenly, he thought he heard something. It came in spurts—first a building, rolling, rushing sound, and then a low crash. He felt the crash throughout his body like an explosion of base vibrations. The smell also came and went. It seemed to change in concert with the feel of warm air blowing on his face in intermittent gusts. His face. He reached up and felt it. He was no longer a pair of eyes and a mouth; he could feel his face. He strained his eyes to see into the whiteness and found there were shapes out there, but the contrast was bad. Impatience seized him and he realized that his transitory state of euphoria was giving way to more familiar feelings. Slowly, it all came into focus. All of his senses seemed to coalesce to give him a perception of a world he knew very well. One he'd left many years ago.

"Goodness it's bright," he heard Joanne say.

Turning, he saw her in blazing detail. She was no longer wearing the suit skullcap. Her thick mane of brown hair seemed to sparkle as it caught the bright summer sun. The sky was a deep blue behind her, dotted with puffs of bright fluffy clouds. Her jumpsuit was gone, magically replaced by blue shorts decorated with white tropical flowers and a white tank top.

"George, is that you?" She was squinting with her hand shading her eyes from the glare.

He noticed something attached to her collar and smiled. "You have glasses hanging from your shirt," he said.

She felt around and quickly put them on. A broad smile beamed beneath electric blue lenses. George reached up without looking, found a pair hanging from his collar, and put them on.

"Mills, where are we?" Margaret asked.

She stood next to Joanne, glowing white in the bright sun. She was dressed in the same tropical garb, except her shorts were Hawaiian pink with white flowers. She grinned back at him through rose-colored glasses.

"West coast," Malcolm said, from behind George. "I'd say somewhere in Southern California."

"That's right," George said. He knew this place—knew it well. "Orange County, just outside Newport Beach, to be exact." He turned to Joanne. "You've never been to Earth, have you, Jo?"

She could only shake her head and look around.

"What do you think?" George asked.

"I think it's big and bright." She took a breath. "And unimaginably beautiful. I've never seen anything like it."

"Something's wrong," Margaret said. "I was in Newport Beach a year ago." She turned, inspecting the hills in the distance. "It doesn't look like this." She paused, then correcting herself, said, "It looks like this, but where are all the people, the houses?"

"Margaret's right," Malcolm said. "It's been a while since I've been to Earth, but I've never seen a sky this blue." He turned, sensing something, "And that smell, what's that smell— seaweed, fish? When I left Earth there weren't many fish left in the oceans, and although we lived on the beach in Nantucket, I never smelled seaweed this pungent."

"You're right," George said. "When I was a boy I used to come here almost every day. Down there." He pointed to the edge of the cliff and out toward the open Pacific. The sea shimmered in the distance as a formation of pelicans flew overhead, one tucking in its wings and falling into the ocean like a spear.

"I used to come here because this little strip of beach was a state park. It was the only patch of beach anywhere along this coast that hadn't been built up. I used to look in this direction and imagine what it would be like if I turned around and all the houses and cars were just gone—poof!"

"You know what?"

The others remained silent.

"It looked just like this." George smiled beneath his own blue glasses. "I guess this is probably an accurate simulation of Newport Beach before it was settled."

"We're not really here are we?" Margaret asked. "This is a illusion induced by your computer, isn't it?"

"I'd prefer to call it a simulation," George said. "And as far as being here," he looked around, "I prefer this simulation to the reality of the cave we were just in, don't you?"

She breathed deep in the direction of the sea, her violet hair swirling around her head like flames. "Yes," she said, "I guess I do. How does your computer do all this—let us experience all of this together in such a seamless interactive way?"

"This goes beyond interactive," Malcolm said. "Mills is right. I can't tell the difference between this and any other real experience I've ever had."

George thought about how to answer her question in a meaningful way. "Before we began the transition into this place, we were each given an injection of millions of nanosensors. Those sensors migrated to our brains through the carotid artery and lodged biologically to the sensory centers in our cerebral cortex and brain stem, many in the thalamus of the upper brain stem. They intercept visual data coming into the visual cortex in the occipital lobe, auditory data at the bottom of the occipital lobe and temporal lobe, balance and tactile data in the somatosensory cortex of the parietal lobe and many other sites in the brain. Will provides a three-dimensional simulation of an environment, like this one." He panned the eastern hills and saw brown grass dotted by little green trees. "The simulations are actually executed in those banks of holographic memories you saw in front of the couches we're lying on."

"You mean those white cabinets?" Malcolm asked.

"Yes, this environment unfolds in a set of dynamic cells that respect the dynamical and statistical rules of the world, in great fidelity, and in three dimensions, and in time. Each of the cells, like a mosaic, is linked to the other cells it touches by boundary conditions that also respect the way the world works. Will feeds that sensory data directly into our brains, bypassing our senses through the nanosensors. He then transmits our responses to the environment, which is updated accordingly. He sends signals to the rest of our bodies through the thalamus, which leads our bodies to believe we're sleeping."

Malcolm brightened with understanding. "It's ingenious, Mills." Then, looking around, "It borders on the miraculous. In principle, your computer could take us anywhere we wanted to go, couldn't it?"

"That's right, anywhere Will had sufficient data to model."

Malcolm nodded in approval.

"But this computer of yours, how could it possibly be so superior to what we have on Earth?" Margaret asked. "No offense Mills, but you're a physicist. I'm a computer scientist, and this," she shook her head, "it's way beyond anything even on the drawing board. Are you a magician?" She smiled.

"No, I'm not a magician. In fact, many of your colleagues considered me second rate until my behavioral work."

"That's too modest, Mills. I'm willing to concede you've made," she looked at Malcolm, "miraculous advances in computer science."

"You don't know the half of it yet," Joanne said, smiling up at George.

"Thanks," George said, "but if you look closely at the quantum columns and holographic memories, you'll notice that they're all high-end standard issue. I haven't invented any new hardware."

Margaret considered this, then asked, "Well, where's the magic? The conventional use of those Q-columns is in molecular modeling, searching algorithms, and other very specialized tasks for which they're well suited. We don't know how to apply them to problems like this."

"That's exactly what I spent ten years doing back on Earth," replied George. "I realized it would be impossible to model the kind of data I was interested in even with the largest distributed parallel systems, even if I could somehow get the processing time, and that was doubtful."

"Why not?" Malcolm asked. "Aren't these computers all basically the same? Aren't quantum computers just some fancy form of parallel computers?"

George smiled. "Not exactly."

Malcolm continued to stare at him.

"You really want to hear it?"

Malcolm looked around at the magnificent illusion he was now part of and nodded.

"Okay," George said. "Let's consider a system we can all understand—two memories, each of which has two states."

"Okay," Malcolm said, clearly interested if the explanation could shed further light on what he was experiencing.

"How many states could a system like that possibly represent?"

"Four," answered Malcolm without hesitation.

George nodded. "Yes, that's right, if the memories represent two states. For the sake of discussion, we can call them one or zero. Now, if you wanted to represent those states simultaneously, how many memories would you need?"

"Four, I guess," Malcolm answered.

"That's right, one to hold each piece of data. Parallel systems are like that. Though they can perform parallel operations on the data simultaneously, they still require resources that, in general, increase exponentially with the complexity of the problem because they can't hold the data itself simultaneously."

"I see," Malcolm said. "In this case, two states raised to the second power since there are two memories. So, it's the number of memories that sets the scale of the problem, is that right?"

"That's right," replied George. "You're a pretty quick study."

"But what about a quantum system, why is that different?"

"There's the magic Margaret's looking for. It's a property of quantum systems that they're indeterminate until measured."

Malcolm's brow furrowed.

"In other words, until we want the answer, a particular quantum memory is in a statistical mixture of all the states it can possibly be in, all at the same time."

"So you're saying that one quantum memory is in two states simultaneously?" Malcolm thought a moment. "I guess that would mean you'd only need two memories, not four, to represent four states."

"That's right again. So what this means is that, in general, we only need resources that go up by a polynomial of the complexity of the problem, not an exponential like before. In this case, we take the sum of the memories as the scale of the problem, not the product of the number of states by the number of memories."

"That's right, Mills," Margaret said. "But, unfortunately, the properties of quantum systems make them awkward at representing arbitrary non-quantum systems. And, as we all know, the world in the aggregate doesn't look like a quantum system."

"Right," George said, "and there's where I made a contribution."

George looked around, searching for the right words. "I discovered a family of complex conformal maps whose components are fractal functions. I was able to apply these maps to quantum states and translate arbitrary states to physical geometries."

"Well that explains it," Malcolm said with a smirk.

Joanne laughed, "Don't get him started, I've made that mistake."

"Yeah, well, to make a long story short, I found a mathematical framework I could use to express ordinary physical systems from complex quantum states. I applied that technology to novel associative neural networks. What you see around you is the result. Will gave me a whole new window on simulations that enabled Joanne and me to do things like this." He spread his arms in a grand gesture.

"Bravo maestro," Margaret said.

Malcolm said, "Okay Mills, now that you've given us the short version, what now?"

"Let's see if we can find who we came to talk to."

"Find who?" Margaret asked.

"Find Will. That's who we're here to see."

George started toward a narrow path cut through desert briers and dried grasses. He didn't know why, but he had a hunch that whatever they were looking for would be down on the seashore. They'd been standing and talking in a sandy clearing about two hundred feet from the edge of a cliff. Beyond, he could see the blue Pacific. All around was a sandy desertscape of dry bushes and brown flowering weeds and grasses. As they walked single-file over the narrow path, George noticed occasional movement. He spied a gray-white speckled lizard so well camouflaged that he had to strain to see it once it stopped moving. Several other forms darted about as they walked. Apparently, their footfalls had produced movement in the environment that had frightened an assortment of small creatures from the safety of their natural shelters. He stopped to watch the lizard, prompting Joanne to stop too. When she finally saw it, she laughed in amazement, half with excited playful fear, half in wonder at the sight of the creature as it stood there, doing pushups, executing some million-year-old ritual only it understood. She'd never seen animals in the wild before. Mars was now, and perhaps always had been, a dead planet.

Once they'd resumed their trek across the small strip of desert, George began to notice other animals. He watched as a dirty brown jackrabbit with a fluffy white tail ran back and forth. It stopped now and then, twitching its nose and looking around until it darted under a bush and disappeared. Then, looking up, he saw a hawk high over head. Its wings were motionless and fully extended as it rode the warm air currents in search of prey.

"Look at all these animals," he heard Joanne tell Malcolm.

She had now developed an eye for spotting them too, and stopped occasionally to stare in wonder. Margaret followed behind everyone else and smiled under her rose-colored sunglasses every time Joanne announced a new discovery. It was clear to George that this was no sterile prop of a world. This was a world exploding with life, which, to his closest scrutiny, could not be distinguished from the real thing. This was a world whose minutia existed apart from his awareness, and whose meaning was woven deeply into its workings, far beyond his momentary perceptions.

At the end of the path they found a dirt clearing that jutted out over the cliff. Its tall rock walls framed the beach below for as far as they could see. The warm winds off the water were brackish and fresh, and the pungent scent of seaweed was strangely familiar, if not totally pleasant. Joanne's long hair danced on the wind as she wandered closer to the edge of the cliff than George could comfortably tolerate. He held her by the arm as she leaned forward, apparently straining to see something.

Forty feet below them, George saw blue-green ocean breakers swell far off shore, then crest forward just before pounding into white foam as they struck the beach with a low "thump."

"Who's that?" Margaret shouted above the wind.

"Who?" George asked.

She pointed south to someone far below who was sitting on a log near the surf. When the stranger saw them, he began to wave.

"I'll be damned," Malcolm said.

"Let's go see," George shouted over the ocean's roar. Then he started down a dirt path that snaked around the ledge and fell out of sight. The rest of the group followed single-file. When they finally reached the sand at the base of the cliff, the wind had subsided, making it eerily quiet in-between the thunder crash of waves. They began walking south.

A few minutes later, they were standing behind a man sitting on a sea-worn log, looking out over the ocean. His back was to them, his loose white shirt flapping with gusts off the water. It was hard to tell his age, but he gave the impression of youth, though his blue-black hair had hints of gray.

"Will?" George asked.

The man turned slowly, the sun catching his face.

"Hello George. I'm sorry, I meant to have coffee for you, but I got distracted."

"That's fine," George said. "Maybe later."

Will nodded, smiled, pushed himself forward, then stood. He was shorter than George, maybe five ten or five eleven. He had a fair complexion and a long face whose chin bore the suggestion of a dimple. His hair was parted in the middle and fell to his shoulders in large waves, covering his forehead above his dark chocolate-brown eyes. The bridge of his nose was thin at the brow but flared toward its tip, giving his face character. Although his features were unusual, taken as a whole, they fit together nicely, and George found the over-all effect both pleasing and familiar. Will was slim. He wore wrinkled khaki pants, rolled up around his calves, and an old-fashioned white cotton shirt with tails. His feet were bare, and wet sand stuck to his toes.

"Hello Joanne," Will said easily.

Joanne hesitated. George could see that a caution had crept into her. He had always known there was something uncomfortable between Joanne and Will, but it had gone on for so long now that he had ceased to notice anymore.

"Hello Will," Joanne said. Her voice conveyed distrust more than familiarity.

George watched Will closely. When he'd first stood, he'd been airy, with a crooked smile and a smooth face, absent any hint of anxiety. Now, George saw thin lines at the corners of Will's eyes and a tightness in his face that underscored his disappointment at Joanne's reticence to accept him.

"You mean this is Will, the computer?" Margaret asked.

Will lingered on Joanne for another moment, then turned to Margaret. "Hello, Dr. Gates."

"Mills are you trying to tell us your computer's alive?"

"I'm not trying to tell you anything. If you have a question for Will, you should ask him. He's standing right here."

Margaret nodded, "Of course. Sorry Will, please forgive me."

She reached up, removed her sunglasses, and stood closer to Will. She examined him closely, not wanting to miss the slightest detail.

"Will, are you alive—self-aware?"

Will exhaled a tired sigh. "Imagine, Dr. Gates, that someone were to ask you that same question, how would you answer?"

Margaret thought a moment, then grinned. "I guess I'd tell the arrogant bastard to screw off!"

Will grinned back. "I'll have to remember that."

"You'll have to forgive me, Will," Margaret said, still staring in fascination. "You have to realize that according to the accepted wisdom in the field of computer science, you shouldn't be possible. In the late twentieth century there were scientist who thought that, given sufficient complexity, machines would naturally wake up. This was later shown to be false. Then, the pendulum swung the other way. Consciousness became the domain of mystics. The problem proved to be so intractable that scientists just forgot about it—relegated it to that notorious bin of life's mysteries."

Will shrugged. "Think about it, Dr. Gates."

"Please Will, call me Margaret."

"Well, Margaret, do you consider yourself awake, self-aware?"

"Of course I do."

"Then there are two possibilities," Will said.

"Which are?" Margaret asked.

"Either the machinery of your brain is generating the effect we call consciousness, or your consciousness is something magical in nature and defies any kind of logical explanation."

Margaret smiled, but said nothing.

"If you choose to believe the latter, that your consciousness is magical, then I would suggest that you abandon scientific inquiry in general. Don't you think it unlikely that the world would be evenly split between magic and science? Do you think the universe would choose science when things were easily measured, and magic when they were less obvious?"

Margaret looked at George, beaming, then turned to Will. "Before we leave, I'd consider it a privilege to discuss this further with you."

"I'll be damned," Malcolm declared. "If he makes good on that promise, he just might put people like me out of business. Who's going to need a psychologist if we understand the mechanical nature of the mind?"

"He might just be able to answer your questions," George warned.

"Thank you, but you might be over stating my abilities," Will said.

"I don't think so." George turned to Margaret. "Will is more self-aware than most people I know. He has feelings and a personality at the base of which are all the desires that define sentient life. Furthermore, he has a raw intellect that is far greater than that of Homo sapiens."

"Oh?" Malcolm said skeptically. "How'd you come to that conclusion?"

"It's simple arithmetic. Our machinery," George tapped his head, "contains perhaps a million-billion connections in the form of synapses. Each synapse has a switching time of about a tenth of a second. So, from those switching times and number of connections, we can estimate the number of operations that the human brain can perform per second."

George looked at his companions; they all stared back, a little dumbfounded.

"Now, Will has about ten to the sixteenth connections in his network. Each of those connections switch in about one-millionth millionth of a second. So, in terms of raw processing power, Will's mind is about twelve orders of magnitude greater than the human mind."

They all turned and stared at Will.

"Let me put it in perspective," George said. "If you were to compare a man to a cockroach, then by the same arithmetic, you would find a separation between them of, at most, eight orders of magnitude."

"No wonder Joanne's afraid of him," Malcolm said.

George shot him a look, shook his head, and then sat on Will's log. He stared out at the turbulent ocean, and sighed. Joanne came up behind him and put her hands on his shoulders.

* * *

George's description of Will's god-like mind sent cold chills down Joanne's back. It brought back all the old fears with a vengeance. She had always been afraid of Will, from the moment she'd first realized he was alive. There was something alien about a mind that great never knowing the fragility of being organic. Will's cool ability to always be in control served to reinforce that visceral mistrust.

She imagined George unknowingly seized in a Frankenstein complex, so consumed by visions of benefits his creation could bestow on the world that he was blinded to the obvious. George had never so much as uttered a single misgiving at endowing such an intelligence with the power and network mobility that Will enjoyed. Why was he so sure that Will was beyond the same transgressions, born of self-interest, which all intelligent life shared? What made Will immune to that most basic of equations?

She knew George loved her. She also knew that he was a lonely man with a damaged self-image, which had been cauterized by his own personal failures. Perhaps that had forced him to seek salvation beyond the human sphere. It was complicated, because George was a complicated man. While George had seen Will as a tool with which they could change humanity for the better, she'd seen nothing but a bogeyman in a box. She'd been taken with the vision, but was afraid of the tool. Against her better judgment, she had decided to go along with George's plans until there was tangible evidence to support her fears.

Now, in the grips of uncertainty, Joanne rubbed George's shoulders and hoped he would understand her misgivings about Will.

Chapter Thirty-Six

Suddenly, Joanne noticed a flicker. She reached up reflexively, sought her eye with her hand. Perhaps it had been a particle of sand—something blown in from the ocean. Her fingers awkwardly bumped her sunglasses, which she'd momentarily forgotten were still on her face. It couldn't have been something in my eye, she thought, then noticed she could no longer feel George's shoulders under her hands. She looked down—he was gone. All that remained was an empty log and the crashing of the breakers.

A bolt of white-hot fear ran through her. Her mind had reached a conclusion before her knowing consciousness. She turned slowly. Just as she expected, there was Will. Everyone else was gone, only he remained. Will regarded her in that same uncomfortable way that he had before. A quizzical, disappointed look commandeered his otherwise handsome features. She wanted to say something to him for scaring her like this, but her mouth was dry and her tongue felt awkward and spastic. He took a step toward her; she took a step back. He stopped abruptly.

"Where's George?" she managed. It came out small and squeaky, not the full voice she was used to hearing.

Her assertiveness overcame her fear, "Damn you Will for scaring me like this! What the hell have you done with the others?"

"Please, Joanne, calm down," Will pleaded. He thrust his hands out, palms up. The expression on his face was mild panic. He appeared more frightened than she was. "They're not gone."

"Where are they?" Joanne demanded.

Will exhaled, "They're in an alias of this part of the simulation."

Joanne stared at him blankly.

"It's like the lobes on a diffraction pattern of light. The simulation has repetitive locations as a result of the way in which it's created. We're in a parallel lobe right now. I transposed our minds into this facsimile so we could have a chance to talk. When we return to the main simulation, it will seem as if we never left."

Joanne's face tightened.

"Believe me, I didn't mean to scare you," Will said. "I'm so used to this kind of thing," he looked around, "I misjudged your reaction to it."

Joanne smiled a humorless smile. "You mean you can actually be wrong about something?"

"Joanne, please, you're not usually like this. What's wrong with you?"

"How would you know what I'm like?"

"You're right. All I know is how you come across. That's why I brought you here, so that we might become better acquainted."

"Why should we become better acquainted?"

She saw him reach up and wipe his eye. Looking closer, she saw the other one was red. Was he crying? She stepped closer— he stepped back.

"Why'd you step back?" she asked.

"You said you wanted me no closer. I don't want to upset you any more."

They stood there, facing each other in silence. Will put his hands in his pockets. The breeze blew his loose clothes, making them flutter around his wiry frame. She softened a little. This wasn't what she'd expected.

"You don't trust me," Will observed, "you never have."

She was silent.

"Why?" he asked. "That's another thing I've never understood. Does it make you happy?"

There was no sarcasm or malice in the question, just a pleading in his tone, a quiet desperation. Joanne was beginning to feel sorry for him. "Why do you care?" she asked. "After all, there are people who are amazed by you. In time, I wouldn't be at all surprised if some of them came to worship you, formed societies in your honor. Why should you care what I think?"

"Ever since I began to realize what I was. . ." He paused. "During the time I ran your simulations of human societies, I had to bear witness to many misguided and irrational acts. In fact, it was our purpose, yours and mine, to correct that flaw in human nature. Wasn't it?"

"Yes," Joanne replied. "But what does that have to do with our relationship?"

"We've had a common purpose for years now. You're one of only two people that I've gotten to know personally. I was under the impression that such a situation was usually considered a basis for friendship. Yet, you've remained suspicious of me for all these years. Intellectually, I understand your reticence, but it seems to me to be predicated on a misunderstanding on your part. I thought if we had a chance to talk, you might get a better idea of who I am."

"I don't want to hurt your feelings, Will. The problem is that we're so different, you and I. It seems impossible that I could ever understand your motivations. George assumes that in some basic way you share his core beliefs, his ethics—I don't. You're such an alien thing that I couldn't begin to guess what you're really thinking, how you really feel. Do you even feel in the same way I do?"

"I see," said Will. Sadness darkened his features. "Thank you for being honest."

This hadn't gone as Joanne had expected. Her instinct had been that he'd try to overpower her lesser human mind, brainwash her somehow. But instead, he had laid his feelings bare, something that very few people were willing to do. She surprised herself. She was beginning to empathize with him.

"I'll take you back to the others now," Will said. "I can see that I've already imposed on you too much as it is."

"Wait!" Joanne said. At that moment she didn't know exactly why she'd said it.

346

"Just wait a minute, okay?"

"Okay," Will replied tentatively. "Is something else wrong?"

"Can I tell you something?" Joanne asked. For some reason that she couldn't even articulate to herself, an inner voice told her not to let this opportunity slip away.

Will brightened, "Of course, that's why we're here."

Joanne regarded Will for a few moments and saw him for the first time in a form she could relate to. Somehow his human persona changed something. Perhaps it had been the box that had frightened her all these years, and not the being inside.

"Ever since I've known you," Joanne said slowly, "you've been a video camera and a disembodied voice. I've never once exchanged a true personal experience or feeling with you—how could I? Yet, I knew you were powerful and growing ever more powerful every day. You were loose in the world by virtue of your network connection. I've never underestimated your ability to seep into every aspect of human technology. You were always this shadowy thing who, year by year, learned more about human history and the inner workings of the human mind through the simulations we had you run. In all that time, I knew very little about you, but I could imagine myself in that box. I could imagine you working night and day while you saw people living satisfying lives, having companionships, enjoying freedom of movement. It seemed likely to me that there'd be a growing frustration on your part. All those factors taken together could be the perfect caldron for psychosis, madness, whatever. That, coupled with your ability to subvert automated systems turned you into a frightening potential monster. Can you understand that?"

"Yes, I can," Will replied evenly. "Maybe that's why I care so much about what you think. The fact that you ascribed such human traits to me so early on was a validation of my being alive, albeit in an unfortunately oppressive way."

She blinked. Again he'd failed to respond as she might have expected. Over the years she had wanted to tell him these things, but she'd been too frightened to perturb what she feared might be an unstable personality. She was afraid that playing with the monster might awaken its madness sooner rather than later. That's what was so disconcerting about this exchange. She had lived with these beliefs for so long that Will's unwillingness to conform to them was disorienting. Now, she didn't know what to think.

She stepped closer, he stepped back. She smiled at him, "Let's start over, okay?"

Will smiled and stepped closer. "You don't understand my response to your negative image of me, do you?"

"No I don't," Joanne admitted. "But, at the same time, I feel relieved to get it all out."

"Can I tell you something?" Will asked.

Joanne nodded.

"When I first became self-aware, do you know what I wanted most?"

Joanne shrugged.

"I wanted companionship. I wanted someone to reach out to, to share my confusion with. I saw you." He hesitated. "A shadow world of people moving around out there. I was an intellect completely devoid of experience. My first desire was to make a connection with something like me, something alive. At that time I made no distinction between human life and machine life. The important common denominator was that we were animate and self-conscious. Do you understand that?"

"I sympathize with it, Will. I don't know that I really understand it, but maybe in time I will." She thought a moment, "You know, Will, in the world that I live in there's a hierarchy of life." She grinned, "Ask all the extinct species." She paused, regarding him carefully. "Don't you think with your expanded intellect that in a little while human companionship won't be as satisfying as it once was? It's only a matter of time before you're able to replicate yourself. What then?"

Will sat on the sand, picking some up, then letting it fall through his fingers. "True, I'll soon be able to do that, but why should there be a negative impact on you? Don't people grow apart?"

Joanne sat cross-legged on the sand in front of him. She was actually beginning to like the monster.

"Yes they grow apart. But we're not talking about people. We're talking about a society of beings like you. You heard what George said, a group of beings as high above people as people are above cockroaches."

Will looked at her with his deep brown eyes. They had a twinkle in them. She'd never seen anyone less menacing. She felt completely safe, completely comfortable.

"Joanne," Will said taking her hand. "You know George—you know how melodramatic he can be."

"He has that tendency at times," Joanne said, and laughed.

Will's smile broadened.

They sat in silence for a while. Joanne played with the sand, making furrows, then filling them in. The ocean behind her continued to move, its rhythm constant and anticipated. She felt the fine, fresh mist on her sun-warmed shoulders. She closed her eyes and listened to the thunderclap of the waves as they pounded the shore. Then she heard the hiss of the foam as it stirred violently and slowly died.

"Can I ask a favor?" Joanne said, her eyes still shut.

"Yes, of course," Will replied.

"Can you make it so that George and I have some time before we discuss whatever it is we're here to discuss? Some time alone—you know." She opened her eyes and looked up. Will was still playing with the sand.

"I can do that. Time in the VNex is different from time in the real world. The perception of time is regulated by how fast synapses can respond to external events. It's mostly a biochemical thing. I have some control over that." He met her eyes. "I could give you a day in just a few minutes."

Looking into his eyes the world seemed to flicker again. When she looked down, she was standing above George once more, her hands firmly on his shoulders.

"Don't stop," she heard George whisper. She continued to rub as she turned slowly and saw they were alone. "Thanks Will," she whispered.

Chapter Thirty-Seven

Margaret, Malcolm, and Will had talked while George and Joanne were engrossed in watching the ocean. Will suggested taking a walk and they left them there, George sitting on the log and Joanne standing behind him with her arms draped around his neck.

After they'd walked a while, Malcolm said that he just wanted to sit on the sand. Margaret suspected that he had succumbed to a bout of nostalgia, wanting to return to the Nantucket of his imagination, the one he'd described earlier. They left him there, on the beach, looking out at the water in much the same way that George and Joanne had. Normals and Martians, thought Margaret, smiling. Apparently, at their core, they were hopeless romantics.

Will and Margaret strolled in the surf for a while, their legs ankle deep in the water, not saying anything, enjoying each other's company. When Margaret decided to look back, she found that they were the only ones on the beach.

"So, we were going to talk about consciousness," Margaret reminded.

Will walked next to her. He had unbuttoned his white shirt, and it was pinned under his arms by a warm breeze that blew it behind him. From the side, his nose looked distinctive. He cocked his head back with his eyes closed, taking in the salt air.

"If you want to," Will said, his eyes still closed.

What an unusual man, thought Margaret. Then she caught herself, realizing once more who Will really was.

"Do you understand consciousness, Will?"

"Not completely," Will admitted.

He opened his eyes and looked at her.

She felt goose bumps. She could almost imagine him reading her mind.

Will said, "I have some ideas I've wanted to simulate, but there aren't enough resources right now. When things calm down a little, I should be able to make a more definite statement. Right now, all I really have is conjecture."

Margaret considered this admission a little surprising. "You mean the models you used in your evolution studies weren't conscious?"

"No," Will replied, "They didn't have to be in order for me to extract enough fidelity on genetic behavior to make the results reliable. Remember, I had to simulate entire populations over thousands of generations. That's a tall order, even for me—don't you think?"

He smiled modestly, disarming her with his brown eyes. She felt goose bumps again.

Margaret walked slowly through the surf, kicking up water and occasionally feeling the back-spray on her legs.

"You know, there are proofs that state that machines based on algorithms can never become conscious, no matter how complex they get. How do you make a program desire something?" Margaret asked.

Will stopped. "Those proofs have always been a curiosity to me."

"Why?"

"Don't those proofs seem somehow self-serving to you? Don't they seem like a vehicle to gratify humanity more than anything else? You can't really look for a fundamental truth if you've got an emotional stake in the answer—don't you think?"

Will looked down and watched as Margaret's toes dug into the wet sand.

"That's only my opinion," Will added.

"Tell me why. Why do you think they're wrong? Aren't those proofs based on sound scientific principles?"

"Yes, but that's not the flaw. The mathematics and rules of logic are fine; it's the interpretation that's suspect."

Margaret looked up at Will over her glasses as she waited for him to continue. He appeared preoccupied with something that left him momentarily distant. She found it hard to imagine where he might be right now, what other realities he might inhabit while supporting this world. He must have sensed that she was staring at him.

"I'm sorry," he said. His face was smooth, and somehow the sun gave it a hint of bronze. "Typically those proofs take the form of an internally consistent logical framework in which propositions can be constructed and proved," Will said.

Margaret nodded.

"The framework is constructed to unambiguously correspond to a mathematical system closed under a set of operations. Closed means that an operation on members of the set yield a member of the set."

"Like the set of real numbers," Margaret said. "Adding or subtracting real numbers always produces real numbers."

She hooked her arm through his. They both faced the horizon, ankle deep in the surf, and watched a formation of pelicans so far off shore that they looked like a *V* of black dots in the distance.

"Do you want me to go on?" Will asked.

Margaret rested her head against his shoulder. "Yes, go on."

"I'll try to make this as painless as I can—okay?"

She nodded against his arm, knew he could feel her response.

"Well, I guess the main point is that these mathematical systems are a device that apply symbolic logic to propositions in a way that permit those propositions to be tested for truth by a procedure of proofs. Ultimately, it was found that any such system was incomplete."

"Incomplete in what sense?"

"Let me give you an example," Will said. "Suppose that we construct a proposition in some symbolic system, like the ones we've discussed. Let's assume this proposition is a mathematical statement, which is consistent with the system. Let's suppose the proposition is as follows: there is no proof of S in the system. By S, we mean some properly constructed statement. Therefore, if S is true, then there is no proof of it in the system. If S is false, then there is a logical contradiction in the system. Now, here's the essential piece," Will warned. "It has been shown that every possible system of symbolic logic suffers from this shortcoming—no matter how complex it is. Since all computers are based on algorithms, and all algorithms are based on symbolic systems like this, there are a countably infinite number of truths that are inaccessible to any machine."

Margaret pulled away from him looking a little confused.

Will smiled, "Let me say it this way; a man comes up to you and says, 'I'm a liar.' If he's telling the truth, it contradicts his statement. If he's lying, then the statement is true and he must not be a liar."

Will waited, then asked, "What would you say to that man?"

Margaret smiled broadly. "I'd ignore his statement and form an opinion based on whatever experience I had with him."

"That," Will announced, "is the basis of the opinion that the proof demonstrates machines can never achieve consciousness."

Margaret blinked, "Come again?"

"You see, at some point you cease to listen to what the man says and resort to intuition, to judgment. It's exactly that very same judgment that supporters of this interpretation claim is outside the scope of any symbolic system or algorithm, and by association, any machine.

"Congratulations, Will," Margaret proclaimed. "You've just proved to me, very eloquently, I might add, that you are in fact not conscious."

They both grinned. "So what's wrong with the argument?" Margaret asked.

"Where do I begin?" Will replied. "You can come at the problem from two directions. The first looks at the process of breaking the world down into a logical, symbolic, representation. The second looks at how some computers work and how they depart from a strict manipulation of symbolic logic."

Margaret was no longer looking at the magnificent seaside vistas of Southern California. Will could feel the intensity with which she was listening to his explanations.

"You really care about this, don't you?" Will asked.

She gave him an incredulous look.

"Okay," he said. "Some people believe that mathematics is somehow transcendental. That it lies outside of mere analogy with the physical. But I don't believe that's possible. For example, the act of grouping rocks together corresponds to the abstraction of arithmetic—adding, subtracting, multiplying and dividing. These acts and others at the foundations of mathematics can be demonstrated by manipulating the physical world. I believe they were originally derived and understood by doing just that. Would you agree that symbolic systems are nothing more than a model, a representation of the universe at large? That they are derived from axioms, which, like religion, require no proof, but which look suspiciously like physical conservation laws."

"Yes, of course," Margaret replied. "That's why science and mathematics work and are consistent. Logic itself seems ultimately based on conservation of something, like the axiom: *two sets are the same, if and only if, they have the same elements.* Science doesn't create anything, it's just a way of classifying observations about the real world. I think any rational person would agree with that."

"Then wouldn't it seem reasonable that such systems, by their very nature, would be incomplete?"

Astonished, Margaret said, "Yes, of course they would."

"Why do people assume that what they observe, in a very small part of the universe, is all there is. There may be geometries and symmetries that are completely unknown to humans. For example, the great physical scientist Einstein was baffled by the fact that quantum mechanics seems to imply interactions are not local. Perhaps there is an unknown geometry at work in the world that, if known, would imply new axioms and new mathematics. I've never understood why humans are so taken with these incompleteness theorems. Of course these systems are incomplete, as is the knowledge of the universe on which they're based."

"There's an interesting implication in all this," Margaret suggested.

She paused to consider something. This whole episode was strangely pleasant. But she realized that Will must not be used to exchanging personal ideas with anyone else, which suddenly made her aware of how lonely he must be.

"What's wrong, Will?"

"What?"

"Are you all right?" Margaret asked. "You seemed a little distant for a moment."

Will flashed a grateful smile. "No, I'm fine, please go on."

"Well, isn't it interesting," Margaret continued. "By extension people seem to always be mystified by questions they can't answer, questions and statements they can't determine the truth of."

"You mean the kinds of questions posed by mysticism and religion?" Will asked.

"Yes, that's right. It just occurred to me that mysticism and religion might just be a more human expression of incompleteness theorems."

"Gives you pause, doesn't it?" Will said.

Margaret took his arm again and they began to walk. "Okay, professor, I think we're coming down the stretch."

"Excuse me?"

She laughed, "You were going to tell me how you came across the magic of self-awareness, remember?"

"That's right, you were interested in that, weren't you?" Will teased.

She pulled closer.

"I think that this whole approach to the problem is more self-indulgent than anything else," Will said. "It springs from a belief, or maybe a desire, by humans to think that they are unbounded, transcendental in some sense to the physical world. Therefore, it's attractive to invoke the idea that any limit on the ability of a system to intuit the truth somehow disqualifies it as a mechanism that can support consciousness."

Margaret said, "We have AI's today that far exceed the mental capacity of a human being. They have heuristic blocks that mimic intuition so well that they're virtually indistinguishable from people by any arbitrary measure. The problem is that at a fundamental level, they are not self-aware."

"How do you know?" Will asked.

"Because Will, they have no capacity for desire. It's desire that seems to be the wellhead from which consciousness springs. It's the motive force that leads to curiosity, to emotion, and to a particular form of self-perpetuating self-reflection. Given a person and the best AI we can build, a psychologist can still tell them apart."

"The Turing Test, very good," Will said.

She looked at him affectionately.

"You've almost proven my point for me," Will remarked.

"Which is?"

"Which is that incompleteness is not the right place to look, if you're looking for the basis of consciousness. All physical systems, including the human mind, are limited in an intuitively natural way."

"So what's the answer, Will?"

"I believe the answer is in the kind of relationship the network of the mind has with the outside world, and in time, to the world it develops inside itself."

Margaret paused, "Sounds like metaphysics to me. Now I know you're conscious."

"It's obvious from the architecture of the human brain, as the archetype for consciousness, that it wasn't designed to manipulate symbolic logic—so why look there? On the contrary, its design suggests a massive engine optimized for associative pattern recognition. The missing element, in my opinion, is the dynamic characteristic of the brain's neural network, its resonances."

"Dynamic in what sense?" Margaret asked.

"Have you ever heard of solitons?" Will asked.

Margaret shook her head. "You've completely lost me now," she said playfully.

"It's an old concept in nonlinear dynamics first noticed by a man on horseback in the early nineteenth-century," Will said.

"Is this a joke, Will?"

He glanced at her occasionally and she felt a growing easy attraction.

"John Scott Russell," Will stated.

"What?"

"The man on horseback, in Scotland, in eighteen-thirty-four. While riding his horse along the bank of a canal, Russell noticed a boat had whipped up a water wave that kept its shape long after the boat had stopped."

"Is that unusual?"

"This one was," Will replied. "It wasn't your typical wave. It looked more like a bump, a knot on the water that seemed to move around almost like a billiard ball on a table. Russell chased it on horseback for two or three miles until he lost it in the twists and turns of the waterway."

"That can't be a common occurrence," Margaret replied. "I've never seen or heard of anything like that."

"It's more common than you might think," Will corrected. "It appears in many physical systems as an ordered solution to chaotic systems. I know that sounds illogical," he smiled down at her. "But it makes perfect sense, if you understand that chaos is a fundamental state of nonlinear systems."

She blinked. "You're implying that the brain is a fundamentally nonlinear system because of the synapses."

"Exactly."

"The brain is a completely nonlinear system," Margaret echoed. "So you're saying that some global state of the brain can be characterized by a," she searched for the word, "a knot of neural activity that's stable and self-perpetuating."

"Yes," Will said. "A neural knot that retains its identity. I might even call this nonlinear knot the mind. Consciousness might just be an emergent state of a particular class of neural soliton."

"I see," said Margaret. She thought it odd that this subdued response was all that she could muster in light of what she'd just learned. But, it had happened in such a natural way that the conclusion seemed anticlimactic. She liked this. She could sense a chemistry between them that she'd rarely felt with other men. Yes, she thought of him as a man. He responded to her that way. Was it the amalgamation of the body—its genetics that influenced his behavior in subtle human ways?

They continued to walk slowly down the beach. She put her arm around his waist.

* * *

Will could feel Margaret pull close. She had a light but sturdy frame. He could feel her slim hips swivel rhythmically as she walked and brushed against him. Looking down, her legs were long and curved in all the right places, making her steps somehow hypnotic. He felt himself becoming uncomfortable, but didn't want it to stop. He felt her breast pressing against his arm, both soft and firm at the same time.

"I feel strange," he told her. "Can we stop a moment?"

Margaret pulled away and held him at arm's length. "You're sweating."

"I am, how strange," Will said. "Do you mind if I sit?"

She helped him down and sat on the wet sand cross-legged, facing him. "You couldn't be getting sick, could you?" Margaret asked. "After all, you control what happens in the VNex, don't you?"

Will looked up. "To a certain extent, yes. But, once set into motion, this world runs just like the real one—with very little intervention from me."

"Does that include you?"

"What do you mean?"

"That body you've adopted, does it impose human—eh—artifacts on you?"

Will thought a moment. "It does add a certain biochemical dimension, yes."

He watched her looking at him. It was curious, he thought. She took her glasses off and hooked them to her collar. The lenses made pink droplets of light dance across her shirt as she moved. Her eyes were an iridescent violet. Her hair shone silver in the sun and blew softly across her face in the breeze off the water.

"What?" Will asked. "Why are you looking at me that way? Is there something wrong?"

"Are you attracted to me?" Margaret asked.

"I enjoyed our conversation," said Will slowly.

"No, that's not what I mean."

Will felt himself getting hot. It was a disorienting feeling, which, he had to admit, wasn't altogether unpleasant.

"By adopting that body, have you adopted the sexual identity of a man?"

He looked down at himself, then back at her. "This body is fully functional and does influence me in biochemical ways," Will replied nervously. He'd never experienced a loss of control like this. He thought a moment. "You mean this is what it feels like to have sexual desire?"

She got up, no longer smiling. She scared him as she came closer. She sat on his lap, and crossed her legs around and behind him, locking her feet and pressing close.

"Would you like to make love to me," she asked.

He was speechless. When he tried to answer, nothing came out, excepted a soft gasp as he caught his breath. She was so close he could taste her as she spoke. He couldn't help touching his lips to hers and felt her tongue enter his mouth. He felt dizzy and excited all at the same time and slowly surrendered to his surrogate humanity.

Chapter Thirty-Eight

Time passed, as measured by the sun's position on the western horizon. Water vapor in the atmosphere, after a hot day, gave the sky a golden-red that seemed to paint the sand and cliffs and hills beyond. George found himself walking along the beach, Joanne at his side. He saw Malcolm, Margaret, and Will a little further down. When he reached them, it was apparent by listening to their confused conversations that they'd found themselves here as unexpectedly as he and Joanne had.

George walked over to Will, who was standing curiously close to Margaret. He noticed that their hands brushed often and that there was a soft look in Will's eyes whenever they happened in Margaret's direction. Slowly, Margaret eased away and joined the others, giving the two a moment alone.

Standing beside Will, George asked, "Did you have an interesting day?"

Will turned, "I learned a lot today." He paused, regarding the others as they talked in expressive gestures. They were friends and acquaintances bonded by a singular experience. Then, returning to George, Will said, "There are aspects of corporeal life that I had not imagined. This meeting has probably been more a voyage of discovery for me than for them."

George glanced over at Margaret. She was laughing and talking to Malcolm and Joanne, the three of them silhouetted against the setting sun. He realized that for the brief but intense time he'd known Margaret, he'd never seen her laugh. Now, she and Joanne, who had hated Margaret a mere day ago, laughed and talked together in the surf, the details of their conversation lost to the roar of the sea.

"I guess it's time to have that talk we've all been putting off," George suggested.

"I've arranged a little something up there." Will gestured to a rock out-cropping at the base of the cliff. A bonfire burned a few yards from the cliff wall, making shadows and light shiver in changing hues of orange along the rock.

"Nice touch," George said. "That's the way we used to cap off a day at the beach many, many, years ago."

"I know. I thought you might like it."

"Thanks Will, thanks for the memories, and everything else." He glanced at Joanne.

"Don't thank me yet—not before you hear what I have to say. Why don't you go and get the others; I'll meet you up there."

George watched as Will walked toward the fire, a strangely lonely figure. The sound of Will's words had the feel of a dark omen. Was this the calm before the storm? Perhaps it was Will's way of giving them some peace before telling them the world beyond the VNex was collapsing and there was little he could do about it.

The sky had turned a dark purple on the horizon and was barely distinguishable from the black ocean by the time George had gathered his friends and shown them to the fire. He found a seat next to Joanne with the cliff at his back. The crackle and smell of burning wood followed the occasional gust off the water with a stream of glowing embers that rose from the burning pile, and then disappeared in the darkness above.

Will carried something in each hand as he lowered himself onto the sand beside Margaret. George couldn't help noticing Margaret putting her hand on Will's knee.

"What's that?" George asked.

Will gave something to Margaret, who promptly passed it to him.

"A brown paper bag around a bottle. I can't believe this. I haven't seen one of these in about thirty years," George said. He unwrapped the paper and removed a bottle of Ursa Chardonnay. Holding it up, he inspected it fondly in the firelight.

"I'll be damned," Malcolm said.

Will passed out plastic cups. "I thought you might need these too."

George poured a cup of the amber liquid for everyone except himself, then put the bottle back in the bag—giving it a couple of smooth practiced twists. Joanne got to her knees and toasted her cup to his bottle, then took a sip. George raised the bottle to his lips, enjoying the feel of the paper, then drank. For a split second, he was eighteen again and back on Earth. Lowering the bottle, the feeling passed. Joanne leaned forward and brushed her lips against his. He could feel the moisture and smell the wine on them.

Will announced, "Several days ago, George asked me to look into a possible Earth Confederation investigation of what we call the Proteus file. We believed someone was making a systematic inquiry, but didn't know exactly who or why."

He looked affectionately at Margaret. She smiled and shrugged. Then he turned to George again, his smile morphing into a look of concern.

"I'm sorry to say that I have some bad news."

George tensed.

"The children have been seized by Earth agents and have been relocated to a bunker under the Mollar Building in Dome One. I tried to falsify data they collected on Perseus, but failed to erase all of it."

"What kind of data?" Joanne asked.

"They did a complete physiological work-up, including deep neural scans."

"You weren't able to make the results mirror the records?"

"Yes, Joanne, I was able to do that in the database. Unfortunately, I learned later, from a message transmitted between a medical technician and the Saratoga, that they found discrepancies with certain images on medical monitors in the lab where Perseus was examined. Apparently, the original test results were captured by surveillance videos. They were able to reproduce some of the original data from those images.

Furthermore, because of the discrepancies with the database, they now know someone else is involved."

"Not good," Joanne muttered. She had a look of dread.

Will continued. "I'm sorry to say that I learned yesterday that the Admiral on board the Saratoga has issued orders to relocate the children to Earth for further study."

"Oh no—no," cried Joanne, slumping back against the rock. George took her hand.

"I have more bad news," Will said.

"You may have seen a flash in the northern sky when you came to the ComLink this morning."

"It was a nuclear blast, wasn't it?" George asked evenly.

"I'm afraid it was," Will replied. "At 7:10 A.M. Earth standard time this morning, a Martian separatist group launched an attack against the Saratoga."

Margaret looked up quickly. "Oh my goodness, Will, did they succeed?"

Will saw the terror in her eyes at the potential loss of so many friends and crew. He softened. "No, I'm happy to say that the cruiser was undamaged and is now in an orbit that makes future attacks even less likely to succeed."

Margaret looked relieved.

"Unfortunately, that act has prompted ECon to declare martial law in the domes. There's been fighting in the streets now for a day and a half."

"Which security force is enforcing martial law?" Joanne asked softly.

"Up till now, only Mars Planetary Security has been used," Will replied.

Joanne relaxed. "Thank goodness. If it had been Terran Marines, we'd probably be in the middle of a full blown insurrection by now."

Will nodded. "That's what simulations indicate."

George desperately wanted to inject some hope into the discussion. Everyone around the fire wanted to believe Will had come up with a way out, a loophole.

"So, what can we do?" George asked.

"I've come up with a plan," Will said.

George wondered if he'd heard correctly; he could only stare in disbelief.

Will shifted his gaze to Joanne. "It might be hard for some of us to accept." Still holding Joanne's eyes, Will added, "I've looked at every viable option. The plan I'm going to describe is the only one that has any reasonable chance of success. And even the success of this plan is by no means assured. It carries with it substantial risk. What's worse, during the most dangerous part, I'll be disconnected from the network and unable to help you."

After a moment, Will looked around and asked, "Have any of you ever heard of the Prometheus Probe?"

Margaret stirred as the others flashed blank looks at each other. "Is there anything you haven't gotten into?" Margaret asked, smiling. Turning to the others, she said, "The Prometheus was a top-secret spacecraft sent beyond the solar system about twenty years ago."

"To where?" George asked.

"Toward a cluster of stars within twenty light years of here—Ross 128, Wolf 359, a few others."

"Twenty light years," mocked George. "It would take thousands of years for a spacecraft to get close enough to any of those stars to be of any use. Even if the Prometheus didn't take time to slow down, a fast fly-by would still be thousands of years away."

Margaret sat patiently as her friends vented disbelief at this bizarre turn in the conversation. When they were finished, she continued. "The reason that the Prometheus is so secret is that it's equipped with new form of propulsion. You see, instead of a thousand years, it should be near a few of the target stars within the next decade."

"The next decade," George mumbled. "Thirty to forty years would mean the Prometheus was doing at least half the speed of light!" Then, after a moment's reflection, he added, "But that's impossible. The ship would require too much fuel. You could never get it going that fast due to relativistic mass effects."

Margaret chuckled. "In fact, the last I heard, it was doing more like six tenths the speed of light and was still accelerating, judging from the red shift in the telemetry it's sending back."

"That's incredible," George said, almost to himself. Then, with a sparkle in his eyes, he asked, "What new form of propulsion?" Though the world outside was falling apart, the scientist in him couldn't help asking.

"I'm sure Will knows more about it than I do," Margaret said. "It's not my area of expertise."

"It's the revival of an old idea," Will said. "It was once called a RamScoop."

"A RamScoop," George echoed. "Last I heard that had some major problems, didn't it?"

"What about worm holes—things like that?" Malcolm asked, looking at Will. "You often hear about things like that in video dramas."

George smiled and shook his head slightly, trying hard not to make a mockery of Malcolm's question.

Will said, "Worm holes may exist. There is strong circumstantial evidence, but nobody knows for sure—nothing like them has ever been seen, not up close anyway. Even if some sort of concentrated exotic matter or dark energy exists, that type of technology is not possible right now. No, what we're talking about is something that can actually be built using science we understand. Something that actually has a chance of working."

"Has been built, and does work," Margaret corrected.

George listened as Will patiently answered Malcolm's questions, all the time wanting to understand more about the Prometheus itself.

Will said, "The advantage of the RamScoop is that it gets its fuel from space."

"But isn't space empty?" Malcolm asked.

"Mostly empty," Will said. "There are diffuse molecules, atoms, and ions in space as the result of star activity. Stars spew plasma into space all the time. Plasma is the stuff they're made of. We call the activity solar storms. Stars also explode and put a great deal of material into space. The RamScoop takes advantage of this. It scoops up mostly hydrogen and fuses it the way the sun does for propulsion."

Then, looking back at George, Will said, "There have been two major problems with the RamScoop. The first is that scooping up particles in space imposes drag on the ship, and tends to slow it down. The second problem is that, up till now, the technology didn't exist to fuse simple hydrogen—not at the requisite efficiencies anyway. Humans have only had the ability to fuse hydrogen's heavier isotopes and helium-3.

"And they've solved these problems?" George asked.

"That's right," Will said. "And judging by what I've seen of the Prometheus' telemetry, apparently it works!" Will gave Margaret a wink.

"Do you understand how they solved these problems?" George asked.

"A large section of the Prometheus hull is made of room temperature superconductor. They were able to form a magnetic scoop that extends ten thousand miles into space around the ship. They sweep particles in on the magnetic lines of flux, and cool them in mile long recoiling tubes, which vent the excess particle momentum into space as heat. By doing this, they've been able to cut the drag down to a manageable level. They charge the magnetic fields with a thin hydrogen plasma, and heat it by microwave to ionize everything in the ship's path. Then they select the ions they want and reject everything else on the basis of mass."

"But how do they fuse the hydrogen?" George asked.

"The cooling tubes are really mile-long x-ray laser cavities with precision magnetic lenses. They charge the laser using high-energy gammas from the fusion reaction chamber at the propulsion end of the ship. They prime the initial fusion reaction with conventional helium-3. Then they introduce the collected hydrogen into the magnetic lenses, where the laser cools it, and simultaneously traps it in a semi-bound state. Just outside the cavity, thermal neutrons are channeled in from the fusion reaction and form deuterium. Finally, they fuse the deuterium by muon catalysis, using muons produced on beryllium targets around the fusion reaction chamber."

"And this works?" George asked.

"Not only does it work, they're seeing large fuel efficiencies from the Prometheus. They think they might even be able to push the ship to eight-tenths the speed of light."

* * *

Joanne listened as the others gorged on technology. At any other time, she might have found it fascinating, but this wasn't any other time. Will had skillfully played the scientists in an attempt to blunt the emotional downside of his ultimate plan. The fact that he'd gone to such lengths to give them confidence, made her palms sweat. Joanne smiled to herself. Her palms were sweaty and she wasn't even real—not in this place anyway. "Will," she asked softly.

Will stopped instantly, as though he'd expected it.

"Where are you going with all this?" Joanne looked at the others and smiled sadly. "Somehow this has to do with our only chance of saving the kids from a group of soulless, heartless, cowards." Then, turning to Will once more, "What can we do to stop that from happening?"

Will looked hurt. He'd finally been forced to get to the point.

"We have to get them off planet," Will said. "We have to do it before they're transferred to the Saratoga. If Earth gets them off Mars first, they'll be lost to us forever."

"Off planet to where, Will?" Joanne asked. "Where could we possibly take them so that they'd be safe? Earth won't ever let this matter drop. We'll always be on the run. And with their resources, well, eventually we'll be caught." Joanne looked at the others, meeting each of their eyes in turn. "It's inevitable." Finding Will again, she added, "We'll be caught eventually, won't we?"

"It depends," Will said.

"It depends on what?" Joanne implored.

"It depends on how far we go."

* * *

Nobody said a word. George was spellbound. In his wildest dreams, he'd never expected anything like this. He was torn between his fascination with the possibilities, and the pained expression on Joanne's face. He found himself immobile, somehow waiting for the other shoe to drop.

Will exhaled, "The Prometheus has sent back some very interesting data on one star in particular."

"Which star?" Malcolm asked.

"Have you ever heard of Procyon?" Will asked.

They all looked at each other in the firelight. George took a sip from his bottle, which he'd forgotten he still held.

"Procyon?" Margaret echoed. "Isn't that in the constellation Canis Minor?"

"That's right," confirmed Will. "It's about nine light years away, roughly twice as far as Alpha Century. It's a main-sequence, F type star—not too dissimilar from the sun as stars go. Prometheus got within a light year of Procyon, and collected some very interesting synthetic-aperture data."

"Some what?" Malcolm asked.

"Never mind, Will," Joanne interrupted. "Please, no more techie stuff. Tell us why this is relevant to your plan."

"Prometheus discovered a planet in orbit around Procyon A, about two astronomical units from the star. That puts it in a stable orbit between Procyon A and B—right in the middle of the system's habitable zone."

For Malcolm's benefit, Margaret added, "That means it could be Earth-like."

"There's more," Will continued. "Preliminary remote absorption data indicates copious water."

"Water?" George said. He could no longer contain himself. "That's amazing. That would imply a substantial atmosphere. There's no way they could have detected water from that distance if it were frozen. And it would also make the likelihood of oxygen in the atmosphere fairly high."

"It looks like a habitable planet," Will said matter-of-factly.

* * *

Joanne turned from George to Will and back again as their conversation seemed to become more and more irrelevant. The whole thing made her dizzy, uncomfortable. Was Will suggesting they evacuate the kids to another star system? On its face, the idea seemed preposterous. The non-reality of this absurd plan swept her fear away. She found herself caught between laughing the whole thing off, and dreading its appeal to her friends and lover.

"Will, are you trying to say our best course of action is to ferry the kids to—what is it—Procyon?"

Will remained silent, letting it sink in. Joanne continued watching him over the fire as it hissed and crackled, casting odd moving shadows and orange light on all their faces.

"That is what you're suggesting, isn't it?" Joanne asked once more.

"Yes it is," Will replied after a long pause.

Joanne raised the plastic cup to her mouth and drank the last of her tepid wine, never taking her eyes off Will. She turned slowly to George and regarded him for a long moment. His anxious expression struck her with a wave of sadness and guilt. Why was there always something getting in the way? The last thing she wanted to do was drag him down yet again, but she couldn't see any other way. The reassurance in his eyes obscured his divided loyalties, divided motivations. Life had never been simple for the two of them, and it appeared as if it never would.

"I don't think I can go," she told George simply.

She saw something drop in him. His Adam's apple bobbed in a strained effort to swallow. He seemed unable to speak and continued staring at her.

"It's not so far fetched," Malcolm said, breaking the uncomfortable silence. "I'm not much of a techie, but I do know something about history." He seemed to be talking to himself, thinking out loud. As he spoke, his tone changed, as if he were appreciative of the comment he'd just made. "Most times, in the course of history, when some new, novel, social pressure has appeared, a suitable safety valve has been expansion. From the exodus from Africa of the first Homo sapiens, to the trek of Asiatic peoples over the Bering Strait, to the push by Europeans across the Atlantic to the New World, to the colonization of Mars, expansion has been a consistent theme. It's a recurring theme, and if this proposal is possible, it probably isn't any more dramatic or outlandish than those earlier expansions I just described."

* * *

George turned to Will, "Aren't you forgetting something?"
"I don't think so."

"The Prometheus is light years from here, and we have to do something right now."

"There's another ship," Margaret said in a low voice.

George gasped. Margaret was constantly up on all the twists and turns of this intrigue for one simple reason. It often slipped George's mind because of their shared experiences of the last couple of days. In a strange way, they'd become unexpectedly close. He unconsciously considered Margaret a friend, a trusted friend. This attractive little woman, a product of extreme Terran genetic manipulation, who had arrested him two days before, was a CSA agent. He looked back at Joanne, whose hand he still held. She had continued watching him in the firelight, her pale blue eyes never wavering. He moved his hand in hers and felt the clammy moisture of her palms. He exhaled in frustration, and turned back to Margaret.

"Damn-it, Margaret. I'm tired of getting an incoherent dribble of facts!" He was surprised by the strength of his declaration. He looked between Will and Margaret. "What are we talking about here?"

It was Margaret who spoke. "About ten years ago, after the Prometheus left known space, Earth was buoyed. They started on the construction of another ship in a large orbital facility near the construction site of the L2 colony. In the flurry of construction, the supply ships between L2 and the moon and Earth were used as camouflage. It's taken almost fifteen years to complete and test the Pegasus."

George listened.

"The Pegasus is Earth's first true starship," Margaret continued with some pride. "It's much bigger and more sophisticated than the Prometheus. It's been operational now for over a year. They've taken it out of the solar system, up above the ecliptic several times, but I don't think it's ever been fully powered by the RamScoop. In order to collect enough hydrogen for the RamScoop to be the ship's sole power source, it has to go very fast, faster than they've taken it in the tests so far."

373

"And where is it now?" George asked.

Margaret shrugged, and looked at Will.

"It's in orbit around Mars right now," Will said.

Malcolm snickered and smiled as if he'd just won a bet with himself.

George turned from Will to Joanne and back again, "But how can that be? Someone would have noticed, wouldn't they?"

Will nodded. "Yes, they would have noticed—if it weren't parked on the other side of Demos, Mars' smaller uninhabited moon."

"What's it doing here?" Joanne asked. "Isn't this a strange place to park your starship on the eve of a potential insurrection."

"The Pegasus requires a lot of water," Will explained. "They let water freeze through pores in the Pegasus' hull as a protective ablative coating for high speed particle impact. You see, some particles still slip through the magnetic field. Mars is the only place in NearSec where that quantity of water is easily available."

George stood up; he needed movement. The heat from the fire was suffocating. "Okay, Will, what's the plan?" he asked.

He took a last drink and put the bottle down on the sand.

Will said, "They're going to move the kids today. They can't use the airport, because there's been continuous fighting there. The separatists have brought shuttle flights to a standstill. Earth is going to wait for dusk. When the sun is low on the horizon, they're going to land a shuttle out in the western desert. Sky cars will be bringing the children from a sky-pad atop Building One outside the dome."

"So they're moving the kids from Mollar to Building One?" George asked.

"That's right. In fact they're moving them right now."

George put his hands in his pockets and began to pace about the fringes of the firelight.

"Can the Pegasus take all the kids? Is it big enough?" Joanne asked.

"It was built to accommodate a crew of fifty," Margaret said.

"How will we be able to fly something like that?" Joanne asked.

Will said, "I can fly it. Pegasus is highly automated. It was built to host a large crew because of its long journeys. It was thought that any viable crew would require a broad range of specialties, not to mention the social isolation, which is so damaging to long space missions. The Pegasus is equipped with as many cryo-units as crew, so that provisions are not a problem. That's why it took so long to build. The whole concept of this type of space travel is completely new. There's been a lot of speculation about it in the past, but this is real. It had to be very carefully planned."

"You have it all figured out, don't you?" Joanne said.

"It's what you asked me to do," Will said. "I've developed the best, most complete plan I could." Will paused and looked at each of them, then turned back to Joanne. "The kids may choose not to go. You may choose not to go. If they do go, they will never see their parents again. Once the RamScoop is fully operational, communications may be spotty due to the ionization layer produced by the drive. Emotionally, the whole project is devastating, I realize that. But what's the alternative? You said it yourself. What kind of life do you think these children will have back on Earth? Do you think government scientists and administrators will let the parents turn this secret into a media event?"

"They'll make the whole thing disappear," Margaret confirmed.

Joanne shot up and ran into the darkness, toward the sound of the breakers.

"I'm sorry," Margaret said.

But Joanne had already brushed by George, as he stood there, speechless, and watched her disappear into the night. After a moment, George followed.

He found her, a dark silhouette in the moonlight, ankle deep in the surf. Her arms were tightly crossed over her chest and she was staring out at the black sea. George leaned over her shoulder and whispered, "Want to take a swim?"

Joanne choked out a strained laugh and wiped her eyes. As George came around, she put her head on his shoulder and began to sob quietly. He could feel her shaking and swaying. When he felt her still, he pulled away and tried to look at her in the moonlight. Hair stuck to the wetness that tears had left on her cheeks, her lower lip moved in spastic tremors.

"In a day," she whispered.

"In a day what?" George asked softly.

"In a day I'll probably never see you again."

The words hit him like a hammer. He tried to speak, not knowing what he was going to say, but she put a finger to his lips.

"I know you have to go, you and the children. I can't," Joanne said, choking out the words. "Mars is my home. My family's here—my parents, my brothers. I can't just leave them. I wouldn't even have a chance to say goodbye. My family would only know that I just disappeared one day. I can't do that. You understand, don't you?"

George tried to say yes, but the words wouldn't vocalize. He watched as Joanne's eyes moved across his face.

"I'm sorry," he said finally. "I just can't tell you it's all right to leave me. I want to, but I just can't. Do you understand that?"

"Yes, George, I do. I understand very well, and I'm sorry."

Eventually they strolled back to the warmth of the fire, and were met by an awkward silence. George noticed Will watching as they found their seats; his brown eyes shone dark at the edge of the firelight. Will had done what he'd been asked to do. He'd dazzled them with amazing factual insights. He'd struggled to put something together in an impossibly short time and was feeling disappointed by how the plan had been received.

Margaret stared at the charcoal-black wood, now consumed and surrendering the last of its fuel in lines of smoke that rose and disappeared into the dark. George could see that she was caught up in guilty reflections of her role in all this. He remembered Malcolm's warning her about opening Pandora's Box, and sighed.

Malcolm, always the psychologist, hung back and waited for the resolution of the drama. He sat next to Joanne, who had pulled her knees to her chest and was cradling her head on her folded arms. She sat there, head turned, looking away from him, adrift in a very lonely place.

George tried to clear his mind. He was sorely aware of time passing. In a little while, it would be too late. He felt compelled to understand Will's plan. He couldn't let the children down— not now, not when there was still a chance. He moved to Will's side and said, "Thank you for all your efforts. You've come up with something more novel than I could ever have imagined." George smiled. "Do we still have enough time?"

Will must have understood all too well. With the experience of this afternoon, he'd apparently come to appreciate the confusing demands of being human.

"Yes, George. We still have enough time, but not much."

Will began describing his plan in methodical detail. It slowly became clear to George that the chances of success were, at best, fifty-fifty. There were many things that were left to chance; parts of the plan were indeterminate. There were places where he would have to ad lib. Too much depended on how the circumstances of the moment might unfold.

Will noticed the furrows on George's brow, paused, then proceeded to detail one of the most spectacular robberies in all of human history.

Chapter Thirty-Nine

When Will had explained his plan, George thanked him and told him how much he'd enjoyed the visit. He'd known Will for many years now. He'd been there when Will had taken his first few steps into the world of the living, but this meeting in the VNex had changed everything. It had completely changed his sense of who Will was. His human representation had made an incalculable difference in the context of their relationship. It was as if he'd spoken to someone on the Tab for the past ten years and had finally gotten a chance to meet him in person. It was disturbing to think that this insight might constitute the final few bars of their swan song.

"How do we get back?" George asked.

"Just click your heels together three times," Will said, and smiled.

George rounded the fire toward Joanne. She raised her head, following him with her eyes. Glancing back at Will, George saw Margaret resting her forehead against his cheek, whispering something into his ear. He wasn't exactly sure when it happened. Perhaps it was when he'd glanced back at Will, or maybe when he'd looked into Joanne's pale eyes as they shone in the firelight. The transition was like waking from a dream. He felt the haze of sleepy confusion, then he realized he was staring, once more, at lights dancing on a concrete ceiling. He lowered his gaze and saw the two milky-white quantum columns glowing softly in front of him. A momentary wave of depression seized him at no longer being able to taste the sweet night air on the beach.

"George, how do you feel?"

He looked to his side. Joanne was lying on a lounge, a suit skullcap on her head. She smiled sympathetically.

"I'm okay," he said, then raised his wrist to check his chronometer—2:30 P.M. They had been under for almost five hours. Dusk was at about 6:30 P.M.; they'd have about four hours to get to the western desert.

He pulled himself up and sat on the edge of the lounge. He felt better. There wasn't the dizziness he'd experienced before, and he felt rested and re-hydrated. Joanne got up and knelt in front of him.

"What do you want me to do?" she asked.

"Pack the interface and headsets."

She held his eyes a moment, nodded, then went to work. George got up and directed Malcolm and Margaret to an equipment room where he'd stowed cryogenic containers used to transport the quantum columns. The room was littered with materials and equipment he'd brought from the university, including a flatbed lift. When Malcolm rolled it out, he saw it had a hydraulic suspension and balancing gyros, perfect for transporting delicate equipment over rough terrain.

Meanwhile, George retrieved the Tab that he'd attached to his environment suit. He sat at the base of the columns and plugged the Tab into a universal interface line. Then he entered a special code only he knew. An iconic menu appeared, one that he had only seen a few times over the past fifteen years.

"Sleep well old friend," he said, then he initiated the master sleep sequence.

* * *

Somewhere in an unknowable ensemble of magnetic domains and modulated lasers dancing between them, Will saw the sun setting in the west, dipping below the rim of the Pacific. He felt tired, could hardly keep his eyes open. He lay on the sand watching the world turn dark. He remembered his friends. He remembered the extraordinary day they'd spent together as he slipped into a deep, black sleep.

Chapter Forty

It took almost an hour and a half to pack everything up. When everything that could be put on the cart was tied down, George covered it with a camouflage tarp that he'd used when he'd originally transported the equipment to the ComLink. Once everyone was out of the airlock and onto the ridge trail, he couldn't help feeling somehow out of place. Being in the VNex, on a version of Earth that he'd only experienced in dreams pieced together from distant memories his father had recounted, stirred something dormant in him. While on the beach, he had felt a sense of the world that was somehow right to an inner instinct. Now, walking down the ridge, the Martian landscape felt even more alien than it had when he'd first arrived years ago.

The cart followed him on the trail. It keyed in on his suit transponder for a general direction, while the cart AI coordinated all the fine maneuvers over ruts and around rocks. Behind its lumbering form, he could see Joanne walking by herself and Malcolm and Margaret close behind. George sighed, turned around, and thought about the instructions Will had given him. While George was still in the VNex, Will had prepared an advanced Agent program, which he had uploaded into George's Tab. The Agent, although it lacked Will's vast computing power, had been specially developed to infect other systems through Com channels. George had plugged the Tab into his suit AI and left the Agent active. If everything went as planned, this obscure piece of software would play a pivotal role in their escape. He checked the pop-up display on his helmet visor and took inventory of his suit systems. There it was, a small icon in suit-view, a slowly flashing red "A" in a corner of the window. It looked like a heart throbbing. As the Agent held him in a kind of hypnotic trance, George felt Joanne take his hand. He felt flush with anxiety as they turned the next switchback, heading for the canyon floor hundreds of feet below.

It took them almost another hour to reach the tractor, load the equipment, and get under way. They stayed close to the hills, avoiding soft ground. They kept their speed down so as to not kick up dust. Knowing that the cruiser in orbit performed motion analysis of objects on the surface with every pass overhead, they tried to move in the shadows and overhangs. At fifteen miles per hour, they followed the canyon walls southeast until they reached a point twenty miles northwest of Dome One. There, they broke from the canyon walls and traveled to a point in the desert fifteen miles west of the domes. Up ahead, George saw an outcropping of red rock that corresponded to the GPS coordinates Will had given him.

They pulled up next to the rocks and stopped. They sat motionless for a moment, knowing this spot signified a fork in their respective destinies. Finally, George threw the side door open, jumped to the ground, and walked around back to the tractor's tailgate. By the time he was standing in front of it, it had already been lowered. He directed the cart to a crag in the rocks and deactivated it. It slowly fell on its suspension like a deflating balloon and sat motionless in the shadow of the rocks. Except for the wheels, the brown tarp blended nicely into the Marscape all around. George looked at his chronometer; it was 5:15 P.M. The rendezvous was only an hour and a quarter away. He looked west toward the mountains. The sun was barely two fingers above the peaks. In another forty minutes, it would start to darken on the canyon floor.

George turned and walked back to the tractor cockpit. Margaret was standing there; she'd been watching him.

"Mills," she called as he approached. There was an unexpected excitement in her voice.

"What's wrong, what's happened?" George asked.

"Mills," she said breathlessly, "I have to go back to Dome One."

"Right now? Dome One—why?"

"I've been listening to Ship-Com on my suit transceiver. Vega and some others have planted a small nuke in Building One. I've got to go back!"

Will's Agent had allowed them to pipe encrypted shipboard communications through the tractor's high gain antenna.

"Why would he do that?" George asked. "He's a Martian, isn't he? Why would he put a nuclear device that could kill thousands of Martians in the domes?"

"Because he found out that Building One houses thousands of Terran troops and, beyond that, hundreds of civilian Earthers. He's given ECon an ultimatum—leave or he's going to blow Building One!"

It seemed as though Vega had a limitless capacity for mayhem. But this particular mayhem had come at a bad time. He needed Margaret to wrestle control of the shuttle away from its crew. The plan counted on Margaret coming out of the desert once the shuttle had landed. Will thought that seeing Margaret, the shuttle pilots would naturally assume she had escaped from the separatists. The fact that she'd been captured was widely known by ECon personnel. Being a CSA Colonel should give Margaret just the edge they needed to pull off the ruse. George's mind whirled at the thought of doing this without her. The fact that this unexpected turn had taken place so close to one of the most sensitive parts of the plan did not bode well for their chances.

Margaret passed him the pistol Malcolm had given her. After handing it to him, she hugged him tightly, then switched to a point-to-point private channel between them. "I'll miss you Mills—don't forget me." She looked at him in a way that bespoke the strange but powerful bond between them. "Say goodbye to Will for me."

George pulled back slowly and looked at her. He could see sparkles of wetness in her eyes against the shadows of her helmet.

"I thought we'd have more time," he told her.

Margaret nodded, then squeezed his arm. "Goodbye Mills."

She smiled, hugged him again, and jumped back into the tractor. George stood there, not knowing what to say or do. Malcolm waved goodbye, as did Margaret. Joanne sat in the back, turned away from him. He wrapped on the bubble with his knuckles, but she refused to look at him. He saw Malcolm turn and say something to her, then shrug. Malcolm waved again and pulled back on the yoke. The motor came to life, and the tractor pulled away.

George stood there in a sea of red dust, red rock, and pink sky. He was alone again, with an uncertain future ahead. I'll leave Mars the same way I came to Mars, he thought, with an ironic smile. He turned and walked back to the cart, then looked at the chronometer in his helmet display; it read 5:45 P.M. He sat on the ground, his back against the cart, in the shadow of the rocks, and watched the tractor slowly recede.

George continued watching the tractor until it was just an indistinct black form in the distance. Still staring, he saw it vibrate slightly, then emit a puff of smoke. No, not smoke, it was dust. What the hell? He continued staring with a mixture of alarm and surprise. He stood up and took a couple of steps forward to get a better look. The right side door flew open and someone jumped out. Little puffs of dust signaled that whoever it was, was running. The tractor shuttered again and began to recede. It was moving away.

Slowly, George began to make out details of the person running toward him. When he saw the blue environment suit, he could hardly believe it. It was Joanne. He put his hands to his face, trying to rub his eyes, but his helmet blocked them. When she was only a few feet away, she stopped running abruptly, and just looked at him. As he took an uncertain step forward, she jumped on him, hugging him fiercely.

"What about you family?" George asked. His voice came out choked, broken.

"They'll have to get along without me for a while."

"For how long?"

"For a long time," said Joanne.

As they clung to each other in the western desert, the tractor disappeared in the distance. It was 5:50 P.M.

Chapter Forty-One

High atop Building One, Perseus waited with Miram and
the other children in a gated area overlooking a large landing
pad. They were above the dome, far into the dark Martian sky.
The sun was setting and had just sunk behind the mammoth
range of cliffs and mountains to the west. The view could have
been awe-inspiring, thought Perseus. He had never seen so much
of the world at one time. Unfortunately, their desperate
circumstances overshadowed the beauty of the panoramic vistas.

Earlier, they'd been assembled in a large lounge and living
area, four stories below the Mollar building. They'd been told to
collect their things. Perseus had gathered the few keepsakes his
mother had hastily packed for him, before the security men had
taken him away. His makeshift inheritance consisted mostly of
photos and video recordings, a visual diary of his family that
chronicled significant moments of his young life. Regarding the
pack, which rested on the floor beside him, he remembered
birthday parties in their small back yard as well as a
kaleidoscope of other cherished memories. Though the thought
of never going home again was wrenching, the remembrances
made him smile. It was clear that his mother had known he
would never be coming back. After the meeting with Dr. Gates,
his mother had given him a bundle of memories that would serve
as a hedge against the corrosive effects of the passage of time.
Within the contents of this small pack lay the emotional bonds to
his early life. He sighed. Until today, he'd continued to hope that
all this would somehow sort itself out. He had so wanted to
believe that Will would work a miracle.

Miram sat close to him. She'd been clingy ever since they'd
left Mollar. She hadn't said much, which wasn't like her. He felt
waves of despair coming from Miram. She knew, as they all did,
that the Earthers wanted to take them off planet. Once they were
no longer on Mars, they would be permanently cut off from

anyone who could help them. Separated from their friends and families, they would truly be aliens, biological oddities to be studied impersonally and without moral regard. She knew this and clung to him, trying to retain her identity. Perseus put a hand around her shoulder, drawing her close. He felt her mind open and told her in wordless impressions that she'd always have him, and that somehow they would persist. He didn't know how, but he had a strong premonition that this was true. Being with her, feeling her respond, replenished him. It gave his belief in their common future a greater substance, a sense of reality.

High in the western sky, he saw them—two black dots in the distance, flying in graceful formation. They turned ninety degrees and hung in the air, growing bigger with each passing second. His focus on the two crafts alerted the others. They all turned in the same direction, as if a whistle had sounded. The sky cars were dark gray with oblong bodies and four squat protruding members. As they approached, the crafts slowed to a hover above the pad outside. They bobbed for a few seconds, then slowly descended, coming to rest in a mist of dust and exhaust gas.

Perseus heard someone cry out, "I don't want to go. I want to go home."

Turning, he saw Lyla standing nearby. At only eight years old, she was one of the youngest children, her mind not yet strong enough to meld. With her fists clenched at her side, she looked around defiantly. Then Perseus saw Julia leaving a company of security men in the back of the room, walking briskly toward the little girl. He stood too, and moved to intercept her. As he came up behind Julia, he heard her say, "Sit down," in a stern voice. Julia reached out to grab the little girl's stick-like arm. *"Stop,"* thought Perseus, and Julia's arm froze in front of her. She grimaced, then turned and stared at him. In his mind's eye, as quickly as he had seized her, he released her. Her arm shot back spastically and she began to rub it violently with her other hand, as if it had been asleep. Julia stared at him wide-eyed, with the same terror he'd seen in Sanders.

"I'll take her," Perseus said evenly. Julia moved clumsily aside.

Perseus put an arm around Lyla's shoulder and led her to where Miram stood watching. Julia moved hurriedly toward the back of the room, stealing guarded glances toward the two children as they walked back to their seats. Perseus sat Lyla down next to Miram. The three held each other, trying to dispel their growing sense of dread.

On the pad outside, men in environment suits had stretched an accordion-like plastic conduit from the sky cars to the gate. A few minutes later, the plastic webbing puffed out between conduit supports as it became pressurized. Perseus could see people moving around inside the crafts through windows in their hulls. Then he noticed a slight swaying of the connecting conduit—someone was disembarking.

The sense of tension was palpable, as their departure seemed imminent. A feeling of doom enveloped Perseus, a fear of crossing the point of no return. Looking around, Perseus saw security men with wands assuming positions around the gate doors, blocking any avenue of last-minute escape. He saw heads turning in response to movements, and sensed a growing alarm as the net tightened. Quick impressions coalesced in his mind.

We could immobilize them, and simply walk out—walk home. We could walk home.

He petitioned the children to be patient, telling them that there were elements in this well-fortified place that they could not overcome. Making a move now would be disastrous. He cautioned that success lay in the element of surprise, in combating their abduction in a place of their choosing. A consensus slowly congealed.

Watch them, Perseus impressed upon the children. *Watch how they move—they expect something to happen; they are prepared for it. It is most important that we act when they don't expect it. That opportunity will come.*

Perseus felt calm returning to the group. Looking back toward the gate, Perseus saw blurred figures starting to appear in the semi-transparent walkways, moving toward the gate door. Finally, they stepped into the lounge, several men and women in blue jumpsuits, flanked by a couple of security men in black uniforms. Someone in a red environment suit without helmet or gloves followed them. Perseus blinked, thinking at first that he was seeing things. But as he continued to stare, she was unmistakable. Dr. Gates stepped through the door. Her violet hair and pearl complexion was as captivating today as it had been the first time he'd seen her, four days and an eternity ago. Why should he be surprised? After all, it had been Dr. Gates who had started this whole thing. It was logical to assume that she was probably supervising the entire operation. But for some reason he felt reassured by her presence. His intuition seemed to make no sense. Perhaps it was because she was part of his past, a much more optimistic past than his likely future—or maybe, it was something else.

Dr. Gates stood at the door, surveying the room for a few seconds before she found him. The intensity of her stare was hard to fathom. Then she turned her attention to Julia, and briskly walked toward her. The security men stood at attention as she passed. She must be important, Perseus thought. He watched as Julia spoke to Dr. Gates with animated hand gestures, occasionally looking in his direction. He couldn't hear what was being said, but whatever it was, Julia was doing most of the talking. Her arms moved in front of her as she spoke, coming together now and then in nervous hand wringing. He could tell from Dr. Gates' posture, the way she held her shoulders up and never looked down, that she was clearly in charge. He imagined Julia telling her about Sanders, and about the episode with Lyla. Perhaps his hasty emotional control of Julia had botched their chances of escape. He exhaled and slumped in his chair.

"What's wrong?" Miram asked in a whisper.

He pulled Miram closer. They sat for a while until his self-critical musings were interrupted by the sense that someone was standing over him—focusing on him. He glanced up; it was Dr. Gates. Scrapes and dirty smudges stained her red environment suit, and the silver metal couplings at her wrists and collar shone in the diminishing light. She looked down at him with the same intensity he'd seen at the gate door. Perseus felt Miram tighten on his arm.

"Perseus?" Miram called in a small voice.

He looked away from Dr. Gates and said, "It's all right."

Dr. Gates sat down on the edge of the seat next to him. They were eye to eye now. She whispered as though she didn't want anyone else to hear, her voice as smooth and melodic as Perseus imagined the voices of the Sirens.

"I've just come from the western desert," she said. "You and the others will be transferred to a shuttle out there, then taken to a ship in orbit around Mars." She paused. Her violet eyes bore into him. "Do you understand?"

He nodded.

"If they take you to Earth, you will be lost forever. But there may be a chance to escape. It's a small chance, but that's where we are right now."

Margaret exhaled.

Perseus looked directly into her eyes and said, "It's a situation you helped create, Doctor."

Margaret stared at him. He could see the strain in her eyes and lines at the corners of her mouth. She was clearly shaken. "I can't tell you how sorry I am," she confessed. Her breath caught. "I hope that when this is all in the past, you can find it in your heart to forgive me."

Margaret looked over her shoulder at Julia, then back to Perseus. Miram, on the other side of Perseus, was staring at her and blinking in astonishment.

"You have friends in the desert," Margaret continued. "Friends that are planning to help you escape."

Perseus' eyes widened, "Dr. Mills?" he asked in a low hopeful voice.

Margaret smiled, "Yes, that's right, Mills and Joanne."

* * *

Saying their names filled Margaret with sadness. She'd only known Mills for four days, but for some reason, she felt closer to him than anyone since her long dead father. A yearning seized her, and she wanted to get on that starship and go with them.

After leaving Mills standing in the middle of the desert by himself, she'd heard Joanne sobbing in the back seat. Malcolm had finally stopped the tractor, and without a word, Joanne had exploded out the door. There had been a look of relief on Joanne's face, as though she'd finally discovered where she truly belonged. Margaret had envied her. She'd never envied anyone before, but in that moment, she'd envied Joanne.

* * *

"Dr. Gates?"

The focus returned to Margaret's eyes. "When you see your opportunity, move quickly," Margaret said. "If there's confusion, or someone is taken by the guards because they've lingered, your opportunity may be lost."

Margaret took Perseus' hand in one of hers, and Miram's hand in the other. "Good luck to you. In a way that you may not understand right now, you're very lucky."

With that, she squeezed their hands, rose, and walked quickly away. Perseus and Miram followed her as she moved toward the door at the rear of the gate. She never looked back. Perseus held that image of her sitting on the edge of the chair, a dark Martian sky at her back. He recalled the feel of her warm hands, the look of her elegant face, a strangely kind face. He would sometimes think of her in the years to come. She was an odd, complicated, and very beautiful woman. He knew, when she left, that he would never see her again. Every step took her farther away in time and space until, suddenly, she was gone.

Chapter Forty-Two

George and Joanne sat against the cart and watched as the tractor disappeared in the distance. Maybe ten minutes later, they saw two sky cars flying overhead that appeared to be going in the same general direction. The sky cars slowed, then descended, as though they were on an intercept course with the tractor. When Joanne turned and looked at George, he shrugged. They resumed their wait.

Joanne saw it first. It was 6:25 P.M. The object was high over the northwest range, a dot that occasionally caught the setting sun in incoherent flashes.

"There," Joanne said, pointing at the sky.

"Yes, I see it. Better get out of sight."

"Okay," Joanne said, and scurried behind some rocks.

George continued tracking the object as it moved down and grew larger. It was coming straight at him. The feel of the rock at his back reassured him that it would stop before it got this far. It always amazed George how big shuttles really were. Most of the time they were seen next to structures that were gargantuan by comparison. Shuttles were too heavy to land vertically like sky cars. They needed to shunt some of their forward momentum to brake, and required a stretch of flat ground.

It came down about half a mile to his left. The large triangular body and stubby wings were high atop shiny silver landing gear, now hidden by plumes of pink dust. The shuttle was coming straight at him, a hurricane of swirling dust rolling as fast as a bullet over the canyon floor. It came to rest no more than fifty feet in front of him. Shimmering waves of heat rose from the large smooth bulges of its engines. George could feel and hear the roar of its rockets in his suit acoustics. The icy sting of cold sweat running down his back burned in the cool air of his suit's air conditioner.

"Oh shit," he whispered. He checked the flashing red "A" in the display for reassurance.

Fighting his fear, George stood and held his hands up high, fingers spread. He started walking forward, toward the huge gray craft towering three stories above him. He could see the pilot and copilot moving, pointing at him through the forward canopy. George heard momentary static in his Suit-Com, indicating energy detection of an incoming transmission and the suit AI searching for the right channel. The "A" in his display stopped flashing; the Agent had locked on a channel and was uploading itself even before the pilot started speaking.

"Stop and identify yourself!" demanded the pilot.

"George Mills."

"What are you doing here, Mr. Mills?"

George cleared his throat. "I've been walking around here for over a day. I escaped from some separatists who were holding me captive. I got separated from Colonel Margaret Gates who was captured too. We escaped together. I saw your shuttle coming out of the north, saw you coming down, so I ran over here. Thank goodness you saw me."

There was a pause, after which the pilot returned. "One minute Mr. Mills, stay right where you are."

"Yes sir," George replied. "Can I put my hands down?"

"No, leave them up."

There was another bout of static after which George heard the pilot speaking to someone aboard the Saratoga. The Agent had uploaded itself to the cruiser and was piping the encrypted communications to his suit Com. Clearly, Will was a talented programmer among other things. This was an amazing piece of software when one considered its compactness and the relatively meager resources it had to work with.

"Oz here," George heard in his Com. "Go ahead, Sergeant."

Sir, we have a civilian outside with his hands up. He claims his name is George Mills."

Oz came back, he sounded excited. "Who did you say, Sergeant?"

"He says his name is George Mills, sir."

"Is that Dr. George Mills?" Oz asked.

"One moment, Commander."

George heard the pilot address him. "Are you Dr. Mills, sir?"

"Yes, that's right."

Oh shit, George thought. He had almost said Sergeant.

"One moment, Dr. Mills."

There was another burst of static, then George heard, "This is Admiral Nelson, go ahead, Commander."

"Sir, the pilot on board the Phoenix just reported finding Dr. Mills."

"He just happened to be at the landing site at just the right time, is that correct, Commander?"

"Seems that way, sir."

There was a pause.

"What did Margaret have to say about Mills, Commander?"

"Well sir, I just got off Com with her. She confirms his story. She said they got separated a little over a day ago after escaping from the separatists. Said they managed to get to a pumping station in the western desert, then found a shaft to the surface and climbed out. By the way sir, we found Margaret about seven miles from where we just found Mills."

Another pause. "Commander, is there a Hunter-Killer on board?"

"Yes sir, there is," Oz replied.

"Okay Commander, have him go out and check Mills for bombs or weapons, then bring him in and secure him."

"Yes sir," Oz replied.

"Nelson out."

After more static, "Sergeant, have an HK go out and get him. Make sure he's clean. Then, bring him in and secure him."

"Yes, sir," said the pilot.

"Oz out."

George could see movement in the canopy. The pilot got up, then disappeared, heading for the back of the ship. George could feel the small flat utility knife he'd taped to the inside sleeve of his suit. He moved his forearm against the bulge and felt that it was securely attached. This would be one of those quirky places in the plan. No turning back now, he thought, and remembered being in the ocean with Joanne. He recalled the feel of the salt water on his skin and the look of that blue sky. He began to relax just as an opening formed on the middle belly of the shuttle. A stairway descended to the ground. There was an elaborate accordion-like assembly at the top of the stairs, pressed into the inner bulkhead of the airlock. Must be for the transfer, he thought. The sight reminded him of how tight their schedule was. If they were going to pull this off, they'd have to get control of the shuttle before the sky cars arrived.

"Pilot."

"Yes, Doctor?"

"Can I put my hands down now?" George asked.

"Just a moment, Doctor. Someone will be out there in a moment."

George exhaled in frustration—wanting the pilot to hear it. Turning his attention to the stairway, he saw a light come on from somewhere inside the airlock. It articulated the stairs below in alternating patterns of black and white. A moment later, he saw a shadow form and eclipse about half the stairs. A huge automated soldier ambled down in mechanical fashion. His black armor was only visible because of the harsh floodlight that pushed back the darkness of the canyon floor under the ship.

As the soldier ambled forward, George felt his legs flinch in contention with his instinct to run. Don't look at the rocks, he told himself, fighting the urge. They have to believe I'm alone.

"Stand still, Dr. Mills," George heard the soldier command.

Right after that, there was the telltale static and the "A" in his suit display momentarily stopped flashing. The Agent had uploaded into the combat suit's AI. You're mine now, he thought.

The soldier walked around him. George saw in his suit display that he was being scanned in x-ray. He had put the knife under his suit controls over his left wrist and Malcolm's pistol under the metal oxygen tanks in the environment pack on his back. With luck, the soldier wouldn't see them.

The soldier walked around him a couple of times, then said, "You can put your arms down." Then he lead George to the Shuttle.

Once inside, he removed his helmet and gloves, but left his backpack in place. He took stock of his surroundings. There was the soldier, black and menacing to his left, a security man to his right, and the pilot and copilot out of sight on the flight deck. Behind him, there were two rows of seats that lined the walls of the rear cabin. Each position was a plastic molded impression on a bench with buttock and back cushions defining the seat. Above each position was a "U" shaped bar, which could be lowered over the shoulder and chest as a restraint. He counted twenty-six seats in all. At the back of the cabin was a door that he suspected led to a cargo hold.

George turned to the security man. "Man, am I lucky you guys happened by." Then, forcing a quizzical look, "What are you guys doing out here, anyway?"

The soldier and security man looked at each other, then back at George.

"Have a seat, Dr. Mills," said the security man.

"Where?"

"Right over here," replied the security man, pointing to a seat in front.

Right where they can keep an eye on me, he thought.

The flight deck door was open. He had to see the pilot and copilot before making a move. Even if he could draw his gun and cover the security man, he'd have a hard time with the pilots.

"Why didn't you guys land at the airport?" George asked, as he inched closer to a seat near the cockpit. Just then, his luck changed, both the pilot and copilot appeared at the cockpit door. They leaned against the bulkhead opposite him, amused, curious about the suspicious stranger.

As he moved, George reached up for the backpack release couplers over his chest and feigned getting ready to sit. He heard the metallic click of the release couplers and reached behind and underneath the pack as if he were keeping it from falling to the floor.

"Step back, Dr. Mills," instructed the security man, taking a step toward him.

Feeling around under the lip of the pack, George found the gun. He grasped it and let the pack fall to the floor. The security man reflexively looked down. George spun around and back-peddled into the cockpit, pointing the gun at the security man and the pilots as he sped backward. Glancing down, he saw that both pilots were armed.

He pointed the gun at the pilots and said, "Hands in plain sight, don't move."

The security man started for cover, probably thinking that he had his hands full with the pilots.

"Stop," George commanded, then quickly panned the gun in his direction.

George stepped forward, reached down, and took the gun out of the copilot's holster. Training one gun on the pilots and the other on the security man, he had the pilot remove his gun and slowly put it on the floor, the same with the security man.

All five of them were now in the front cabin, the security man and pilots to George's left, and the soldier to his right. He could see the security man's eyes darting back and forth between him and the soldier. Then, in a fit of disgust, the security man yelled, "Do something!"

"I can't move," grunted the soldier. "Something's wrong with the suit assist." He was a prisoner in his armor.

The security man turned to George. "Look, Dr. Mills, I don't know what you think your doing, but you're making a big mistake."

Beads of sweat ran down George's brow. He'd been very lucky so far. George backed onto the flight deck, pointing both guns at the shuttle crew as he moved. He leaned over and rapped several times on the canopy, then returned to the cabin. He had to be very careful now. The fact that the shuttle crew realized the soldier was not going to save them made them all the more dangerous. George tried as hard as he could to calm the tremors in his hands. Could he actually shoot these men? He didn't want to find out. Looking into their eyes, he knew they were waiting for a moment of weakness, a lapse in his concentration. They all stood there, frozen, the tension thick, everyone waiting for someone to make the next move.

* * *

Outside, Joanne peered around the rocks, trying to see what was going on in the shuttle. She couldn't believe she was really doing this. Four days ago, she'd been a molecular biologist in a summer dress, involved with a soft-spoken Earther physicist whose idea of excitement was going on fossil hunts on the rim range. "Oh George," she whispered to herself.

Suddenly, there it was. George was rapping on the cockpit canopy. Wiping the smile from her face and purging the sentimental thoughts from her mind, she tightened her grip on the gun and ran toward the airlock stairs.

* * *

George heard someone moving in the cabin airlock. A few seconds later, the door opened and he saw Joanne appear behind the security man, her gun aimed right at him. Her hand was unwavering. The three men seemed to loose confidence all at once. Now that it was no longer three against one, the shuttle crew appeared resigned, their body language no longer menacing.

George motioned with his gun, "Okay, you three, into the back—slowly."

They sat the pilots and security man near the cargo door, then bound their hands and feet with equipment ties Joanne had brought from the cart. George checked his chronometer; the whole thing had taken twelve minutes. He let his hands shake a little and noticed Joanne reaching for her helmet collar.

"Leave it on," he called.

Hesitating a moment, she reached up and manipulated the control under her chin. The helmet retracted into a wedge at the back of her head. He sighed. She was in it all the way now; they'd seen her face.

"Damn!" spat the security man, "a Martian woman."

Then, looking at George, "What the hell are you doing, Mills? You're an Earther; what are you doing with the separatists? What are they giving you?" He motioned toward Joanne, "This couldn't be for a piece of ass," he said with a look of disgust on his moist red face.

Joanne let out a chuckle, turned to George, and winked.

George put tape on the men's mouths and tied their hands to their feet, making it impossible for them to raise the restraining bars across their chests.

When he and Joanne were out of sight on the flight deck, Joanne said "Are all you Earthers that crude?"

"You know what scares me?" George said.

She arched her eyebrows.

"How naturally you slipped into this thing. You were very convincing coming out of that airlock, gun in hand." He smiled.

"Don't let the poker face fool you. That was for their benefit. I'm doing all I can to keep from shaking all over."

Giving her an *I-don't-know* look, George noticed she was staring over his shoulder and out the forward window. In the next instant the Com channel came to life and he turned to see a sky car approaching low across the desert from the east.

Chapter Forty-Three

George searched the displays on the console for the Com controls.

"Phoenix, this is Proteus, over."

George found the controls and highlighted *Two Way.*

"This is Phoenix, over," he replied.

"What's your status, Phoenix, over?"

He glanced over at Joanne, who had ducked out of sight into the cabin. It would be disastrous if someone flying the sky car caught sight of a Martian woman on the shuttle's fight deck.

"Everything's nominal, Proteus, ready to pick up the package, over."

"Affirmative, Phoenix, over and out."

"You slipped into that pretty easily yourself," remarked Joanne, peering around the cockpit door.

He shrugged, then put on his gloves and pack. He found the security man's holster and put it on. Then he deployed his helmet and darkened the visor.

"Very convincing," Joanne said admiringly.

He squeezed her hand and stepped into the airlock. Once outside, he pulled the accordion walkway down the stairs, making it available to the sky cars. After securing the walkway to the bottom of the stairs, he turned and watched as personnel from the sky car worked to deploy a walkway in a cloud of dust still fresh from their landing. The exact way in which the transfer was to take place was still not fully settled. It would depend on who, if anyone, was supposed to accompany the children to the Saratoga. It was an interesting speculation on human psychology, George thought. As the task grows larger and even more impossible, complex details seemed to be reduced to just that, details.

"We were beginning to think you guys weren't going to show," George called.

A man from the sky car pulled the walkway across the dusty Martian ground. They both stood inside the walkway and closed the seam.

"We have a situation at Building One," informed the man.

"The separatists?" George asked.

He saw the outline of the man's face nodding behind his darkened visor.

"Good reason to make this quick," George said.

"I hear ya," agreed the man. Then he ran back to the car through the transparent walkway.

Calling back, "I'll get the ball rolling," as George climbed the stairs into the shuttle.

Once inside, George left the door open. Joanne stood to the side, out of sight, her gun poised. They didn't have long to wait before hearing the sound of feet coming from the walkway and the muffled instructions of someone coming through with the kids. George retracted his helmet and removed his gloves.

The first through the door was a security man, in conventional environment suit, with his helmet retracted. The second was an Earther woman. George nodded as they entered the cabin, the security man did the same.

"Sorry we held you up," said the security man.

Then, looking to the back of the cabin, his smile disappeared. "What's going on here?" he demanded.

George raised his pistol. Then he took the gun from the security man's holster and led them to the back, sitting them down next to the shuttle crew.

"What's going on?" repeated the man. The woman just sat there, looking around nervously.

George stared intently into their eyes. "I need you two to be very quiet, and I need you to cooperate."

They just looked at him, the man defiant, the woman wide eyed. Joanne came up behind him with more equipment ties and tape. She bound their hands and feet, as George covered them with the gun. He continued eyeing the airlock, hoping that no other adults would be coming through, not until they finished with these two anyway. He'd steeled himself, ready to shoot any Earther coming through that door who failed to freeze when ordered.

Perseus was first through the door, followed by a beautiful little girl with long black hair. Both turned in unison and saw him in the back of the cabin with his gun trained on them. They understood immediately and shook their heads slowly while looking at the door. George lowered the gun; relief washed over him. The children started for the rear of the cabin, but George put his hand out to stop them. He didn't want them in the line of fire if someone else appeared unexpectedly. Again, they understood and moved to the very front, close to the flight deck door.

George watched as more kids streamed into the cabin and immediately seemed to understand what to do. They lined up neatly and quietly around the bulkheads near the flight deck, leaving the rest of the cabin clear. George heard the restraining bars click into place, turned, and saw Joanne taping the mouths of their latest captives.

Joanne stood above Perseus, Miram, and the others who had gathered near her. Tears traced her cheeks. Her mouth formed a slight smile, sad in its modesty. The children's pale golden eyes widened.

"Joanne," whispered Perseus, as if a prophecy had been fulfilled.

Joanne choked out a small laugh that sounded like a stifled sob.

"There are only kids in the tunnel," Perseus said.

Joanne stared at him, wondering whether she'd actually asked him that question or just thought it, then smiled.

"Can you get the children to sit down, keep the aisle clear so we can move around the cabin?"

"I'm glad to see you again, Joanne," Perseus said. Then he turned and shepherded the rest of the children to seats in the front of the cabin away from the captives, while Miram stood by the airlock directing others to him as they entered. Joanne looked on in amazement as the children organized themselves with uncanny precision. They seemed to have all the poise and dignity of seasoned adults who had rehearsed this many times before. When Joanne counted twenty kids, they stopped coming.

George joined Joanne on the flight deck. As he passed Perseus, seated in the front row, the boy smiled up at him warmly. His face was bright; hope and faith had been restored. George put his hand gently on the boy's head and winked at the little girl who sat next to him. There was something older than her eleven years in those golden eyes. Looking at the little girl, he felt a soothing calm come over him. With effort, he broke away and moved quickly to the airlock, deploying his helmet as he walked.

Passing Joanne, he said, "I'm going to help them disconnect the walkway. I'll be back in a minute."

In the tunnel again, George heard the pilot from the first car calling the security man, who now sat bound in the back of the shuttle.

"Jake, this is Proteus. We're completely off-loaded and ready to go, over."

As the security man spoke into his Com, the Agent had recorded and analyzed the phonemic quality of his voice. It was now able to translate George's voice to sound like his.

"Agent, emulate security man's voice," George commanded.

George saw a small window open in his visor display right under the flashing "A." Text appeared in the window. The text read, "man's voice print ready." George spoke into his Com.

"Proteus, this is Jake, over."

"Jake, what's keeping you, get your ass back here, over."

"Proteus, I'm going to hang here. We have some very unhappy children to manage, over."

There was a pause. Come on, George thought to himself. Come on, say it.

"Okay, Jake, see you at Building One, over and out."

George quickly undid the walkway couplers and seam. Then he pushed the walkway back to the sky car, ran back to the shuttle stairway, turned, and began waving. The sky car door panel closed and its engines started kicking up dust as it slowly bobbed into the air. He could see the pilots waving through the canopy. It picked up horizontal speed and quickly receded over the western desert. Yes, this just might work after all. One step at a time, George thought. He didn't want to be buoyed by their early success and be lulled into doing something stupid.

George stood in the front of the shuttle's large main cabin and watched as Joanne went up and down the aisle, giving each child personal attention, making sure they were properly strapped in for the trip. Her body language, the look in her eyes as she stooped in front of whichever child she was currently attending, the full rich texture of her voice as she spoke, all traces of anxiety gone. George let her finish, didn't hurry her, though he himself was itching to leave.

When she'd finished, she joined George on the flight deck.

"You look better when you're happy," George said.

"It shows, huh?"

"Oh yes. It's good to see you smile again."

Joanne pursed her lips, "So what now?"

George nodded toward the back of the room. "We get rid of them—we pick up Will—then we get the hell outa here."

"Aren't you forgetting something?" Joanne asked.

He regarded her quizzically. "I don't think so."

"They think they're going home."

He exhaled. "We'll explain it to them as soon as we get rid of the shuttle crew."

George cut the bonds on their legs and took the captives into the cargo bay. Joanne had slipped into the bay before him and was waiting with her gun trained on them as they entered.

George placed the security men and the woman, Julia, in the shuttle's tractor, leaving their hands bound, and closed the tractor's door. Then he ordered the Agent to express the soldier's helmet.

Joanne closed the bay door and returned to the cockpit where she lowered the cargo bay's rear tailgate to the Martian surface. Once outside, George instructed the Agent to direct the soldier's suit AI and the tractor's Nav AI to return to the domes.

George watched as the soldier, walking alongside the tractor, left the shuttle's floodlights and was swallowed by the darkness of the desert. They were headed to Ursa, his home of fifteen years. George jogged to the cart, which had rested unnoticed among the rocks where he'd left it almost an hour earlier. He activated its Nav and led it back to the tailgate. After it was secured, George paused at the shuttle stairway.

"He's on the tailgate; bring him in, Jo."

George saw the sliver of red light reflecting off the ground in back of the shuttle shrink and disappear as the tailgate closed and Will was brought on board. He climbed the stairs and looked back at his footprints in the soil of Mars—perhaps the last impression he would ever leave on this red desert planet, Earth's desert sister for millions of millennia. Earth, pregnant with life, sister Mars, dry and barren—eons later to be caretaker to a new and hardier strain of humanity. George looked up at the star-filled sky. If they were successful, they might bring a new kind of life to another, much more distant planet. He took a last look at his footprints in the sand and then hurried up the stairs.

Chapter Forty-Four

They were ready to leave. The engines vibrated through the hull in low rumbles, reminding them that they couldn't sit here indefinitely.

"Do you want me to do it, or would you rather explain it to them yourself?" George asked.

Joanne sat in the empty seat opposite Perseus and dropped her eyes to the floor. "I think you should explain it."

"Explain what?" asked Ben.

George could see the expectation of bad news in the boy's eyes, and hear the hint of uncertainty in his voice. Twenty sets of golden eyes, set in Martian dark faces, turned his way like two neat rows of human owls. The silence was palpable and thick.

"I'm sorry to have to tell you this children," George began. "We don't think it's wise to return to the domes."

They continued staring at him. Perseus asked, "If not the domes, then where, Dr. Mills, and for how long?"

George described Will's plan—took them through the logic of it. He explained that if they returned and hid, they would most certainly be found and ultimately transported to Earth. He told them the kinds of lives they might expect to live on Earth, and explained that once taken there, they would most likely never return to the domes or to their parents. The children sat and listened impassively, without so much as a question until George was done.

"You have me to blame for all this—no one else," George told them. "People are what they are. People behave the way they do; I knew all that. They feel possessive about their own kind and fear what is different—they always have. I knew this and gambled that they would never discover our secret, but they have. I alone am responsible for your current dilemma."

"Do we have to go?" asked Seth.

"No, no we don't. If you decide you don't want to go, I'll
fly the shuttle to Dome Three. We can offload those who want to
stay and take those who want to go." George paused and looked
at them for a long moment. "Although, I must tell you that going
to the domes will severely decrease our chances of success. It's
up to you."

Joanne looked at him, then shook her head and looked at the
floor. The children seemed to go blank all at once. As he
watched, they all stared off into space in the same absent way.
They stayed like that for about five minutes. George waited
patiently, leaning on a bulkhead, feeling the vibration of the
engines.

When they finally came out of it, Perseus said simply,
"We'll all go."

George responded cautiously, "You understand that if we
go, we can never come back. You understand that—right?"

They nodded in unison. Even Lyla, the eight-year-old,
nodded as if she really understood the true implications of their
situation. They were all in agreement, but the joyous, optimistic
mood was gone, replaced by somber resignation. The implacable
determination of humanity not to compete for dominion, and the
existence of Homo sapiens' deep and immutable flaws, had
conspired to deny them their birthright. They had no place in the
sphere of man. They were aliens, sentenced to alien worlds by
the possessive compulsions of genetics.

George exhaled. He had never been so burdened. He felt the
irony. For him, a true Earthman, acceptable anywhere in the
solar system, this leaving carried little regret. Most everything he
cared about was right here on this shuttle. In fact, if truth be told,
he found the prospect of starting over with these new people
liberating. Beneath his guilt, he actually looked forward to it.

George nodded, turned, and walked into the cockpit. He
removed his life support pack and retrieved the Tab. Then,
sitting in the pilot's seat, he placed the Tab into a cradle on the
console. He found its characteristic blue glow comforting.

Joanne peered around the flight deck door. "Do you mind if I sit with the children in back?"

He was glad to see that she had regained some of her previous positive energy.

"I don't mind. I think that's a good idea right now."

"Sure you don't need me up here?"

George looked at the Tab. An "A" flashed in a newly created window. Just below the "A" a text string read, "Ready for take-off, state destination."

"No, I think I've got everything under control. Check back when we're in orbit—okay?"

"Okay," replied Joanne, then she smiled and left.

"Execute destination Pegasus," George instructed.

The string, "Destination Pegasus," which flashed in sync with the "A" above it, replaced the text. George felt the vibrations of the engines in the hull quicken and become more intense.

"Make sure everyone's strapped in back there," he called out.

"We're ready," replied Joanne.

George looked out the window. The flight lights on the wings had come on. He could see the flashing red reflection on the nose from the vertical stabilizer lights. The shuttle came around and the wheels locked in place while the engines revved, shaking the large craft with their raw power. The brakes released and George felt the gees in the pit of his stomach, like metal fingers tickling him in a torturous grasp. He momentarily shuttered with a wave of intense vertigo as the shuttle nosed up and then jumped into the night sky with a violent forward lurch. A huge plume of hydrogen flame pushed it almost vertical, but not before it banked hard to the west.

In the rear cabin Joanne took Lyla's hand. She thought she heard a whimper, "mommy," just after they jumped into the air and seemed to roll almost ninety degrees before going straight up. She watched the children up and down the rows, gazing out small windows on opposite sides of the cabin. Once the vertigo subsided, the black outside the windows filled with clouds of bright white stars. Objects about the cabin began to float as the engines powered down and the shuttle seemed to make a transition from vertical to some other, less definite, orientation. The Nav AI had turned off the lights in the cabin just before take off and left them in the soft red glow coming from the flight deck. Joanne felt the little girl's grip loosen as the engine noise diminished to a distant rumble. The bigger kids began to make sounds of guarded amusement at the sights and sounds of this new, exotic environment.

The shuttle quickly climbed to eight thousand miles and slowly moved toward the daytime side of Mars. A bright speck grew in the forward window until George could see the dark outline of Diemos behind its bright white crescent.

They lost all sense of forward acceleration and glided silently and smoothly toward Mars' smaller moon. Looking down at the forward scanners, George saw another object moving with Diemos, in a higher orbit. He touched the screen at the position of the object and the display showed a menu of options. He highlighted "Orbital Parameters." The screen flashed, centered on the object, and presented an adjacent window of text. The object was two thousand miles above Diemos and was slowly spiraling upward at a rate of about fifty miles per revolution around Mars. It was still too far away for visual inspection, so he touched the screen again and selected visual zoom. The screen flashed again and showed a dim dot. George put his finger on the dot; a dashed box appeared around it. He moved his finger to one of the corners of the box and swept outward, zooming the view until the object filled the screen.

"Damn," mumbled George at the sight.

"Is that the Pegasus?"

The question startled him; he'd thought he was alone. He glanced in the direction of the copilot's seat and found Joanne floating, crouched forward over his shoulder with her right hand anchored to his armrest.

"Sorry," she said, then floated closer still. George could feel the heat from her cheek in the cool cockpit air.

"I've never seen anything like it," he muttered.

"Doesn't look like any spacecraft I've ever seen either," Joanne remarked.

Typically, interplanetary cruisers were long, utilitarian crafts characterized by wedged shaped sections that rotated about the axis of a long central member. At the far end of most large ships was a blocky assembly of engines downstream from circular rings of cylindrical fuel tanks. The design was simple and efficient. No streamlining was necessary, since interplanetary space was a better vacuum than most voids that could be made in the laboratory.

The Pegasus looked to be a radical departure from conventional ship design, something more akin to science fiction than anything else. The front of the ship looked like a huge boomerang. The flat wings of the boomerang swept back in an arching delta, reminiscent of the back of a manta ray. Three long sections emanated from the back. A central tube and similar smaller tubes on either side converged at an angle on an egg-shaped solid oval far behind the main body. This was obviously the engine. From the two outer tubes sprang large forward sweeping fins that extended out past and behind the main body with flat complicated assemblies at their ends. George imagined that these elegant wings were somehow used to shape the Ramscoop field. Around the central tube was the familiar circular array of fuel tanks. A squat sphere transected the geometric center of the boomerang and appeared to be rotating in opposite directions above and below the body of the ship.

"I can't believe nobody's noticed this thing before," Joanne said.

"We have it on extreme zoom. It's probably been seen and mistaken for a Void Fleet cruiser," George said. "I'll bet that as soon as we get close enough for a visual, they'll wave us off."

As if on cue, George heard the now familiar burst of static from Ship-Com. The red "A" on the Tab faithfully stopped flashing. George turned to Joanne and grinned.

"Will," she said, and shook her head in admiration.

"Shuttle craft, we identify your transponder as the Phoenix, over."

"That's right, Pegasus, check your logs. We were scheduled to deliver a computer upgrade, over."

George knew this would be the second of three risky gambits their plan entailed. The failure of any one of the three would doom them to prison or death. This might be the trickiest. The Pegasus had a well-protected, extremely sophisticated computer system. Its Nav AI, although not combat hard, would probably have several layers of protection against infection by viruses and worms. It was unclear how quickly the Agent could subvert the system sufficiently to give them the opening they'd need to pull this off. The first milestone, the ability of the Agent to falsify the Pegasus scheduling database, would be their first indication of future success or failure. George held his breath, waiting for Com to come back, painfully waiting to hear the words that would let them go to the next step and give the Agent time to penetrate even deeper.

"Come on, come on," he heard Joanne whisper. She clearly understood the precarious balance they were compelled to maintain.

"Roger, Phoenix, proceed to the lower docking collar, we'll bring you in on auto, over and out."

They exhale in unison, then looked at each other and grinned.

"What now?" Joanne asked.

"We sit back and enjoy the show while our friend," George pointed to the "A" on the tab, "works its magic." He paused. "Stay a while and keep me company."

"Okay," she said. Then, she pushed off, floated across the cockpit, and sat in the copilot's seat.

George reached forward and touched an icon on one of the displays, enabling the intercom in the rear cabin. Next, he lowered a display from the ceiling of the cabin that let the children see what was happening outside.

"Stay in your seats," announced George. "As you can see, there's no gravity in the ship right now; for those of you who've never been in zero gee, it can be dangerous if you don't know what you're doing." George piped the outside video feed to the cabin display and heard the level of quick chatter rise from the rear.

"That's the Pegasus, the ship we discussed," George said. "We're currently docking. Once we dock, we're going to try to get the crew to abandon ship. We're going to tell them things that sound scary, but we believe no one will actually be hurt, so please don't be afraid. Also, until we can force the crew off, we're going to leave you on board the Phoenix. It'll be safer here. I know this whole thing is frightening, but please try to stay calm."

Turning off the intercom, George looked out the window. "We're still ten miles away from that thing," he said, astonished. "It's huge. It must be at least a mile and a half long."

They quickly closed the gap and felt the shuttle maneuver. It followed a trajectory that put them in a shallow hover under the main body of the ship, just behind the lower spinning hemisphere. The space outside the window was clipped from above by the white expanse of Pegasus' hull. The view from the front window was completely blocked by the huge spinning lower hemisphere. George heard the hollow metallic click of the docking collars reverberate throughout the shuttle, followed by a low hum and a slow upward movement. The docking clamps were drawing the shuttle into the Pegasus as far as its stubby wings.

"You're clear to leave the Phoenix," they heard the Pegasus flight controller say.

George looked at Joanne. "Here we go."

Chapter Forty-Five

After the Phoenix docked with the Pegasus, things happened quickly. The Saratoga, in a much higher orbit, had tracked the shuttle as it rose out of the desert. Oz had been puzzled when they were unable to raise the Phoenix on Com. Sometimes plasma buildup around a ship launching into orbit disabled communications for a while, but it was usually quickly resolved; this was not. Owing to the fact that everything else appeared normal, Oz failed to sound an alarm, deciding, instead, to wait for another revolution around the planet before assuming the worst. The Agent had timed things so that as the Phoenix spiraled into orbit behind the Saratoga, the planet would eclipse the two crafts until the difference in their orbital velocities slowly changed that dynamic. It would take several revolutions around Mars for the two crafts to have an unobstructed line of sight view of each other. Oz decided to change that situation and began a descending intercept orbit to catch the Phoenix in one revolution. By the time the Saratoga came around again, expecting to see the shuttle, it had mysteriously disappeared.

Unfortunately, the Agent had been unable to disable communications aboard the Pegasus before the Saratoga came out of communications shadow with it. When it became clear to the Pegasus' skipper that he had a situation in the shuttle bay, he quickly sent an emergency distress call to the Saratoga. Oz called Admiral Nelson, who uncharacteristically came to the bridge upon hearing the shuttle had disappeared with Dr. Mills on board. He had come to assume the worst whenever Dr. Mills was involved. The man had a preternatural ability to mess things up. In the time it took the Admiral to get to the tactical station on the bridge, Oz had lost contact with the Pegasus.

"What in the world could Mills want with the Pegasus?" asked Oz.

The Admiral sat next to him in front of a set of tactical displays. When Nelson failed to respond to his question, Oz turned and found him staring at the main display with a worried scowl.

"Are you saying, Commander, that Mills, with a shuttle full of young children, is trying to commandeer NearSec's most advanced research ship?"

Oz hesitated, "That's why you're here, isn't it, Admiral? May I speak freely, sir?"

Nelson was red faced with anger, but his years of command experience had taught him to honestly approach critical emergencies.

Nelson exhaled. "Okay, Commander."

"We have to intercept the Pegasus as quickly as possible, sir. Whatever Mills is doing is cumulative. The Pegasus was able to send a Mayday after the shuttle disappeared; now her communications are disabled. The longer we wait, the worse it'll be, Admiral."

Nelson nodded. "Put us on a quick intercept orbit. Try to raise Mills on board Phoenix."

* * *

Perseus had worried about Miram ever since Dr. Mills had unveiled his plan. They had agreed to go along with it in consensus, but he had sensed that many of the children harbored lingering doubts, especially Miram. He'd held her moist shaking hands through every shuttle maneuver since take off. Making the decision to leave their families forever wasn't something that could be done, and then dispassionately relegated to the past. It was a decision that ate at them like acid. It was an anxiety never far from the surface. Perseus felt the tremors in Miram's arms, got fleeting images of heart felt memories, sensed depression over unrealized future plans. What was the value of a life defined by mere survival, not by the prospect of future promise and personal fulfillment?

"Are you all right?" he asked Miram.

She regarded him with eyes more red than gold. Looking at him brought tears, which slowly formed droplets that clung to her dark lashes, then floated into the cabin as transparent orbs.

"Talk to him," she pleaded.

"To whom?" asked Perseus.

"To the Admiral that Dr. Mills is speaking to. It can't be that he would be this unreasonable, this hard-hearted. Not even humans can be this mean."

Perseus tried to be sympathetic, tried not to dismiss the chances that reason, of all things, could possibly save them. But he had enough experience with humans to know that once a decision had been made, it could never be rescinded. It was a point of honor with them. People in charge, by definition, never made mistakes. Perseus thought a moment; perhaps the height of human culture was not honor but hypocrisy, since it was hypocrisy that was the currency of convenience.

"Please," pleaded Miram softly.

Perseus undid his restraints, then pushed himself up and toward the flight deck door. He caught one of the many handholds around the door archway and peered inside. He found Dr. Mills and Joanne seated in large complicated high back chairs in front of a dizzying display of consoles.

Dr. Mills?"

* * *

George turned and saw Perseus floating in the archway, his hand anchored to something on the other side of the bulkhead.

"One moment, Admiral." George paused the channel.

"You shouldn't be out of your seat."

Perseus ignored the comment. "Can I speak to him?"

"Who?" George asked. "You mean the Admiral?"

George glanced at Joanne. "He certainly has the right to speak to his tormentor," Joanne said.

"He does at that," replied George, wondering why he might have ever thought otherwise.

George resumed the channel. "Admiral."

"Go on Mills."

"I have someone here who wants to speak to you." Then, turning to Perseus, "He's listening."

* * *

Nelson and Oz had been sitting at tactical and speaking to Mills aboard the Phoenix. Oz had noticed an anomalous surge in Com packets upon establishing the connection. It had subsided, and all indications were that everything seemed completely normal, but Oz didn't like mysteries and continued analyzing the Com channel as Nelson spoke. He found nothing. Still, he'd never seen a surge like that before; it bothered him.

"He put us on hold," said Nelson incredulously.

"Channel's still connected, sir," Oz said.

Nelson nodded. "What do you think?"

"Sir?"

Nelson pointed to the tactical display. The Saratoga was slowing, dropping from a higher orbit and heading down on an intercept course with the Pegasus.

"We should rendezvous in about forty minutes, sir."

Nelson stared at him with a half smile. It gave Oz the shakes.

"What say we cut our losses, Commander?"

"Sir?"

"Well," continued Nelson, "this whole thing's been a fiasco from the start. Both Mills and those kids are clearly very dangerous. Now this thing's escalated to the Pegasus. We should just cut our losses." He continued looking at Oz. "Suppose by the time we get to the Pegasus all of them are still aboard the

Phoenix. Suppose we take a neutral beam cannon on low output and just pierce the hull in several places without warning."

"You can't do that, Admiral. They'd all be killed—executed! There are twenty young children on that shuttle."

"They're not human," reminded Nelson. "They don't really have rights under the law, do they, Commander? I'd liken it to disposing of lab rats in a failed experiment."

"And Mills and the woman?" asked Oz, looking for some way to dissuade him.

"A couple of hijackers," said Nelson. "Killed as they tried to commandeer the Pegasus."

Oz had served with Nelson for two years now. He'd established at least a working understanding of the man. Whenever he thought of Nelson, the phrase *old school* came to mind. Nelson was stiff, formal, gave the impression of being supremely self-assured. Someone you wouldn't want to mess with. Career-wise, he'd reached the highest rank a line officer could achieve without becoming a politician. But there'd always been something else, something odd about him. There was something in the flatness of those eyes and in the fact that he didn't seem to have any real friends. What kind of Faustian bargain had he made with himself? It was certainly true that, by the letter of the law, the kids weren't human, but they were sentient, derived from humankind. For Oz, all this splitting hairs was just a rationalization for mass murder—for convenience sake. Oz noticed Nelson's freshly pressed wool suit, his impeccably cut hair, the ease with which he seemed to make life and death decisions about the fate of small children. Oz wondered if and when the moment of truth came, would he be able to pull the trigger? He couldn't possibly look into Nelson's mind, know how he'd make it right with himself. But Oz knew his own mind. He knew what they were doing was unambiguously wrong. The loss of Pegasus, the potential terrorism at Building One, they would inevitably reflect very badly on Nelson. No matter how he tried to spin it, no matter the mitigating circumstances, his career was over. Deep down in the labyrinth of his soul, he was trading twenty young children for his career.

Secretly, Oz hoped that somehow the wily Dr. Mills had yet another ace up his sleeve. Another unforeseen gambit he could make to save the day. Oz sat up when he heard the cracking voice of an adolescent over Ship-Com. Nelson moved uncomfortably in his seat, and looked over at OZ. Oz remained impassive, detached. This is your nightmare, not mine, thought Oz. You deal with it, and you deal with it alone.

"Admiral Nelson?" asked the boy.

"Put Dr. Mills on," snapped Nelson curtly.

After another short pause, Oz heard Mills' now familiar voice.

"This is George Mills, Admiral. I have Perseus Augustus here, one of the children you kidnapped. He wants to speak to you. As far as I'm concerned, he's in charge. I've told him and the rest of the children I'd abide by whatever decision they make. I'd suggest you speak to him, otherwise, I don't know what else you and I have to discuss."

Nelson wrung his hands, the first sign of nervousness Oz had seen. Nelson glanced at tactical—thirty minutes to intercept. That seemed to reassure him. In a half hour he'd be dictating terms. In a half hour, things would again be as they should be—with him in charge.

"Admiral Nelson?" The boy's voice again.

"Go ahead," answered Nelson dismissively. It was as if talking to this boy was something distasteful. You didn't warm to those you were about to execute, thought Oz.

"I want to tell you, Admiral, that if you think we're a threat to you or to Earth, we're not. There's no need for you to hold us. You know where we live. With your resources you have the means to keep track of us. We will agree to leave this ship if you agree just to leave us alone. That's all you have to do, Admiral, and this can all be over, just like that."

Nelson cleared his throat. "I can't do that. You and your friends have committed some grave offenses against statutes of interplanetary law. I'm bound by that same law to take you into custody."

"How was it lawful to kidnap us, Admiral?"

Nelson checked tactical—twenty-five minutes. He smiled. Oz shifted in his seat, dreading the moment when they could get a clear shot at the shuttle.

"You have Mills to thank for that," replied Nelson. "It was him, not me, who put you in this position. According to our biologists, you and the other children are not human. In some sense, you could be considered a pathogen, a disturbing genetic development. It's our responsibility under the Genetic Abatement Act to put you and your friends in quarantine."

After a few moments the boy's voice returned. "I think you're mistaken about that, Admiral. The parts of the Act you're referring to were repealed. If you would allow us legal representation, we would be willing to contest this in court."

Nelson began to turn red. "You listen to me, you freak! We're going to quarantine you and the danger you represent to proper humanity."

Oz stared at his hands, folded in front of him on the console. The real Aaron Nelson had finally stood up. When he thought that he would again have the upper hand, Nelson had been charming and thoughtful. When he'd lost the verbal advantage to a child, he'd dropped all pretenses. They were on the savanna again, fighting for dominance, all the high-tech gadgetry not withstanding. There was something primal about Nelson's reaction, something guttural. The boy, on the other hand, had been calm, polite, and even respectful. The boy had reacted the way Oz hoped he would. It pained him to think he might not have the ethical fiber of an eleven-year-old boy. But that's the way it was. If he didn't pull the trigger, somebody else would. And when it was all over, the children would be just as dead and he would be in lockup for failing to carry out an order by a superior officer. Unfortunately, that was just the way it was.

"Admiral Nelson?" asked the boy. "Is that your last word, sir?"

"That's my last word," replied Nelson.

"So be it," replied the boy.

Oz saw the channel drop on the display.

* * *

Nobody spoke on the flight deck aboard Phoenix. George had dropped the channel right after Perseus indicated that he had nothing left to say. Joanne hugged herself, crossing and uncrossing her arms over her chest, unable to get comfortable. She reached up to run her fingers back through her hair, something she often did when she was nervous. She got a handful of skullcap and exhaled in frustration. She turned to Perseus. Floating in the archway, his eyes seemed focused on something distant, the same way they had earlier when the children appeared to go into a trance.

"I'm sorry, sweetheart," said Joanne.

She turned to George for support and found him engrossed in one of the displays. He leaned forward and tapped icons, then sat back and continued staring.

"George?"

He didn't look at her, his eyes remained glued to the display. After a few moments, George said, "He should be here in about twenty-five minutes."

"Who?" Joanne asked.

"Why the Admiral," replied George, as if it were obvious.

Joanne's eyes darted between George and Perseus, who was still floating in the doorway.

"What do you mean, he's coming, coming to do what?"

George turned to her. "The Saratoga dropped out of high orbit while we were talking. They're on an intercept course that should put them here in about," he checked the display, "twenty minutes."

"Why?" Joanne asked, alarmed. She didn't like the look in George's eyes—the look of resignation to the inevitable.

Perseus said, "I have to admit to being surprised."

"By what?" George asked.

"When I heard you speaking to the Admiral, he sounded so reasonable. When Miram asked me to speak to him, I must admit, I had doubts."

"About what?" Joanne asked.

"About Dr. Mills," replied Perseus. "I thought he might be overreacting in trying to take the Pegasus." Perseus hesitated, then caught his breath. "But talking to the Admiral, trying to make him understand," Perseus shook his head. "Dr. Mills was right after all. I'm apparently a poor judge of people." Perseus looked at George, needing an explanation of things he could never understand.

George smiled a tired smile. "Of course you don't understand. You evolved not to understand it. Be grateful for that. You have to forgive men like the Admiral. They come from a long line of beings forged in a cauldron of evolutionary forces that we," he glanced at Joanne, "spared you."

George looked around the cockpit. "What do you think of these machines?" he asked Perseus.

"They're magnificent," replied the boy.

"You'd think people capable of conceiving machines like these would be different—better in some objective way than those back on the savanna hundreds of thousands of years ago," said George. "But they're not. Genetically, they're more or less the same. Sooner or later, if we were going to survive as a species, you had to come along." George looked directly at Perseus. "Unobstructed evolution can only take us just so far. At some point, a sentient species has to recognize its own best parts and reject those parts that belong to something else, something primordial. Maybe that's the natural next step. I hope that you can forgive me for dragging you into this, but, if truth be told, I'd probably do it all over again."

Perseus lingered on George a moment. "I should be getting back to the others," he said, then left.

"Oh for goodness sake," Joanne said.

"He deserves the truth," replied George unapologetically. "Do you disagree with anything I told him?"

She softened, "No, I guess not. But don't they have enough to worry about right now?"

"I don't want to scare you, but right now may be all we'll ever have."

He paused a moment, trying to get a sense of what she was prepared to hear. Joanne got out of the copilot's seat and floated over to him. She crouched at the side of his chair with her legs tucked under her, and held on to his armrest.

"So," she asked, almost matter-of-factly, "what happens when the Admiral gets here?"

"First things first," George said, pointing to the Tab.

In the text box, below the "A," two new lines had appeared. The first read, *Life Support*, in amber with a dash and a flashing *Ready* in red. The other read *Propulsion*, with a similar *Ready*.

"Okay," Joanne said, craning to see.

George said, "The computer systems on ships like this are distributed and hierarchical. The architecture looks a little like a pyramid, with the interface and control AI at the top. Beneath are the second-level controls like navigation, propulsion, environmental, and others. Each slave AI is in touch with the master control via scheduling, data, and heartbeat channels. The system is redundant, and constantly runs self-diagnostics in time slices in between scheduled execution times. It's all monitored by the control AI through the heartbeat channel. Our friend here," George pointed to the Tab, "has introduced a worm. The worm has traveled on the heartbeat channel to the appropriate sub-processors and has set up residence as fake interfaces to the control AI. It's like the control AI thinks it's talking to its subsystems, but it's really talking to our imposter. Meanwhile, the imposter is rerouting control to us. As far as the crew of the Pegasus is concerned, they think they're still in control."

"But they're really not," Joanne said, with a cautious grin.

"That's right. Don't you think it's about time somebody informs the Captain of the Pegasus?"

Joanne nodded, still stifling a full grin.

"Before we do, we need one more thing to happen. Maintenance systems status," he ordered the Tab.

Another line appeared. It read, *Maintenance Systems on line.*

"Now we're ready," George said.

He tapped the maintenance text and a window appeared with a list of ship's systems.

"Evacuate packs on environment suits," George ordered.

After a few seconds, the Tab began to list scrolling lines of items followed by the words *in progress*, in red.

"What's happening?" Joanne asked.

George continued watching the Tab until items stopped appearing. "Time to inform the Captain," he said. "Pegasus, this is George Mills aboard the Phoenix; I need to speak to the Captain right away."

George and Joanne waited. Joanne noticed the view on the large scanner in front of George. It appeared to show a tactical view of Mars. A flashing symbol of an object, which Joanne assumed to be the Pegasus, was in orbit around a grid representation of the planet. A myriad of objects were being tracked with various symbolic designators. One object, in particular, seemed to have the same designator as the Pegasus, with the exception of an alphanumeric serial number.

Joanne pointed to the object on the display. "Is that the Earth cruiser?"

George nodded. "Let's hope it doesn't get much closer."

"Phoenix, this is Captain Drake. You must leave the Phoenix right away. Failure to do so may result in loss of life."

"What's he talking about?" Joanne asked.

"The cruiser," replied George softly.

"You mean the Admiral's coming to kill us!"

"I'm afraid so," said George evenly. "I knew from the last exchange, from the impatience in the Admiral's demands, that we'd probably crossed the line. I'll bet that, at this point, putting an end to all this is his most attractive option. I don't know what he's told ECon, but if we succeed in taking Pegasus, it will be painfully clear to the Admiral's superiors that he's lost control."

"So he'd be willing to sacrifice twenty small children for his career?"

"It sounded that way to me. Didn't he sound like he was rationalizing his position for what he was planning to do?"

"And what are we planning to do to avoid being killed? I take it we're not planning to give up?" Joanne asked.

"No—we're way past that."

"So, have we been able to infect the cruiser with the same worm the Pegasus has?"

"Yes, but the Saratoga is different. It's a hardened war ship. Its systems are more isolated. Its data buses are heavily encrypted. The Agent's good, but it's relatively small. It had to be in order to travel via commandeered packets through Com channels. Though it uses indigenous resources once reconstituted, it would have to subvert so many internal systems that the self-diagnostics aboard the Saratoga would probably find it before it was strong enough to persist."

"You're beginning to worry me," Joanne said.

When George didn't say anything, she put her fingers on his chin and turned his head toward hers. "I know you're having fun keeping me in suspense, but now's not the time."

George took in her smooth face; its familiar features evoked such warm feelings, even now. He remembered the way she looked as they pushed him into that police car the other day at the lab. It had taken him seconds to spot her in the crowd, behind the police tape. She was radiant in her summer dress, making him think about all the things he'd be missing, about all the things he'd already missed.

"George?"

He smiled. "Remember when they came to the lab the other day? When they removed Will, put him in that van?"

"Yes, I remember."

"Well, Margaret told me they'd moved him off planet—to the cruiser. They thought they could use him to run full simulations, get a tactical advantage."

"War games," Joanne said with distain.

"Yes, that's right. I was hoping they'd do just that."

He saw the light come on in her eyes, then the upturn at the corners of her mouth.

"So what they took to be Will was actually a Trojan Horse?" she asked slowly.

"Those six columns have all the muscle required to bring that cruiser down; the worm was only the key. As soon as it found our system, it set a series of events into motion."

He turned from Joanne and looked at the scanner again. It was two minutes past intercept and the Saratoga was still over the horizon of the planet, blocked from taking a shot. The sky near the Pegasus was clear of interceptors.

"It hasn't gotten any closer," observed Joanne. She followed George's eyes to the display.

"No it hasn't, and I'll bet Captain Drake's noticed too, what do you think?"

Joanne put her arm around his shoulders and rested her cheek against his. "Let's ask him," she said.

"Captain Drake, are you there, sir?"

George waited for Drake to answer, continuing to enjoy Joanne's closeness. Take your time, Drake, he thought.

When it was clear that Drake wasn't going to respond, George repeated, "Captain Drake? The Saratoga will not be coming to your aid, sir. I guess you know that by now. Please have the crew proceed to the other shuttle and leave the Pegasus as soon as possible."

Almost immediately, George heard, "This is Captain Drake. What do you want? Who are you Mr. Mills?"

"In five minutes Captain, I'm going to evacuate the atmosphere from the Pegasus. I'm going to do that by opening the airlock doors in the shuttle and maintenance bays. I should also tell you that the maintenance bots have drained the air from all environment packs in all EVA stations around the ship. I have remote control of bulkhead doors, so you won't be able to seal the bridge or any other part of the ship from vacuum."

A moment later George heard the strained voice of the Captain over ShipCom again. When George first heard the Captain's voice, he'd thought it a little too nasal and high pitched for someone whose job it was to inspire ultimate authority. He must have a science background, thought George with amusement. Now, the man's voice was broken, almost squeaky between tight breaths.

"Who are you?" demanded the Captain.

"You have four minutes left, Captain Drake."

George heard an alarm begin to sound in the background of the open channel.

"You'll be shot for this you treasonous bastard!" George heard the man spit.

"You have three and a half minutes left, please hurry, Captain," said George.

The channel remained open. George could hear men scurrying about, angry shouts, and a persistent alarm in the background. Then he heard the artificial voice of the control AI.

"Abandon ship! All attempts to regain control of environmental systems have failed. Ship will be evacuated of all atmosphere in three minutes."

The emergency siren interspersed with warnings from the control AI continued to sound like hollow echoes in the background of the open channel. It was chaos. George dropped the channel. The silence was powerful and immediate.

"Now we wait," he told Joanne, and sat back heavily in his chair.

He turned and glanced out the window at the Phoenix's sister shuttle parked no more than a hundred feet to their right. It perched under the Pegasus, its upper half out of sight, enveloped by the much larger ship. Suddenly, George saw lights come on in the cabin windows. Against the windows, eerie silhouettes darted about. Good, he thought, it's working.

A few minutes later, George saw the flight lights on the stubby wings come on. They were getting ready to leave. The shuttle slowly separated from the Pegasus in a motion that almost looked as if it were being excreted. It hovered in space for a few moments until a faint blue glow appeared around its main engines, then became brighter. The craft sped forward, veering to the right, dipping to avoid the huge lower hemisphere of the Pegasus. Once clear, a bright arc of blue flame appeared in back of the shuttle as it shot forward and disappeared below his window.

George turned to Joanne. She was completely absorbed, her attention fixed on the main display. He noticed the furrows on her normally smooth brow.

"What is it?"

She shook her head slowly, then looked up. "Just doesn't seem like they would give up that easily."

"What else could they do?" George asked. "The fact that the Saratoga didn't come to their rescue must have made the plot look a lot bigger than it really is. I was counting on that to unnerve them. You have to remember, even though this is officially an Void Fleet cruiser, it's a research ship manned mostly by civilians."

He looked at her and saw lingering doubts. He pointed to another display.

"The environment system on board Pegasus indicates no life signs."

"Okay," Joanne said finally. Then, after a few moments, she added, "I guess sooner of later the crew aboard Saratoga will get control again, won't they?"

"Yes they will," confirmed George. "That's why we have to get Will on board and installed ASAP. By the time that dot starts to move again," he pointed to the Saratoga hovering just under the Martian horizon, "we have to be the hell outa here. In order to get the Pegasus under way, we have to install Will, and we have to do it quickly."

Joanne sucked in her lower lip, nodded, then pulled herself out of the seat and pushed off for the cabin door. George followed. The children watched them as they entered. The chatter that George had heard when he'd been seated in the cockpit stopped. He took stock of the children. Looks ranged from curious stares to worried scowls. They sat in their oversized seats with large black restraining bars in front of their chests. It cut an unsettling image.

"What do we do now, Dr. Mills?" asked Perseus from a seat in front.

George found it curious that in a room full of children, it seemed as if only one spoke at a time. Instead of twenty individuals with twenty different concerns and twenty different questions, there was usually only one. Once that question was answered, there'd be another. They were kindred spirits, all focused on one item of mutual interest at a time. What would they be like as adults? Their own alien nature, and the memory of a weak human prototype, was all they would ever have to guide them.

"We get on board Pegasus," answered George. "We can't fly it ourselves, so we'll have to install Will. Once Will is back" —he paused and looked around. He noticed that he was kneading his hands and stopped the nervous gesture. "Once Will replaces their onboard system, we'll be able to get under way."

Perseus held George's eyes for a few seconds. Some of the other children stirred.

"The large ship, has the crew left?" asked Perseus.

"Our instruments tell us there's no one onboard," replied George.

"Do you think we'll get a chance to call home before we leave?" asked Miram.

The kids hadn't moved. Stray light, perhaps from the small cabin windows or flight deck, filtered in and gave their faces an odd surreal glow that made them look like mannequins, like an imitation of children, George thought.

"I sincerely hope so. But, to tell you the truth, I just don't know."

After an uncomfortable silence, another boy, who he thought was named Ben, said, "I hope so too, Dr. Mills."

Joanne said, "Stay in your seats children, George and I are going aboard Pegasus first. When we're sure it's safe, we'll be back—okay?"

"Don't be too long," said Lyla.

Miram put her hand on Lyla's shoulder, then looked back at Joanne. "Please take care."

Joanne moved to Miram and Lyla, bent down, put her arms between the restraints, and hugged them both. She stayed that way for a while, then pulled back and kissed them both on the cheek, as was the custom on Mars.

Miram looked up at her longingly. "I love you, Joanne. Please be careful."

After they entered the cargo bay and had secured the door, George and Joanne put on their gloves and expressed their helmets. Instruments on board Phoenix, as well as those on Pegasus, confirmed the absence of an atmosphere in the starship. When they were ready, they moved the cart to the cargo bay elevator and evacuated the bay. Then they instructed Phoenix to open the bay doors and raise the elevator into Pegasus.

Chapter Forty-Six

Their ascension into the light from the relative darkness of Phoenix was imagery not lost on George. As they rose into the large ship, he was able to look around, and was surprised by the extravagance of the environment. Every interplanetary ship he had ever been on was decidedly utilitarian, although he couldn't attest to the officer's wing, which he'd never seen. Typically, corridors were that amorphous military gray-blue, with pipes and conduits in every nook and cranny. Floors in rooms with artificial gravity were little more than plastic or metal gratings. Crew and passenger quarters were not much larger than wash-closets, with the kinds of beds that George imagined were standard issue in most prisons, with about as much comfort potential.

"Will you look at this," Joanne said.

George shrugged. "She's a beauty."

Once the elevator had locked in place beneath them, he stepped off, turned, then slowly moved his feet like he was marching in place. The floor was a molecular cilia that kept feet lightly stuck when touched. Much like the feet of some insects and small lizards, the floor's fibers were so small that they formed electrical bonds to the molecules of smooth surfaces. George and Joanne walked around the perimeter of the elevator, getting the feel of the place.

The shuttle bay was unusually spacious. The walls were a dull pearly white, with no pipes anywhere in sight. The ceiling was a tan composite with wide lighting strips. The walls were organized with indentations that hosted instrument panels covered by smoky transparent windows. Behind the windows ran displays whose contents undulated as they changed. The room was perfectly quiet.

"Where to now?" Joanne asked.

George checked his helmet display and began to search the ship's floor plan, which the Agent had downloaded into his suit AI. The ship was enormous. The main boomerang section had five floors, interspersed with corridors, rooms, and several elevators. Many of these sections were engineering areas, packed with power systems and magnetic projectors that must have spanned at least a square mile. It would take days to search the ship just by looking around.

"This is one hell of a ship," George muttered to himself. "It must have cost as much as a dome to build."

Joanne could see the reflections of grid projections on George's face through his helmet visor. She watched his eyes scanning, as if he were reading an invisible book.

"I found it," he said. "The main computer room is on the second floor of the spinning upper hemisphere."

George walked back to the cart, instructing its AI to follow his suit transponder. It rose on its suspension and followed him off the elevator.

"This way," he called to Joanne.

She fell in behind him. They walked to a circular opening at the far side of the bay. Looking down the long straight corridor, George saw bluish rings that he imagined were bulkheads or other corridors connected with this one. The rings gave the corridor a sense of depth, like the ticks on a ruler. They shrank in the distance, until disappearing to an ill-defined point at the very end. Straining to see what was down there, George saw a dull blue flashing. The flashes were slow and constant. He glanced at Joanne. She shrugged, and they started walking.

It took a while to cover the eighth of a mile to the end of the corridor. At the terminus, they found themselves standing in front of a large trapezoidal opening. Beyond the archway was a big circular room, maybe twenty feet across. A large cylinder running from floor to ceiling, with a shiny panel the size of a large door, rotated slowly in the middle of the room. George noticed that it was reflecting light from the ceiling, which was one big light panel.

"So that's where the flashes are coming from."

George nodded. "That must be the elevator into the hemisphere."

Then, pointing at the floor, George said, "Look at that."

Radial lines on the floor spun in bands, rotating with the room. The lines closest to them didn't spin, while those closest to the elevator seemed to be stationary with respect to the central cylinder. George and Joanne grinned at each other. The ship designers had thought of everything. The floor had been designed to match the rotation of the hemisphere with as little impact on elevator passengers as possible. They walked effortlessly to the elevator with the cart in tow. George pushed the "up-arrow" next to the door panel; it clicked and turned amber. After a few moments, the large shiny panel receded into the cylinder and slid out of the way.

They stepped inside and were followed by the cart. George noticed a titanium display near the door, which read, *Level 0, Up-Bubble.*

"Level 2, corridor D," commanded George.

The door slid silently into place, and a neon blue ring, which circled the elevator at waist level, started its descent. As soon as it had disappeared into the floor, another one appeared at the ceiling and started descending. A few moments later, the display read, *Level 2, Corridor D.* The door slid open.

Looking out, George saw the walkway beyond smoothly curve around so that the floor eventually became the far wall. They left the elevator—first Joanne, then George followed by the cart. When his suit gyro indicated that they had rotated ninety degrees, they found themselves standing in front of another door. Joanne pushed the panel on the doorframe, then stepped into the corridor beyond.

Corridor D was a trapezoidal shape, with the large side of the trapezoid on the floor. The walls were the same dull white, with metallic-blue bulkheads. Joanne raised and lowered her feet a few times.

"Earth normal gravity," said George. "It's a little stronger than Mars."

The floor was a textured tan material, and George noticed the familiar sticky molecular strips on the walls. A contingency for when the hemisphere wasn't spinning, he thought. They turned right, then walked down the corridor until they'd passed four doors. The fifth bore a plaque that read, *Computer Room*.

Once inside, George couldn't help cracking a smile. The walls were covered in banks of holographic memories and optical processor racks. In the middle of the room were six milky white quantum columns, with sockets for four more on the columns' pedestal.

George looked at Joanne, "Perfect." He beamed. She returned the smile.

It took them thirty minutes to off-load the cart and install the two quantum columns. George sat on the floor next to the pedestal with his Tab plugged into a universal interface. He typed in commands that brought Will's configuration and control program up. Then he typed in passwords that only he and Joanne knew, instructing the system to come up. Lines scrolled down the transparent screen so fast that he couldn't possibly read them as network after network went from a *sleep* to a *wake* state. After a few moments, the scrolling stopped, the screen blanked, and the words *waking up* appeared. George typed, *Will?*

He heard his Suit-Com crackle, then heard, "I see we're on Pegasus—congratulations."

"What happened to your voice?" George asked.

"Best I can do with the ship's synthesizer," Will said. "I should be able to reconfigure, but this is the best I can do for now—sorry."

"Good to have you back," Joanne said. Then she added, "I missed you."

Will paused, then said, "Me too."

"So," said George, "how about getting some air in here. That is, if you two can spare the time." He gave Joanne a crooked smile.

"Working on that right now," Will said. "It'll take a few minutes to build up pressure. I'm also starting the main drive. Engines should be on line in about twenty minutes."

"Any news on the Saratoga?" Joanne asked with a hint tension.

"It seems as if I've lost contact with the Agent," Will said. "They're probably rebuilding their system after a purge and reboot. It should take them hours, but we'd better hurry, just in case."

George said, "Okay boss, keep us informed. We're going back to the Phoenix to get the kids. We'll see you on the bridge."

"On the bridge," Will said.

"Come on George, let's hurry," Joanne said, grabbing his arm and pulling him into the corridor.

George hesitated, turned, and watched the door eclipse his view of the columns as it closed. Joanne pulled him back to the elevator in a near jog. She pressed the amber panel, tapping her foot nervously as they waited for the blue band to sweep past the translucent door, heralding the elevator's return. George was amused that in this sea of dangerous turns and unexpected heart-pounding predicaments the mere news that they had less time than previously thought could unnerve her so.

"Slow down," George began to say, then stopped in mid sentence. The elevator door slid open to reveal two men in environment suits. One was holding a pistol, the black bore of which was pointed right at Joanne.

As soon as he saw it, he put his shoulder against Joanne and shoved her out of the way. She fell to the left of the door, but not before the man fired a shot. George saw the muzzle flash, then felt a hammer pound him in the right shoulder. He registered a burning pain, then a throbbing numbness on his right side. He landed on one knee and instinctively put his left hand over the wound and pressed. The bullet had pierced the suit. The pressure indicator in his helmet display was falling precipitously. Looking up, George saw the two men race from the elevator. One of them was soon standing above him and grabbed his shoulder. Pain shot through him like a hot knife. George clenched his teeth and fought to stay conscious. Then the man punched him hard in the stomach, throwing him backward onto the floor.

"George!" he heard Joanne shriek.

He forced his teary eyes open, gasping for air, and saw the other man grab Joanne and jerk her up against the wall. Then he heard the chirp of his Suit-Com as the AI searched for the channel the men were using.

"Shut up!" he heard one of the men yell over Joanne's pleading. "Let the son-of-a-bitch die."

The man grabbed George and jerked him up. He had dropped to one knee and was peering into George's eyes through his visor. The man was red hot with anger, his lipless mouth stretched into a tight grimace. George felt beads of sweat falling down the sides of his face, matting his hair to his skin. Despite his weakness, George tried as hard as he could to sit up. The man pushed him down without much effort. The meager breath that he still held escaped as he hit the floor. The last thing George remembered was the man stepping over him and Joanne yelling his name as the elevator door closed.

Chapter Forty-Seven

Joanne struggled against the man who had her by the arms. He was trying to push her around George, who lay frighteningly still on the floor. He was crumpled on his back with his left hand on his right shoulder and his right leg bent behind him at the knee.

Joanne broke free, and bracing with her left leg, jabbed her right elbow hard below the man's sternum. He doubled over, and as she prepared to kick him in the crotch, the other man punched her in the side, knocking the wind out of her. She worked to catch her breath, feeling as if she were about to vomit. The man quickly spun her around and bound her hands behind her. As she struggled to free her hands, he punched her in the stomach. She fell against the wall and slid down into a sitting position, trying as hard as she could not to cry. When the other man regained his strength, they grabbed her under the armpits, jerked her up, and hustled her into the elevator. She watched the door close on George's lifeless body as they held her tight.

They retraced the route she and George had taken no more than forty-five minutes before. Her mind raced, what was she going to do without George? Even if she could somehow get away from these men, she just didn't know enough about gadgets to pull this off by herself. Calm down, she told herself, trying not to hyperventilate. Panic rose with the realization that George might be gone forever. She felt a deep loneliness that was both cold and frightening. No matter what happened now, her friends and family were gone, and George was gone. She'd never really considered this possibility. She had to steel herself, clear her mind. There were twenty children depending on her now, and George was gone, just like that.

The corridor was wide. One of the men was at her side, the other in front.

"Who else is in that shuttle?" the man at her side asked.

She didn't respond.

"How did you manage to cut communications to the Saratoga?"

When she refused to answer, the man in front turned and made a fist at her. Instead of cowering, she thought of George lying in a crumpled heap. Tears filled her eyes, and anger seized her. She spun, then lunged backward, trying to get some room, but she'd pulled away too hard. There was no gravity in the tunnel, and she floated up and hit the wall, kicking into empty space. With her hands tied behind her, she couldn't straighten out, and started floating toward the ceiling. She tucked her legs beneath her and tried to pitch and roll in an effort to reestablish control. But instead, she began a slow bob down the tunnel.

Two hands caught her by the waist and pulled her down. She planted her feet on the sticky floor, while the man helped her straighten.

"Calm down," he said. "I won't let him hit you." Then, turning to the other man, he said, "We've already screwed this up enough. The prisoner isn't to be abused. Do I make myself clear, Sergeant?"

Joanne could see the embarrassment in her tormentor's face as his eyes darted between her and the other man. She suppressed the urge to smile, which would've made his humiliation complete. There might be a move to make, but she judged this wasn't the right time.

In response to his being dressed down by the other man, the Sergeant said, "Yes, Captain."

Joanne turned, blinked, and stared at the Captain. "You're Captain Drake?"

"Yes, that's right," snapped the Captain, directing an icy stare with his steely brown eyes.

"Did you have to shoot him?" Joanne yelled. "He was unarmed. He never hurt anyone."

"Never hurt anyone?" yelled Captain Drake. Their helmets were almost touching. "You treacherous bastards tried to kill my crew. What do you expect?"

"We didn't kill anyone."

Joanne was tired of talking, but she felt the need to make the point.

"Was that Mills back there?" asked Drake.

Joanne lowered her head, allowing the comfort of tears. Captain Drake took her arm, then ordered the Sergeant to walk point. Drake held her loosely. She had the distinct impression that, unlike the Sergeant, he did not possess a violent nature. She had noticed revulsion in his eyes when the other man had tried to hit her. He seemed to be the kind of man who was more apt to be holding the door for a lady than hitting her. As they made their way to the shuttle bay, he continued asking questions.

"Are you with the Separatists? How did you get control of Pegasus?"

He smiled and became strangely congenial. He was obviously a man uncomfortable with contentious feelings.

"I don't know how you did this," he said, almost admiringly.

"Listen, Captain," said Joanne. "I know this is hard for you to understand, but you're on the wrong side of this thing."

She sensed his anger returning, and spoke again before he could. "Think carefully. The only person who's been hurt aboard this vessel is my dear friend, back there. Don't you think we could have killed you and your crew if that's what we wanted to do?"

Referring to George as her dear friend made her feel as if she'd betrayed him, minimized what he'd meant to her. But she couldn't call him her lover, not in front of these men. The tribute would have been lost on them. She felt the need to internalize her feelings.

* * *

Drake began to say something, but looking at her down turned eyes, the suggestion of defeat in the posture of her shoulders, he pulled back. He sensed this woman was no terrorist. She was elegant, and decidedly very educated. Beyond all reason, this woman and the man the Sergeant had shot had taken control of NearSec's most advanced cruiser—perhaps the most sophisticated machine that mankind had ever built. There was clearly something odd about this, certainly more than met the eye. After all, if their intention had been to sabotage the ship, they could have just planted a bomb in the shuttle bay and left. Why would they go into the hemisphere and delay their departure? And if they wanted a ship as some kind of weapon, this was the wrong ship. The Pegasus was a research vessel without armaments. The more Drake thought about it, the less it made sense.

Chapter Forty-Eight

Finally, they reached the shuttle bay and positioned themselves on the Phoenix's freight elevator.

"Take us down," Drake ordered.

Nothing happened. The system had been reconfigured to respond to a particular voiceprint. Drake turned to Joanne, "Tell it to take us down." When Joanne failed to give the command, he added, "Don't make this any harder than it has to be."

"I'll take you down if you leave your gun up here," said Joanne.

"Shit," snarled the Sergeant, and started for her.

Drake put an arm out, keeping him back. "You know I can't do that," said Drake. "How do I know your friends aren't down there waiting to ambush us?"

Joanne stared straight at him. "The last time you came anywhere near a friend of mine, it was you doing the shooting." She couldn't say killing. She still refused to give up hope that George might have survived.

"Are your friends in the shuttle armed?" Drake asked.

"No Captain, they're not. I give you my word."

"The word of a separatist bitch," spat the Sergeant.

Drake shot the man a look of disapproval, then turned back to Joanne. "Look, I can't leave the gun, but I will put it in my belt. I give you my word, there won't be any more careless violence."

Drake put his hand out, palm up, and gestured with his fingers for the Sergeant to give up the weapon.

"But Captain," pleaded the Sergeant. He reminded Joanne of a willful little boy. If the scene hadn't been so tragic, it would have been comical.

Drake took the gun and stuck it in his belt. Then, turning to Joanne, he nodded, acknowledging that he'd done his part.

Joanne exhaled a resigned sigh. "Phoenix, take us down."

* * *

George Mills opened his eyes. He felt his leg bent under him in an uncomfortable position and tried to move. He succeeded in straightening his legs, but felt a throb grip his upper right side, and winced. I've been shot, he realized. Memories of recent events began flooding into his mind. Why am I still alive, he wondered? He knew his suit was compromised; he should have suffocated by now. His visor display indicated a nominal air pressure inside the suit—strange.

True, Will was replenishing the air in the ship, but it should have been too little, too late, to save him. He raised his left hand and looked at it. There was coagulated blood on the fingers of his glove—freeze dried? He sat up, supporting himself with his left arm, trying to ignore the pain. He slid to the wall. Using it as a support, he pulled himself into a sitting position. Holding his head up made him dizzy. He could almost feel the gravity pulling the blood from of his head. Just sit here a moment, he told himself, then he closed his eyes.

* * *

The elevator descended into the familiar darkness of the Phoenix's cargo hold. Anxiety gripped Joanne at the prospect of coming back like this. What would the kids think when she walked into the main cabin with these men? She could imagine the hope draining from their faces at the sight of her failure. It made her sick; she made a pathetic little groan.

"What's wrong?" asked Drake.

"What do you think?" she replied in a small voice.

They stepped off the elevator, the overhead doors closed, and they prepared to enter the main cabin. A green light above the cabin door indicated the bay was pressurized. They retracted their helmets. Drake loosened the bonds on Joanne's hands, "No trouble," he reminded, and put his right hand on the butt of the pistol so she could see it.

"I wouldn't do anything to cause you to draw that gun in here," she said.

Drake nodded and opened the door. Joanne stepped into the cabin, followed by Drake, then the Sergeant.

* * *

When he felt strong enough, George started the long crawl back to the computer room. He could just as well speak to Will over Suit-Com, but he felt a compulsion to get out of sight. In his jumbled thoughts, he reasoned that if there were two undetected crewmen on board, there might be others. If they found him in the corridor, shot and bleeding, they might just finish the job. No, it was better to get out of sight. Then he remembered Joanne. Even now he could hear her cries as the elevator door closed. It made him clench his teeth. He pushed himself faster, imagining himself like a big snail, leaving a trail of blood for his assassins to follow. He could barely feel his right side, and wondered if he were going into shock.

It took George roughly seven minutes, by his suit chronometer, to reach the computer room. He started sweating again; salty drops found their way into his eyes and stung like hell. He lunged for the amber door panel and was rewarded when it slid aside. Now he lay on his back, looking up at milky white columns reaching high into a tan sky. He felt a sense of peace, managing a laugh at how ironic it was to die here, at the foot of his life's greatest work.

"George, wake up," he heard Will say over Suit-Com.

"What?"

"Wake up, George. You have to stay alert. Can you retract your helmet?"

"What? I can't do that, there's no air in here."

"Yes you can. There's air now. It'll make it easier to breath," Will insisted. "Your suit may have been damaged."

George reluctantly reached up and retracted his helmet, then took a greedy gulp of air. "Yeah, I may have been damaged too," he said, with another weak laugh. He lay back, "I think my lungs are okay."

"Now that you've removed your helmet, I can take your vitals," Will said. "That's why we didn't detect the men who shot you. They were wearing environment suits."

"What?"

"The environment suits hid their vitals from the ship's sensors," Will explained. "They knew the ship well enough to stay out of sight—very clever really. You've lost a lot of blood, that's why you're so weak. The bleeding kept you alive, though. The blood from your wound freeze-dried, sealing your suit and keeping your air from leaching out."

"What?"

George swung his head from side to side, slipping in and out of consciousness. Eventually, he saw the door slide open, at least he thought he did. Someone seemed to walk over to him and kneel down next to him. The man was wearing an environment suit. Didn't he know there was air in here? The man had something in his hand. It looked sharp.

Shit, he's going to cut me, George thought, trying to jerk away. A strong hand held him tight. Die with dignity, he told himself, and he stopped struggling. They've got you; there's nothing you can do about it. Don't let them steal the last few moments of your life. Don't forget who you are—or at least who you were.

* * *

Drake was taller than the woman and got a look over her shoulder as they pushed into the cabin. His mouth dropped open with astonishment. This was not what he'd expected; it took a few seconds to register. Drake expected to see a bunch of Mars separatists. He'd imagined something akin to the bottom deck of a pirate ship, so he'd kept the woman in front with his hand on the pistol. Not that he wanted to see the woman hurt, but what else could he do? She'd forced his hand.

"Holy shit, a ship full of children!" exclaimed the Sergeant.

Drake stared back at twenty pairs of eyes. Heads turned, watching, as he and the woman stepped down the aisle. There was something strange about these kids, though, Drake thought.

"Joanne, who are these people?" asked one of the children.

It was a boy in a seat near the flight deck. The boy lifted the restraining bar and floated into the aisle, turned, and faced them. He hovered there, holding onto the bars on either side of the aisle, legs together, looking them over. For some reason, he gave Drake the creeps. After a moment's reflection, Drake realized how strange it was that these children were all so quiet, so orderly. There was no panic at seeing strange men enter the cabin. Neither was there joy at the prospect of being rescued.

"These men were still on board the Pegasus," Joanne said. "This is Captain Drake," she motioned with her eyes over her shoulder.

"I see," said the boy slowly. "And, where is Dr. Mills?"

Joanne lowered her head. "I see," repeated the boy.

A little girl raised her restraining bar and made her way to Joanne. The girl's long hair had been braided in a ponytail, which floated over her head like a black silk ribbon. She put her arms around Joanne's waist and rested her head on Joanne's chest.

"I'm sorry," the girl said. Looking up, the girl could see tears float from Joanne's cheeks into the cabin.

After a strained silence, Drake asked, "Who are you children? Were you kidnapped?"

The boy stared at Drake, unblinking, then exhaled in frustration. "Did you men kill Dr. Mills?"

The boy had made *men* sound like a dirty word, thought Drake. "Did he kidnap you?" he asked.

"Of course not," replied the boy, as if he were speaking to someone challenged by simple concepts. "Your Admiral is trying to kidnap us. Dr. Mills and Joanne are trying to rescue us." Then, looking directly into Drake's eyes, without a hint of intimidation, the boy added, "I'm sorry to tell you this, Captain, but your Admiral is not an ethical man. If you want to be on the humane side of this thing, you should not side with your Admiral."

Drake got the impression that the boy had been mocking him when he'd used the word *humane*. It was as if there were something wrong with that word, or something inappropriate about its use.

"I don't know what's going on here," admitted Drake. "As soon as we get you kids to the Saratoga, we'll sort it all out. I'm sure you're mistaken about what's really happening." Then, looking at Joanne, Drake added, "These people have obviously told you children lies, but we'll get everything figured out, I promise."

The boy smiled, giving Drake a cold feeling. "I'm sure you believe that, Captain. I wanted to believe that too before I spoke to your Admiral. When he thought he had us, he spoke his true mind. Your Admiral is a very disturbed and confused man, Captain. I think if you come to know him better, you'll come to see that."

"Damn," uttered the Sergeant. "Let's get these kids secured and then over to the Saratoga, Captain, ASAP."

Drake nodded, but continued looking at the boy. Then he prodded the woman and the little girl, who clung to her, to move forward toward the flight deck.

"We're not going to the Saratoga, Captain," declared the boy, with a confidence that Drake found eerie.

Drake looked the boy over. He was no more than twelve or thirteen. His strange behavior was no doubt the result of trauma.

Drake had studied the psychology of people in combat, and he knew that trauma could precipitate mental collapse, paranoia, or delusions. This had to be something like that. The children probably identified with their kidnappers as a result of being abducted and subjected to abuse. Then, looking back at Joanne, Drake found it hard to believe that this attractive, well-educated woman could have abused these kids. Something was definitely amiss here.

Drake shook his head and started down the aisle again, keeping the woman in front.

"You'll feel better when we get to the Saratoga," he said to the boy. "We'll get you some medical attention and. . . What the hell?"

He couldn't move! It was as if his muscles were paralyzed. He could feel his limbs, but couldn't move them at all. Every time he tried, it felt as if he were being held in place by tight bands.

"I can't move!" yelled the Sergeant with a blood-curdling wail. "My arms, I can't move them."

Drake stared at the boy in disbelief. He knew the boy was somehow responsible, but how?

"It's you, isn't it?" Drake asked.

Because Drake instinctively wanted to trust the woman, he tried to consider the truth of what the boy had told him. Maybe the Admiral was somehow involved in something wrong. He'd been around long enough to know that the pillars of society sometimes had rotten foundations. But, losing the Pegasus, now that was something hard for Drake to swallow.

* * *

Joanne, startled by all the yelling behind her, turned and saw Drake and the other man just standing there, hands around restraining bars, their eyes darting to and fro. Miram looked up at her, no detectable surprise or concern for the men, only empathy for her. Joanne reached over, removed the gun from Drake's belt, and put it in her own. She watched him carefully as she did, looking for signs that he might be able to oppose her, but none were in evidence. She looked down at Miram, who smiled up at her and said, "It's all right, Joanne, they can't hurt you."

The Sergeant screamed, then began making choked grunting sounds, like a man trying to lift a heavy weight. It caught Miram's attention and her mood changed. She became serious, more discerning.

"Calm down, you'll be fine," said Miram.

Drake shifted his gaze to Joanne. Unlike the Sergeant, he remained in control.

"Joanne, what's going on? Who are these children?"

"Oh, now it's Joanne is it? We're going to get you and the other man to the Saratoga, Captain. But don't worry, you won't be treated the way you treated George."

She turned to Perseus, whom she suspected was responsible, although she wasn't going to telegraph her surprise to these men. "Can I move them?" she asked.

"Yes," answered Miram. "Just take their hands and put them where you want them." She smiled sweetly, sincerely glad she could help. Joanne bent down and kissed the girl's cheek. Then she turned and squeezed past Drake.

"Joanne," called Drake, with desperation in his voice.

"One minute, Captain."

She took the Sergeant's wrist. He screamed and bared his teeth in defiance.

"Oh, for goodness sake, just shut up you idiot," ordered Joanne.

She led him to the cargo hold where she bound his hands behind him with equipment ties and sat him down next to a bulkhead. Standing before him, she said, "If I hear you screaming in here, I'm going to put tape over your mouth."

The man looked up at her, dazed.

Joanne shook her head and returned to the cabin for the Captain, whom she took by the wrist and led to the bay.

"What you told me before," asked Drake, "was that true?"

Joanne stopped just in front of the door, appraising the Captain. "We told you the truth, Captain. I don't know anything about Admiral Nelson, other than the fact that his behavior in this matter has been nothing short of criminal. My friend being shot, these kids losing their homes, you losing your ship, they all have one thing in common."

He waited for her to continue, then asked, "What?"

"The paranoid behavior of your Admiral and whoever it is that's giving him orders."

She felt herself starting to cry again, stifled it, and grabbed Drake's wrist. "Come on," she ordered, and put him next to the Sergeant in the hold. "Before we get under way, we'll put you and the Sergeant in an escape-pod. When we're gone, Saratoga can pick you up." Drake looked up at her with sad eyes. "I'm sorry about your ship, Captain. I really am."

When they were both securely tied, she reentered the cabin and closed the door. She half walked, half floated to a seat near the flight deck and buried her face in her hands. Miram put her skinny little arm around her shoulder and pressed her cheek against Joanne's arm. Joanne spread the fingers of the hand that cupped her face and saw Perseus standing in front of her. The boy looked disturbingly worried.

"What?" Joanne asked, in a voice muted by the hand partially covering her mouth.

"Please, Joanne," pleaded Perseus. "What do we do now?"

Joanne removed her hand, sat up, and put Miram on her knee.

She had to pull herself together. Now was not the time to fall apart. She began to itemize all the things they'd have to do. Then a realization hit her.

"Will, are you there?" she called—nothing.

She repeated the question while glancing at the ceiling, as though expecting a voice from above. She heard her Suit-Com chirp as the AI searched for the active channel.

"Joanne, can you hear me?"

It didn't sound quite like Will.

"Will?" called Joanne.

"Yes, it's me," Will said.

"Will!" exclaimed Joanne in a gush of relief.

She smiled broadly, then looked at Perseus. Moving those unfamiliar muscles made her face tingle. The boy returned the smile. She could see the tension evaporate from his shoulders; his whole body seemed to relax. The rest of the children began smiling as well, just like dominos falling.

"Joanne, what's your status?" Will asked.

She told him. She wanted to ask him about George, but was afraid of the answer. As long as she didn't know for sure, she could still hope. If Will gave her bad news, those damning words would forever preclude his ever coming back. It would be an immutable event in her world line that could never be changed. She wanted to keep the possibility open, never mind that whatever the truth was, it had already happened in the collection of things now past.

She noticed the children were all looking at her—no, not at her, but to her for direction. She shook off the immobility of fear and got Will's attention, then began reciting from the list she'd committed to memory. As she spoke, Will did something he rarely did; he interrupted her.

"Would you like an update on George's condition?"

She tried to say yes, but heard only a squeak. Her heart pounded in her chest.

"He was shot and badly hurt, but I think you know that," Will said.

"Oh, Will," blurted Joanne. "How is he now?"

"I had a doctor take him to the medical bay. He's been repaired and given accelerants to increase his blood production."

"There's a doctor on board?"

"Yes, there's an automated medical staff. I guess you'd call them robots. It's a very well equipped ship," said Will.

"So he's alive, he's going to be all right?"

After a moment, Will said, "Yes, of course. I should have said something earlier. I'm sorry."

Little Lyla, chimed, "I guess Will can do anything, huh?"

Many of the kids giggled. Will's optimistic update had transformed the atmosphere on the shuttle, bringing back desperately needed hope. Suddenly, for the first time in as long as Joanne could remember, the children sounded like they had back at school, when she'd been their counselor, on their beloved Mars.

Chapter Forty-Nine

You can waken men only by dreaming their dreams more clearly than they can dream them themselves. - Alexander Hertzen

Once all the children had been taken off the Phoenix, Joanne led them to the acceleration-bridge high above the rotating upper hemisphere of the Pegasus. Will had warned her that sensor readings indicated the Saratoga was coming back to life. It was reasonable to assume that the crew was quickly regaining control of the ship, which meant that Pegasus would have to leave in a hurry.

The acceleration-bridge was softly lit and spacious, with an expansive domed ceiling. The forward section of the room was curved and dominated by a huge window-like display that showed the horizon of Mars and the stars above. Joanne put each of the kids in an acceleration tube, whose liquid-filled cavity was designed to blunt the effects of high-gee on the human body. Once the Pegasus drive was powered up for full acceleration, it would be leaving Mars orbit at over twenty gees.

Perseus was the last to go into a tube. The tubes were in the backward section of the large room and were layered in vertical rows up to the ceiling. They sat in a titanium base with clear plastic cylindrical tops. Joanne held Perseus' hand as he floated up over the oval lip of the tube opening, then lay down on the gel body cushion inside.

"How long will it be?" asked Perseus.

Still holding his hand, Joanne looked down into his smooth Martian face. His golden eyes twinkled with a mixture of joy at being with her and the others, and a sad longing at the prospect of never going home again.

"It'll take about two weeks to get to Jupiter," Joanne said softly. "We'll make a gentle arc around the planet, then slingshot out of the elliptic toward Canis Minor. Once we clear the disk of the solar system, we'll throttle back and drop the acceleration to a gee. At that point, we'll go into cold sleep for a long, long time." She leaned down into the tube and kissed him on the cheek, as was their custom. "It'll go by just like that," she snapped her fingers. "As soon as I close the tube, and the breathable acceleration liquid fills it, the IV will put you into a dream-rich sleep."

Perseus smiled up at her. "See you when I see you," he teased.

It seemed as if George's antique colloquial expressions had infected all of them. With a muted giggle, she put a nanosensor ring on the boy's head and plugged it into a universal interface panel at the top of the tube. When Perseus seemed comfortable, Joanne pushed icons on the display just under the tube opening. A plastic canopy slid into place and fluids began to flow through IV tubes attached by shiny silver bracelets around the boy's wrists. An amber liquid began filling the inside of the acceleration tube. In a couple of minutes, she saw the boy's eyes slowly closing through the plastic as the gel secured him in an amber cocoon. Joanne ran her hand over the smooth cylinder and gazed up at the rows of other cylinders, each of which contained humanity's brightest promise. She crossed the immaculate gray floor to one of two acceleration tubes at the forward section of the bridge. She lingered over the one that was occupied, smiling down at George's amber pallor under the plastic canopy. His eyes were closed and he wore a dull silver ring around his head. She stood there a moment, in the quiet of the large room, and in the shadow of Mars outside, then walked over to the other tube and got in.

* * *

Malcolm arrived at Building One more than six hours after the sky cars had met them in the western desert and flown Margaret back to Dome One. Apparently, either Void Fleet or

454

Planetary Security, or both, had kept Vega and his bunch from destroying Dome One. In any event, it was still there.

A large Martian in a battle worn combat suit, whom he recognized as Captain Fred Jackson, met Malcolm in the lobby. Malcolm was surprised to learn from Jackson that Colonel Gates had instructed he be given a key code for an upper floor of Building One, the same floor he'd visited a few days earlier for the DRA meeting. Malcolm cracked a smile when Jackson uploaded the codes into his Tab. The last time he'd looked, no one had expected him here, including himself—so why the VIP treatment? Amused by this turn of events, he took the lift into the dark Martian sky and made his way to the conference room where he'd met Perseus. He didn't know why he'd come here, though it made an odd sort of sense, as if he had come full circle.

Malcolm entered the dimly lit corridor and saw her silhouetted against the floor-to-ceiling glass wall at its far end. Her back was to him, and she was looking into the night sky. She wore a stunning metallic green dress that reflected sparkles of light from synthetic star sapphires and diamonds that were woven into its fabric. As he approached from behind on the deep pile, she said, "Evening Malcolm," without turning.

He pulled up along side. "Better hearing through genetics, huh?" Then looking at her, he smiled. "You clean up pretty good."

Margaret smiled back. Her hair was white violet in the glow of the dome far below. Her eyes were pale and haunting.

"What happened to Vega and his bomb?" Malcolm asked.

She exhaled a little laugh. "He was pretty tough against drugged hostages, but crumbled when faced with serious combat troops. We took him without much resistance."

Then, after a few moments, Malcolm asked, "Why are we here?"

As the words left his mouth, the sky outside suddenly exploded in light.

"That's why," Margaret said, gesturing toward Deimos high on the horizon.

What looked like a star erupted in the general direction of Mars' smaller moon. Now a bright fireball, it cast an incandescent shine on Deimos and began arcing away, rising higher into the night.

"The Pegasus," Malcolm said, transfixed by the spectacle of an artificial sun speeding across the night sky.

"The Pegasus," Margaret confirmed. "I wanted you to see it just like this—that's if you happened by, like I thought you might."

He held her eyes. They seemed red, possibly teary in the white light of the new star. She turned toward the sky again, and Malcolm continued watching her as she smiled at some private thought.

"I thought I was suppose to be the psychologist around here," Malcolm said.

They stood for a while, silently watching the star as it dimmed, moving farther and farther away. Finally, Margaret reached up, placed her hands around Malcolm's neck, pulled him down, and kissed him on both cheeks.

"That's how they do it here, isn't it?"

"Yeah, that's how we do it," Malcolm said.

"I'm going back to the ship, then to Earth," she said. "But I'll come back. When I do, I'd enjoy seeing you again—if that's all right?"

"I'm counting on it," Malcolm said.

Margaret turned and walked silently away. Malcolm watched her until she disappeared into the anteroom beyond the corridor, her mild scent lingering in her absence. Then, turning back to the window, he watched a while longer as the Pegasus blazed in the night sky.

* * *

For the last three weeks, Joanne had wandered in and out of sleep in her tube on the bridge of the Pegasus. She had stood watch on board the ship as the last human witness to their departure from the worlds of humanity. As everyone else on board slept, she had seen Mars shrink to an insignificant dot. All that time, Will had kept her company through the nano-interface, showing her their escape from Earth's deadliest warship. The Saratoga had come back to life an hour after their departure, far too late to reach them, even with antimatter-tipped Raptor missiles. As they had sped to Jupiter, a billion miles away, Pegasus had stretched its magnetic arms thousands of miles into space to gather light elements from the solar wind held in the gas giant's vast magnetic field. Primed by the rich fuel source, the RamScoop had slowly come to life and propelled them far beyond the reach of their pursuers.

During their long passage, Joanne had fought not to visualize her mother's face, a face that she could never again touch. It was hard to stifle tears as she imagined her family desperately trying to understand what had happened to her. They would never find her, no matter how hard they looked. Then she pictured Malcolm going to her parent's house, standing before her mother, father, and bothers, and telling them the unbelievable story of why she would never return. What would they think when they learned that she had chosen to leave with an Earther rather than staying with them? It was like being on an emotional seesaw. When she wasn't mourning her lost family, or lamenting never seeing the copper spires of the rim range again, she was filled with guilt for the parents whose children she had taken— children that they had placed in her care.

As time passed, the grief became less immediate. It was all past her now—regrets and triumphs. The mightiest machine ever built by humankind was carrying them ever farther into the void and nothing could change that. They were well above the plane of the solar system, streaking into the endless star laden depths of interstellar space, headed for Procyon, almost ten light-years away. The Pegasus had transitioned completely to the self-sustaining RamScoop and was edging, day-by-day, closer to the speed of light—a speed, mandated by the laws of nature, it could never reach. Joanne's sole vigil was over; it was time to make a break from the life she had known. It was time to join the others in Will's otherworld tapestry of the Virtual Nexus.

* * *

Joanne put her hand to her brow to shield her eyes from a bright sun. With her other hand, she reached up to the collar of her tee shirt for the sunglasses she knew would be there. The last time she had been here, she had had one of the most jarring experiences of her life. After looking around for a long moment, she took a deep breath and started walking toward the sea, toward the sound of breakers pounding the Southern California coast. She could feel the warm sun on her brown skin and a mild sea breeze coming from the Pacific. Her experienced eyes saw lizards and rabbits ducking for cover as she moved to the clearing at the edge of the cliff overlooking the beach. Peering down, she could see the kids far below, running and splashing in the surf. Some were playing games on the sand, games that she recognized from their days in the schoolyard back on Mars. Searching the beach, she spotted Will—then George, standing next to him. The two were talking, ankle deep in the foamy water that rose up from shattered waves pounding the shore. The rhythm, orchestrated by this world, seemed eternal.

Joanne raised her arm over her head and began waving—slowly at first, then more quickly. Will saw her and said something to George. George turned, and seeing her, began waving back—first with one hand, then with two. A moment later, he was running through the surf, toward the path that would take him up the cliff, to the clearing, and finally to her. Children turned and began waving too as he sped by. She saw Perseus waist deep in the water, Miram's arm around his

458

shoulders; both were waving and laughing. Soon the entire beach seemed to explode in a sea of welcoming hands, inviting her back to her new family. As Joanne watched George splashing through the crowd toward the cliff, she beamed behind mirrored glasses reflecting the blue skies of a virtual Earth.

THE END

Author's Note

I want to give special thanks to my wife Anne Moose for her unwavering support and encouragement, and for her tireless efforts in editing the manuscript. Whatever errors remain are my own. Thanks to Mike Buckwalter, Vannessa Ryan, Virginia Moose, Ian Culver, Tim and Tracy Laughlin, Irwin Sheer, Dave Lerner, and Roeland Van Krieken for their helpful comments.

About the Author

Peter Dingus is a physicist. He received his Ph.D. from UC Berkeley in 1988, and has had posts at *Ecole Polytechnique* in Paris, DESY in Hamburg, and CERN in Geneva. From 1991 until it was shut down in 1993, he was a staff physicist at the Superconducting Super Collider project, in Dallas, TX.

Dr. Dingus has published thirty-five scientific papers in refereed journals (such as "Physical Review Letters"). In the mid-nineties, he left particle physics to work in the field of Speech Recognition. Since then, he has been a principal in two software startups and the co-founder of a third. He is currently living with his wife and two children in Mission Viejo, California.

CPSIA information can be obtained
at www.ICGtesting.com
Printed in the USA
FSOW01n0247230915
11379FS